'**An ambitious novel with deeply felt and perennially interesting themes** . . . The emotional and psychological damage of war, and its effects on the men and their families, are sympathetically and sharply dramatised, while some of **the writing is lovely**'

Elizabeth Buchan, *Daily Mail*

'The ebullient Obadaiah Nelson, a black boxing fan from Louisiana and fellow legionnaire . . . is the main narrator of the major's war story and he tells it in **rich voice** peppered with slang and wit . . . **A book of great ambition and power**' Antonia Senior, *The Times*

'A sweeping novel of guilt, loss and misunderstanding' *The Lady*

'A **powerfully emotive** family drama featuring **well-drawn and sympathetic characters** set against a little known but momentous event in US history, which will strike a chord with those who enjoyed Pat Barker's *Regeneration* and Richard Flanagan's *The Narrow Road to the Deep North*' *We Love This Book*

'A story about fatherhood and family, about how there are some things we never, ever get over, about how love is enduring, and about how society can let down those who sacrifice most for it . . . **Mandanna deftly weaves a spell that brings [the story] to a moving conclusion**'

Girl!Reporter

Sarita Mandanna is from Coorg, India. Her debut novel, *Tiger Hills*, was longlisted for the 2011 Man Asian Literary Prize, selected for the TV Book Club, and was Editors' Choice in the *New York Times*. It has been translated into fourteen languages around the world.

Also by Sarita Mandanna

Tiger Hills

GOOD HOPE ROAD

Sarita Mandanna

First published in Great Britain in 2015
by Weidenfeld & Nicolson
This paperback edition published in 2016
by Weidenfeld & Nicolson,
An imprint of the Orion Publishing Group Ltd
Carmelite House, 50 Victoria Embankment
London EC4Y 0DZ
An Hachette UK Company

1 3 5 7 9 10 8 6 4 2

A CIP catalogue record for this book is available from the British Library.

978 1 780 22905 8

Typeset by Input Data Services Ltd, Bridgwater, Somerset

Printed and bound by Clays Ltd, St Ives plc

www.orionbooks.co.uk

For my parents,
Col Ben Mandanna and Dr Rani Mandanna

There come times in a man's life that change everything. He looks about him afterwards and sees that the leaves have turned, as if in an instant. The river has altered its course, no longer flowing southward or anywhere familiar at all. It is changed, the ripples from hidden trout seeming to flow up-current, the stones in its bed flipped over, exposing pocked bellies so long buried in the mud.

PROLOGUE

France • 1915

There's mud in the South too, all sorts of it. Hard mud, under a sun bakin' down so strong that the birds be fallin' dizzy from the trees and near barbecued on the hot ground. Mud packed so tight that it sets the dogs to pantin' as they hunt for shade, liftin' their paws quick and delicate like, 'cause the ground, it burn them so. Not my feet though, they too rough used to notice – I been paddin' 'bout barefoot most of my boyhood, all across the dirt roads and back ways of the Quarter. There's soft mud, after the rain, she fall and loosen the soil so next year's crop can come singin' outta the earth. Red mud, light mud, in-between, Creole-coloured mud.

I seen all kinds of mud.

Upon all my borned days though, I ain't never, not ever, known as much mud as there's here at the Front. The fields, the woods, all torn up and left insides-out. Flowers gone, the grass, trees even, as if they all been sucked deep into the earth until only mud be left. Brown and black, the sort that stick like tar and blackstrap to guns and gear. The kind that suck at marchin' boots and spit up the dead – not two days since they been buried when the mud, she churn and turn and heave them right out again. Itty bitties of them: elbows, knees and feet; pieces of the broken men lyin' below.

There this boot I seen once. A trench wall gone and collapsed from the rain, right on to a sleepin' soldier. His buddies, they scrambled hard to get him out, but turns out they started their diggin' at the wrong end – by the time they uncovered one of his boots, it was already too late for him. The more they dug, the mud, it started to slip and fall again, until there was nothin' to do but smooth the mud best they could and leave the poor bastard with his boot stickin' straight out from the wall.

That was 'bout all the burial he got, but it since become a habit with every man to spit on our palms and give that boot a quick polish as we walk past, until darned if it ain't become the shiniest, spiffiest hobnailed boot in all of wartime France.

A real good landmark it be too – 'right by the dugout, past the duckboards, left by the boot' – couldn't miss it if you tried. It ain't the feet that get to me, but the fingers and hands. They stick up from the mud, as if the dead, they diggin' free of their graves. Sometimes when the wind blows, they look to be wavin' at me.

'Obadaiah. Hey, Obadaiah! Obadaiah, you hear me? Get me outta here.'

One of the first such I see, it lie not two paces away. We'd moved to the sector just the night previous, and the Boche sent up a real humdinger of fireworks to say Hello. Whizz bangs, ash cans, potato mashers – everythin' the Boche got, they thrown our way.

We hear the shells come a-whistlin' and a-roarin', and back in those early days, before I learned to tell by its sound just how close a shell was goin' to fall, I be 'fraid every time that this here shell, it makin' straight for me. No place to run, nowhere to hide; we crouch in the trenches, coverin' our heads with our hands as if this goin' to save us when a shell comes singin' our names. All day long the shells fall and when finally they stop – and the earth, she stops buckin' – I get up on my feet. My ears still ringin' as I climb on to the fire step, dazed like, to have a look through the sandbags.

There it was, the hand, stickin' straight up from the mud.

One of ours, that the first thing that come to my mind, but no, I look around at our part of the trench, and we all done good this time. Gaillard, he sittin' up and cussin' somethin' fierce. James start to whistle, coolly brushin' the dirt from his legs, but his breath don't always come into the whistle and the tune comes out choppy like.

Bop. De. Bop. De. Boop.

Mud still dribble-drabblin' down the walls of the trench; it always do, I will soon learn, after a shellin'. Somebody is screamin' some distance away, to the left. Someone always be, after the shells. I tell you this: ain't no human voice meant to make such pain-filled sounds, and no person made for hearin' them. This man, he screamin' somethin' awful; all of us listen, although we try not to. I stare at the hand, and in between the hollerin', and James' whistlin', and the soft, scratch-scratch sounds the mud make as it settle, I hear somethin' more.

'Obadaiah. Obadaiah,' the hand seem to call. 'Over here.'

By and by the screamin' slows. The man who been wounded, he taken to the dressin' station, but it don't look so good, we learn. Still, it's been a lucky evenin'. The trenches, they all held under the shellin', ain't none that caved in. That legionnaire, he our only casualty. Well, him, and Danny, who be visited by Miss Dia Rhea once more. She been his loyal companion for a few days now. It ain't as bad as it could have been – Dia be less potent than the other Rhea sisters, Pia and Gonna, but try tellin' that to a man shittin' his guts out into a latrine bucket.

'Maybe we set Danny up on a '75, and send over some of that ass gas to the Boche,' I suggest. 'Clear them out in a hurry.'

A weak joke, but we laugh anyhow, glad to shake the tension that stays on after a shellin'. Like wires on a banjo after the music's been plucked from them, twangin' quiet like, back and forth.

For some reason, I say nothin' 'bout the hand.

The Captain come by in a while. Ain't no orders to attack tonight, he say; seem like the shellin' is the last show for the evenin'. The field between the rolls of bobwire go quiet as the sun fold up and the light start to die. Up and down the trenches, men curl white and tired in their coats. I find it hard to sleep. I keep thinkin' 'bout that hand, stickin' so straight and alone from the mud. It a French hand, Boche, or English? I wonder. A man's hand is 'bout all I can tell. I stretch out my own, wrist stiff, fingers wide; the first stars throw a cool light over the lines in my palm.

I touch the gris-gris in my pocket and think suddenly to send up a prayer. For that hand, and the man it once belonged to, for the wounded this evenin', for all of us.

The prayer, it one I ain't said in a while, one Pappy taught me moons ago. I repeat the words silently, holdin' the gris-gris in my fingers. It a right powerful gris-gris, brimful of protection and magic, and as I rub the fur on the rabbit's foot, Pappy's schoolhouse come floatin' into my mind. The wooden floorboards with the crack to one side. The window stuffed with rags – the glass been broken so many times with a brick or similar thrown hard and bitter, made sense to stop tryin' to fix it and just leave it broke. Pappy, so serious, holdin' the Bible as he teach.

'Obadaiah,' I hear again, a whisper over the wire. My eyes fly open and the schoolhouse is gone, just like that, disappeared into the night.

The minutes tick past so awful slow that it's a relief to get on guard duty. I climb up on the fire step, leanin' my rifle against the wall as I brush away the night crawlies litterin' the elbow rest. Some 'rest' – most these trenches been built for one size of man – a not so big man – and I always got to fidget some to get comfortable. I set my eyes to the loophole. My sight takes some adjustin', from hours of lookin' at nothin' but this way to Danny shittin', to that way at Gaillard bayonetin' every toadfrog he find – and there be plenty on the water-filled floor – to straight upwards at the peel of grey sky. Feel good, to let my eyes stretch into the night.

A temporary truce was called in this sector two days ago, we heard tell, so that both sides might bury their dead. There's the faint bite of chloride of lime in the air, from where it was sprinkled 'bout the trenches and across No Man's Land. The field before me all hacked up once more from today's shellin', but the bobwire belts still look fresh repaired. Ain't nothin' lyin' snagged on them tonight, no fallen men, none of their gear. I run my eyes real careful over the wires, post to post, one end to the other, and wonder just where the snipers are lyin' in wait. I look over the heaps of earth, and the shell holes filled with silent, gun-shine water.

The hand is still stickin' from the mud, so clear in the starlight that a sniper could take out every finger, one by one, if he wanted. *A Boche hand, or English or French?* I wonder to myself again, but ain't no way to know. It's a man's hand, is all. Young, I figure – the skin fits tight over the fingers. Ain't been dead too long either; not yet been time for it to turn green, to bloat with gas and stench.

A man on guard duty, all kind of thoughts start to go through his head as he stand on the fire step. Nothin' to do for two hours but pick over mist and shadow, wonderin' if the Boche gonna attack on his watch. Minute after minute tick past with ain't nothin' happenin', and slowly his mind start to wander, this way and that. The whisky smell of Perdido Street, the dolls shakin' their hips so fine. The blind praline vendor, the Rexall on the corner, and watermelon, red to the rind. He grin in the darkness, 'memberin' old fights where he won, drum his fingers thinkin' of them that he lost. He fuss and worry over things he might've done different, dream of all that he goin' to do, all the places he might get to after the war.

Tonight though, all I can think 'bout is that hand. I wonder what it been doin' before it came to rest here in the mud. The man it belonged to ain't never worked in no cotton fields like I done, his skin, it the wrong colour for that. Never stepped inside no ring either I bet, never practised no swings at sacks of river sand – ain't no scars or bumps to show. Maybe he played the piano someplace where the ladies smelled fine, or tennis in one of those clubs where they serve sandwiches so small, it take thirty to satisfy. Maybe he been a teacher like Pappy, or a writer like James? A passin' cloud casts a long, low shadow over the fingers; from where I stand, the shadow, it looks like an ink stain.

A writer, then?

A writer, I settle.

I think of all the words those fingers might have written before the war, whatever language they been in.

Food. Sex. Vin. Musik. Cher. Woman. Heart. Sun. River. Père. Papan. Gott.

All the words that poured from that hand before the mud, before this endless, graveyard mud.

'Obadaiah,' I seem to hear him say, 'Obadaiah.'

Even when my watch is over, I find it hard to sleep. I smash the butt of my rifle against the rats that scratch around our boots. Once or twice, I get one and hear it squeal. Don't stop them though, never do, so I stop. I can hear them runnin' across coats and haversacks, and try not to think 'bout what they be eatin' as they root in the mud, or how they be growin' so glossy and fat they look more like house cats than rats. I think 'bout the hand, stickin' lonesome and defenceless from the mud, and what those rats might do to it. I hold my rifle closer. If they come upon it, I will shoot, I tell myself. It goin' to fetch me all sorts of trouble with the Captain, I know, but Lord, I goin' to shoot . . .

Close to mornin' when bone tiredness take a hold of me. I fall asleep, sittin' with my back against the wall of the trench, rifle in my hands. I dream of Pappy's schoolhouse, 'cept there ain't nobody inside.

The daily stand-to alarm go off an hour before dawn, shakin' the sleep from me. It take me a moment to figure out where I am before I get to my feet. All of us legionnaires line up on the fire step, rubbin' at stiff shoulders and sleep-filled eyes, weapons ready in case of a 'surprise' attack. The foolishness of this war: across from us, beyond the bobwire, beyond the stretch of No Man's Land and then the bobwire belts on the other side, the Boche be doin' exactly the same.

I'm slow gettin' to the fire step; when I do, James is standin' where I been last night. From where I am, I ain't able to see the dead soldier's hand. This bother me bad. I look over at James – surely he seen it by now? His expression give nothin' away. He stare straight ahead, movin' the plug of chaw in his cheek. I search through the loophole in front of me, but all I see is mud, and wire, and a slowly lightenin' sky.

I can't hear it no more neither; ain't nobody callin' my name.

We wait there an hour, stampin' our feet and shiftin' 'bout to get warm, until the dawn is fully upon us. The stand-down sound and men start to move 'bout the trench, fixin' to clean their rifles, do repair work, mend the duckboards and such. Danny sayin' somethin' to me but I ain't payin' no attention as I mosey along the fire step to where I been standin' last night. I think of them rats, and for a moment, I'm right afraid of what I'm goin' to see. I set my eyes to the loophole.

A weight lift from my chest and I grin, from one side of my mug to the other. There's my buddy's hand, stickin' from the mud, five fingers, clear as day.

It just a hand, a dead stranger's hand, but in those five stiff fingers, in that silent, unmovin' palm, I see all of his life that's passed before. He no longer just another dead soldier, but a man, once with breath and body and a heart beatin' with want – a man, same as me. When I see his hand still there, unharmed through the night, it as if that fallen soldier, he gone and survived after all. As if everythin' that come before – all that those fingers did before the war, the words they wrote, the hands they touched, the rifle they held at the end – all those things, they ain't been for nothin'.

I grin through the loophole, uncarin' of who's lookin' at me.

'Good mornin',' I call to it, man to man. 'Good mornin'.'

ONE

Raydon, Vermont • March 1932

Jim Stonebridge waded deeper into the river. It extended before him, the grey of winter giving way to a brisk, clear blue, and where the afternoon sun caught it, a quicksilver sheen. He waded slowly, not so far that the water breached the tops of his rubber boots, and with an economy of movement that set off hardly a ripple. Ahead and to his left, an outcrop of rock thrust its shoulder over the river. The water that lay beneath was shielded from the sun, dark and still as a pane of glass. The river ran deep there, he knew, and in those cavernous hollows, trout. Fat-bellied rainbows, he was certain of it.

He stopped, bracing his legs against the silt. A slight breeze nudged at the ends of his canvas shirt. It hung over the river for an instant, weighted with the smell of wet earth and pine. The scent it carried lingered, dense and familiar. He took a deep breath, drawing it in. Tree oil. Resin. Mud. Spring seeding the woods.

Everywhere, the quiet sounds of water. The river flowing freely once more, the floes of ice, speckled with twigs and the debris of last year's leaf litter, the only remnants of its winter carapace. Water in the woods, dripping from thawing bark, pooling in snowmelt ground. Ice cracked, breaking down, rippling in the ridges marked by his boot, seeping into the frozen earth and awakening the soil.

He ran a thumb over his fishing rod, along the silk that threaded its length. A casual glance at the overhang of rock to anchor his bearings. A controlled flick of his arm, backwards, forwards. Fly, leader and line arced overhead.

A movement in the trees caught his eye. A squirrel, losing its grip on a nut or acorn, bounded along a branch. Idly, he followed its flight, measuring without conscious thought the distance from where he stood. Slipping into the boyhood pattern of old – judging the angle of the muzzle, the trajectory of the hypothetical shot.

A dab of colour on the horizon, drawing his eye further upwards.

Just above the stand of grey, bare branches reaching for the sun, a patch of red, marking the sky.

An apple? was the first thought that jumped into his head, despite its obvious incongruousness. He began to reel in the slack line as the object floated clear of the tree line. He watched puzzled as it sailed overhead, trailing a rippled shadow over the river.

A balloon?

He heard the drone of the plane almost immediately after. Little more than a dull vibration in the back of his teeth at first, but steadily rising in volume, the sound grating in the air. He recast the line, annoyed.

Flatlanders, come from Boston to holiday in hill country with their rich-boy toys.

The noise of the plane grew louder as it came wheeling into view. Stubbornly, he refused to acknowledge it, reeling in the line as if the plane simply did not exist, even though the sound of its engines was now strident enough to spook the fish. He glanced again at the outcrop of rock, got his bearings, flicked his arm. Fly, leader, line in a perfect cast, but the sound of the engine was impossible to ignore, the peace of the afternoon now firmly a thing of the past.

'Fuck.' Reeling in the line again, he squinted into the sun.

It was a small, twin-engine affair, flying low enough that he could make out the man in the cockpit. Behind him, someone obscured by a mass of balloons. An absurdly large number of balloons, even more than he'd seen in the marquee tent of the carnival that stopped by the town each summer. They streamed from behind the pilot's seat and out from both sides of the plane. Red. Each the same bright shade of apple red.

The plane banked and flew lower, directly over the river, in an explosion of sound and colour sure to scare even the deepest-lying trout.

'FUCK.'

He watched it approach, standing stock still, rod in hand. Closer yet, the noise infernally loud, the balloons parted and now he could make out a face. A girl, her hair loose and wild, startlingly red in colour, almost exactly the same tint as the balloons she held. She waved at him, sending the balloons bobbing this way and that. She was laughing, he saw, as she waved again.

He smiled. She leaned to shout something to him, her words lost in the roar of the engines. Had she been closer, she would have seen his smile for what it was – a cold, angry thing that barely touched his eyes. Still smiling, he lifted his arm straight above his head and gave her, the balloons and that damned plane an unmitigated Stonebridge finger.

She slackened her grip, taken aback, and the balloons in one fist at once spun free. The plane passed on by, banked to the right and accelerated as it swept over the trees. He watched it grow smaller until it was finally lost to sight. Balloons skipped helter-skelter in its wake, like a flock of red-winged birds whose cage had unexpectedly been sprung. Some floated higher, some lower, bursts of apple red blossoming in the clouds and snagging on the wintered tamaracks. A solitary balloon floated towards the river, bouncing off the outcrop of rock before landing on the glassy pool beneath. It settled there, the red of its skin taking on a deeper hue as it touched the unlit water like a dark, slow-blurring stain.

Jim turned and waded towards the shore.

'How many?'

He hesitated as he nudged the andirons closer to the fire. He pushed a fallen log into place, feeding it into the heart of the flames. 'None.'

His father grunted. 'Told you it was too early.'

Jim straightened, turning around so that the fire warmed the backs of his legs. 'Saw some rising.'

'You saw nothing. Too early in the season, that's all. Damn fool's errand and a waste of time.'

Jim tossed the tongs back on their hook. They landed with a clang, sending dandelion wisps of soot parachuting into the air. 'They were there,' he insisted edgily. 'It was the aeroplane that spooked them.' Soon as he said the words, he wished he hadn't.

'Plane?' Major James Stonebridge's eye twitched. The left one, betraying, as it always did, the tension beginning to fester inside. It squeezed shut, fluttered open, fluid pooled in its corners. 'Boche? A Boche plane?'

'No. Not Boche, not Germans. Not here.'

The Major stared at his son, his eye starting to water in earnest.

'It wasn't the Boche,' Jim repeated. 'Just a couple of flatlander asses showing off.'

'How do you know?' the Major snapped. He pawed irritably at his eye. 'You don't know for certain.'

'The one behind – she was a woman.'

'A what?' The Major's jaw slackened with surprise. 'A *woman*? No, not the Boche then.' Frowning, he looked down at his clenched fists, as if they were foreign appendages, new, unfamiliar. 'Not the Boche,' he repeated. He opened his fists, flexed his fingers. 'Flatlanders. Of course.'

'Here,' Jim said quietly, 'why don't you sit awhile.'

'I'll sit when I want to,' the Major said sharply. He did. With a small thump as he eased his cane out of the way. He swiped at the moisture dribbling down his cheek and cupped a palm over the still-quivering eye. He sat in his customary place, before the fire, his armchair positioned with its back to the window and the magnificent views that lay outside.

Jim turned away, pretending to fiddle with the flies laid out to dry atop the mantel. Trying to spare his father the humiliation of being caught in open field; of such naked, misplaced apprehension. He felt the seep of the older man's discomfiture keenly nonetheless, the sour tang of it mingling with the smell of the Major's whisky breath, of mulch and woodsmoke, hanging heavy and unspoken between then. He smoothed the patch of canvas on which the flies lay, watching his father all the while in the mirror overhead.

The mirror hung over the mantel by means of a thick chain of brass. A massive oval. Its size marked it as out of the ordinary, but was not by itself its most unusual feature. Instead of the customary clear, silver-backed glass, the surface of the mirror was black. Deep, obsidian black, like something forged of rain and pushed up through the stones, or the egg, perhaps, of some nocturnal, giant-winged bird. From where it squatted on the wall, it commanded a view of nearly the entire room. The overstuffed leather armchairs, the rocker in the corner, the maroon and beige wallpaper with its jumble of roses and reverse printed foliage. The silhouette pictures of his great-great grandparents, the samplers on the far wall, picking out family names, births and marriages in a precise cross-stitch. The radio with its dully gleaming knobs, the fishing tackle from that afternoon leaning against the side door, old pictures from magazines, that someone had framed. A pine cone upon a shelf. Mourning pictures worked in silk, the threads come undone from the embroidered arcs of willow and oak, the once white gowns of the women now yellowed with age. A pewter tray. A musical box, its key rusted. A host of amber tankards.

The detritus of six generations of Stonebridges, all captured and compressed on to the convex surface of the mirror. The blackness of the glass absorbed both colour and light, its opacity rendering the reflected images flatter, less vivid. The apple trees framed in the window, the edge of the barn just visible, the winter sun – all as if diluted when viewed in the mirror, sundered from frost and shine and the depth of everyday living.

His father's face was no longer florid, the vein in his forehead smoother, the pallor of his broad but finely formed hands accentuated as he drummed on the arms of the chair, stopping now and again to sop up the moisture that still dribbled down his cheek. He'd squeezed the errant eye shut to control the twitching, but Jim saw how the other one darted still, from this corner of the room to that, as if hunting an unseen enemy.

'Can never be too careful,' the Major said abruptly. 'Tricky bastards, the Boche.' He drummed his fingers on the arms again, frowning as a thought struck him. 'This woman,' he said suspiciously, 'she could have been—'

'Just tourists,' Jim repeated.

The Major looked up sharply, recalling the mirror on the wall, and was suddenly aware of his son's scrutiny. Their eyes met, the small subterfuge of the son evident in the slight and momentary widening of his eyes; a percussive flush of shame. Then anger, in the father's at the concern he saw in the other's face, at himself, for placing it there. Both faces grew shuttered in the very next instant; nothing left to see but a studied blandness. The mirror leaching the blue so thoroughly from both pairs of irises that the years between them seemed to fall away: two pairs of matched, water-colour eyes, watching each other in the dark mirrored glass.

Jim flipped the flies over with deliberate casualness. 'Flatlanders. Early this year. Flew so low, they spooked the fish.'

The Major stared coolly at his son. He nodded. 'Flatlanders,' he agreed.

A wind came whistling up towards the house, rattling the shutters and reaching draughty fingers under the kitchen door. The Major hawked his throat in response, spitting a rich, dark-coloured stream of tobacco juice into the fire where it hissed and spluttered in the flames.

He frowned. 'You ought to have waited. They'd have returned. The *fish*,' he elaborated irritably. 'After the sound quieted, they'd have come back.'

TWO

Jim did not think of the girl from the plane in the days that followed. Still, when he saw her next, in the general store two weeks after, Jim knew it was her at once. She stood with her back to him, examining bolts of some pale fabric at the counter. It was her hair he recognised. Rich red, as deeply coloured as he remembered from when he'd seen it streaming behind her in that plane. It curled loose about her shoulders now, a lush, vixen pelt.

She glanced briefly over her shoulder as the door chime sounded, before turning back to her scrutiny of the fabric. For some reason it annoyed him, the brevity of her attention, as if he'd expected her to recognise him too. He let his gaze linger, taking in the way the blue dress she wore moved with her, moulding to the supple waist, the long legs, the surprisingly defined calves.

'Jim.' Mrs Dalloway beamed from behind the counter. She stood on her tiptoes to kiss his cheek. 'Your father, how is he?'

He shrugged.

She took the grocery list from him, not bothering to read through it as she began setting out packs of smoking tobacco on the counter with practised ease. 'Do you know, I almost ran out of these? One of those flatlander tourists came in looking for a few just the other day. Said I was all out though, knew you'd be coming by soon enough . . .'

'Excuse me.' The girl smiled at Mrs Dalloway. 'I don't mean to interrupt, but may I have a look at the teal, over there?'

'Of course, dear.' Glancing apologetically at Jim, Mrs Dalloway bustled over, donning the pair of spectacles that dangled permanently around her neck. 'Now, which one is it that you wanted? The green-blue one over there – or is it blue-green? It's pretty, isn't it?'

'You been out yet this season, Jim?' Mrs Dalloway called. She nodded at the flies tied in a corner. 'The river's running again.'

He looked involuntarily at the girl, as if she might somehow connect this mention of the river, and fishing, with him. 'Still too cold for the fish, I reckon.'

'Oh, I don't know, with this spell of sun that we're having . . .' she gestured at the chairs set around the old potbellied stove. 'Been keeping even the regulars away, that's how warm it's turned.'

Jim had passed old Asaph and Jeremiah Thompson beside the church earlier that morning, sunning themselves on the benches around the large maple. 'They'll be by. Isn't anyone strong enough to keep away from your coffee, Mrs Dalloway.'

She laughed, her cheeks turning pink with pleasure at the compliment. 'You could be right, you could be right.' She turned back to her customer. 'So, what do you think, dear? It does suit your colouring.'

'I'm not sure . . . They are all so pretty, it's hard to decide.'

A hint of iron entered Mrs Dalloway's voice. 'Well now, you need to make up your mind, dear. Here, why don't I let you decide while I finish up with Jim.'

She resumed stacking the tins of tobacco on the counter. 'Flatlanders!' she mouthed to him, rolling her eyes. 'Now let's see. Coffee, flour—'

'Hi, you there, in the overalls. Help a girl out, would you?' Jim turned, startled. The girl had two different swathes of fabric draped over her, tucked over each shoulder and about her waist. She cocked her head, smiling, and that mane of hair fell to one side. 'The teal, or the rose?'

He began to say something, caught off guard, then shrugged, embarrassed. The girl laughed, a low throaty sound that seemed to him all kinds of knowing, making him feel like a fool.

'Well, that decides it,' she declared. Unwinding the bolts from about her, she piled them onto the counter. 'I'll buy both, and that's that.'

She sauntered over, her heels loud on the wooden floor as Jim handed his father's card to Mrs Dalloway.

'Why, is that a veteran's card?'

'Yes, dear.' There was still a touch of asperity in Mrs Dalloway's voice. 'It's Major Stonebridge's – Jim's father. He was in the war.'

'The town must be proud.'

'That we are,' Mrs Dalloway agreed, her tone softening at the girl's interest. 'He was decorated in France you know. A real Yankee doughboy.'

The girl turned to Jim, intrigued.

'Do you think we might meet him? My friends and I, we have a summer theatre camp going. Well, spring camp, I suppose. We thought we'd begin early this year, no point in waiting about when we were all quite bored. *Any*way, we're working on a play. It's about soldiers. And the Great War. Do you think your father might accord us the pleasure of his counsel? Lend some authenticity to our shenanigans?'

'No.' Jim didn't bother elaborating the bald refusal, still prickling from his earlier fumble.

'He's a private sort, dear, the Major,' Mrs Dalloway piped up helpfully. 'Keeps to himself, a real stay-at-home. Why, I don't think I've seen him in years, isn't that right, Jim?'

'Yes, but I'm sure if he knew . . . Oh!' The girl paused, her mouth rounding dramatically over the 'Oh'. 'Why, how rude, I've yet to introduce myself!' She extended a slim-boned hand, not put off in the least by his reticence. 'I'm Madeleine. Madeleine Scott.'

After that morning, he thought of her. That rich red colour. Suddenly, it was everywhere. In the roan of a cow, in the threads unravelling from the velvet of his father's smoking jacket. In a portrait on a wall, a past Mrs Stonebridge wearing something red and sparkling about her throat. In the seams of the leather armchair, and the bridles glistening with oil against the wall of the barn. In the apples that lay fallen around the oldest tree in the orchard, arcs and moons of red on snow-patch ground.

Jim turned from the window, glancing restlessly at the black mirror. He could still see the tree, grafted from the earliest on the orchard. It seemed to list even more crookedly towards the barn when viewed in reflection, the memory of last year's storm in its jagged crown and gnarled, arthritic stem. The littered apples seemed at once attenuated and exaggerated, the red of their skins muted, but taking on a strange, subterranean glow, as if they were on an illustrated plate in one of his great-grandfather's books.

The image jogged Jim's memory, reminding him of a book he hadn't thought about in years. He waited until the Major had stepped outside, vaguely guilty as he watched him make his way through the dooryard. Only then did he head upstairs. He pulled out the book from the corner cupboard, shaking it to dislodge any insects that might be roosting within its pages despite the cedar roses that Ellie had thought to place along the shelves.

He whacked it against the windowsill and a puff of rust-coloured rot rose from the leather spine. It hung in the air, soft and amorphous, before drifting down, obscuring and then revealing the blurred image of the Major through the thick-paned glass. Jim studied his father for an instant, watching as the Major stooped and fussed around the fruit trees that were trained over the stone walls of the orchard. He turned his attention back to the book. It was a cyclopedia of painters and paintings. He flipped through the plates of reproductions, and there she was, just as he'd remembered her.

Venus Anadyomene.

'*Aphrodite*', the Major had pencilled in the margin. '*Made famous in a much-admired, now-lost painting by Apelles. Said to be inspired by Phyrne, the famous Greek courtesan, who, during the festivals of the Eleusinia and Poseidonia, was given to swimming in the sea, naked.*'

The woman in the black-and-white illustration was full-hipped and bare, squeezing the water from hair that hung over one shoulder. The lack of colour rendered the image flat, antiseptic, but nonetheless he still remembered the thrill he'd felt as a boy when he'd first happened upon her. The illicit tingle of pleasure as he'd taken in that expanse of unclothed skin.

'It's a very famous painting,' the Major had explained to his young son. 'Well, a painting of a painting, although no one knows for certain what the original looked like. Titian. He was the artist. His name also means "a shade of red".'

He'd said nothing in front of his father, but later, he'd stolen open the book and coloured in the woman's hair and the tips of those perky, gloriously naked breasts with a stick of bright-red Crayola.

A good thrashing it had earned him too, he remembered as he stared down at the page. Venus – or Aphrodite – who had once appeared so alluring now looked to him doughy and lumpen. The hair though . . . he touched a finger to it, tracing the strokes of red crayon, smudging the colour gently into the paper. *A blue dress. A mane of red hair, tumbling down her back.* He trailed his finger lower, down the exposed throat, to the chest, to the tips of the woman's breasts.

There was a flare in his groin. Suddenly restless, Jim shut the book with a snap and put it back in the cupboard, the rot settling on to his corduroys like soft, rust-coloured soot.

The third time he saw her, it was in the woods again. When Ellie came in the following Wednesday to cook and tidy up the place, she told Jim about a bobcat sighting, over by the Garland place, said that her kid had mentioned it to her. He set out the next morning, not particularly hopeful of bagging the creature without a dog to trail and tree it. Still, a bobcat sighting could hardly be ignored, not with the bounty paid by the State for each furred head.

He walked about the brush where the animal had last been sighted, methodically combing the ground. Sure enough, there they were: a neat set of tracks. His gut told him that if the cat was headed anywhere, it would be to the ridge that lay eastward, towards the river. Plenty of rocks and ledges there for resting places, and the wetlands teeming with hares and such for prey.

The problem was, the ridge lay plumb on the Garland property. It didn't seem like anyone was around though, not this early anyhow. The Garlands usually just came up from the city in the summer . . . He hesitated, only momentarily, before crossing the dirt road and passing the posted trees that marked the land as private property.

The acre or so of woodland that skirted the road lay in a depression. Filled with shade and thick with trees, the place seemed to him unusually silent. The ground was largely free of snow but yet winter-hardened, frozen solid in the slew of frosted nights that had followed on the heels of the warm spell. Jim headed deeper into the woods, glancing now and again at the ridge ahead as if he half expected the cat to be lying there in the open, sunning itself.

The trees grew fewer, a thin, clear light shimmering between them. A lone icicle hung from a branch. He touched a finger to the droplet beading its tip. A couple more days of sunshine like today and the few remaining patches of snow would melt as well, the creeks beginning to run in earnest once more. Cradling his gun, he walked on, mulling idly over the quiet.

He paused before a loose stand of sugar maple. The full-sap moon had risen the previous week. Low, blue over the woods, marking the start of the sugaring season. The maples had stirred in response, the sap slowly released from the wintered heartwood. The weather that had followed – days of sunshine and frost-tipped nights – had been ideal for making the sap really start to flow. All across the hills, the maples, still bare-boughed, were turned parturient, surging with quiet tides.

Jim rested a hand against the trunk of a maple, weighing in his mind the sap that lay pooling within, when it struck him: the tree wasn't tapped, and neither were any of the others. That's why it was so quiet – there was no *plink-plink* of maple sap dripping into buckets. He frowned to himself. Soon these maples would bud and the sap would turn, no longer suitable for syrup. Flatlanders! Frowning at the waste of it, he glanced again at the ridge looming directly ahead and walked on.

The soil was wetter as he approached the river, the beginnings of a spring creek evident in a shallow ditch, its border of snow still pure white and pristine. A few feet ahead, another crystalline stretch, but this one lay dimpled, ice piled in telltale granular furrows about its length. He extended a foot, the ice crunching beneath his boot as he shoved it aside; underneath, the meaty, speckled spathes of a skunk cabbage. The spring flower of the woods. It simultaneously curled about itself and thrust upwards in a red, fecund heat, melting its way through the ice.

A stray, boyhood memory: placing a spathe of cabbage in his mouth; the burning an instant later, like a hundred needles piercing his tongue. The Major, holding him above the kitchen sink, washing out his mouth.

He was shaking the ice off his boot when he spotted the scat. A sizable pile beneath a gnarled oak, bare of foliage and thick through the butt. He hunkered down over the droppings and when he glanced again at the ridge, there she was, out of nowhere.

Madeleine Scott. She stood with her hands on her hips, calmly watching – nearly startling the crap out of him too.

'This is posted property.'

'Didn't see no signs.'

She laughed. 'They're everywhere! Douggie likes people to know what's his.'

He stood up, brushing his hands on his shirt.

'Oh, don't leave, for God's sake.' She grinned. 'I won't tell if you don't.'

She came down the slope towards him, hair fiery against the

backdrop of grey bark and clear sky. She stamped her feet as she reached the bottom, a light gesture that barely dislodged the mess of pine needles and soil from her boots. She seemed neither to notice nor to care.

'I won't tell,' she repeated, shading her eyes as she looked at him. 'Besides, if you go, Jim Stonebridge, how am I ever going to find my way out of here?'

She'd remembered his name. A frisson of pleasure, followed by annoyance at himself for caring either way.

She bent over the scat. 'What are these? Droppings?'

'A bobcat's.'

'How do you know?'

He shrugged.

'How?' she persisted.

'Been hunting them a long time.'

'Still,' she said doubtfully, 'how can you be certain?'

'The ends,' he said, exasperated. 'See how they are blunted and not tapered? That's typical for a bobcat. There's a lot of it too – the scat, it's in bits and pieces.'

'Bits and bobs of bobcat scat.' She laughed. 'You learn something new every day. So what else can you teach me, Hunter Stonebridge?'

He looked at her, a swift, sideways glance, but she appeared to be genuinely interested, her expression guileless. Their eyes met for an instant, held. 'Their tracks are rounded,' he said stiffly, 'more so than those left by coyotes or fisher cats.'

She nodded, and he found himself wondering what else she might find interesting. That bobcat claws were retractable and didn't always show in the tracks? The way they had of crossing a logging road as soon as they came upon it, instead of padding cautiously alongside like other creatures tended to do? That some folks called them Wood Ghosts; that to see one was a good omen, and he had seen one, once, years ago on the frozen river, a spectre carved from ice and woodsmoke?

'They've summer and winter coats,' he offered, 'silver in the winter, brown and red,' – he glanced at her hair – 'in the summer.' Abruptly self-conscious, he turned from her as if to scan the ridges.

'How long have you been tracking this one?'

'Not long.' He hesitated. 'A couple of hours. Goes better with a dog,' he added defensively.

'Don't you have one?'

'Gave her away.'

'Oh. Why? Was she no good?'

'She was great.'

'So why did you—'

'Why are you here anyway?' he demanded. 'Are you really lost or just following me around?'

She laughed. 'That's right. First I lie in wait at the store and now I'm stalking you through the woods.' She seated herself on a large rock, tilting her head as she looked up at him. 'I'm a trifle lost, I have to admit. It was such a lovely morning that a walk seemed like just the thing, but now—' She sighed dramatically. 'I can't quite figure out my way back.'

'Damn fool thing to do, wandering about alone when you're not familiar with the woods. What would you have done if you hadn't seen me?'

'Climbed a tree or something? Walked to the water and waited there?' she shrugged, unperturbed. 'I'd have thought of something.'

He shook his head, amused despite himself. 'There are snakes around these parts, you know.' He gestured towards where she sat. 'Rattlers, under rocks and such.'

She shot to her feet. 'Rattlers?'

He grinned. 'No.'

'That's not funny.'

'Come on, let's get you back.' He started back towards the dirt road that bordered the woods. 'I take it you're staying at Doug Garland's place then?'

'Yes. But what about your bobcat?'

'Long gone. You talk far too loud for it to have stuck around.'

'I do not,' she said calmly. 'A lady never raises her voice. I don't think there was a bobcat here in the first place. In fact, I don't think you know what you're talking about, Jim Stonebridge.'

He turned around at that, just like she knew he would. 'Oh, I don't, do I?'

She settled back on the boulder and shook her head. 'No, I'm afraid you don't. What's more, you've been very rude to me every time I've met you.'

'Have I? Third time's the charm.'

'A third time!' She laughed. 'You're very confident that there will be a third.'

He looked quizzically at her, neither letting on about that first encounter of sorts at the river which would make this the third time they had met, nor disabusing her of the notion that he fancied meeting her again.

When he told the Major that Madeleine would be visiting, Jim waited, shoulders unconsciously tensed, fork poised over Ellie's boiled dinner, unsure how his father would react.

The Major continued to chew his food. He took a slow sip of whisky and nodded as he set down the tumbler. 'Flatlander?'

'From Boston,' Jim replied, relieved.

Jim said nothing more about how they'd met, or how, despite meaning to drop her off at the road that led to the Garland place, he'd found himself dawdling.

They'd meandered back as he pointed out the skunk cabbage he'd found, and another patch of ice, honeycombed in the light. She told him that her father taught economics at the University in Boston and was doing some research for Douggie on the side. The invitation, when it came, had worked out well, her theatre group had been looking for a place to practise and . . .

'What's your play about?' he asked.

'It's called *Catharsis*. An interpretation of the Great War through modern dance. Here,' she said by way of explanation. Standing in the middle of a clearing, the sun picking out all kinds of colours in her hair, she folded her body in half, bending over an extended foot like some graceful, long-necked bird. She turned, arms outstretched, light streaming down over creamy skin and fluid muscle.

He said nothing then, but he would think of that moment often. The glory of her hair, the grace of her body, sunlight flowing over her as if over the surface of a river. 'What do you want with the Major?' he'd asked brusquely, to mask his discomfiture.

'Your father? He sounds interesting.'

'He never talks about the war.'

'Alright.' She smiled. 'It doesn't matter, it was just an idea.'

Of course, now that she didn't seem all that keen to meet the Major, perversely, he wanted her to. He wanted her to see the old house, discover for herself how erudite his father was, to show her the apple orchard, and the books in every room.

'Even if he doesn't talk about it, you should meet him.'

'Alright,' she said again, simply. 'When?'

He looked now at his father. 'This Wednesday,' he said, in response to the Major's question, and the latter nodded.

That was the end of the conversation, father and son fell back into their daily routine of eating at the twelve-seater carved dining table together, but mostly in silence. Jim slathered mustard on to his portion of beef and began to tuck in heartily, thinking again of his meeting with Madeleine in the woods. He'd just dropped her off near the gates of the Garland estate when he'd turned, on a whim:

'Some folks call them Wood Ghosts,' he'd called out. 'Bobcats. It's good luck if you see one. Spotted one by the frozen river once, not far from where we were today. Just sitting there, staring into the woods. Like a statue carved from ice. Its breath had frozen into icicles about its nostrils and frost had bearded its face.'

THREE

Despite the fact that the Major had not once mentioned Madeleine's upcoming visit since that brief conversation at the dinner table, he hadn't forgotten. That Wednesday, when Jim came in from the barn, he paused, startled in the doorway. Then he grinned. 'Going somewhere?'

The Major ignored him and continued to read his newspaper with great dignity, as if his being all gussied up in a tweed coat and bowtie was a matter of course.

Ellie stuck her head out from the kitchen, face rosy from the oven. 'Doesn't your father look handsome?' she beamed. 'And what about you, mister?' She pointed an accusatory spatula as Jim peeled off his gloves. 'Surely you aren't going to receive your young lady dressed like that?'

He glanced down at his overalls, rubbing at a spot of grease. 'Whatever do you mean, Ellie?' he asked innocently.

'Jim Stonebridge, you know exactly what I mean. You were brought up better than that, go on upstairs and get yourself cleaned up.'

The Major lowered his newspaper. 'He looks alright to me, Ellie,' he commented, unexpectedly coming to his son's defence. 'The young lady is visiting a farmer's home after all.' He lifted the paper to his nose once more, effectively ending the debate.

They stared at him astonished, then shaking her head, Ellie disappeared into the kitchen once more.

'Ellie,' Jim called after her, amused. 'She isn't my young lady, I barely even know her. Besides, she's coming to see the Major, not me.'

He'd just about stuck his head under the faucet when the Ford turned into the drive. Grabbing a washcloth, he rubbed the steam from the window, catching a glimpse of the automobile before the glass fogged over once more. Tossing the washcloth aside, he cranked the window open, the cold raising gooseflesh along his arms as he watched the roadster noisily change gears and careen up the drive.

Turning off the ignition, Madeleine stepped from the car, holding the collar of her coat close against the chill. Her head tilted as she took in the house. She wore her hair sort of wavy in front and fastened at the nape of her neck, a rich, auburn knot, large as his fist.

He tried to read her expression, suddenly anxious for her to love this old, sprawling house as much as he did.

The front door opened. He could hear the slow scrape of the Major's cane. 'You must be Miss Scott.'

'Do call me Madeleine,' she replied, smiling.

'What beautiful woodwork,' Madeleine said, admiring the carvings in the front door.

The Major nodded stiffly, still formal and reticent as he pointed with his cane at the date inscribed above it.

'1 September 1773,' Madeleine read aloud, intrigued. 'Has the house been in the family all the while?'

'There've been Stonebridges in these parts since the town was founded.' He cleared his throat, tapping his cane on the floor as if debating whether he should, before awkwardly offering her his arm. She was gracefully looping her hand through it with a 'Do tell me more!' as Jim loped downstairs. Their eyes met, and she smiled.

Gradually, the Major began to let down his guard. He told her about that first Stonebridge, responsible for the house and that date over the door. A seadog if ever there was one, he'd stumbled upon his true love late in life: these mountains. It had proved a lasting affair. Although Captain Stonebridge still left periodically for the sea, it was here that he returned each time. His great-grandson, the Major's father, came out of the Civil War missing two fingers and afflicted with a violent case of wanderlust. He'd headed for Canada after the war, making his way across the Eastern Townships and the logging camps along the Laurentian, before joining a whaling ship off the West Coast.

'Ocean air and salted spray,' the Major said wryly, 'tidal persuasions, passed on through blood.'

Jim watched bemused as his father, so long unaccustomed to playing the role of host, graciously offered to escort Madeleine on a tour of the downstairs floor. 'My father was gone a long while,' he continued. 'When he returned, it was with a tiger skin that grew mould in the next spring thaw, that ivory tusk you see in the corner, velvet-lined boxes filled with whale teeth, porcelain place settings from Karlovy Vary, two wagonloads of books, and an army of cabinet makers and shipwrights on loan from a shipyard-owning friend.'

The men had set to work, expanding the original façade of the house, he explained, building upwards and behind. The symmetry of the original windows was maintained, but more were added and skylights introduced here and there. A library was built, fireplace mantels were carved from imported Italian marble, and brass hardware and claw-footed tubs were installed in the bathrooms upstairs. The Major pointed out the hem mirror installed along the fireplace in the formal parlour. 'Women would check their skirts there,' he said, 'back when the Stonebridges threw all sorts of grand soirees and dances.'

'Don't you host dances here any more?' Madeleine asked. She tapped the parquet floors with a foot, glancing mischievously at Jim. 'These floors are so beautiful, they just beg to be waltzed upon.'

The Major stared at her white leather Mary Janes as she tapped her feet. 'No,' he said, his voice suddenly distant. 'No, not any more.' He removed her hand from his arm, a frozen expression on his face.

'Major Stonebridge,' Madeleine began, 'I meant no—'

'Jim, I've bored your guest enough with my ramblings,' the Major interrupted. 'Show her around the rest of the house – the library, perhaps.' He limped stiffly from the room, the sound of his cane echoing on the parquet floors.

'Whatever did I say?' Madeleine said, bewildered, to Jim. 'I'm sorry, I didn't mean to upset him.'

Jim shrugged. 'He just didn't fancy a waltz with you,' he said mock solemnly, trying to lighten the moment.

'Oh, but I wasn't . . . you *know* I wasn't suggesting that he dance with me!'

'It was nothing you said.' Jim paused, his face tightening as he searched for the right words. He shook his head. 'Nothing that you did.' He opened the door to the library. 'Here, what would you like to see first? The family hoard of whale teeth, or Captain Stonebridge's journal?'

'Why don't you have dances here any more?'

'We used to, when I was little. Things changed after the Major got back from France. And after my mother died . . .' He shrugged again.

She took the box of whale teeth he held out, absently opening and shutting its blue velvet-lined lid. 'How long ago?'

'My mother? Soon after the war, about a year or so later. I was ten.'

'I'm sorry,' she said simply.

He turned to the bookshelf, pulling a weathered pigskin journal from a shelf. 'A journal that belonged to my worthy ancestor. The good Captain wrote every day of his adult life.'

She opened the journal, turning pages at random. 'Tidal longings . . .' she murmured. The light from the casement windows threw diamond patterns across the walls and the russet of her bent head. 'So do you harbour them, too?' She looked up, a smile playing about her lips. 'The Major told me that it skips a generation sometimes, but surface it does, time and again – the Stonebridge men and their fondness for the sea.'

Jim chuckled, settling himself against the desk. 'Sure, I think about it sometimes. What it'd be like to live at sea, nothing around but wind and high water. But no, this is home and the Connecticut's more than enough for me. The Connecticut river,' he elaborated. 'Fishing. Swimming. Canoeing. If you behave yourself, I might even take you there sometime.'

Shutting the journal, she reached behind him to place it on the desk then straightened to look him square in the face, parting those soft, ruby, contoured lips. 'And if I don't?'

Their eyes met, held. Before he could come up with a suitable retort, she'd stepped away.

The Major sat in his armchair and stared unseeing into the black mirror. The afternoon had been a mistake from the start. He should've known better. It was the way the boy had mentioned her visit though, the studied casualness of his tone, as if it didn't matter much either way, when clearly, *she* did.

The bowtie he'd put on with such care only a couple of hours earlier felt close and stifling. He tugged at it and it came apart, the ends hanging about his neck.

He should've known better. Too long. Too long since he'd last played host, and it was probably too late now. When a man had lived for a time with only the very familiar, the smallest unknown variable could upset everything. Even the most innocent of questions came fused with fault wires, threatening to destroy the shaky equilibrium so hard won, so painfully assembled over the years, exposing the bleached bones of memory long buried.

Dances, she had asked about, tapping her heel on the wooden floor, and it was as if the years had rolled back in an instant.

He could clearly hear the band, as if it were still playing from the stage set up in the corner of the dance floor; a mighty go they were having at the song too. The light from the sconces was reflected in the polished gleam of their instruments, flaring from the brass mouths of the trumpets and the hoops of the drums.

'When Yankee Doodle came to Paris town
Upon his face he wore a little frown
To those he'd meet upon the street, he couldn't speak a word
To find a Miss that he could kiss, it seemed to be absurd.'

The room felt close, stuffy, belying the snowdrifts that lay outside. So many people, the entire town it seemed, had turned out for this homecoming of one of their own. Suntanned, shiny-medalled, Raydon born and bred Yankee doughboy, on furlough from Paris and the war to end all wars: Major James Arthur Stonebridge.

A chorus of partygoers belted out the lyrics to the song, whatever they knew of it at least, mostly seizing enthusiastically on the word 'Yankee'. The noise hurt his ears. He started at each crash of the cymbals, his hand jerking reflexively to his shoulder for a rifle that wasn't there.

'But if this YANKEE should stay there awhile
Upon his face you're bound to see a smile
Soon YANKEE DOODLE he left Paris town
Upon his face there was a coat of brown
For every man of Uncle Sam was fighting in a trench

Between each shell, they learned quite well to speak a little French.'

He especially hated it when they came up on him from behind. An unending stream of guests, shaking his hand, taking his arm, slapping him on the shoulder as they offered their congratulations.

'Good on you, James!'

'Gave the Boche a taste of Yankee spirit, I bet.'

'I tell you Stonebridge, if I were younger, I would've been right there in the trenches with you boys. Pow, pow pow, giving those Germans a right good shellacking.'

It was so hot indoors. Sweat trickled down his neck, pooling slowly under his collar. He glanced longingly at the windows, picturing the clear, frosty night that lay just outside. The maples outlined in blue, thrusting bare-armed shadows over the ice.

He nodded at yet another guest come to felicitate him, barely making out the man's words. His back itched as the sweat crept down his spine and for a disorienting moment, it was as if he were back at the Front. Unwashed and under-slept, so filthy that his entire body itched and he couldn't tell if it was from the mud drying on his skin or the cooties in his uniform.

Reaching for his pocket square, he wiped the sweat from his forehead.

A woman leaned in, eyes bright with interest. 'How many of the Germans did you get, James? I mean, personally? I hear some men kept count, like notches in a belt?'

The excited twitch of her lips as she awaited his reply, those vulgar, suffragette, blood-red lips that had suddenly become de rigueur and perfectly acceptable in polite society while he'd been gone.

Overcome with loathing, he set down his glass and turned abruptly to his wife. 'Let's dance.'

He limped about the periphery of the dance floor, pain shooting up his damaged leg. It had been bothering him all evening, but he was too proud to use his cane and give these jackasses something more to chatter about. Why had he ever agreed to this mayhem? It had been his wife's idea, alarmed as she was by the stooped, silent husband who had returned to convalesce from his wounds, with dark circles under eyes that seemed so lifeless.

'I could hire a band from that new hotel in Montpelier,' she had suggested tentatively. 'A winter ball, it's been a while since we've hosted one of those . . .' It had been easier then just to nod in agreement than acknowledge the anxiety that she tried so hard to hide each time she looked at him.

He kept to the edge of the dance floor now, so that there was nobody at his back. His face expressionless, but his eyes darting ceaselessly from one end of the room to the other. It was foolish, he knew. Yet he could no more help this constant vigilance than deny his time at the Front. Round the room they went, his wife gladdened by his offer to dance, mistaking it for a glimpse of the husband she'd once had and laughing as she sang along.

'When YANKEE DOODLE! gets back to Paree
He'll break a million hearts take it from me.
When YANKEE DOODLE! learns to Parlez vous Francais
Parlez vous Francais, in the proper way
He will call each girlie 'Ma Cherie'
To every Miss that wants a kiss he'll say Oui Oui.'

A whirligig of feet on the floor, twisting, pirouetting, dancing. Round-toed and high-heeled, suede and supple, polished leather. A wave of anger swept over him as he recalled the inane conversation he'd had with yet another guest that night.

'See what you boys have gone and done, Stonebridge,' Doug Garland had said insouciantly. 'Now they're saying that the puttees you wear in the trenches would make good aids for hunting.'

'I saw something in *Vanity Fair,*' Mrs Garland helpfully piped up. 'A long length of wool, wound about the ankle and up to the calf. They're all the rage in men's fashion I understand. What colour would you suggest I get for Doug though? Khaki would be the most authentic, I suppose?'

Garland had grimaced, pulling on his cigar. 'The ugliest trend, and one that I hope is soon put to an end . . .'

The Major's face tightened as he remembered, the anger inside knotting into a hard, impotent rage. It all felt so wrong – the carousing, these effete men in their kid-leather shoes. What of all those worn, frost-stiffened boots? That bone-wearied tread, men marching mile after interminable mile, whether towards oblivion or deliverance, they hardly knew and were too tired to care.

He glanced towards the windows again, perspiring freely now and longing for air.

The music grew louder, the feet around him moving dizzyingly fast. A woman's white slipper, tap, tap, tapping on the floor. His wife said something to him, her words lost in the raucous sound. He shook his head to clear it. 'What?'

She leaned closer to repeat what she'd said, then changed her mind. 'Nothing,' she mouthed, laughing as she shook her head.

His nostrils flared as he caught a whiff of her perfume. Sweetly floral, mingling with the other scents in the room: of firewood, citrus, alcohol and musk. The balm of the civilised world. All false. Artificial. These lights, this bonhomie, the inanities of people who would never understand what it was really like over there.

A wave of bile rose in his throat.

Footsteps sounded in the hall, shaking the Major from his reverie. Suddenly aware of his watering eye, the Major clapped a hand over it, filled with longing for the solitude of the orchard.

Jim eyed his father's reflection in the glass, warily noting the strained tautness of his face and trying to gauge his mood. Before he could say anything, however:

'A Claude mirror!!' Madeleine was staring wide-eyed at the black mirror.

'Why . . . yes,' the Major mumbled, surprised.

'I've never seen one this big, in fact the only one I've ever seen is one that a friend of my father's owned. And that was tiny. This . . . this is . . .' her hands fluttered before her as she tried to formulate the words. 'It's *so* beautiful.'

'A clothed mirror?' Jim asked, puzzled. He'd never heard his father call it that, or anything else, for that matter. As far as he knew, it had always just been 'the mirror'.

'Claude,' she laughingly corrected. 'Pronounced like "road"; the name, as in Monet.' She walked, entranced, over to where it hung, examining the convex black surface of the glass. 'Beautiful,' she repeated.

She turned to Jim. 'They were used by artists to get a better feel for landscape compositions and colour. There are so many tones in a single colour, so many variations of shade, from light to dark, and they're notoriously difficult to capture on canvas. The Claude mirror,' she gently tapped the frame, 'it separates the tones so that only the most prominent are visible, making them easier to replicate. The old masters frequently used mirrors like these, setting one or more around their chosen subject and then painting the *reflection*, rather than the actual image.'

She hesitated, smiling at the Major. 'Do you think . . . May I take it down, examine it more closely?'

He hated anyone handling the mirror, but the Major nodded reluctantly, the palpable sense of relief emanating from his son as he did so making him feel even more of a heel.

He sank deeper into his armchair, trying to regain his composure, brushing surreptitiously at the last of the moisture from his eye as Jim brought down the mirror from the wall. Madeleine bent eagerly over the glass. There was something so guileless about her absorption, her enthusiasm so contagious that the Major gradually began to feel righted again. The old memories beginning to blur about the edges, their vividness receding, sifting into shadow.

The rasp of his breathing eased, and slowly it began to feel feasible once more to buy into a notion of normalcy, to make believe that the past could be left to lie where it had fallen, stripped away like an undertone of no importance. That this was all that mattered: a fire in the grate, the pool of light it cast, and three people, spending an evening in its warmth.

Madeleine continued to examine the mirror, resting its base on a table and swivelling it this way and that as she explored the room through the reflection in the glass. Now tilting it to the ceiling, now towards a knot in the floorboards, returning time and again to the faces of the two men in the room, one young, the other not, both with identical, summer-sky eyes.

It was dark outside when she said she really ought to leave, flurries of snow beginning to swirl silently through the dusk. Quietly remarking that it was far too cold for him to step outside – a charming, and rather obvious subterfuge, given his weather-beaten cheeks – the Major excused himself, so that Jim and she might end the evening alone.

'He's lovely,' she said as she buttoned her coat. That coquettish tilt of her head. 'So what happened to the son?'

'It skipped a generation, the loveliness,' Jim said solemnly as he escorted her to the Ford.

She grinned, holding out a hand to a descending flake. It held there a moment, then drifted gracefully towards the ground.

He opened the door of the Ford for her and tucked in the edges of her coat before brushing away the frost that crusted the windshield. He came around to the driver's side and she lowered the window.

'Douggie Garland is throwing a grand gala the Saturday after next,' she said. 'He's even ordered peacocks, real live peacocks, from some place down South.' She leaned forward, grasping the wheel with gloved hands. 'You should come.'

'I should? And what if all I have to wear are beat-up overalls and a hunting cap?'

She laughed. 'Well, then that's what you'll have to wear. Give everyone something to talk about.'

'Maybe I will. Get my hunting rifle, bag a couple of peacocks while I'm at it.'

She laughed again. 'So I'll see you then?'

He shrugged. 'Maybe.' He pointed at the open window. 'You really should roll that up, or the windshield will get fogged up.'

'Mmm, I'll take my chances.'

'You will, will you?'

'Yes. With the windshield, maybe even with men harbouring all sorts of secret *tidal longings.*'

'You know,' he said, leaning forward to rest his arms on the open window, 'my father left out something. What he didn't tell you is that no matter how strong the fever, or how far the Stonebridge men might go, they always return in the end.'

'Well, Jim Stonebridge,' she said insouciantly as she started the engine, 'they must know a good thing when they see it.'

He waited until the lights disappeared down the drive and was whistling as he walked back into the house. It was quiet; his father must have gone to bed. He hoisted the mirror back on to the wall, and stoked the fire. Struck with a notion, he took down the mirror again and held it to the fireplace, watching as the dark surface of the glass came alive. The colours of the fire, red and orange, black, gold and blue, each muted but distinct in its reflection.

'Clau-de mirror,' he said, under his breath. He ran a finger over the frame, thinking of the way her hands had looked against it, slender, so delicate. He shook his head, feeling foolish, but grinning all the same as he hoisted the mirror back on to the wall. Settling into his father's chair, he fiddled about with the knobs on the radio, and was soon absorbed in the game.

Upstairs, the Major lay curled up tight in his bed. Knees drawn in, hands tucked under, his entire body compacted, as if this forced density might anchor him, might hold him fast in the present. There was a pressure building within his chest, so intense that it hurt to breathe. He knew that ache well. Soon the voices would begin. Just a distant buzz at first. Then the shapes – of men and trees, blackened and torn. Of horses silhouetted against orange shell burst. A whinny of terror that cut to the bone; the voices growing louder, calling, reaching for him with phantom limbs.

The room was freezing cold, the bedclothes icy. When he had come upstairs, leaving Jim and Madeleine to their goodnights, a draught had nipped at his ankles, blowing frigid air across the landing and into the bedrooms. Worried that a shingle might have collapsed, he'd tracked the draught to the bathroom and seen that the boy had foolishly left the window open earlier that evening. Snow had been drifting in from the eaves for hours, powdering the windowsill and melting on to the floor. Still, buoyed by how well the evening had turned out, the Major had been more amused than annoyed.

He'd been looking for something to mop the floor with when he'd happened to glance outside. Something shifted within him, the quiet humour of an instant ago dissolving in the faint gleam of snow from the darkness outside. A memory, dredged from the past, of the final denouement of that evening long ago.

A man, dancing, or what passes for it. He looks at the windows, thinking longingly of the ice-rimmed woods. Damp with sweat, he limps on. His wife leans in to say something; his stomach turns, and falling to his knees, he throws up. The meat from his dinner, the copious amounts of wine that he has drunk – he brings it all up, continuing to retch even after there's nothing left. He rests his forehead against the floor, eyes closed, when he realises that it is very quiet in the room. The band has stopped playing.

'Too much to drink,' someone says.

The lurch of shame is replaced with a sudden, cold rage, an

unspoken fury against these fools with their white slippers and dance parties and no idea of what it is like out there. He staggers upright, throwing off his wife's hands as she tries to help. There is only one thought in his head: to be as far from here as possible.

'Please, continue playing,' he hears his wife say tremulously to the band as he leaves the room.

He stands in the hallway, staring towards the living room, drawn inevitably to the mirror that hangs there in knowing silence. He is gripped once again by the sense that this is all a dream, this world outside the war. Except he is slowly coming to realise now that it is not the world, but he who has changed, and that nothing here can ever make sense to him again. His body is coiled tight, choked with despair. He wants only to leave, to head out the door and keep walking, through the blue silence of the woods, past the frozen river, to the very ends of the earth, with only starred sky and cool, crisp snow to catch him as he falls. Blindly he stumbles towards the mirror, uncaring of – in some ways even welcoming – the pain arcing down his leg.

There is a movement in the shadows and he freezes, muscles tensing instinctively into combat mode. His eyes are wide, the pupils dilated in the half-light. It's not the Boche, however; only his boy, waving a hand through the railings. The child is thrilled at this unexpected company, leaning over the balustrade and beaming from ear to ear as his father comes up the stairs. A gap-toothed smile; he lost a tooth earlier that week. The staircase is in shadow and the boy cannot see the expression on his father's face.

The man is filled with fury, an unreasonable, unthinking, adrenaline-fuelled rage. He bounds up the stairs, two at a time, the adrenaline masking the white hot pain in his leg. A couple of strides and he is upon the child.

'What are you doing here? Didn't your mother tell you to go to bed?'

The boy looks blankly at him, only making him angrier. He smacks his son across the face with so much force that the child is nearly knocked off his feet.

'Stay in your room. Stay in your *room*. Didn't I tell you to stay down?' The child bursts into tears and runs to his room, cradling his stinging cheek in his hand and nearly tripping over his nightshirt in his fright.

'Restez en bas!' the man shouts furiously at his retreating form, 'I told you to stay down!'

It is only then that he realises he's speaking French. He's been shouting in French at the boy all along, who understands not a word.

Moving tiredly as he remembered, every joint in his body suddenly that of a much older man, the Major had shut the bathroom window. Picking up the washcloth that Jim had tossed in the corner earlier that evening, he had mopped the water from the floor.

FOUR

April 1932

It still hadn't stopped snowing, even a week after she'd left; at least it seemed that way to him. The sluggish passage of the days, the dreariness of leaden skies, the oppressive monotony of snow, collecting against the walls. Where once he might have taken pleasure in the gleam of rime frost on a leaf hanging solitary on a branch, or in the paw print upon some lonely bank, now all he felt was restlessness. She'd been, and gone, and there was shape and heft to her absence, a weight to the space she left behind.

The house felt stifling. The Major was sunk in one of his drinking binges, seemingly bent upon finishing as much of the bootlegged Canadian finest stockpiled in the cellar as was humanly possible. Bottles littered the side table and the floor around his armchair as he stared emptily into the Claude mirror. There was little to see except the reflection of the snow as it fell outside, each flake contracting then expanding as it traversed the curvature of the glass.

Jim had thought that the Major and Madeleine had got along well. So lighthearted had he felt after her visit that, accustomed as he was to his father's sudden shifts in mood and withdrawals into stony silence, the Major's subsequent disavowal of the evening caught him by surprise. The Major did not refer to her visit at all, not the next morning, nor in the days that followed. Jim waited, but when there was nothing forthcoming – 'She said you were charming,' he offered, almost shyly, in a bid to open the conversation. He shoved his hands in his pockets, drew them out again, fiddled with his belt. '"Lovely," I believe is the actual word she used.'

The Major said nothing in reply and at first Jim thought he hadn't heard, until he saw the giveaway twitch of his father's eye and knew otherwise. He waited an instant longer, for acknowledgement, for something, anything, but all the Major did was lift the whisky to his mouth once more.

Jim strode from the room, filled with a tight, hurt anger.

He spent most of his time in the barn after that, tinkering with the motorbike; when Ellie came in later that week and brightly asked how the young flatlander's visit had gone, both men said nothing. She saw the bottles, and the look on Jim's face, and knew better than to press further. She cleared away the litter without comment and busied herself in the kitchen, offering what comfort she knew: an apple pie with raisins plump with brandy from the cellar and just the way Jim liked it, a toasted, cinnamon scent warming the house to the eaves all that evening.

Still the snow fell, a soft, insidious rebuttal to that first thrust of spring. When it got unbearable, the silence, her absence, Jim shouldered his gun and headed once more for the woods. Too stubborn to go where they had met, by the Garland property, he circled his old haunts instead. There was nothing to be hunted, he never once lifted the muzzle, but still he walked, through the low, grey light, past sugar brush and pine, until he came at last to the water. The pines along the shore stood dark and brooding in the half-light, sentinels, bridging this world to another. Snow drifted delicately down, sideways, feathering the pines, dusting his face, sifting over the slow-moving river. Where once a balloon had floated, red and swollen, now white ice touched black water; a brief dance, as one slowly dissolved into the other, and still the snow continued to fall.

He stood on the bank, motionless, watching its dark rippled flow. Abruptly he shifted, making up his mind. He would attend the gala.

Perhaps it was the turn in the weather, the way the morning light played over the window panes. Maybe it was the clocking of enough days and the consumption of enough whisky that had served to recess memory once more into dormancy. Whatever the reason, the Major awakened on Saturday, on what – although he didn't know it yet – was also the morning of the gala, to a blessed, internal stillness.

Instead of reaching automatically for the bottle that lay on the floor, he blinked instead, at the quiet. Dawn was seeping through the windows, the edge of the bureau revealing itself in inches and quarter angles in the soft glimmer of morning.

Aurora, he thought to himself, recalling the ancient Goddess of the dawn. *Aurora, riding forth from her saffron bed.*

The pressure within his chest had eased; the abyss of the past no longer gaping wide. His pupils shifted, examining the pillow beneath his cheek, a single tuft of goose feather sticking upright through the fabric. His gaze moved lower, taking inventory of the contours of thigh, calf and foot beneath the bedclothes. He lifted a hand and cautiously flexed it. He spread the fingers, absorbed in every ridge and misshapen knuckle, like a newborn discovering the boundaries of its body for the very first time. Shakily, he raised himself, and holding on to the headboard for support, lowered his feet to the floor. A wave of nausea; he squeezed his eyes shut, opened them, focused on the rumpled sheets, stained yellow with sweat.

Saffron bed . . . he thought again, faintly amused by the irony.

The water from the faucet stung his skin, so cold that it hurt his teeth, but it cleared some of the fuzz from his tongue. He limped slowly downstairs, staying close to the balustrade, and in the kitchen, tacked cordwood on to the smouldering remains in the stove.

A spark flew out, caught on the front of his flannel shirt, flaring into a brief, fierce orange before spluttering out. He picked at the spot of soot, flicking it from him. A sense of accomplishment even in so small a task, relief over finding himself in the present once more, at being able to participate in the mundane events of the day. He ran over the facts in his head, taking comfort in this litany: a spark had lit out. The belly of the stove was bright with fire. It was April 1932.

Pulling on his boots, the Major stepped into the dawn. The apple trees beckoned through the mist like old friends. He limped among them, touching a familiar hand to bark and bough. Angling to the right, he continued along the old stone wall that bounded the orchard, waist high and scattered with snow and fragments of moss. The wall dated back to the first Stonebridge claim on this part of the hills, and was built from rocks cleared from the land. Some gneiss, a few stretches of limestone, but mostly granite of varying dimensions. Just a stone wall, no different from the others to be found winding about these hills, except that this one he knew like the back of his hand. The three largest stones were arranged next to one another about half a mile out. Bill, his brother, had liked to sit astride the wall there, whittling at pieces of wood with his penknife. And here, on this stone, at the base of the wall, covered now by grass, two sets of initials, carved a lifetime ago. His own, and a girl's whose name he no longer recalled, but with eyes of vivid green.

Sunlight caught the wall, coaxing fire from brumal stone, morphing jut and thrust into rose and a deep, burnished amber. He pushed on, panting now from the exertion, a stooped, solitary figure among his beloved trees. Just ahead, there, by the Baldwin that had taken seven years to bud, a man had once run, his young son bouncing on his shoulders, his hands gripping the child's legs. Laughter, the man's and the boy's, echoing through the trees. Had it been him and his father? Or was it him carrying Jim? The Major paused for a moment, unsure. It didn't matter, he decided, chary of probing the memory any further and risking it crumbling to nothing.

He quickened his pace through the thinning mist, going as fast as he was able, reclaiming these scattered bits of his life as they revealed themselves to him, piecing together as if from broken glass a picture of the person he once had been, of the life lived before.

Before the war, before France, before everything.

At last he faltered, the ache in his leg too pronounced to ignore. He leaned against the wall for support, waiting for the spasm to ease. Slowly he turned back towards the house, an imprint of his hand left in the snow that topped the stones.

He came around to the kitchen, breathing heavily as he unlaced his boots. The familiar creak of the armchair as he lowered himself into it. He leaned his head against the backrest, the tranquillity of the morning still held close inside him. There he sat, hardly moving, watching the sun swim across the surface of the mirror, the last strands of fog clinging futilely to the apple trees before vanishing into the day.

The morning grew steadily clearer, the sun holding firm court over the skies. It buoyed Jim just to look at it – the wash of light over the hills, sweeping aside shadow, restoring palette and definition to a smudged, undertone world.

He whistled as he brought in the backlog of mail – bills, a catalogue from Monkey Ward, and newspapers of nearly a week – whistled as he walked back up the drive, snow melting around his boots. A dark sweep of wing over the roof line – a barn swallow, in solitary, joyous flight. He looked up, squinting against the sun and was reminded in an instant of Madeleine, the way that she'd stood just about here, the tilt of her head as she'd looked up towards the roof. His carefree whistling stalled, and in its stead came a nervousness that he was entirely unaccustomed to, at the thought of seeing her again.

It was this feeling of being slightly off kilter that made him approach his father once more. He'd noticed that the Major had risen early, but Jim had given him a wide berth all the same, still hurt from being so profoundly shut out all these days. Now, however, he hesitated behind the Major's chair.

'I'm headed out this evening,' he said. 'There's a gala.'

So startling was the notion of this boy of his – rough-hewn, given to solitary wanderings – attending an evening soiree that the Major temporarily forgot the mirror, swivelling around instead to look directly at his son.

'A gala,' he echoed, astonished. 'Where?'

Jim cleared his throat, tapping the roll of newspapers in his hand. 'The Garland place.'

There was a silence and then the Major nodded. 'Douggie Garland.' The springs of his chair creaked as he turned away.

'Madeleine – she's going to be there. She's the one who invited me.'

'Did they print it?'

'What?' Jim asked, confused.

'The letter.' The Major nodded towards the newspapers. 'Did they print it?'

'No. I don't know. Haven't looked.'

'You probably don't remember the Garland mansion – you were young, but it's grand alright.'

'I remember. I was seven, old enough.' Jim hesitated. 'I'll only be gone a while.'

'I'm not your keeper, boy,' his father said, more sharply than he'd intended. 'Go, and there's no need to rush back either.'

A stiff silence followed. The Major drummed his fingers on the arm of the chair and glanced at his son in the mirror. 'And I wouldn't wear overalls,' he offered gruffly.

He had meant the comment to be wry, but the boy started as if stung. He tossed the roll of newspapers on to the side table. 'Butler's dropped out of the Senate race,' he said shortly, changing the subject.

The Major reached for the newspapers, frowning. 'Shame.'

Jim shook his head irritably. 'He was running on a dry ticket. Yes, I know, long-serving Marine, Medal of Honour, what not and all, but still, dry as they come.'

His father nudged the bottle of whisky that still lay by the armchair. 'Every man's allowed a vice,' he said lightly, 'and he has his – temperance.'

Once again, it was a badly misjudged attempt at humour. The sight of the nearly empty bottle angered Jim anew. He started to say something, changed his mind, and without another word, turned and left the room.

The Major's face flushed a dull red. 'And it's two-time,' he called tightly after his son. 'Major General Butler is a *two-time* Medal of Honour awardee.'

'An analysis of the solid 2–1 victory of US Senator James J. Davis over his dry opponent, Major General Smedley D. Butler, shows that the results of Tuesday's Pennsylvania primary will stand as a weather vane for the rest of the nation.'

The Major shook out his newspaper and read the sentence yet again. That fragile sense of peace he'd found earlier seemed lost. The mention of Garland had been jarring, but it was the exchange with Jim that had cut him to the quick. He stretched out his leg and slowly massaged the aching knee, gripped by a deep melancholy. The memory from earlier that morning, of a man running through the orchard, his laughing son bouncing on his shoulders . . .

Cutting a fresh plug of chaw, he tried to keep reading. *'The unabashed and vocal support that the ex-Marine has provided to the proposed Veteran Bonus Bill is suspected to have contributed to Tuesday's outcome.'*

The Bonus Bill. He knew it. It wasn't the fact that the General had been running on a dry ticket, it was his position on the Bonus Bill. *'The Bill has encountered severe opposition . . .', 'The Bill has . . .'* When he found himself going over the same words for the fifth time in a row, he gave up. He folded the paper, and set it on the table.

The bottle of whisky caught his attention. The look on Jim's face, the scorn he'd seen in his son's eyes reflected starkly in the mirror. Ashamed anew, he reached for the bottle, filled with the urge to fling it from him, to smash the accursed thing in the grate, but his hand stayed, slowing almost to a caress as his fingers curled about its squat neck. Shame turned to resentment and a deep, burning thirst. The Major lifted the bottle closer, tilting it this way and that as he examined the dregs. He started to twist the cap open, but again came that searing sense of shame, and abruptly he set the bottle down.

He shut his eyes and rubbed his forehead. A thought occurred to him and, rising to his feet and leaning heavily on his cane, the Major limped upstairs.

Jim stayed in the barn all morning working on the dirt bike, finding absorption in the clank of chain and machine part. The sun grew in strength, pouring in through the small, high windows of the barn, casting bands of haze over the dark wood walls and drawing meadow scents from the hay that carpeted the floors.

When finally he came back to the house, he found a cummerbund left immaculately folded on his bed. One belonging to his father. A peace offering of dark blue silk and smelling of cedar roses.

FIVE

Paris • June 1914

The ticket to the fight cost me nearabout a month's wages. It's most of what I got in my pocket, but hell if I care. I'd have emptied my pockets and given my pants too had it come to that, but no way am I goin' to miss watchin' Jack Johnson.

I hold on to that ticket all the way to my room in the 12th arrondissement. What with the fight the next evenin', and the Grand Prix the day after, Paris was 'specially crowded, and I ain't 'bout to let no quick-fingered thief pickpocket that ticket from me as he hustles past. I hold on tight, lookin' down now and again at it in my fist. Just the sight of it got me grinnin', from one end of my mug to the other like some soft-brained fool.

Ain't nobody seem to pay me much mind – things different here in Europe. Maybe these Frenchmen just more polite, or better at hidin' what they really think. Maybe it just the magic of the City of Light – it bein' one of those soft-smellin', slow-movin' summer afternoons, everythin' all bee-stung and honey-swollen. Anyhow, there ain't been one person starin' or mutterin' somethin' unholy as I pass; one or two men even nod and tip their hat to me. By and by, I get over the novelty of this, and begin to tip mine right back. I come across a powerful comely cher, all chocolate eyes and swellin' curves, and I sweep my hat off my head and bow low. She look over at me, and her eyes, they twinkle as she smiles.

I laugh from the pleasure of it, and walk on, a bounce in my step. I start to hear it, the secret music of the city, its hummin'bird chords in the gardens, slip-slappin' note by note through the Seine.

La Ville-Lumière, they call Paris, but this ain't so much a city of light but a city of music. A man might sit at any one of the café tables in the Rue de la Paix and what music might burst from his fingers! Treble and bass clefs, and the sax baritone. Beat patterns in every corner – in a bridge that curve just so, in all the carvings of the Notre Dame, through all of these old, old stones. And colour, so much colour – blue, green, and the chocolate of a woman's eyes, all of it comin' together like notes in a chord.

I see the music in my head, can feel the keys of the piano start to dip inside of me, and before I know what's what, I'm whistlin' a tune out loud. Grinnin' like a fool and holdin' on to my precious ticket, hummin' the music of Paris right across town.

I get to my room and hide the ticket behind the one picture frame that sits on the wall. I wink at the old dame frownin' down at me. 'Jack Johnson, doll,' I tell her. 'I'm gonna watch him in the ring tomorrow, and don't you wish you could walk right outta that frame and come along.'

Jack Johnson. I'm talkin' 'bout *Jack Johnson*. The Galveston Giant. Four-time defendin' world heavyweight champion, twenty-one time defendin' world coloured heavyweight champion. He's been champion since 1908, with eyes turned now to 'White Hope' Frank Moran to see if he can take the title away from the Giant. The papers on both sides of the Atlantic been full of the upcomin' match and I be goin' over each article so many times, I can repeat the words with my eyes closed.

Moran got age on his side – just twenty-seven – while Jack a long-in-the-tooth thirty-six. Moran been in serious trainin' all the weeks leadin' up to the fight, hell-bent on droppin' fifteen pounds before he step in that ring. I hear tell that on top of his runnin' and jumpin' rope, he be gettin' his sparrin' partner to sock him hard in the jaw. Hard as he can stand – it toughen the bone to pain. There's that right-hand punch of his too: Moran calls it Mary Ann – on account of it bein' such a knock-out and all.

Jack on the other hand, just be Jack. Motorin' around Paris in fancy cars, eatin' hard and liquorin' harder, gold teeth flashin' as he crack jokes 'bout his consumptive condition.

Even still, there ain't the littlest doubt in my mind over who goin' to win. Moran, he been on a good run – sixty-nine professional fights, thirty-nine wins, thirty-one knock outs, sixteen losses and fourteen no-decisions, but he ain't never been up against 'Giant' Jack Johnson before.

See, I grown up somethin' like Jack done, on dockyards and such. Ain't nothin' like sluggin' it out every mornin' on the docks just for the right of showin' up and doin' your job, that toughen a boy up right quick and proper. After you been in a few Battle Royals, where you and a bunch of other kids been blindfolded, and you gotta slug it out among yourselves till only one of you is left standin' – well, a boy learn to move mighty quick after that, and he sure learn to hit hard.

Moran might be tough, but he ain't never met nobody like the Giant before.

Soon as the fight was announced back in March, I been of a mind to watchin' it. I made my way to Philly and steady hung 'bout the docks, and by and by, got myself a gig on a four-masted vessel headed for France. We docked at Le Havre earlier this week and soon as I could, I hightailed it to Paris. The skipper, he told us just where to room in the 12th, the landlady bein' an old acquaintance of his and all, and here I am, with a ticket to the 'Fight of the Century', as the papers been callin' it.

I ain't got much left on me after payin' for the ticket, but there one thin' I got to buy prior. If you seen any pictures at all of Jack outside of the ring, then you know that along with a likin' for white women, Jack, he got a thing for black top hats. I'm hankerin' for one just like his, to wear to the fight tomorrow night. I stop a few men on the street and ask where I might find a hat fine as theirs. The wonder of this city – ain't nobody seem to find my request outta hand. They all point the same way, towards Chappelerie E. Motsch on Avenue George V.

The shop, it real frou-frou, like everythin' else on that street. Big gold letterin', glass and marble everywhere, and nothin' like I ever shopped in before. I pass it twice, first on this side of the street, then that, before I feel up to walkin' inside. That hidden music I hear, well in this part of the city, it ain't jazz no more but full-on opera, the kind you feel like you be needin' a monocle and a moustache to understand. I don't feel much better once I get up the nerve to enter – there's marble as far as I can see, and everyone speakin' in low, Sunday church sort of voices as they bend over the hats. I fiddle and fidget and feel like a fool, wonderin' just what I'm doin' in this rich man joint. My nerve starts to fail me proper and I nearabout turn and jump out that door, when a salesgirl asks if she can help me.

I tell her, bashful like, and she warms some when she hear the French fallin' from my tongue. She say they mostly do custom fittings, and I tell her I ain't got that much cash or so much time, but

I gotta have a hat just like the Giant's for the fight tomorrow.

'*Ah, la boxe*!' She shakes her head. 'Why are you Americans so crazy about this boxing match?'

'Boxin' match? This ain't just no boxin' match!' I say hotly, settin' her straight. Forgettin' all 'bout bein' bashful, I tell her 'bout 1910, when the Giant fought Jeffries in Reno. I'd have been right there watchin', 'cept I been in this bit of trouble with the law at the time. I followed that fight all the same, round by round. It was telegraphed live, and all around the world and every corner – Times Square in New York, bar-rooms in Washington and Tennessee, outside the Tribune offices – that Sunday evenin', everywhere you looked, there were crowds around a telegrapher. We even gotten a pool runnin' in County Cook prison, with the wardens arrangin' to have one of the inmates operate the telegraph keys. Ten to six and a half, the odds were, Jeffries to Jackson, and I wagered everythin' I got on the Giant.

Fifteen rounds they went, and when they announced the Giant's name at the end of it, man you should have seen the way the city went wild. Well, our parts of the city anyhow. It was a Fourth of July too, and I heard tell after that the fireworks that gone off that evenin' were somethin' to see alright.

There been ugliness, sure, in some parts of the country, broken bones and worse for some of our kind, but that only made the rest of us all the more loud. The champ, *our* champ was champ of the world once more, and we gone boo coo crazy happy, figurin' the fight that evenin' gonna shut those folks up for good.

I'm talkin' 'bout the folks burnin' bad over the fact that a coloured hold the world championship title. Even if Jack been holdin' on to that title for six years now, since 1908.

He first won it from Tommy Burns, and I'd have given everythin' I owned to watch that match, 'cept it was held in Sydney and what I owned at that time, it weren't hardly enough to get me even as far as New York. Jack, he won the title fair and square, but the papers said all kinds of things – that the match been fixed, that Burns been in decline anyhow. Them folks, they gone and badgered Jeffries outta retirement – someone got to teach this cotton pickin' blackbird a lesson, they said – until finally he agreed to the match in Reno.

Jack beat him proper, smilin' the whole time; the papers said the next mornin' that his win been so effortless, *obvious* it was fixed.

Ever since, them folks been out there, trawlin' the coal mines, farms and dockyards, huntin' for someone tough enough to beat the Giant. The Great White Hope they been callin' it, the hope that a white man gonna bring back the championship to their side of the colour line, where by their account, it rightfully belongs. Well, Jack, he believe no such thing and for the past twenty-five matches, he been reignin' king. They hate his guts and his hard drinkin', his proud, unashamed ways, and when he take a white woman for a wife, they slap a case of immorality against him. Jack, he got no choice but to leave America, makin' his way to London and now Paris.

Still them folks been searchin' and finally now in 1914, they gone and found themselves a new Hope in golden-haired Frank Moran. Tomorrow's fight ain't just some boxin' match, I tell that salesgirl, it much bigger than that. The Giant, he stand for more than just being a champion fighter, he . . . he . . . I struggle to explain what Jack Johnson come to mean to men like me.

'He's a *champ*,' I say finally, 'he *my* champion.'

The salesgirl look at me funny and I think at first she laughin' at me. But she tell me to wait, and damned if she don't go into the backroom and come out some minutes later with a hat fine as can be. There a slight fade to the brim, one you can't hardly see, but on account of which the price is only a bit of what it would have been otherwise.

I stand there, turnin' the hat this way and that under the lights. I tell you, it been one of the most beautiful things I ever held in my hands, chers included, and there been a fair number of them through the years.

The salesgirl ask what I plan to wear with the hat. 'These,' I reply, pointin' at the clothes I got on.

She shake her head. '*Incroyable*.' She quickly write on a piece of paper and hand it to me. 'Go here. They are costumiers for the opera. Tell Yvette that Celine sent you.'

I hardly know how to thank her, and she grin when I try. 'Ah, it's okay. Maybe you come by later and tell me about *le boxe*, yes?'

I tuck the hatbox under my arm and bendin' low, kiss that angel's hand. 'I promise, Mademoiselle.'

*

So it is that on the evenin' of 27 June 1914, Obadaiah Nelson, who never had no pair of shoes till he was well past ten years of age find hisself standin' outside the Velodrome d'Hiver, a song in his heart, ticket in his hand, and lookin' swell, dandy fine.

The stovepipe top hat sit real jaunty on my head. A thing of such beauty, the brushed beaver fur dark black in the settlin' light. Its silk linin' stamped with the crest of the shop, the words 'E. Motsch' over a shield, with two lions balanced on what looks to me like a ship. This last I 'specially like, given that it was a ship that brought me here to France. The rest of me look pretty fine too, in full evenin' clothes, borrowed from the good Yvette. A walkin' cane in my hand, shiny – and somewhat tight – black shoes on my feet and even a silk scarf around my neck.

I preen somethin' fierce in those borrowed feathers as I hand over my ticket and enter the Vel' d'Hiver. The din inside is somethin' else. By all accounts there were twenty thousand people at that fight in Reno back in 1910, and I reckon there at least as many here tonight, if not more. Many are women. Not the kind I seen at fights back home, hangin' around cellars and back rooms so smoke-filled you can't hardly see nothin', just the one naked bulb hangin' from the rafters. These are women of class, in expensive gowns; the jewels in their hair twinkle like stars.

It unsettle me some at first to find them lookin' at me, a few from the corners of their eyes, others more open as they turn my way and look me up and down. Then it hit me – the Giant, he a big man, 'bout six foot two, and I'm pretty high standin' myself. With this hat on, one just like his, and these clothes – why, those women must think the Giant and I are kin! I hold myself even taller at the thought, so proud and struttin' that tail feathers near start to grow from my rear. I hear a few American accents as I make my way to my seat. I cheerfully tip my hat to them, as if we grown up in the same sort of homes, gold-painted halls, marble floors and all.

I take my seat just as they announce the names, and boy, when I see the Giant, I forget 'bout preenin', I forget 'bout everythin' else, I just sweep the hat from my head and cheer like surely nobody never cheered before. He climbs cat-like into the ring. I whoop and holler, drinkin' in every detail, his hands hangin' easily at his sides, his jestin' and jollyin' with his minders, the way he shrug off his robe and saunter over to the centre of the ring.

The ring 'bout sixteen feet long and covered by a canopy strung with so many electric tubes that under their light he look almost grey. The light do funny things to blond Moran as well, turnin' his skin green, like copper left out in the rain. As relaxed as the Giant looks, standin' there with his hands on his hips, Moran seem tense, sort of bunched into hisself. I don't blame him one bit.

The megaphone crackle to life again and the announcement of the fight echo round the velodrome. The crowd fall silent for a moment.

'Go Moran!' a man calls.

'Jack!!!' I holler in return. The couple seated in front, they turn round to look at me, frownin', and I grin.

They go twenty rounds, and from what I see, it ain't no match at all. Every now and then, Jack's wife, she yell from the front row.

'Go Daddy! Give it to him, pop!'

Someone should've told her to save her breath, 'cause the Giant, he don't need no such encouragement at all. In fact, he make the match seem so easy that people start to complain.

'Fake!' they hiss, 'fix!'

I know there nothin' fake 'bout his win at all. This ain't no fixed match. Moran, he try his hardest, but the Giant is just that good.

Moran don't land even one of them Mary Ann punches. Each time he try, Jack just dance out his way, this way, then that. Round two, Jack land an uppercut in Moran's face. It break the skin and the blood start from his nose. Round ten, another cut, this time below the eye. Round fifteen, Moran so tired, he nearabout holdin' on to the Giant just to keep hisself on his feet. Five more rounds he lasts, and I tell you one thing – Moran, he got grit and he got stayin' power. Full twenty rounds he go against the Galveston Giant, and ain't many men who can say that.

Close to midnight when the match finally ends. The referee declares the Giant the winner, and I yell his name somethin' hoarse. Jack Johnson just proved that he still the champ of the world! I race down the stairs that lead to the centre of the floor like a madman, not even noticin' those too-tight shoes that been pinchin' my toes all evenin'.

The ring awful crowded and the Giant just 'bout drowned in champagne. He surrounded by folks pumpin' his hand, slappin' him on the shoulder. I push my way to the ropes and I'm lookin' up at him, wavin' the hat to catch his eye and 'bout to call his name, when somethin' 'bout his expression makes me pause.

There all this ruckus around him, so much laughter and talk and congratulation that Jack, he should be the happiest man alive. But there he stand, with the strangest look on his face. Tired, he look, worn out, and suddenly very old. It stop me cold. I just stand there, the hat in my hands, lookin' up at him and at that deep tiredness in his face. Slowly placin' my hat on my head, I turn and start to make my way out of there.

The exits are crowded and I guess I weren't payin' too much attention 'cause I never did see who it was that knocked the hat down. Could have been any one of them – the fellow walkin' a blonde right behind me, the Americans to my side. The hat, it roll off my head and right into the feet of the crowd. I push my way down in my fine dandy clothes and all but it keep gettin' caught under all those feet, and by the time I catch up to it, its brim is dented somethin' awful. There's a tear in that fine black fur, and a shoe print on the linin'.

I pick it up and dust it off the best I can, my heart damn near breakin', 'cause that been one proud, beautiful hat and now it ruined.

Take me a long time to get to sleep that night. An awful long time, and when I do, I sleep right through the mornin'.

I wake to a right commotion in the corridor outside. When I ask, they tell me that the Duke of Sarajevo was shot a little while earlier.

I ain't fully followed the how or why, but the German Kaiser, he go and declare war on Austria in return.

SIX

The afternoon sun is hot on my skin. Still, after nearabout a month in prison, it sure feel good. I lift my face to it, and it beat down on my closed eyelids with a sharp, white light that clear La Santé from my mind.

All these past weeks, I been coolin' my heels in there, inside a stink-filled cell hardly tall enough to stand upright in, and crowded with three other men besides. Leanin' against the peelin' walls stained with mould and dried piss, dreamin' of the chers I'm going to get with soon as I'm outta here. Brown-eyed dolls, the kind who smell real nice, with skin like warm honey silk. Most days I been dreamin' of those girls, and in between, cussin' out that skipper and his lyin', weasel neck.

It was his doin' that I ended up here in La Santé. Soon as that Serbian count was killed, Paris been struck with talk of war. Rumours spreadin' wide, a treble riff cuttin' right through the heart of the city. Jazz bars start to lie empty as all the tourists leave. Like rats from a troubled ship, 'cept these rats, they run fast as they can *towards* the ships, squeezin' into every spot there is and payin' triple, sometimes five times the regular price to get away before the Boche arrive. Instead of havin' to pay wages, skippers suddenly gotten entire crews willin' to work for free, just for a safe passage home.

When I mosey on over to the docks at Le Havre for my balance wages, the skipper say he owe me nothin'. What's more, he say, cocky as anythin', if I want to get back to Philly, I got to pay *him* proper.

'I ain't doin' no such thing!' I say heatedly, warnin' that weasel that he'd better pay up if he know what good for him.

'I'm jesting, is all,' he protests, grinnin' his oily grin. He make a big show of countin' out part of my wages, sayin' he need a few days more, to sort through the rest of the accounts. Why wait here at the docks when I could go back to Paris, he say. He can send the rest of the money and my papers to the landlady there.

Ain't that much to do in Le Havre, and the money he put in my hand, it enough for a few days more of summer lovin'. *Laissez le bon temps rouler*! Fool that I am, I hotfoot it right back to Paris – a powerful good time I had that night too. The next mornin', the police, they come bangin' on the door, fussin' to see my passport and other papers.

'The skipper got them back in Le Havre,' I tell them. The skipper the one who reported me to the police, they say. One thing lead to another and what with tensions already high with talk of war and enemy spies, and my not havin' any sort of identification on me, I land behind bars in La Santé.

The way things work here in Paris, a man can be put in prison before even being charged. Most of July I spend locked up in La Santé, waitin' my turn before the judge. All the while, talk of war keep spreadin' outside, like jungle drums bein' beaten, deep inside the city's heart. I feel the bass notes of their warnings as I cool my heels in that stink hole, feel them rollin' through the sewers, pushin' up along the floors and walls. On Saturday 1 August, the warnings come true: mobilisation notices posted across Paris as Germany prepares to declare war on France.

At first, there's dead silence at the news. Even from inside the prison, I feel the quiet, the thickness of it, coatin' the city's tongue. Paris been stricken dumb. The French, they didn't ask for no war, they ain't invaded no country or anythin', but war been pushed upon them all the same. A shock-filled silence and then the city *explode* in sound. Bugles and trumpets, and the thrillin' notes of the Marseillaise.

'*Allons*! *Enfants de la Patrie, le jour de gloire est arrive*!'

The French, they didn't seek this war, but now that it at their doorstep, they gonna put up a fight. Motor cars and trucks crank up and down the roads outside the prison, soldiers march past to the sound of loud cheerin' and there the clatter of horse hooves at all hours as the French cavalry rides off to war.

'*Vive La France*!' The cry is taken up by voices across every arrondissement, as church bells ring out over the Seine. '*Vive La France*! *Vive l'Armée*!'

I raise up on to the balls of my feet, pressin' my chin against the small windowsill to look outside, my fingers restlessly a-tappin' on the bars of the window.

A right grand affair it look to be, the cheers of the crowd rattlin' the walls of the prison and lightin' a fire in my blood. Men bein' requisitioned for the Front from around the country, we hear. Everyone between the ages of eighteen and forty-five been called up, not that folks be waitin' for their official papers before linin' up in front of the registration offices. Proper soldiers they goin' to become, for as long as this war goes on, set up with full gear, shiny rifle and all. By all accounts, it shapin' up to be one grand, slap-up fight and it got me hankerin' somethin' bad to be outta this cell, out there in the sunshine and in the middle of it all.

Some weeks later, when a captain from the French Foreign Legion visit La Santé, it feel to me like my first stroke of luck in a long time.

'Prisoners held on minor charges are permitted to enrol in the Legion,' he informs us.

If we volunteer to sign up for the length of the war, our offences will be pardoned. I know that I ain't even had no trial yet, but this sound like a right sweet deal to my ears anyhow. Out of this stink hole into the real world once more. And how bad can the Front be? A couple months of ruckusin' 'bout there, then back to Paris for the victory celebrations. I ask, cautious like, if folks like me can sign up, men of colour, and the Captain look surprised.

'Yes, of course,' he say.

My hand 'bout the first to shoot up in the air.

The Captain laugh. 'Not so fast. Every recruit joinin' the Legion is given a day to change his mind,' he explain. The same rules goin' to apply to us; he gonna be back tomorrow with a doctor for the physical examination. I can't hardly wait, countin' down the hours. The next day, he return. The doctor turn away quite a few, one man for no more reason than his rotted-down teeth. When it my turn, I send up silent thanks to my mammy and pappy for the pearly whites they passed down to me and open my mouth wide.

I pass the physical easy, and that how me and a few others come to be soakin' up the sun outside the main gate of the prison. We waitin' for Gaillard, the legionnaire sent to escort us to the headquarters of the Legion at the Hotel des Invalides, to finish his cigarette. The sun, it's hot alright, and I look curiously at him as I roll my sleeves higher.

He sit on the wooden bench screwed into the brown brick wall of the prison, hardly even lookin' at us as he smoke. Real comfortable in this heat, in a jacket that's fully buttoned, even the collar, the crease in his red trousers as sharp as if he just put them on. He got a few years on me, somewhere in his late thirties I figure, not too tall and real thick through the chest, with arms that bulge under his jacket. He got a tattoo on his bull-like neck; the sun and years have faded the writin' to near the same blue of his collar.

'*Legio Patria Nostra*,' it say, around a drawin' of two guns and a thorned rose. The Legion is our Fatherland.

Puttin' out his cigarette, he adjust his cap and look us up and down, as if noticin' us for the first time. '*Le meilleur de La Santé*,' he say, dry like. The crème de la crème of La Santé.

'*Comment avez-vous rejoint la Légion*?' I ask, interested.

He glare at me with narrowed eyes. '*Merde*!' he snap. 'You never ever ask anyone in the Legion when and how he signed up. *Never*. Not even a man who may have joined before he was fully grown. Maybe because he had to get away from his village because all the girls, even the richest, the prettiest of them – ' he make melon shapes with his hands – 'fell madly in love with him. All of them, at the same time, makin' his life a livin' hell – "pick me, choose me" – until there was nothin' to do but run away, as fast as he could, and join the Legion.

'*Non*,' he continue, 'you *never* ask anyone why they joined. Once you're in the Legion, all your past is forgotten.' He sweep his hands out wide, the buttons on his jacket shinin' like gold. 'Gone!'

We walk the hour or so it take to get to the Invalides. So many done left for the Front, that the cheerin' crowds are gone, but trucks still roar past on Rue d'Assas, loaded down with tarpaulins, nettin' and fat rolls of bobwire. The French flag everywhere, in the windows of apartments, hung from lamp posts and planted in the flower beds. Bright-coloured buntin' – red, white and blue, same colours as the flag – is tied 'bout the iron balconies. It litter the street, just like it do after Mardi Gras. I push at a bit of buntin' with my foot. Like after Mardi Gras, with the party already moved on, and just leftover itty bitties in the streets to show the way . . .

I look up at the family walkin' towards us. The young mother, the father in uniform, each holdin' a hand of the little girl skippin' between them. The man say somethin' to his wife, noddin' at the child, and she smile. The little girl suddenly breaks free of her parents.

'Attrape-moi, Papa, attrape-moi!'

She take off runnin' down that street, the bows in her hair jigglin'. She right giddy with excitement over this little game, and her father chase after her, laughin'. The mother is comely, and I steal a look at her as we pass. The smile from a moment ago gone as she stare ahead. She don't even notice us, eyes only for her husband as he run after their daughter; there's so much sadness in that pretty face that I look away.

Gaillard march past her, stone-faced. *'Les salauds,* les Boche,' he mutter under his breath.

Rue de Grenelle is a long row of iron shutters. The shops all closed; where there been hats and watches and all colours of candy, now there only notices posted by the drafted proprietors.

'Maison Française,' the notices say. *'Maison Ultrafrançaise.'*

Gaillard point at one of the shutters. 'You could get the best croissants in there,' he tell us. 'Crisp. More delicate than you could ever imagine, crumblin' in your palm if you held them too close. Melt to nothin' in your mouth they would, leavin' only the taste of warm butter.' He pause, lost in the memory of those croissants that sound so good my stomach start to rumble. 'Now there are no croissants to be had anywhere in Paris,' he continue in disgust. 'The bakers are all at the Front, and the Government has ordered that only the simplest of breads be baked.'

He spit noisily in the gutter. 'Bastard Boche! Thanks to them, there's nothin' in the bakeries no more but dry *boulot* and *demi fendu.'*

Changed as the city is, it's only at the Invalides that it truly sink into me that France now at war. I must have passed by them buildings dozens of times before, on my way to jazz bars and such, and not given them a second look. Now, though, the golden dome look to me like the crown of some old king, standin' firm as he face the enemy. I run a hand along the sun-warmed chassis of a motor car, one of hundreds parked in the courtyard. Civilian vehicles, called up for the war effort, Gaillard tell us. Row after row of them, more than I ever seen in any place before, of all makes and sizes. I 'member the stories Pappy used to tell, of warhorses all suited up in armour and lined up for battle . . . Them cannons in front of the buildings ain't been used in years, but somethin' so charged 'bout the air that I bet none of us would be much surprised if those guns, they suddenly begin to buckle and fire. Legionnaires everywhere, on the stairs, walkin' quick and purposeful-like through the corridors, and watchin' them makes me want to hold myself taller.

'Napoleon,' Gaillard point out, jerkin' his chin, and we look up at the statue of Msieu Bonaparte hisself, starin' silently at us, a hand tucked into his coat. 'He is buried here,' Gaillard say casually.

When it is my turn to walk into the room, the officer ask only a couple of questions.

'An American, I see. Do you wish to give up your citizenship?'

'*Non.*'

'Do you wish to change your name?'

'*Pourquoi?*' I ask, surprised.

'Some men do,' the officer shrug. 'Once in the Legion, a man can leave his past behind, if he so wishes. A pregnant girlfriend, a broken heart, worse.'

'*Non.*'

He show me where to sign the form, and easy as that, Obadaiah Nelson free of prison and become a legionnaire.

They tell me that my gear gonna be handed out in a few days – it still early days in the war, and supplies ain't yet caught up with the number of recruits. I'm given three francs and a blanket, and shown a room to sleep in. Now that room, it already got six men in there, one of who is slowly pickin' at his swollen, stink-filled feet. When he starts to work the cheese from under his toenails and flick it to the floor, I figure I can do better. I ask what time I need to report the next mornin', and stayin' just long enough to clean up some, head on out to the Latin Quarter.

It ain't long before I meet a cher, fine as can be, with some English on her tongue and a friskiness in her bones. 'Three francs' all I got,' I confess. 'But I'm leavin' for the Front soon and sure could do with a goin' away party.'

She laugh and lean in for a kiss, and it ain't long before we on her bed and I'm sinkin' deep into her warmth. She hold my head in her hands. '*Vraiment*?' she gasp. 'You are really going to war?'

I manage to nod, tryin' not to break that sweet rhythm, my hands full of soft, yieldin' woman flesh.

She laugh again and wrap her legs 'bout my back. 'Who would have thought it. *Les Américains*, fighting our war. My American *poilu*!' I ain't up to pointin' out right at that moment that I ain't all that hairy. Only later that Gaillard tell me that '*poilu*' – hairy one – is how the French fondly call their soldiers. Anyhow, she still talkin', 'So you're one of the comers then, not the goers?'

'What?' I manage, confused.

'So many of the foreigners, they couldn't wait to run away at the first mention of the Germans.' She squeezes tight and begins to rock beneath me. 'The goers. You, my dark-skinned *poilu*,' she gasps, 'you are a comer, yes?'

Yes'm, I surely am!

Those francs, they go unspent. She tuck them back into my pocket when I try and hand them to her the next mornin', and kiss me on the cheek. '*Bonne chance*,' she say. 'Good luck, *mon poilu*.'

When I foot it back to the Invalides, I'm instructed to report to the 2nd Division. To my surprise, I find there's other American recruits here too.

Big Rene Phelizot, he been huntin' elephants in Africa all this while. He book passage to France soon as he hear 'bout the war, the Boche gettin' him all the more riled up by confiscatin' all his ivory in Antwerp. Frank, he been chicken farmin' in Virginia. He was sick of them egg runs, and the hens be slow-layin' in the autumn anyhow. There's Eugene, a butcher from Woonsocket with a carvin' knife packed in his things. Nick the Greek been sellin' bananas under the Sixth Avenue Elevated Station in Manhattan, and Bert been a cab driver in Paris.

Turns out there's a bunch of us, from all parts of the States, though listenin' to some of them talk, our paths ain't crossed none too much back home. College graduates these are, many with a heap of family money, talkin' of ponies and opera and such, of holidays in London, and their frou-frou college clubs, Delta Sigma Kappa Crappa Pi Pee.

I stay quiet at first, mindin' my business as I listen to them jabber. Once the war was announced, each of them been of the same mind it seems: to get over to the Front and see for themselves what all the fuss 'bout, and if they could help out any.

There's two brothers from Tennessee, with real fancy clothes, long reachin' family tree and all. The very kind of folks who, if you saw them walkin' down a street in the South, you'd do well to heed your mammy's tellin' and cross on over to the other side. I thought I known everythin' there to know 'bout boys like them. Here, these two though, milky pale Southern skins and all, seemin' like they don't care one bit 'bout no colour line, jibin' free as can be with Bob Scanlon, the boxer from Mobile.

They get to talkin' 'bout boxin', and Bob, he mention the reason he come to Paris in the first place was Jack Johnson.

'You seen the match?' I interrupt, clean forgettin' my notion to stay silent.

''Course I did,' he exclaim. 'You go too?'

'You bet I did!'

We stand there beamin' at one another, two men of colour, sharin' our pride in our very own champ, but not inclined to say too much more. Jack still a touchy topic with most, and we ain't lookin' for no trouble.

'It was fixed,' one of them college boys scoff, and I feel the heat rise in my face.

Before I can say anythin' though, a voice cuts in.

'I doubt that.' The speaker is tall, not too broad of shoulder but his hands got real wide span. He been sittin' in a corner all this while, readin'. 'Johnson is just so good he makes it seem ridiculously simple.' Settin' down his book, he glance cool like 'bout the room. 'I watched him fight in Reno. When a man's that good at what he does, he makes every match seem fixed.'

'You a Johnson fan?' I ask surprised.

He shakes his head. 'I was counting on Jeffries actually, in Reno.' He's silent some, then adds, 'Still, after that match, any man who denies Johnson's the best fighter out there is a jackass and a damn fool.'

That was the first time I laid eyes on James Arthur Stonebridge. I taken a likin' to him at once.

SEVEN

Toulouse • October 1914

The more I see of James, the more I come to realise that he the least-speakin' man I ever met. An East Coast Yankee he is, come from some place up in New England. Keeps mostly to hisself and somethin' like my pappy he is, his nose always stuck inside some book. There plenty thoughts in his head, but not many that come to his tongue – and when they do, it a week with seven Wednesdays that he don't call someone a jackass or a damn fool.

Three weeks we been in Toulouse now, drillin' and marchin' and wakin' at the devil-spawn hour of five every mornin'. We sure luckier than the bugler standin' out there in the still-dark grounds, but this fact ain't made me no better disposed to havin' to jump outta our beds soon as the reveille come tootlin' through the windows. All the same, after that month in La Santé, this here camp in Toulouse feel like one long picnic, and I ain't complainin' none. The Front seem awful far away, but suit me just fine to just ease up some and catch my breath here for a bit.

Different for them college-boy recruits though – mighty restless they are, and itchin' bad to get to the Front. The veteran legionnaires – the *anciens*, we call them – poke fun at their eagerness, but this only egg them on all the more. James 'bout the only one who stays quiet, listenin' to the others yarn. The number of Boche they goin' to take down! The parties once the war been won! They got it all planned, and truth be told, it don't sound too bad to me at all. Thanksgivin' on the Front, and Christmas in Paris. New Year's back home or wherever takes their fancy, at victory parties that turn all sorts of crazy, with the liquor flowin' free and chers steady swingin' easy.

'What about you, Stonebridge?' someone calls.

James look up from the notebook he writin' in. 'It's a damn fool of a man,' he say slowly, 'who thinks the war will be over by winter.'

He nods at the beat-up rifles we been issued. 'I'd wager the Kaiser has outfitted his men rather better than this,' he comment, and lift up his pen again.

He a real serious sort he is. When Gaillard come around, askin' for *'Un homme de bonne volonté,'* I hold back, fixin' to learn more, but Yankee James, he the first to raise his hand. How straight he stands! So brave he look, rock-solid, set on doin' whatever it is that needs to be done, this top secret mission, as Gaillard thumps him on the shoulder.

How crushed when the next moment, Gaillard hand him a mop and a bucket and point towards the ripe, overflowin' latrines!

I near fall over laughin' at the look on his face. Pappy, he always said it'd be my big mouth that'd get me into trouble, and he surely right. Gaillard rounds on me and in two shakes of a duck's tail, there I am, standin' right next to the Yankee, a mop and bucket in my hands too.

Gaillard claps us on our backs. 'Get to it, *mes enfants,*' he grin.

Turns out by the by that a talent for shovellin' crap ain't the only thing that Yankee James and I got in common. Even with all the different roads we taken, him with his low-speakin' New England ways and me, a Louisiana gumbo ya-ya boy, we still got things we share.

First, of all the new recruits, it's him and me who speak the best French. Sure, his be the highfalutin' Paris-parlour version, while mine's pure Southern Creole, strung through with swamp moss and the flow of the Mississippi, twistin' and turnin' like no proper French ever could. Even still, James and me, we've become translators for the rest. 'Specially when the other drill instructors start yellin' at us *jeunes* to form all sorts of formations and most of the recruits be lookin' blank like back at them, shiftin' from foot to foot and not understandin' one itty bitty word.

Then there's the motion pictures. These first weeks in the Legion, we kept plenty busy durin' the day, but most evenings we got to ourselves. I run into James often times in town, waitin' in line for the westerns they screen here, straight from the good old US of A.

'You a John Finch fan too?' I ask and he shrug as if he don't care one way or the other. 'See you often enough here,' I press.

'They show them for free,' he says, as if that explain everythin'.

*

Slowly, we start to get the ins and outs of being a legionnaire. Oh we still yelled at plenty every day durin' the drills, but the number of times we hauled up for showin' up to the grounds a minute or two late, for not standin' straight enough and such, those become fewer. We figure out how to tie the long blue sash that goes on beneath our belts – it goes easiest with two men. James, he got the bed next to mine, so the two of us pair up. I hold one end of his sash, real tight. He start at the other end, twistin' it 'bout his middle, turnin' round and round towards me till all nine feet go on, flat and smooth. Then he do the same for me. Sometimes I shake things up by puttin' a little rhythm in my step, a click clackin' of my heels and fingers, a little dippin' and bowin', with real sharp turns. He look startled at first, but then I see the twinkle in his eyes.

Then there's System D. *Demerdez vous,* or System D, simply mean this: do whatever you gotta do to get yourself outta shit. Or as James translates it, more polite like: fend for yourself.

James and the other college boys have a harder time with System D, but I been livin' with it most of my life and ain't got no trouble with it at all. Time for drill already and your gear ain't in order? *Demerdez vous*: 'borrow' someone else's. That rifle lyin' shined and proper polished on someone's bed, the shirt, freshly washed and left unguarded on the clothesline – all fair game for System D, *merci beaucoup*!

It work well for food too. We awful hungry all the time – the Legion, it sure feeds its recruits, but only as much as it needs to, and not one itty bitty crust more. The company cook's a right ornery bastard besides. He touched with *le cafard,* the *anciens* say – the illness of the brain that befallen many of them after the Legion's Algerian campaign. 'Like black beetles crawlin' inside your head,' Gaillard tell, a sickness brought on by the desert sun. Durin' one of those endless marches there, the cook gone and passed out, tumblin' ass over head. When he finally woken, he gotten up as if ain't nothin' happened and everythin' okay. Everythin', 'cept for this: from then on, he been fixated on the notion that he the double of King George of England.

Mind you, there's some resemblance between the two. 'Bout the same height and broadness, the same shape of the head with the hairline startin' to pull back, and them big, far-spaced eyes. The cook though, he convinced they look like twins. From now on, he must be called by his rightful name, he insist, and in the humour-filled manner of the Legion, everyone agree, even the officers, callin' him King George.

George, he be guardin' the kitchen supplies like the treasury of all England. We try our luck, and even bribes when we got them, but ain't no second helpings comin' our way.

I start hotfootin' it to the patisseries in town as often as I can. My legionnaire wages of one sou a day don't stretch none too far, and even when I make a little on the side – games of poker, a boxin' match or two, and a laundry service that I start up in the barracks – it don't add up to much. Too many waterin' holes in this town besides, and I ain't never had too many coins left for cakes and such.

Et voilà: System D. I set myself instead to learnin' my way around the chers that work the counters at the patisseries. Here in Toulouse, the bakeries, they still open, and I set 'bout schoolin' them chers in this and that, and our back-home ways of lagniappe. They don't believe me none at first, that our bakers down South be throwin' extras for free into our bags, but I swear on Pappy and all things bayou that it be true, and soon they been givin' me some lagniappe too. Extra cake and left-over marzipan, sometimes even a *corniotte* or two.

I seen James hangin' 'bout the patisseries enough times to figure that this here Yankee, he as sweet on chocolate and spinned sugar as any bayou born. I figure he got some money of his own 'cause the low wages never seem to bother him none. Even still, damned if the man don't take forever in front of the pastries, figurin' out which ones be the best bargain, and which of those be the thickest, the tallest, the most covered with chocolate.

'*C'est combien*?' he ask, pointin' at a custard tart. One sou, the madame tells him.

He frowns. '*Celle-là ? C'est quoi*?'

'*Une St Honoré*,' she replies patiently, and for him, only two sous.

He moves on. 'That one?' Walnut torte, that one over there is a fruit tart, and those are chestnut creams, she tell him.

He look them all over before pointin' to another. 'That one.'

So sure he seem of his choice that Madame reaches in to cut a slice. '*Non, non*,' he stops her. 'How much for it?'

Before Madame go so boo coo crazy that she throw her rollin' pin at the lot of us, 'Stonebridge,' I call out, shakin' the paper bag in my hand. 'Here. I got plenty for two.'

Now that bag, it hold somethin' real special. I been tellin' the chers at the patisserie all 'bout bayou livin', talkin' to them of gumbo and *étouffée,* and warm beignets. Well, damned if them dolls don't go and rustle up a batch of beignets special for me. *Beignets*! They still warm and so thick with powdered sugar, there's only bits of golden brown that you can see here and there through the white. A right slap-up job them chers have done, and I know from the way James near swallows his beignets whole that he think the same.

'These here beignets be a speciality down South,' I say, proud like.

He shrug like he ain't one bit impressed. 'They're alright,' he say, 'but nothin' like the apple pies you get in Vermont.'

My mouth just 'bout fallen open at that. The Yankee, he's been sittin' there lickin' the sugar off his thumb and checkin' his fingers for every last itty bitty beignet crumb! I just start to laugh at his cussedness. He makes at first like he don't notice, and this get me chucklin' all the more.

He look over at me sheepish like. 'They're very good,' he admits. A sudden grin, the first I've seen on him – it makes him look young – 'Thanks.'

We share the rest of those beignets while they're still warm, and we ain't thinkin' 'bout no Boche and no war as we sit in the square eatin'. There's sugar dust on our hands and the sun on our shoulders. It's a warm day, so bright you can see clear to the Pyrenees. There's music spillin' from the open windows of the cafés. We get to talkin', 'bout huntin' and country ways, 'bout growin' mirlitons, and the smell of apple orchards in springtime Vermont. He ask plenty questions 'bout fishin', 'bout cold-eyed gators and the pirogues we cut from cypresses to float downstream, and tell me 'bout grouse season, and the woolly mammoth tusk they found one time, in the peat bogs not far from his place.

When payday come around, a few of us plan on an evenin' out, and I invite James along. It must be a powerful hard-hittin' cider that his family been brewin' up there in Vermont, 'cause the Yankee sure can drink. Turns out he ain't so quiet no more either, not with a few down his throat.

Our talk turns natural to country things again, to fields and summer pastures, to cotton stackin' and bundlin' hay. One thing lead to another and soon we locked in a friendly bout of arm wrestlin', ginnin' bale against farmyard hayrick. The Yankee's face go red from strainin', the sweat tricklin' down my forehead, both of us being exactly equally matched. I try hookin' my wrist around his hand, he respond by twistin' his grip higher. Back and forth, givin' and takin' in its and bits of an inch as more and more of the legionnaires gather round, cheerin' us on. Ain't no use, ain't nobody goin' to win this one though, and we finally call it a draw. Gaillard slam his glass down on the table and only now do I notice the bunch of *anciens* gathered 'bout us too.

'*Eh bien*, if it isn't my translators,' he grins as he drags up a stool. 'Tell you what,' he say, 'how about we have another match? Either one of you, against me.'

James and I, we look at his bulgin' arms, the knotted veins, thick as rope under them tattoos. '*Non*,' we say, together.

'Come on,' he push. 'I will make it easier – I will go with my left hand.' He take out his purse – it made from his own skin, I heard tell – and empty it on the table, the coins rattlin' down on the wood.

Gaillard's left arm, it don't look any less hefty than his right. We shake our heads again.

'*Merde*!' He throws up his hands in mock disgust. 'Although it is bad form,' he points out, 'to ever ask a man outright, let me tell you why I joined the Legion. When I was but a growin' boy, I fell madly in love. She was the prettiest girl in our village. In all the world. Eyes like . . . like . . .' Gaillard wave a fist large as a ham, tryin' to find the words. '*Beautiful* eyes. Hair like silk, the most glorious girl you could imagine. The only thing was, she was in love with someone else. He was rich, handsome, a bit older, and I knew it was all quite hopeless. She would never notice me.

'That summer, there was a wrestling match organised in the village. All ages, all sizes. *Et voilà*! My chance to shine, and I grab it. Maybe now she will throw a glance my way. I fight with everything I've got, slowly working my way through the rounds, until it's just me and her boyfriend left.

She comes to see me the evening before the final match. For a second, I hear violins, I see tiny angels,' his fingers jab the air, 'playing the harp. *She came to see me!* She looks at me with those lovely eyes. She's watched me fight, she says. She knows I am going to win tomorrow. Could I, she begs, throw the match? If her boyfriend were to lose, it would be too hard on him, the indignity of losing. Well, what could I do? I threw the match. I let him win, let him beat the shit out of me, staring at her all the while. And afterwards, I climbed down from the ring and walked away. Walked out of the village, down the road, just kept on going till I found the Legion. No women here, no matches to be thrown, just men, fighting with real heart.' Gaillard heave a mighty big sigh, rubbin' his hands together. 'At least that is what I thought, till we recruited you lot.

'You see the sort of *jeunes* we've got this time,' he complain to his friends. 'Only good for reading books and cleaning out the crap holes. No fighting spirit at all.'

That rile us, like he known it would. 'See here,' I begin hotly, but Gaillard cuts me off.

'Tell you what,' he say, crackin' his knuckles real slow, one by one. 'Final offer. Me against both of you, together.'

'Together? Two men against one?'

'Oui.' He shift the pile of coins to one side. 'Both of you together, and the winner – or winners – takes it all.'

Now *that* be an offer that make sense to me. I look at James and he shrug. We add our coins on the table too, and the match is on. *Ancien* against *les jeunes*, and now the whole bar is gathered around, placin' bets and cheerin'.

We should have known better. James and I, we push until our eyes 'bout ready to pop from their sockets, but it's like tryin' to move an oak with our bare hands. The veins in Gaillard's forearm stand out, blue and knotted as he hold his position. A small, easy-lookin' shift of his wrist and – slam! – both our arms lie flat against the wood.

The *anciens* burst out laughin' – clearly this a game they seen before. Gaillard grin as he scoop together all the money on the table. 'No fighting spirit,' he chuckle, shakin' his head.

'How about a rematch?' James ask.

'Wait a minute,' I start, but he lift a hand, quietin' me.

'A rematch,' he repeat. 'Just me, against you. If I win, I take the winnings. If you do, I clean the latrines for a month, unasked.'

Gaillard's lookin' at him like he gone crazy. Hell, we *all* lookin' at him like he gone crazy. 'One more thing,' James say. 'How about we try a different technique? New England special. You turn your arm the other way – make a fist and turn the fingers towards you, and I hold on to your wrist.'

'That goin' to give him all the leverage,' I say urgently to James, but he don't pay me no notice. The Yankee's gone boo coo crazy.

Gaillard grins. 'How about you use two hands?' he offer generously. 'Both hands at once, and okay, we go with your method.'

James nods.

They set up once more, each squatted on a stool, elbow to the table. Gaillard turns his fist inwards, James latches on with both arms. Too easy, this goin' to be way too easy for Gaillard. The *ancien* begin his move, this is it, I can see it in his eyes, the muscles in his arm shiftin' position. Just as he start the powerful yank inwards, James, he lets go.

He let go. Gaillard's fist swing back like a piston, straight into his own face. He knock hisself so hard in the jaw, he fly clean off the stool.

My mouth is hangin' open, there's a dead silence around the table. All eyes on Gaillard, who sit up real slow, a stunned expression on his face. '*Merde,*' he say softly, as he register the joke that James just played on him. '*Merde*!'

The Yankee in for it proper, I think, and me along with him. I'm fixin' to put up my fists when Gaillard, he start to laugh. He hold his already swellin' jaw and hoot with laughter. He wave a fat finger in James' face and clap him on the shoulder, and now all of us laughin' and cheerin'.

'Drinks all around,' Gaillard yell, and takin' his winnings, slam them on to the bar.

Gaillard become real fond of us after that. He stop by our table later and sling those huge arms 'bout our shoulders. His jaw turnin' a ripe colour. I try not to look at it.

'You are both from America, yes?' he ask. 'I have a cousin, also Gaillard, in Buenos Aires. Perhaps you know him?'

'That's in *South* Am—,' James begin.

'No,' I interrupt. 'No, we ain't met him, not as yet anyhow.'

Gaillard rub his jaw tenderly. 'I read a book on America once,' he say thoughtfully. James look so shook at the notion of the *ancien* with a book, it makes me want bad to laugh.

'*Le Dernier des Mohicans,*' Gaillard continues. 'Maybe you know it?'

Can't say that I do, but James is noddin'. '*The Last of the Mohicans.*'

'I liked it,' Gaillard say stoutly. 'Took me a few years to get through it all, but I liked it. All those names they had for each other. Hawk Eye. Long Rifle. Subtle Fox. Do they still do that in America?'

'Sure thing,' James say with a straight face. 'You just make one up, accordin' to the man. Obadaiah, for instance, he'd be—'

'Hawk Eye,' I suggest.

'– he'd be Chief Talk-A-Lot.'

'And James here, his name would be Brother Jackass Damn Fool.'

Gaillard grins. 'And my name?' he ask, goin' along with the game.

'Mighty Heart,' James say, just as I say: 'Strong Oak.'

'Strong Heart Mighty Oak,' James suggests, mixin' the two.

Gaillard repeat the words, testin' them slow like on his tongue. 'Brother Strong Heart Mighty Oak,' he agree delightedly, and thumpin' us on our backs, yells to the innkeeper for another round.

It's a right good time we havin', but as curfew draw close, James start to straighten hisself up. 'The *boîte,*' he point out. 'Foolish to get thrown into the barracks prison for being drunk.'

'We ain't goin' to.' I wave my glass towards Gaillard and the other *anciens* who been here at the inn even longer than we have. 'We just go in behind them.'

James look unsure. 'Safety in numbers? That would work, I suppose.'

That ain't what I meant, but I figure he goin' to see for hisself soon enough. When we finally tumble out from the café, it's a beautiful thing is what it is, to stagger back to the barracks behind the *anciens*. If us lot is drunk, they so pickled, they weavin', zigzaggin' from side to side as they walk. They singin' too, or what pass for it, at the top of their voices. Right rude songs and sailor ditties, 'bout the comely chers of Toulouse, their sisters and mothers too. When a window open and a shoe come flyin' through, Gaillard mistake it for praise. He catch that shoe, mighty touched, and bowin' real handsome from the waist towards his unseen admirer, start to sing even more loud.

So it go, until 'bout twenty yards before the barrack gates the magic happens, like it do every time. It like a magician's wand been suddenly waved over the *anciens*. Their singin' stops mid-song, they straighten their shoulders as if on dress parade, and march in perfect silence, givin' a right smart salute to the sentry as they pass.

Behind them, us *jeunes* automatically do the same.

I grin at James. 'See? We just follow them in.'

Soon as everybody of us are safely inside, the *anciens* start roarin' their songs out loud again. All of us join in, Yankee James too, beltin' out the words.

EIGHT

October 1914

We still coolin' our heels in Toulouse as more and more recruits sign up. We rubbin' wax into our leather belts and polishin' our gear one mornin' when someone so strange come walkin' in that we all stop to look. Dressed from head to toe in English khaki he is, complete with leggings and a trench coat. A spyglass hangin' around his neck and what looks like a brand-new rifle over his shoulder. He got a map in one hand, a canteen in the other, and such a don't-care look on his face that the two *anciens* escortin' him in, rifles drawn, they look almost embarrassed.

He was goin' around Toulouse enquirin' 'bout our camp, they tell the Captain, and well – *look* at him, they say, they weren't certain if he were a spy or what.

'Allow me to introduce myself,' the stranger say in a foreign accent. 'I am Karan Singh, and I would like to offer my services, such as they are, to the Legion. I was acquiring an education in Cambridge – literature, the ancient classics primarily,' he explains, 'when the dashed war broke out.' He tells that when he sent a telegraph back home to his folks in India 'bout wantin' to enlist, his father told him not to be a fool. Karan lift a khaki-covered shoulder. 'Well, I couldn't just wait around and do nothing, could I?'

No point joinin' the British Army, his father would've just pulled strings to see that his son got nothin' more than a desk job, sittin' pretty for the rest of the war. Only thing to do was to run away, quick as he could, and make his way over to France in search of the Legion.

Only one small problem; his father, soon as he heard, or maybe, expectin' it, gone and frozen his bank accounts. Karan pull out a fistful of hundred-franc notes from his pocket. 'Once these are gone . . .' He shrug. 'I'm sure we'll be done fighting by then anyway. Or my mother will make him come around. It'll all be fine.' He spend freely that evenin', buyin' round after round for just 'bout anyone who asks.

For all his high-flyin' ways, Karan's real quick to settle into the Legion. He learn the ropes of System D right away and he use it far better than any of us done so far.

When he hear 'bout our *cafard*-brained ornery old cook, Karan start to loiter casual like 'bout the camp kitchens. The cook come rushin' out, wavin' his rollin' pin and bent on makin' sure Karan ain't stealin' none of the supplies when – 'Why, if it isn't King George!' Karan exclaim.

That stop the cook cold. George hold in his stomach, haulin' hisself up to his full height.

'Such an incredible likeness, why, it's as if you have both been drawn by the same hand!'

George blush like a little girl. 'We are alike, *n'est ce pas?*'

'Alike! Why, you are His Majesty's very twin.' Karan shakes his head wonderin' like. 'You *must* be related.'

The thought ain't occurred to George before, but now that he thinks 'bout it, it make complete sense.

'You *have* to be,' Karan continues. 'A long-lost cousin, a court intrigue perhaps, a royal bloodline lost forever.'

'*C'est possible, c'est bien possible*!' George nod. 'And you, *jeune* legionnaire?' He point the rollin' pin like it a sword in his hand and Karan, a knight he especially like. 'Where are you from?'

Karan sighs. 'Like you, I've been disavowed by fortune. The second son, when the eldest must inherit all. And so –' a dramatic sweep of his arm – 'I've stepped out to seek my fortune. My father, born a king, and I a prince by birth, and yet here I am, making my humble way through the Legion.'

George, he right moved by this. 'Wait here,' he order, and disappear inside. When he come out, he got half a roast chicken in his hands. 'Here. Say nothing of this to any of the others, mind you.'

'Come again,' he call as Karan takes his leave. 'Come tomorrow. You and I, we will talk 'bout our kingdoms.' He raise a finger to his lips. '*Mais*, say nothing to anyone else.'

From that day on, Karan always got an extra bottle or two of wine in his *musette,* a hunk of meat, a round of cheese, all gifts from good King George. Funny thing is, Karan, he don't seem to eat or drink all that much hisself. What he gets, he freely shares; sittin' back, smokin' a cigarette and smilin' while the rest of us dig in.

Soon after, they ask for volunteers for an advance to the Front. I look at Gaillard out the corner of my eye, but since there don't seem to be no dirty latrines waitin' this time, I quickly raise my hand, along with everyone else there. There's so many volunteers that the officers, they figure to pick the most experienced soldiers of us lot. They ask what battlefield experience we got prior, and it downright astonish-makin', the number of campaigns that come up. The sort that ain't nobody ever heard of before. Central America, South America, the Mexican Army, with Karan rattlin' off the tongue-trippin' names of fully a dozen wars back in India.

A curious thing, the Captain say – all these wars we been in, all this experience we gotten prior, it sure ain't seemed to have improved our drillin' any.

'*Vous*?' he ask as James step forward.

'Five years,' James say gravely.

'Yes, yes, but where? Mexico, I suppose, along with all your other brothers here?'

James shake his head. 'Five years,' he say poker-faced, 'with the Salvation Army.'

They let us all through.

Lucky for us, those rickety-crack, first-issue rifles goin' to be swapped out before we leave. Only, they being replaced with salvage from the Front.

We watch as the trucks rumble in through the barrack gates, a long line of dusty metal. One of the drivers set his fingers to his mouth and whistle sharply, hollerin' for us to come help unload. We drag our heels goin' over – there's a raw stink 'bout the insides of them trucks. Under the tarp covers, their bellies loaded with bayonets, spare ammo and boots, laced together and blooded around the toes and heels. Pickin's from the dead. The war, it gotten real close all of a sudden.

Us *jeunes* given fatigue duty, to clean the boots proper. For once, ain't none of us got anythin' to say; there's no smart mouthin', no cussin' – we work at those stains with scrubbin' brushes and water in silence.

When they issue the overhauled bayonets, I pick mine up and the blade, it feel both hot and cold to the touch. I try not to think of the legionnaire in whose hands it once been, or what become of him. Still, as I turn it this way and that, checkin' out the tip and grip, I feel as if there's another man there, at my shoulder. I catch sight of him in the blade. I see his peaked cap and coat, with the buttons all muddied, not like ours here in the barracks, proper brassed up and shined. Feel like a dream as I bend closer, tryin' to make out his face, but the lines, they all start to run into one another. Only the eyes remain, dark as two pools of rainwater, raisin' the gooseflesh on my arms.

I turn away sharp like, when I catch James lookin' my way. He must think I'm spooked, the way I've been bent over the thing.

He clear his throat. 'These are hardy weapons,' he offer. He open a tin of chaw tobacco and cut a plug. 'A foot and nine inches long, four grooves, a half-inch diameter in the hilt. Eight-chamber rifle.' He nod like he approve. 'They're sturdy,' he say, tuckin' the chaw in his mouth.

I'm still kind of embarrassed and lookin' to change the subject. 'Why'd you join the Legion anyhow?' I ask, for somethin' to say.

He look surprised. 'My grandfather was in the Civil War.' He shrug, as if this explain everythin'.

'My pappy liked to spend his time in a school house,' I point out, 'but you don't see me standin' before no chalkboard.'

He frown. 'The Canadians are here, as are the British. It's the right thing to do. If nothin' else, for all that France has done for America in the past. For Lafayette, for 1776, for the munitions and men she gave us when we needed them the most.' He look at me. 'How could I not?'

It sound awful noble and so good to me that I feel like I ought to be standin' straight and salutin' or somethin'. I don't bother none tellin' him why I joined up – La Santé, it don't measure up so well against Lafayette.

It boo coo crazy how much we got to fit into our knapsacks. We're strugglin' with the mountain of gear on our beds, pushin', tuckin', foldin', tryin' to cram it all. I'm just 'bout ready to chuck the whole damn pile out the window when Gaillard stop by our barracks and show us how it done. Whistlin' all the while, he pull out shirts, a neck muffler, the white cotton sleepin' hat from the pile, foldin' them all in seconds, sausage fingers movin' fast and clever as a lady's maid. He smooth the creases and measure the folded pieces, makin' sure each be the same length, from the fingertip to elbow, before rollin' them into tight bundles and placin' them easy as can be into the backpack.

We follow as best we can. We're to take everythin' along, even them jackets that are all the same size, too small for most our shoulders. A half-loaf of bread each, a can of sardines, one and a half cans of fish paste. I sniff cautious like at the block of cheese – it don't smell too appetisin' to me, but the hunk of chocolate sure is welcome. Reserve rations of two tins of canned meat, hard tack, salt, pepper, tea, coffee and sugar. There's a blanket, half of a shelter tent with poles, and a hundred and twenty rounds of ammunition. By the time I settle all of it in and heft the sack on to my shoulders, feels like it weigh close to a fine-boned cher.

I lace up them hobnailed boots I been avoidin' and finally try them on. They heavy and I feel like I got to make a special effort to go liftin' my feet. Same as a horse must feel, I figure, after its hooves been newly shod.

I don't want to think too much 'bout the soldier who worn these boots before me, or just how they came to be taken off of him, and for somethin' to fill my mind, pull them off again and start to count the nails in the soles. I ain't never been too good with numbers growin' up, so Pappy, he figured a way to make the learnin' stick to my bones. He gave the numbers names, he did. I count the nails now the way he taught me and figure there's just about one hundred and sixty-two in both them soles together. One six two. One and six, sixteen, sweet as can be, and two, shaped like a duck sailin' by the levee. A sweet duck, and I got me one in these here boots . . .

All that countin' and thinkin' 'bout ducks and such gets me 'memberin' the bayou. From years ago, racin' barefoot through the mud with the other boys. The ducks, white on brown water, as we go slip-slidin' through river moss and swamp. I think 'bout Pappy and what he'd have made of me, all spiffed up and fixin' to head out to war, what he'd have said 'bout the butterflies waltzin' in my belly.

James is sayin' somethin' I realise, and I look up with a start. He hold up his boots. 'We literally,' he repeats, 'are going to walk a mile in someone else's shoes.'

*

Them butterflies, turns out they been flutterin' in other bellies too. Everybody on edge that evenin', nervous sudden like of the war that coming up right round the corner. 'Fraid we ain't readied enough for it and angry over being 'fraid at all. Soon enough, a right hearty disagreement broken out between a Greek and a Pole. How they even got to arguin' I can't say, 'cause each don't understand a word of the other's language. This just make them all the angrier as they yell and holler, Greek to Pole and back, louder and louder, neither even understandin' what the other's sayin', when James step in.

There's a Pole in the group who understands a bit of French, and James pulls him forward. They should settle this argument before it gets outta hand, he say to him in French. He offer to translate from Greek to French, suggestin' that the Pole then translate whatever he can back into Polish.

The Yankee speaks Greek too? I always figured him for a smart man, but this I did not know, and I am settin' up to be all kinds of impressed when somethin' strikes me as not quite right as I watch. The Greek turns to James and yells all kinds of jibber-jabber for a full five minutes, wavin' his hands and stampin' his feet. James nods serious like. He turn to the Polish interpreter and translate all that talkin' and yellin' that the Greek just done simply into this:

'Ta mère est une pute.' Your mother a whore.

The insults just get worse after that, the Yankee translatin' between Greek and French, and before you know it, the Greek jump the Pole and they begin to slug it out.

James step back, and cool as can be – 'Who's up for a betting pool?' he ask.

We gather around, placin' our bets and cheerin' the two of them on. I pick the Greek – I like the way he moves, cat-like he is, and light, while James goes with the heavier Pole. We never find out who wins though, 'cause that fight, it turn hog-wild in a hurry. All the Greeks and all the Poles in the group start hammerin' away at each other, and more of us jump in, just to keep them company.

I get in a couple of punches and get slugged in return. It hurt good, and feel even better, to move and kick and holler, and get some of those butterflies outta us. By the time the sentries come to break up the fight, it's a right lively soiree.

'Didn't know you spoke no Greek,' I say later to James.

He hold a bit of ice against his head. 'I don't.'

It slowly been dawnin' on me these past weeks that this here Yankee, he might not be so Sunday school uptight as he looks after all. 'That translatin' you did – he never said no such thing 'bout his mother, did he?'

He levels those blue eyes at me, and all of a sudden, they twinklin'.

'Sonofabitch!' I exclaim.'What 'bout all them Greek insults you rattled off?'

His eyes twinkle some more as he rub his head. 'From a book.'

'Sonofabitch!!'

'*Poutanas gie*,' he translate gravely. 'Got that one from a book too.'

We head out the next mornin' by train to Camp de Mailly. The fight's long forgotten and everybody's loosened up and in right good cheer. I ain't 'fraid no more – there's a wildness bubblin' inside of me. Goin' to be a right ruckus at the Front, and we just itchin' now to have a go at the Boche. There's all kinds of flag wavin' and hollerin', and song, plenty song.

'Kaiser Bill went up the hill
To take a slice of France
Kaiser Bill came down the hill
With bullets in his pants.'

We pass wagon trains along the way, and all sorts of civilian vehicles called into service. Paris school buses, fancy automobiles, the kind that should have a comely cher in the back, a covered cart with *Violet Parfumerie* written on the sides and violets painted across.

'We're gonna whip the Kaiser
That's what we're gonna do
And that is just as certain
As two times one is two.
We're gonna whip the Kaiser
No matter what you say
For Christ the Lord is with us
To help us win the fray.'

Our voices, they wing out the open windows, singin' different songs, in so many different languages, but all comin' together in a single tailwind, risin' above the sound of the whistle as the train rush forward. The last of the summer light in the colourin' trees, and children run after the train as it race through the small towns, chasin' along the tracks, callin' and wavin'.

We at Camp de Mailly for two weeks, drillin' and marchin' through the battlefields of the Marne. We practise, firin' plenty blank cartridges on fields still littered with shell casings from the battles fought here in September. Twisted and broken bayonets in the red and orange leaves startin' to fall from the trees. The guns firin' to the north now, from Reims, and the lines around the Meuse, and their sound, it like blood-scent to a hound. Between the *bonds de vingt metres,* when we drop down, ear pressed to the grass, we feel their faraway rumblin', beatin' through the ground like percussion drums.

We gather 'bout after sundown, over games of poker and such, but we keep liftin' our heads towards the north and the sound of them restless-makin' guns. With the fightin' moved on, most villagers come back to their homes here, and the smell of cheap wine and fryin' potatoes in the air. The lamps, they throw movin' shadows on the walls of the barn we in. The hay on the floors real thick and golden, and here and there, the dud shells we brought back from them fields. Always talk turns to the Front – *how many, how soon, so many, more than you, more than you'll ever know how to count, oh yeah, well I'm gonna get more than your mama has lovers, that's how many, more than you, more than all of you, and when the war is done, next summer, we'll tally our numbers, we'll party when the war is done, jeez, don't they ever stop, do they ever stop, the guns, wait for us already, we'll be there real soon, give the enemy a licking we will, and when we're done with the war . . .*

We drink more of the wine, and start to spill it on the hay. The sound of them guns in our ears, but we strong, we true. James, he spring to his feet, startlin' us all, and pickin' up one of them bum shells easy as if it were a ball, toss it clean out the open window, towards them boomin', never-sleepin' guns. The moonlight catch the metal of the shell and we watch it go sailin' over the hillside, cool and blue, the lamps throwin' fire in all our eyes.

*

Our marchin' orders come at last. We got a three-day road ahead of us to the Front. The first day go easy. We pass through villages so old that there's gaps in the outer walls where the stones have turned to dust. We sing as we march, and that night, are billeted in warm farmhouses with the scent of fruit and hay 'bout them.

The second day is when our feet start to make a fuss. The *anciens* still cheerfully singin' but us *jeunes* fallen dead quiet. One foot in front of the other, mile after devil-spawn mile, our sacks feelin' like they stuffed with rocks, them boots we got on nippin' and bitin' at our heels.

James, he sufferin' somethin' bad. I can tell from the way he walk, a rollin' sort of shuffle, shiftin' his weight to the balls of his feet. He don't say nothin' though, and watchin' him, I'm set on keepin' right on marchin' myself. Still, I'm awful tempted when Karan throw up his hands. 'I'm walking in marmalade,' he say, fallin' out by the side of the road.

When he take off his boots, sure 'nuff his feet blistered awful bad, the skin peelin' off and bleedin'. Now Danny examinin' his own pulpy feet – one by one, more *jeunes* fall outta the column until I give up too. Our poor, achin' feet! They in right bad condition, we gonna need medical attention for sure.

'James,' I call, but he don't stop, don't look left or right, just keeps shufflin' along. Mule-headed Yankee, when he can get a ride in a medic wagon all the way to our destination.

We sittin' there, waitin' there for the medics, when our Colonel come ridin' up.

'What is the hold-up here?' he demand, annoyed.

We limp towards him, salutin' heroic like. 'We're all in, *mon Colonel*. Our feet are pulped to bits, like fresh marma—'

'March!' he roar, in such a temper that we nearabout fall over one another in our rush to get our boots back on. 'March!' he roar again, and that just what we do, trottin', pantin', fast-shufflin' down the road, until we catch up with the rest of the section.

I steal a look at James, but he don't say nothin'; just shift his chaw from one cheek to another, his face real tired but a look in his eyes like he laughin' on the inside.

We billet in the grounds of an old chateau that night. The red brick walls glow hot as coals as we pass with our lamps. There's chickens,

I notice, roostin' in a corner of the yard. A door opens in the back of the chateau and an old lady steps out. She stare at us, no words of greetin', no smile, nothin'.

'Don't chase the chickens,' is all she say, and begin to go back inside.

James looks thoughtful like at her. *'Poulet de Bresse?'* he ask quietly.

She starts in surprise on the step. *'Oui,'* she nod then. *'Mon fils . . .'* she clear her throat, turn to look him in the face. 'My son bred them.'

'Poulet de Bresse,' James explain, when I ask later. 'You can tell from the comb and feet.'

Only now do I notice the blue feet of the birds, their red combs like blood against their white feathers.

'The queen of chickens, and the chicken of kings,' James say, 'is how Jean Anthelme Brillat-Savarin put it in 1825.'

'He was a renowned gourmand,' he explain when I look blank-like at him. 'There's still folks who hold that these chickens are the finest tastin' in the world.'

It strikes me that with their colourin', these some mighty fine, patriotic chickens. Red, white and blue, same as the French flag, same as the Stars and Stripes, and I take it as a right lucky omen that we seen them.

Gaillard hawk noisily and spit into the straw. 'She should put a couple of these in the oven for us,' he grumble. 'Do her bit for France.'

James and I, we don't say nothin', but I know he's thinkin' like I am, 'bout the son the old lady talked of, and just where he might be right now.

We packin' up to leave early the next mornin', when she come out, carryin' somethin' in her apron. It's six eggs, still warm from the hens. She hand them to us, not a hint of a smile on her face. *'Bonne chance,'* she mutter.

She stand there, alone on the steps of her chateau, watchin' silently as we leave.

Gaillard teach us to rub tallow on the inside of our boots, to ease the rubbin' and the blisters on our feet. We march on, through more villages, small, old, broken. More chateaus, all black and empty. The fighting's been more recent here, and the villagers just 'bout startin' to return; they stand in their shelled doorways and open walls and wave slowly as we pass. Ain't no farmhands here no more, hardly no young men at all. They all at the Front. Only old women left now, too mule-headed to leave their homes.

We push north, past the marshes of Saint Gond where we hear tell fifteen thousand French and twenty-five thousand Boche have been killed. The numbers, they too big to make sense; when I try and imagine how many men that might be, I get lost. I think instead of one Frenchman, who liked nothin' more than to raise red, white and blue chickens.

I think of that old lady's son and wonder if he here, in one of the many fields we pass, where patches of beets still growin' 'bout the newly dug graves. Soldiers' caps, the red *kepis rouge*, hang on wooden crosses, lookin' from a distance as if the fields fully in bloom.

NINE

Verzenay • October 1914

There's the smell of war around Verzenay. Sharp, bitter – it bite the back of our throats. The stink of cordite, machine oil and axle grease hang thick over the road that leads to the village. We see a couple of Boche aeroplanes – for planes they been steady flyin' over this here part of the Front, we hear tell – flyin' so low that Gaillard say he can make out them Boche airmen wavin' mockin' like at him.

The clink and clank of iron and steel all around, the rhythm of a thousand boots. Automobiles honkin' down the roads, and horses so nervous, they toss their heads and stamp. Sparks shoot from under their hooves as they hit against the stones. Colonial troops everywhere, veteran soldiers and new recruits, grey-beards and boys with the growin' still in them, talkin', singin', cussin', the square crowded with all kinds of uniforms. French poilus, British Tommies and Canadian troops. Karan call out to a band of brown-skinned soldiers from India and they fold their hands and bow in greetin'. We pass a battalion speakin' a strange tongue – it seem awful familiar but I can't make out not one word. James, he assure me it English they speakin', regular old English, spoken with a bonnie Scottish accent, is all.

Men everywhere, hootin' and hollerin', cuppin' their hands and yellin' at the Boche. The battle lines lie on the hillside below, close enough that we can make out the long white trenches and the dust clouds movin' up and down the lines as the shells fall. A rattlin' in the background, from the French mitrailleuse machine guns, mixed with the sharp crack-crack of rifle fire. We so close to the Front, we even hear the French officers shoutin' to their men. Their voices carry in itty bitty pieces, like snatches of song.

The music of the war, and it both light a fire and run cold as ice inside of me.

*

There's a sudden tootin' and honkin', from a row of vehicles makin' their way up the streets. The crowd parts clean down the middle, to let them through.

'Easy!' James says sharply, as a crush of bodies pins us to the sides of the buildings. We thinkin' it some grandee general and his staff goin' hell-bent for breakfast, but the honkin' come closer, louder, and now I see the big, red cross painted on the sides. This ain't no general's convoy, but medic wagons, back from the Front.

They pull up right in front of us, before the entrance of the lean-to hospital where stretchers bein' rushed out. The crowd go silent, watchin' as the wounded are offloaded. They covered in blood and dirt, most cannot walk, and those that can are so beat up, they stumble on the cobblestones, some sinkin' right down with their eyes closed. Soldiers with holes torn right through their bodies, men missin' eyes and hands and legs, and there's a dead quiet as it sink in, really sink in, just what we all headed for.

This ain't no rinky dink fight we been marchin' towards, but war, full-blown war, the likes of which none of us ever seen before.

'What's it like then, over there?' someone ask, hesitatin' like.

The Tommy he speakin' to is tryin' to make his own way into the hospital, usin' his rifle for a crutch. He barely look up. 'A real bloody picnic,' he say as he limp away.

An angry buzzin' start to build among us. We cuss out the Boche proper, swearin' to take revenge for all they done, for each and every one of these terrible wounds we see before us. A soldier sittin' on the ground look up, his eyes so weary there ain't enough sleep in all the world to take the tiredness from them.

'We did the same to them,' he say quietly. Ain't no boastin' in his voice, no anger, ain't much of anythin' at all, only a long, drawn-out emptiness.

'You hear?'

James look up from his writin'. 'Tonight,' he nod.

That wounded Tommy from earlier today, he stuck in my head, makin' me right restless. Most of the *jeunes*, they gone drinkin', Karan being set on gettin' as drunk as he can get on the finest champagne he can find. I don't feel up to it, and instead, go wanderin' 'bout on my own. Ain't no purpose to my walkin', down this street, then that, tryin' to quiet them butterflies in my gut. It get quieter the further I go from the centre. By and by I come to the end of the village. The houses come to a stop sudden like, and up ahead, there a clear view in all directions of the hills. Ain't seen nobody around for quite some time that I been walkin', but who should I see now but a single legionnaire, sittin' on a kerbstone overlookin' the hills and scribblin' away in his notebook.

Yankee James.

'We head out tonight,' I repeat. I shade my eyes and look towards the trenches. 'Goin' to be us there soon.'

Them thoughts that been goin' round and round my head all afternoon, they start up once more and before I know what's what – 'We goin' to make it back, right?'

Soon as I blurt the words, I feel foolish. He goin' to think I'm 'fraid, is what. ''Course we makin' it back,' I say quickly, answerin' my own question. 'We makin' it back, and come New Year's Eve . . .' My words fall away, hangin' between us. He don't say nothin', just keeps starin' at them hills.

'I charge by the page,' I say jestingly, to change the subject.

'What?' He look at me, confused.

I nod at the notebook in his hands. 'That stuff you always writin' in there. If it a story, and I'm in it, I charge by the page.'

He grins.

'So is it? A story?'

'A journal.' He hesitate, tappin' his pen against the leather cover. 'But there might be material here for more. I'd like to write a novel, based on my experiences perhaps. After we're done. With the war. After we make it back.'

We both quiet awhile. The evenin' glow with the special light that be late October's. It that in-between time, before sunset, after most of the day is done, with bluest sky and a last bit of sun before dusk come rollin' through. A sudden burst of cloud, not from the sky but risin' like a mushroom from the trenches on the hillside below. Now I hear it, the explosion. That cloud, it slowly break apart, black-gold in the light.

'They're still pickin' grapes,' James observe. He ain't lookin' at the trenches, but at the hillside opposite, planted with vineyards touched root to stem with evenin' shine. Only now do I notice them, the last grape pickers of the day. Their skirts swing as they move through the vines. I hear their singin', real faint, in between the guns and the faraway voices of the officers as they command their men below.

I strain my ears to listen and slowly I begin to make out another, older, softer tune. The quiet song of evenin', and the woods we come marchin' through. Of trees turned fire-coloured, of an iron bench in a lonesome park. The rhythm of the stones in an old, old church, so age-soft they feel smooth as a woman's skin beneath my hands. All the rattle and shake of the war on one hillside, and on the other, the slow hum of the windmill that is still whole, how, nobody can say. It stand tall, untouched by the shells, its long arms circlin' the evenin'.

I ain't got the words to describe how I feel, so I don't say nothin', but standin' there, that wounded Tommy heavy on my mind, takin' in the trenches, and the grape pickers steady singin', I feel like the world, it been torn clean in half.

James point with his notebook, towards the vines and the windmill and the hills that roll gently away towards Paris. 'That's what we're fightin' for really, isn't it?'

The world, it been cut in two. Verzenay, she stand right in the middle, and lookin' out at the hills on this clear fall day, I finally get just why this war so important. The hills rise around us. Here, these golden vines and there, the roarin' guns and men, covered in smoke. Don't know what lies ahead, don't know what goin' to happen to us out there. But this much I do know now: it ain't no grand, slap-up ruckus we headed for but somethin' much more than that. It like there two sides to the world. On the one side lie everythin' good and bright and worth our days on this earth; on the other, all that threaten this.

That's what we fightin' for, that's why we here. That's why this war, this war to end all wars.

TEN

Past midnight, and we still waitin', standin' in drill formation in the dark. The officers, they keep checkin' their watches while the cold drizzle drippin' down our necks. I pull the collar of my too-tight jacket closer, not that it make much difference, as I watch the lights. Flickerin' and dancin' through the rain, all along the hill.

'Artillery fire,' James mutter. He shifts restless like, lookin' at his watch. 'What the fuck are we waiting for?'

I wonder if I should say somethin', 'bout the wagon train I heard 'bout. The *anciens* were talkin' 'bout it – the train was hit by shell fire earlier tonight, right on the road we supposed to take to the trenches. That the reason for our late departure – on account of the added cover of darkness, sure, but also 'cause the officers don't want no wet-behind-the-ears *jeunes* troops such as us to see the dead and lose our nerve.

'I hear tell that a supply train—' I begin, but the words don't go no further.

James look hard at me. 'What's that?'

I clear my throat. 'They sure lettin' off all sorts of fireworks tonight for our welcome,' I say, pointin' at the lights. I don't say nothin' 'bout those blown-up wagons. As if by not tellin', maybe, just maybe, we not even notice the dead as we pass by.

The rain, she finally stop, givin' way to a thin, water-filled mist. James nod at the slice of moon, all fuzzy 'bout the edges, and say it as if it gotten hoar frost. I wonder what it mean, hoar frost, but we set out just then, and under strict orders for silence.

We march single file, down wet streets on which the fallen rain shine like oil. Down a quiet side road, and then we branchin' off, findin' our way along a narrow hillside trail. The mist lies thicker here, turnin' the moonshine blue. A light of witches, a night for haints. Verey lights shoot now and again over the sector, givin' us our bearings – sharp white, even through the mist, like stars burstin' over the lines. Our breathin' the only sound, that and the small suckin' of our boots on the wet mud.

Further, through fog that got the smell of rain-washed earth in it. Until it don't no more and there a sudden blooded, butcher-shop stink in my nose. We've come upon what left of the wagon train. Behind me, I hear James take a sharp breath. Maybe I should've told him after all. I slip my hand into my pocket, reachin' for my gris-gris. My fingers awful cold as I hold on to its familiar rabbit-foot shape.

'Keep moving,' Gaillard whisper fiercely.

Somethin' make me look up, as we pass under a bunch of trees. A horse gone and climbed a tree. I blink, look again, and now I see it just the backside of the animal. Just the hind legs and haunches, sent flyin' into the air from the force of a shell.

'Hock and hoof and long plumed tail,' I hear James recite under his breath. His voice awful calm, like he takin' stock of what left of the animal.

Someone start to throw up. The *anciens*, they shush him angrily, the Corporal threatenin' him in a whisper with the *boîte* and worse – all the noise he makin', the Boche gonna have no trouble findin' us at all.

'*Avancez*!'

We fumble past, tryin' not to see, but searchin' through the mist all the same to sort out the men, what left of them anyhow, from the torn-up shapes around us. The dead horses, their legs stick upwards, like thin tombstones in the night.

When we get to the reserve trenches, they lie before us dark and silent as a grave. After the ruckus of earlier this evenin', the sector gone awful quiet, a watchin', waitin' silence 'bout the trenches. Every detail seem powerful clear – the mud fallin' down the sides of the walls, the sound of it; a small, scratch-scratch rodent noise; the first rungs of the ladder, all greased up with mud; the smell of old sweat and damp clay risin' from the darkness. The *anciens* uneasy too – they veteran soldiers alright, but these here trenches as new to them as to us. Gaillard shift from foot to foot, fiddlin' with the straps of his sack.

'Avancez' the Captain whisper, and grabbin' hold of the ladder, lower hisself down into the trench.

'Avancez,' Gaillard echoes. He straighten, flash a quick grin and swing down after the Captain. That break the spell and now everybody rushin' at the ladder. A press of bodies before me and behind, that ladder slippery as hell from the rain, go careful, Obadaiah Nelson, you—

'*Merde*!'

Someone slip, slam into the man in front, try to grab hold of the legionnaire behind for support and with a powerful crash of tin kettles, cartridge belts and sacks, we lose our footin', tumblin' ass over head down the ladder. We land at the bottom, in a soup of wet, sticky mud. If these tunnels look like graves, well, that racket we just made comin' down, it loud enough to wake the dead. We sprawl there, the breath knocked from us, mud in our hair, all over our faces and gear, the echoes of our grand entrance bouncin' and clatterin' down the trench.

I see the pale blur of James' hand as he try to wipe his face clean. 'Humpty Dumpty,' he observe, 'had a great fall.'

The Captain's cussin' us out, fit to go blue in the face. 'Forward, you idiots, advance!'

We scramble to our feet, slippin', rightin' ourselves, gatherin' up our gear with even more noise, wadin' through this devil-spawn mud that reach sometimes ankle-deep, sometimes right up to our calves as we press forward. The trenches go this way and that, sharp turns left and right, with all sorts of lesser trenches that lead into the main lines. Our eyes still ain't used to seein' down here – just as we get our feet outta a 'specially deep mudhole, bam! there we go rammin' right into a wall.

'Close in! Close in!' the corporals hiss, tryin' to get us to go single file, to close up the gaps in the column, but men keep gettin' lost, turnin' into the communication and sap trenches that go branchin' off from the main trench, stumblin' in this mud that clings like molasses, bunchin' up here, held up there.

A sudden noise up ahead, a squelchin' of many pairs of boots. My heart start to hammer as I strain to see. We in the French part of the sector, I *know* we in the French part of the sector but all the same, I grip my rifle close. It grows louder, the racket, and now the battalion we replacin' come stompin' into sight.

'Thanks for showing up at last, assholes', they growl. 'You're three hours late! Make yourselves at home.'

The sour, unwashed smell of them as they push past, their gear knock us in the stomach, poke us in the eyes, and then they gone, melted into the night.

Home is a rabbit hole of rickety dugouts and half-fallen parapets. The mist has thinned somewhat and moonshine fall pale and blue on torn sandbags, twists of bobwire, empty cartridges and shell holes filled with scummy water that got the stink of piss and worse 'bout it. There the chemical bite of chloride of lime, but ain't no amount of it that can hide the stink that lie 'bout these forward trenches – a foul, crap-hole, rotted-meat stench.

'*Reposez-vous*,' the Captain orders.

'What, here?' Karan asks alarmed. 'There's *shit* everywhere.'

'It builds character,' Gaillard answer for the Captain. '*Reposez-vous*,' he advise, takin' the sack from his shoulders. 'Get some rest.'

We settle down best we can, wet, dirty, pickin' out the clumps of earth fallen down our jackets, tryin' to get the stickiness off our fingers, squattin' small so we don't touch no more of the slime that coat the floor of the trench than we need to. The stink, such a stink! I take out that block of cheese from my kit and hold it to my face, grateful for the sharpness it send up my nose.

A Verey light shoot high into the sky, risin' white over the lines. I'm blinded for a moment by the sudden brightness, and now I see faces, gear and parapet, standin' out sharp against the night. A crackle of rifle fire and a faint cry of '*Aux armes*! *Aux armes*!' somewhere out to our left.

A couple of bullets come whinin' over our heads and hit the wall of the trench. We throw ourselves down into the slime. '*Merde*!' Someone pick up his rifle and start firin' blindly over his head. That send all of us into a right panic and we all firin' now, at no target we can see, to the front, to the left, even to the back – who knows where the goddamned Boche be? The corporals and captains yellin' for us to stay down damn it, stop firing, *stop firing* you idiots, and slowly the shootin' die away as we figure we ain't in no immediate danger.

My heart still thumpin' somethin' fierce; my knuckles hurt from grippin' so tightly on my rifle. Sentries are chosen from among the *anciens* to stand guard in the outposts while the rest of us huddle together like frightened pups and try to get some sleep. Them lights, they keep shootin' into the air, rifles cracklin' in small bursts all night, from one part of the sector to the next.

ELEVEN

Raydon • 1932

Nobody watching Jim saunter through the room, hands nonchalantly in his pockets, would have guessed just how out of place he felt. They'd thrown balls at home, back when his mother was still around. He remembered her and Ellie arranging armfuls of flowers in the huge brass urns and crystal vases that were all packed away now in the cellar, as the band hired for the evening set up in the corner, the single notes and snatches of music echoing through the house as they tuned their instruments. He remembered the carpets rolled up and stacked away, the trucks with trays of food coming round to the back entrance, and the way the lights glittered in the ballroom, magnified in the gilt-framed mirrors around the walls, infusing the diligently waxed floors with an overlay of gold. Later in the evening, watching on tip-toes from the windows of the washroom upstairs as the guests arrived, and then lying awake, listening to the sounds of music and laughter from the rooms downstairs.

Grand as they'd seemed to him then, those evenings had been nothing like this affair tonight, of that he was certain. He wondered again just how he was supposed to find Madeleine in this crowd. 'A gala,' she'd said, and while he'd known it wouldn't be just her and him, he sure as hell hadn't anticipated this monkey show.

'Peacock parade,' he corrected himself dryly. It was hard to miss the theme of the evening, from the appliquéd motifs on the waistcoats of the staff, to the massive topiaries flanking the entrance to the mansion that had been trimmed and moulded into dancing peacocks, tails fanned high.

He glanced at the palm trees that lined the walls. Inside the Garland mansion it was already summer; a lush, tropical summer, not of these hills but some exotic haven. The palms were arranged on either side of the room, their fronds arcing together in a luxurious canopy below the white-and-gilt moulded ceiling. A sparkle of starburst from among the foliage: fairy lights; brilliant, tiny, each no larger than a thumbnail. Paper lanterns were strung along the walls and windows, dozens, hundreds of them, painted elaborately with peacocks, their colours lacquering the room.

'Sir?' A waiter politely proffered a drink-laden tray.

Folks around here had obviously heard neither of the Depression nor Prohibition, Jim thought, as he took in the kaleidoscope of flutes, goblets and sundry glassware so thoroughly flumed and plumed he hadn't the slightest idea what they were called. He eyed the peacock feather positioned archly alongside.

'You got any beer?'

A flicker of empathy crossed the waiter's face. 'Just the cocktails here, and bourbon and single malts at the bar.' He passed a jaundiced eye over the cocktails. 'You could try the Abbey,' he suggested, 'doesn't look too bad.'

Jim grimaced. 'The bar, you said?'

He made his way past the mammoth tubs of magnolia and red-daggered birds of paradise, the light from chandeliers overhead dancing across the laughing, animated crowd. People were thronged three and four deep around the bar, the harried bartenders trying their best to keep up. He pressed his way in, the blur of faces starting to set his teeth on edge, when he happened to glance to his right. There she was, Madeleine, not a foot away.

She sat with her elbows propped on the marble top of the bar, deep in conversation. He tapped her on the shoulder. Pale, freckled. Bare, exposed in the low-cut dress she wore. He had to tap her again before she looked up.

'Jim!' She smiled. 'You came.'

'What's that supposed to mean?' he asked, frowning. 'You invited me, remember?' The music from the jazz band was so loud, he had to shout the words into her ear. She wore no jewellery, neck, arms and earlobes bare of adornment, just that inviting expanse of cool, milky skin.

She laughed. 'I did. You said "maybe".' She turned to her companion. 'Freddie, Jim.'

Jim noticed both the proprietary arm that Freddie draped around her, and the fact that she didn't seem to mind.

'So where are the peacocks anyway?'

'In the greenhouse.' She gestured about her. 'They'd be skittish here, with so many people around.'

She leaned across the bar. There was a single peacock feather tucked into the braided bun she wore at the nape of her neck, its colours startling against the richness of her hair. Without waiting to ask what he wanted to drink, she ordered him a malt whisky, their fingers touching as she handed it to him.

'I see you got the dress code?'

He looked at her surprised, and she brushed a hand over his cummerbund, his stomach contracted at her touch. 'Greens and Blues.'

'You didn't tell me that.'

'Oh, I don't believe in dress codes,' she said blithely, passing a hand over the ivory silk of her dress. Her eyes were impish, daring him to comment on the feather in her hair. Greens, and blues.

'You wanted me to show up in overalls,' he accused, only half jokingly.

She laughed. 'That *would* have been something. Well, that cummerbund is perfect. Vintage,' she pronounced, examining it. 'The Major's?'

'Your father?' Freddie butted in, trying to get in on the conversation. 'A veteran, Madeleine said – you should be proud.'

They ignored him.

'Come on.' She set down her drink and slipped from the stool. 'I'll introduce you around. My parents are here somewhere as well. Freddie,' she called over her shoulder, 'be a dear and save our places.'

Professor Scott stood nursing his drink with Douglas Garland and a knot of other men, all similarly bass-voiced and large-bellied. 'Good to meet you, son,' he said affably, shaking Jim's hand. He put an arm around Madeleine's shoulders. 'Cookie here told me about your father.'

'So how *is* the Major doing?' Doug Garland asked. 'We used to hunt together,' he informed the group. He waved his cigar about. 'Haven't seen him in years though.'

'A veteran?' one of the men asked with interest. 'And what does your father make of Smedley Butler?'

Jim shrugged. 'He ran as a dry. Not the easiest ticket to win over voters.'

Garland laughed. 'No, nor was it the wisest.' He clinked his glass to Jim's. 'Prohibition's had its run, I wager. There's more money to be made in taxing alcohol sales than in outlawing it. One way or another, men are going to find a way to drink, and men like Butler simply don't get that.'

The superciliousness of his tone irritated Jim. 'My father supports him. Says he's done more for our vets than most any other politician.'

'Ah, yes, the veterans and their Bonus Bill. Veteran doughboys, dear, from the Great War,' Garland elaborated, for Madeleine's benefit. 'They think the Government owes them dues because they went over to France. They've been petitioning the administration for a payment of arrears.' He pulled on his cigar. 'We're grateful as a nation, of course we are, but where's the money for this "bonus" going to come from? Not to mention that most of these men are hale and hearty and perfectly capable of earning a living – it's been fourteen years since the armistice, for God's sake. Isn't it enough that we have that lot in the dust bowl to feed, without having to worry about paying off these fellows back from France?'

'My father's a "fellow back from France",' Jim said coldly. 'Not that he'd say it, but the fact that men like him went over there, and the fact that they made it back, ought to make folks like you thankful. If it hadn't been for them fighting – and winning – the war, who knows how much of this,' – he gestured about the glittering room, 'would have remained.' He set down his drink. 'This was a pleasure,' he said acidly.

'Jim!' It was Madeleine. 'Wait up.' She caught his arm. 'What, you're just going to leave?'

'Garland's an asshole.'

'It's just talk, that's all. Politics. Why'd you have to get all bothered?'

He was quiet.

'Come on, let me show you the peacocks. Oh, don't be so dreary! Come *on*,' she cajoled, and wanting to be mollified, he followed her.

She led him down a hall and through a door at the far end. It opened on to a quieter, perfumed passageway, gently lit. 'The rose hall,' she said. 'You should see it during the day. Masses of roses everywhere, it's like something out of a magazine.'

They walked for a while, the strains of the band growing fainter, their footsteps echoing on the marble. Their fingers touched, once or twice. Another door ahead. She pulled it open. '*Et voilà,* the birds.'

The room had been converted into a large, high-ceilinged aviary, housing a family of peafowl. Seven in all, two males and five peahens, roosting on the ledges built into the wall. One of the males cocked its head at their approach. It spread its short wings and sailed to the floor as they drew nearer, its tail sweeping behind the richly hued body in a magnificent, six-foot-long train.

'Look at the colours,' she said softly. 'Have you ever seen anything so beautiful?'

He shrugged, still smarting from Garland's comments and bent on being contrary.

'What's with "Cookie"?'

'My parents call me that. You know, Cookie, as in French.'

He didn't, but nodded anyway. The peacock looked contemplatively at them, the crest on its surprisingly small head bobbing to and fro. It raised a clawed foot, holding it in mid-air as, slowly, its tail started to rise. It grew higher, fanning into an orb of hammered gold. Jim watched in fascination, almost forgetting his earlier rancour. An eruption of ivory quills, feathered in glittering colour – copper, emerald, and silken black; at the apex of each quill, a single cobalt eye.

The bird began to dance, the colours leaching into one another as it swayed and quivered. Petrol-over-water colours, the sheen of a fin upstream. They stood in utter silence, watching spellbound, and watched in turn by those shimmering, myriad eyes. The tapping of the bird's feet was the only sound in the room: a symphony without music, fluid, haunting; a message composed in code. The edges of their palms touched. She lifted her hand, a quiet, unfussy movement, and placed it in his. It felt entirely natural to close his fingers about hers.

He registered the smoothness of her skin, the specific, slotted fit of bone and palm and angled wrist of her hand in his own. The peacock danced. As if in a dream, Jim turned towards her, just as she lifted her face to his. The soft heat of her mouth. Her lips parting, deepening that first, gentle caress, sending a tremor through his body as her tongue flickered hungrily against his own.

'Madeleine?'

Footsteps sounded in the hall outside. The peacock stopped

abruptly, its tail drooping. She pulled away, slipping her hand from his just as Freddie entered.

'Wherever did you go?' Freddie demanded petulantly. 'I've been hunting all over for you. Dinner's been announced.'

'We—' Her face was flushed. 'I was just showing Jim the peacocks.'

Freddie put a possessive arm about her. 'Will you be joining us, Stonebridge?'

'Of course he is.' She didn't disentangle herself from his hold, though.

They began walking back. Jim was quiet, still strangely affected by the bird, the way it had danced, as if only for them, his skin still tingling from the unexpected heat of that kiss. He knew from the way she touched her palms to her cheeks that she felt it too.

'I don't think I got what you do, Stonebridge?'

'That's because I didn't say.'

'Jim's family have apple orchards and a farm.'

'That can't be easy,' Freddie said pompously. 'With the economy . . . I own an aeroplane – Cookie and I like to go flying,' he said, squeezing her shoulder, 'and it's a shame to see all those rundown, hardscrabble holdings, falling into ruin. It's a hard living.'

'Freddie!' she exclaimed, frowning, but Jim interrupted.

'It's a hard living, but someone's got to do it, right? You know what else about us hardscrabble types?' He stepped angrily forward, and Freddie blanched. 'When pretty-boy flatlanders fly their dinky toy aeroplanes over our woods and rivers, causing no end of headache and spooking all the fish, why, we give them a real hardscrabble salute. Just like this.' Jim raised his finger, right in Freddie's face.

'I'm leaving,' he said to Madeleine. This time, she did not stop him.

He tried to put her from his mind after that. 'A flatlander,' he said to himself, 'and too used to getting her own way.' They had nothing in common, he reminded himself, her with her dancing and theatre groups and flying about in noisy planes, whereas his life was here, amidst these woods and stone-rutted hills, rooted in the soil of this farm. And yet, the memory of her lingered – how natural it had felt to kiss her, the feel of her hand in his own.

He went hunting, and despite the grouse being especially skittish and the drumming hard to locate, he bagged himself a brace. The larger of the two had a beautiful set of tail feathers; he saved the longest, striated in brown and white, not admitting to himself that the reason he did so was that she might find it interesting.

The Major asked, awkwardly, how the evening had gone. 'Garland said Hello,' Jim lied. His father looked at him sardonically and Jim turned away, unwilling to meet his eyes. He rapped his knuckles aimlessly on the table. 'Her folks call her Cookie.'

The Major looked puzzled. 'After "madeleine",' he said, his brow clearing. 'It's a French cake,' he elaborated, 'like a soft cookie, I suppose.'

Jim said nothing more but later that week, with his father out of earshot, he asked Ellie if she knew how to bake madeleines. 'They're French,' he explained, with a studied casualness.

Ellie looked at him over the tops of her glasses, a quizzical expression on her face. She didn't know no fancy French food, she said, but if he wanted some Indian pudding, there were three baking in the oven.

Restless, he called a girl he hadn't seen in some time. It made him both guilty and irritated to hear the lilt in her voice, knowing it was there because he'd called. He leaned in to kiss her after the movie they went to but when she pretend pouted and drew back, eyes wide, he shrugged and turned the key in the ignition.

'Jim!' she said, clearly hurt, 'it's been a while, that's all.' He stopped the engine, feeling like a heel. 'I missed you,' she said afterwards, and not knowing what to say, he pulled the tail feather from the dashboard and gave it to her. 'For me?' she exclaimed, and tucked it behind her ear.

He patted her arm, disliking himself, but unable to stop thinking of another woman, dressed in ivory silk, the chandelier picking out blue and green highlights in the peacock feather she wore in the braid of her russet hair.

The girl started to call again after that, with increasingly desperate frequency. Each time, he instructed his father and Ellie to tell her he was out. Ellie shook her head disapprovingly, but reserved comment. When at last Madeleine called, she arched an eyebrow.

'Her call, you'll take, I'm guessing?'

'No,' he said, coolly, 'same message.'

The other girl finally gave up. Madeleine, however, was not so easily put off. She continued to call, sometimes a day, maybe two passing after her last call, but call she did. Jim stubbornly refused to speak with her, although it was hardly lost on the Major, the way his son asked offhandedly at the end of each day if anyone had called.

Finally, it was the Major who, exasperated by this jackass charade and the ringing of the damned 'phone, called an end to the impasse. 'You should come over,' he said tersely to Madeleine when she next rang, before she'd even had a chance to ask for Jim. 'He's in the barn.'

He was tinkering with the bike when she showed up. He looked up as the door of the barn cranked open, and there she was, graceful against the light.

'Hello.'

He continued to grease the chain.

'I called a few days ago, left a message. Did you not get it?' she pressed.

'Wasn't anything for me to say.'

She laughed. 'Well, that's why I thought it best to come.'

He sat up, wiping his hands on his overalls. 'And did you bring your precious Freddie with you?'

'No. No, I didn't. As a matter of fact, I've told Freddie that it's best he head back to Boston.'

'That's a shame,' he said caustically. 'The two of you sure make a handsome couple of flatlanders.'

'Well, then that *is* a shame,' she agreed, sitting down in the straw next to him. She touched a finger to a spot of oil and lifted it to the light, examining the smudge on her skin. Her hand seemed to him like a bird, delicate of wing – a thing of porcelain slightness.

She took his hand in hers, raising the hairs on his arm as she gently rubbed the oil into his wrist. 'The thing is, Jim Stonebridge' she said ruminatively, 'I might be going country.'

At first, he stubbornly refused to meet her gaze. When he did, it was with a still angry, shuttered expression that gave nothing away. She looked steadily at him as he bored into her eyes with his own, and the tautness of his expression began slowly to yield. A series of fleeting, warring emotions in his face – anger, desire, resentment – gave way to an unaccustomed vulnerability. Still she looked into his eyes, and gradually he let down his guard; reluctantly, he let her in.

Swallows swooped and called in the sun; from somewhere in the distance, the sound of a horse neighing. He noted these only vaguely, focused on her, on those large, dark-fringed eyes. Two people, caught in a moment, on the hay-covered floor of an old, red-painted barn. Staring at each other, drinking each other in. Seeing and being seen, beyond the utilitarian membranes of word and gesture. Searching out the hidden shoals and secret bends that lie at our cores, deep, dark and filled with promises for the unlocking.

TWELVE

Spring took firm hold of the hills, belying its fitful start, in what Jim would secretly come to view as a natural mirroring of the way things happened between Madeleine and him. They took the horses out deep into the woods, riding down old, forgotten paths. Oaks, their branches felted with the fuzz of new leaves, threw dappled patterns across the ground. He pointed out the gullies carved by ancient rivers and primordial ice; in those folds and pleats of earth, one morning, a rare pink lady's slipper.

Digging up a skunk cabbage, he cut through the rootstock that lay just beneath the soil. He pushed back the tight layers of unborn spathes to reveal a bud, still dormant, but already a deep, wine red. It would flower next spring. A few leaves in, another bud, naked and pale – it would bloom the year after that. Five buds in all, each smaller and tucked further in than the last. A quintet of spring seasons, hidden beneath the earth, patiently biding their time.

He showed them to her, then doubting that she would understand, felt foolish. He became brusque, slicing through the rootstock and tossing it on the ground, but she picked it up, parsing through the leaves with a solemn, dedicated wonder. On the way back that evening, they came upon two painted turtles, one following the other in a slow, ponderous motion across the dirt road, their shells wet and gleaming, as if varnished.

At first, the Major, still unsettled by the flashback memory that her first visit had provoked, stayed out of Madeleine's way. He'd go deep into the orchard, or shut himself away in the library just as she was due to arrive. Jim, too, contrived to keep Madeleine's visits to the farm as few and brief as possible, whisking her away for long rides on the motorbike, or arranging to meet her elsewhere. Whenever she asked about his father – 'He's tied up with his correspondence,' he'd say glibly, or, 'He's resting.'

'Resting? It's ten in the morning,' she countered once.

'It's his leg. Been bothering him.'

She nodded, not believing a word. 'Douggie said they used to hunt together years ago,' she said suddenly. 'How come you never told me that?'

A barely perceptible stiffening of his shoulders.

'It was a long time ago.'

'So why'd he stop? The Major – hunting, I mean?'

'What's this,' he said exasperatedly, 'an inquisition?'

'Maybe.' She leaned forward to kiss him quickly on the lips. 'So why did he?'

'They used to hunt together, alright? From before the war. Garland and his flatlander buddies would come down from Boston during hunting season, and the Major would show them around the woods, take them to where the easiest coveys lay. When I was old enough, he'd take me along too. After a while though, after he came back from France, things changed. He changed. It didn't interest him any more, hunting.'

She didn't press further, not letting on that Douggie Garland had said a whole lot more when she'd asked him, soon after the gala. The Major had grown increasingly bellicose and unpredictable, he'd said. 'Out there in the woods, you've got to have full confidence in the men you're with. Those are real guns we use, not some trifling toy, and a single mistake can prove fatal. Stonebridge was a good enough sort, but when he showed up drunk one time . . .' He'd taken the Major aside, suggested it was perhaps best that he went home. 'It didn't go down too well,' he recounted dryly.

Although she said nothing of this to Jim, he knew instinctively that Garland had told her what had happened. What she didn't know though, was how it had ended.

He'd tugged on his father's hand, trying to pull him away. Judy, still only a six-month-old pup, cowered behind him, frightened by the raised voices, tail tucked between her legs. It had scared him too, the look on his father's face. The Major shook free of Jim's grasp, furiously cussing out the men. It was only when Jim stumbled backwards over the pup and nearly fell that he seemed to recall the presence of his son.

'Come along, Jim,' he said roughly, 'we don't need this.'

They'd headed west, in the opposite direction to the group, the

Major limping forward at such a punishing pace that Jim struggled to keep up. Judy loped back and forth between the two of them, first alongside the Major, then turning loyally back to the boy, confused by this fractured progress. Jim reached down to pat her head, trying to reassure her and she whined and pressed her nose into his palm.

The Major had pushed on, scaling the ridges so rapidly that he was frequently lost from sight. Judy started to labour, tongue hanging out, puppy legs buckling. Jim hoisted her into his arms, staggering under her weight. He blundered through a bramble thicket, drawing the cuffs of his canvas shirt over his hands best he could to protect them from the thorns. A branch whipped across his cheek, leaving a thin, bloody scratch. He emerged at the other end of the thicket to silence. He stood still, listening for his father's footsteps, but all he could hear was the pounding of his own heart. No sign of his father, nothing around but trees and sky. He drew a shaky breath, quelling the sharp prick of tears in his eyes. Judy whined again, sensing his distress.

There! A faint crackle through the brush. Ignoring his burning muscles, Jim hurried towards the sound.

At last, the Major's pace faltered. He lowered his gun, the injured leg dragged behind him. Jim bent to let Judy out of his arms and she gambolled happily around father and son. He looked tentatively at his father, trying to read his expression. He wondered if he ought to suggest they return home.

Judy dropped suddenly into a point, body stiff, her left leg folded into her chest. A rustle, a panicked whirring of wings and a grouse flew out from practically under her nose. The muzzle of the gun lifted, a bang; the dead bird spiralled down. Jim's heart lightened, bursting with pride. 'You got it!'

His father had nodded, as if in a trance.

The Major began to dress the grouse. Laying it on the ground, he smoothed the feathers and placed a foot on each extended wing. He grasped its legs, one in each hand, and in a swift movement, north to south, wrenched them apart. The breast popped cleanly out.

He had cradled the meat in his palms, his face so devoid of expression that Jim had thought at first that the tears were just from the trick eye, the one that watered with neither warning nor explanation. The Major made no sound, just the tears – *tears,* Jim realised with a shock – coursing down his cheeks. Jim blinked, utterly crushed, the happiness of just a moment ago, gone. He squatted miserably on the leaf litter, an arm around Judy panting by his side. Hating to see his father so vulnerable, feeling somehow as if it were all his fault. The Major cradled the dead bird in his hands and silently wept, shoulders heaving, as Jim sat staring at the ground, feeling helpless, angry and ashamed all at once, and grateful, so thankful that Garland and the other men were not around to witness his father's breakdown.

He looked down now at Madeleine's fingers interlaced with his own. 'We should get going,' he said shortly, slipping his hand from hers.

'Jim—'

'We should go.'

She followed pensively, knowing he was upset but unsure what to say.

With Freddie leaving so unexpectedly for Boston, the rest of the theatre club had held together only a short while before disbanding. 'Let's be in touch, get back together after the summer,' they said halfheartedly to one another and Madeleine laughingly went along.

Her parents left for home a few weeks later, as did Garland. She wheedled them into letting her stay a while longer. 'It's for my art,' she explained. 'There's something about these hills – the colours make me want to sit before a canvas all day.' Her mother had pursed her lips, incredulous, but powerless before her daughter's wilfulness.

'The colours, or is it the Stonebridge lad you intend on studying?' her father had asked gently. Madeleine had the grace to blush as she kissed him fondly on his cheek.

It was Ellie who talked the Major into having Madeleine over to tea once more. She had grown so sick of Clara Dalloway going on and on about how she had been the one to introduce the two youngsters, right here in her store over by the fabric counter. So ruffled were her maternal instincts by the fact that she had yet to clap eyes on this flatlander who had obviously captivated her Jim, that she nagged and niggled at the Major until he had no choice but to agree.

'Fine,' he snapped, 'do what you want, but leave me out of it.'

'Whatever do you mean, leave you out of this – it's your home, isn't it?' she demanded.

'I'm . . . Just set up my tea in the library when the young lady is here.'

'I'll do no such thing! You're the host, James Arthur, and you will have tea with the rest of us,' Ellie said firmly.

The Major turned, an expression of such bitter anger on his face that for a moment, Ellie quailed. His left eye started to twitch just then, however, the skin tightening and juddering. Pressing the heel of his hand tightly over it, he got up and limped from the room without another word.

'It'll do him good,' Ellie muttered to herself as she watched him go. She started to polish the table vigorously, still somewhat shaken. 'Do us all good.'

That's what she told Jim as well, when he said it wasn't a good idea. 'Look what happened the last time she came over,' he reminded her.

'It's high time the Major got used to having people around him again.' Her voice gentled at the worry in his eyes. 'Don't you fret,' she said. 'I'll be here this time, it'll all be fine.'

Haunted by the aftermath of Madeleine's last visit, the Major grew increasingly tense and tightly coiled, his left eye twitching and watering without notice, setting Jim so on edge that he wanted nothing more than to call the whole thing off. Perhaps anticipating this, Ellie had wisely arranged the tea for as soon as was possible, on the day after the next. Before father and son knew it, the afternoon was upon them.

'Madeleine,' the Major said stiffly when she arrived. He extended a hand, but she kissed him on the cheek instead, entirely disarming him. For a second, he was at a loss. 'It's a pleasure, my dear,' he mumbled then, flushing, 'a pleasure to see you again.'

'Jim's been keeping you all to himself!' a beaming Ellie exclaimed. 'I was having no more of that.'

'I can't . . . no, really that's far too much . . .' Madeleine protested faintly as Ellie piled her plate high once more from the avalanche of food on the table. Three kinds of pies, an assortment of sugared cakes, a chocolate pudding, two braided loaves, jam, a large pat of golden country butter, thick and moreish apple butter, maple syrup, a pot roast, jell-o-moulds garnished with pineapple, and a glistening ham, its caramel skin scored into diamonds and studded with cloves.

'I wouldn't argue,' Jim counselled, spearing a slice of ham. 'Not with Ellie, you'll never win.'

He glanced again at his father. The tension that had gripped the Major these past couple of days was no longer evident, his gnarled frame relaxed as he tucked into his third helping of the pot roast. Jim grinned. 'Food's great, Ellie.'

'Eat up, eat up, dear,' a smiling Ellie urged Madeleine, hands on her hips. 'Men like women with some meat on their bones.'

Jim rolled his eyes.

The Major had been sitting silently in his chair all this while, Ellie's nonstop chatter serving as a barrier of sorts, behind which he could safely withdraw, relieved to be able just to enjoy his food and listen in on the conversation. Now, however, he stirred, feeling compelled to intervene.

'Ellie, that's enough,' he remonstrated mildly. 'Madeleine,' he asked, gallantly changing the subject, 'what do you think about the mural contest at Radio City Hall?'

'Oh, Georgia O' Keefe deserves to win!' she said. 'Those vibrant, fantastical flowers of hers – the city could use some of that lushness amongst all that steel.'

The Major smiled, saying he was betting on Davis' abstract of Manhattan instead.

'Yes, yes, that's all very fine and fancy,' Ellie scoffed, 'but who'd like some pie?'

Later, Ellie whisked Madeleine off on a tour of the rooms upstairs, showing her the exquisite sets of pearls and garnets that had belonged to Jim's mother, and her antique tortoiseshell combs, still wrapped in tissue paper. Opening a drawer, she took out a handful of old photographs. She looked at each one before passing it on to Madeleine, her expression suddenly wistful.

'The Major with his older brother, William,' she said, pointing to the two laughing young men standing shoulder to shoulder. 'Nearly five years between them, but they were a pair all right. You'd always see them together, out and about, hunting and fishing side by side. So different in their ways, but devoted to each other. Bill was the loud one, with an eye for the girls and a natural at just about anything he tried. Football star, and captain of the swim team too, if I remember correctly. Went off to West Point and it was all he'd ever wanted, to be an officer, right from the time he was a child, is what I heard. The Major now, he was the quieter one, always reading. Took his own sweet time to get to know anyone new, but once he opened up . . .' Ellie smiled.

'So where's Bill now?' Madeleine asked curiously, trying to reconcile the image of the Major, so young, still only a slender-faced teen and laughing with such abandon in the photograph, with the man downstairs.

Ellie sighed. 'Got thrown from a horse not long after he joined West Point. Wasn't much anyone could do and he died soon after. It tore the family apart, with the Major taking it especially hard.'

She sighed again, sifting through the stack in her hands before finding the photograph she wanted, of Bill in his cadet's uniform. 'Something to think about isn't it, how different things might have been if Bill hadn't had that accident, if it'd been him, like it was always meant to be, going off to war? But that's not what happened. It was the Major who went off to enlist, insisting it was the right thing to do.' She shook her head. 'Maybe it was right, or maybe he was just trying to do what his brother would have done, but whatever the reason, turns out that it was James who became Major Stonebridge after all, not Bill.'

She drew another photograph from the stack, this time of the Major and his wife, on their wedding day.

'How come they didn't have any more children?'

'She wanted to. He did too, before. "Five children," she'd always say, "one for each day of the week". "That's a damn fool notion," he'd reply, "what about the weekend?" "The weekend being for rest," she'd say to him, laughing. With the war though . . . everything was different after that. He made it back home alright, which was a blessing, but—' She shook her head pensively again. 'He was never quite the same. I'd catch her crying.'

She straightened her back, face brightening as she handed Madeleine yet another photograph. 'Now this one – you recognise him, don't you?'

'Jim.'

It was a photograph of the family, taken beneath the old apple tree. Madeleine ran a finger over the freckle-nosed little boy, his bare knees pressed into the earth, an arm close about his dog.

'Judy,' Ellie remembered. 'The setter, her name was Judy.'

'Mrs Stonebridge looks kind,' Madeleine said softly.

'She was. It was a hard day for Jim when she passed.'

'He never talks about her.'

'Not one to talk much at all, is he now? But take it from me, that boy feels things deep.' Ellie laughed and patted Madeleine's hand. 'Well, you'll see that for yourself, I'm sure.'

'You sure were a hit with Ellie,' Jim said indulgently as he saw her off later that evening. Sliding his hands about her waist, he drew her close.

She laid her hands on his chest, spreading her fingers wide and then closing them again, back and forth, like the pleats of a fan. 'Not bad for a flatlander, I take it?'

He grinned. 'Not bad at all.'

She'd stayed a while after Ellie had left, so that it had been just the three of them, sitting beside the fireplace. She'd been unusually quiet, still thinking about the photographs that Ellie had shared, quiet enough that Jim looked enquiringly at her; she'd smiled and laid her head against his shoulder. He'd brought out the ivory chessboard from the library while the women were upstairs, and the two of them sat down to a game. The Major shook out his newspaper and turned on the radio, Jim listening with half an ear as he concentrated on the chessboard.

Madeleine had dreamily watched their reflections in the black mirror, father and son, and her as well, in this montage of simple domesticity, and as she did, she became slowly aware of a deep-rooted contentment. A sense of womanliness, warm and full, a sensation, entirely novel, of being needed, as if she were the link, so long missing, that rendered this tableau complete.

They'd played for a while, stopping when the snores emanating from the Major's armchair indicated that he'd fallen soundly, peaceably asleep.

Madeleine looked teasingly up at Jim now, her hair picking up the colours of the sunset. 'I believe I'm a hit with the Major too.'

He shook his head regretfully. 'Nah, you put him to sleep.'

She laughed. He drew her closer still, sliding his hands down the curve and flare of her spine, further, cupping the swell of her buttocks. She gasped at the press of his fingers. He began to slowly knead that soft, yielding flesh and she arced her hips against his, sparking a deep hunger inside him as he bent his face to hers.

Madeleine came over more often after that visit, and the Major gradually grew increasingly at ease around her. She instinctively avoided all talk of the past now, except for what information he might suddenly volunteer – that the beams in the kitchen came from a ship that his grandfather had sailed on, for instance, or that Jim, one Christmas, had thought to present his mother with a dead toad. She'd unwrapped it and screamed with fright, flinging it right across the room and startling them all with the strength of her throwing arm.

The Major had kept something aside for Madeleine one afternoon. 'Here,' he said, 'I don't believe you'll have seen one of these in Boston.' He handed her a framed letter, the writing on it faded and thin. 'A rat letter,' he said drolly, 'penned by my great-grandmother. Folks used to say she had a witchy sense about her. She came up with this spell to rid the house of rats.'

She'd placed the letter in a box of punched tin and hidden it in the cellar. Years later, when the Major was helping his father replace a creaky floorboard, they'd found it in the hole beneath, beside a handful of river pebbles and a doll mould made of copper, coated with verdigris. The Major recalled the hole being narrow and deep, just large enough for a boy's hand. The doll mould had been especially strange, with its green-tinted head and stiff limbs. Inside the box, they'd found the rat letter, written on paper fashioned from linen rags.

> I have borne with you till my patience is gone. There are no words adequate to express my displeasure. You raid our seed corn, make holes in more apples than you can eat in a hundred yellow lifetimes. You create a ruckus at night, waking the baby who cries something awful through daybreak.
>
> Devils, spirits of the bottomless pit, heed me now, and depart with all speed. Look not back! Begone and never come here again, for *we are now in arms against you*! I hold nothing back – you shall hear the whole. We are preparing water to drown you, fire to burn you, cats to catch you, dogs to skin you and clubs to maul you. Unless you wish to be dyed in fire and brimstone, you Satans, quit at once.

Go to Hannah Watkins' instead.

(This is for the cellar rats. Please give notice to the chamber and garret rats as well, for *we are plotting against you all.*)

Madeleine started to laugh. 'She had a temper, that's for sure! Poor Hannah Watkins, whoever she was. Did the rats leave?'

'They certainly did,' the Major said, a twinkle in his eyes. 'Whether or not to Hannah's, I can't say, but they never did return here, not once in all these years.'

'Now if only great-great-grandma had come up with something for the rats in the barn,' Jim observed laconically, and the Major grinned.

When Madeleine asked if she could take the Claude mirror outside so that she might paint the old apple tree in its reflection, the Major hesitated, but nonetheless agreed.

'He's grown very fond of you,' Ellie remarked later. 'To hand over his precious mirror like that – he gets all kinds of antsy if he's away from the thing for too long.'

'Was it Mrs Stonebridge's?' Madeleine asked.

'That monstrous thing? No, he brought it back from France. Mrs Stonebridge didn't say anything, she wasn't the sort to, but I knew she didn't like it, not from the start. It gives me the creeps too.'

Madeleine looked incredulously at her. 'Why? It's beautiful.'

Ellie snorted. 'To look in it, it's as if the colour's been taken away from everything. Whoever heard of a black mirror, anyhow? In earlier days . . .' she paused, remembering. 'I shouldn't be saying so much, but in earlier days, after the Major had just returned from the war, all he'd do was sit before that thing. Sit and stare into it, rain or snow or shine. Sometimes through the nights even; I'd come in the next day, and there he'd be, still in his chair, looking into that blackness.

'The thing is, there was nothing to see. I mean, at night, sitting there in the dark, *what* was he looking at, all those hours?'

Madeleine leaned against the stone wall of the orchard. She set down her brush, staring at the mirror propped beside her. There was a spare beauty to the reflected trees, the green of their leaves dulled to an elemental glaze. They were almost lovelier leached of colour, she thought, an inner honesty revealed.

'Do you think it's spooky too?'

'The mirror?' Jim looked at her, amused. 'Ellie, I'm guessing. Don't go setting too much store by what she says, she gets these odd notions sometimes.'

'I've heard that some mirrors hold ghosts, that images of people are locked inside the glass. If you look into one between the light from two candles, you'll see someone who's passed on.'

Jim chuckled.

Madeleine touched a finger to the mirror. Its reflection seemed pale and wraith-like in the glass. What was the Major looking for, Ellie had wondered.

What, Madeleine thought suddenly to herself, *or was it 'who'?*

THIRTEEN

The Major flung the newspaper from himself with such force that it flew against the mantel, scattering in a flurry of pages across the wooden floorboards. 'They voted against it,' he said bitterly. 'They vetoed the Bonus Bill.'

Rising to his feet, the Major began to pace back and forth, muscles coiled so tight that the damaged leg seemed almost to be mounted on some stiff and disparate spring as it jolted and dragged behind him.

'It was only the House Ways and Means Committee,' Jim said carefully. 'There's still the Senate hearing.'

'Damn fool politicians. Crooks, the lot of them. Crooks! How could they veto it with a clear conscience? This is back pay for God's sake, owed to every man who shipped out with Uncle Sam's Army. But they don't care. They don't give a damn.' The Major banged a palm on the table. 'Look at the coverage it got, for crying out loud – a measly couple of inches – while that Lindbergh case has been on the front page for weeks.'

'It's Charles Lindbergh's son!' Madeleine protested, startled. 'The poor little thing, not even two years old, and kidnapped!'

The Major paused to stare at her, eyes cold and glittering like two chips of blue ice. 'Indeed. Dashing Mr Lindbergh, hero aviator, beloved of the public. His son snatched from his very crib in the middle of the night. Why shouldn't this country be transfixed for weeks? It isn't as if there's anything else of consequence going on, is there?'

Madeleine flushed. 'I—'

'That's not what she meant,' Jim interjected. He stepped forward to gather up the pages of the newspaper, a casual, seemingly nonchalant gesture that nonetheless inserted him between his father and Madeleine. 'The Bill still has to go before the Senate,' he repeated evenly. 'It still has a shot.'

*

The Major shut himself away in the library all that morning, emerging only as Jim and Madeleine were headed out, to hand Jim a thick, cream-coloured envelope.

'Give it in when you get into town.'

Jim pocketed the envelope without comment.

'What is it?' Madeleine asked curiously, as she climbed into the truck.

'Nothing.'

'A letter? Give it in where?'

He said nothing, starting to whistle instead as he guided the truck down the drive. Deciding it was too beautiful a day to pout, she tamped down the flare of irritation. Besides, she'd see soon enough for herself, she thought.

She started to hum, keeping tune with his whistling. Reaching over, he affectionately massaged the nape of her neck.

The church bell was calling out the hour as they rode into town, the old bell pealing faithfully over the surrounding hills, past shingled roof and painted barn. The sun caught its massive frame as it swung back and forth, infusing it with changeling litheness. Everywhere, the hop and twitter of birds, in budding branches and blooming shrubs. The black locust by the malt shop had flowered, the perfume from the creamy white racemes wafted delicately through the open windows of the store.

Old Asaph and Jeremiah were sitting at a table, spooning down their sundaes as Jim and Madeleine entered. They turned around to regard her with an unabashed and guileless curiosity.

'Madeleine Scott,' Jim said by way of offhanded introduction. Her eyes danced at the way he stood right beside her, close enough to stake indisputable claim and belie the casualness of his words.

At the general store, Clara Dalloway bustled from behind the counter to kiss them both on the cheek. 'The Major, how is he?' she asked, as was her habit.

Jim shrugged. 'Fine,' he said, as usual.

He'd loaded the groceries and they were pulling out of the lot when Madeleine asked at last – 'Aren't you forgetting something?'

'Nope.'

'He asked you to mail that letter.' She waited. 'Are you going to say anything about it at all?'

They drove in silence. She rolled down the window and cupping her chin in her hand, stared outside, hurt by his reticence.

He glanced at her, then looked back at the road. 'He didn't mean the post office,' he finally offered. 'He wanted me to hand it in at the office of the *Gazette*.'

'So why didn't you? And what is it anyway?'

'Because they're not going to print it, that's why. It's the same article, pretty much, that he's been sending in there for years, and nobody's interested.'

'What does he write about? The war?'

'No, not the war. He never talks about the war. The Bonus Bill. For years now, he's been writing about it, but no one wants to hear.' He drummed his hands on the steering wheel. '"Too much of a downer," the editor at the *Gazette* said, all those times that I tried to give it in, "tell him to write something upbeat."'

Abruptly, Jim turned off the road and up a dirt track. She held on to the handle of the door as the truck jolted over the stones.

'Come on,' he said, stopping under a pine tree. 'I've something to show you.'

'I want to read it.'

He hesitated, briefly, before handing over the envelope. She slid a finger under the flap and pulled out the monogrammed sheets inside.

Since time immemorial, ever since man invented empire and war, this has been the conundrum faced by nations worldwide: what to do with the returning soldier?

Whether in Roman times with Sulla's returning hordes, or in Elizabethan days, when wandering soldiers were outlawed from the City of London on pain of death, governments have long regarded the returning veteran as a public oddity at best. At worst, an untenable drain on the exchequer and a direct threat to the safety and stability of their administration.

Our doughboys left for the Great War under the flutter of the Stars and Stripes, amidst cheers many thousand-fold strong. When they returned, plenty were the parades, the fetes, the grand welcome-home galas.

Then everybody forgot.

War, once it ends, whether in resounding victory or grim defeat, is a shameful truth best abandoned; the men who return from the Front, an inconvenience.

A dead or disabled soldier is labelled a hero and he, or his widow, is issued some form of government 'support'. It is rarely enough. What price on the loss of one's limb, of an eye, or worse?

And what of those others, the men who return from war whole in body but altered in ways the civilian world cannot begin to understand?

Our doughboys shipped overseas for the pittance of $1.25 a day, less than they would have earned had they stayed home. They fought hard and they fought strong, but when they returned, it was to a nation all too eager to forget. The jobs they held before the war had long been filled, their hard-won experience on the battlefield of little worth in peacetime.

All our boys are asking for under the Bonus Bill is fair compensation for the time served overseas, in other words, for rightfully earned *back pay*. This is no 'bonus' that these men seek, this isn't charity that the nation must find within itself to donate. This is rightful *payment, promised and owed* to each of these men for their service. A debt, owed by every man, woman and child of this free and proud nation. It ought to have been paid in full in 1918 when the war ended. It wasn't. It wasn't even paid in 1924, when the notion of a 'bonus' was first brought into law.

It has been fourteen years since the war ended. This is blood money we are sitting on. Blood money, and it must be paid today.

'They won't print this?'

'We're in the middle of a depression, you know,' Jim said lightly. He rubbed absently at a smudge of dirt on the windshield. 'Folks aren't interested in this stuff, not with things the way they are. No jobs to be had, banks failing, all those shenanigans on Wall Street . . . Nobody wants to hear about veterans and their dues.'

'My father knows people in publishing.'

'He tried sending around his articles.' Opening the door, Jim hopped to the ground and, coming around to her side, swung her down. 'He tried, and then gave up; it's nothing but a fool's errand now with the *Gazette*. He tells me to submit a piece, I don't, but tell him that I did. When the newspapers come, he checks to see if it's been published, which, of course, it never is. In time, he writes another piece, and there we are again.' He shook his head. 'Come on,' he said, effectively ending the discussion as he strode into the woods.

Madeleine followed, so lost in thought over the Major and his letters that when they broke through the tree line, the tumble of the river was a surprise.

'Here,' he said, and she stood beside him, directly across from a large outcrop of rock, its shoulder thrusting over the water. 'Look familiar?' She shook her head, brow furrowing.

'Look up, at the skyline. Does that help?'

Shading her eyes, she looked into the cotton-candy sky. 'What am I looking for?' she asked, puzzled, when something about the view held her. She turned to look upriver, and down, and saw how, if she were seated in the back of a low-flying plane, a clutch of balloons in her hand, that outcrop of rock might appear familiar.

She laughed, a low, throaty sound. 'Poor Freddie. He was quite shocked you know.' She slipped her arms about Jim's waist, tilting her head to look at him. 'You were rude,' she stated matter-of-factly.

'It was loud.'

He folded his arms around her and she rested her cheek against his chest.

'It makes me sad, your father's letter.'

He said nothing, bending to gently kiss the top of her head.

She buried her face deeper in his shirt, breathing him in, his heartbeat steady as the river chuckled and spun beside them.

'Why balloons?' he asked suddenly.

She smiled. 'Why not?'

The Lindbergh kidnapping remained headline news as the month unfolded. A sighting here, proved false, ransom paid there, to no avail. Increasingly though, Madeleine found herself searching through the papers for news of the Bonus Bill, tracking its progress as it made the rounds of Capitol Hill. It continued to make its way through hearings and petitions, getting passed all the way to the Senate, where it was ultimately defeated.

Still, encouraged by even this modicum of progress, veterans across the country began to rally. The notion originated, some said, in Oregon, others, San Francisco – a decision to march to

Washington and petition en masse for the reconsideration of the bill. Wherever it began, the idea rapidly gathered momentum, amplifying as it spread, shooting sparks down shanty towns and the coal dust of mining camps, streaking across the prairies to the shores of the mainland.

The Bonus Bill. It fired the imagination of these men past the flush of youth, come to grips with the realisation that perhaps the best of their lives now lay behind them. Most were out of work, many had been for some time. They'd tried, moving their families from town to town in search of a job, any job. As the Depression took firm root, however, their efforts had withered. They sat around, watching ashamed as their wives took in washing in order to make ends meet. On Sundays, they found some pretext or the other to skip out for a few hours, so they wouldn't have to face the humiliation of relatives and well-wishers stopping by after church with handouts. Some skipped out on their families altogether, joining the army of hoboes that crisscrossed the country aimlessly.

Worn down by the struggle to earn a living, and deeply scarred by their inability to provide, they were galvanised into action now by a single, electric thought: *A march to the very seat of the Government, a petition for their rights, in person, that surely nobody would be able to deny.*

Grabbing at the sense of purpose this allowed them, this illusion of control over their lives, all across the country, veterans began to move. In twos and threes, in groups of twenty or more, on foot, in beat-up jalopies, hitching rides on hay wagons and packed into deadhead passenger trains and freight cars. Some with empty sleeves, others leaning on canes, still others with rough, slap-dash patches over a sightless eye. Veterans were strung out along the dirt paths and paved roads, about the railroad tracks and hills of the nation like some extraordinary human chain. Men travelling alone, family men with wives, children and thin, downy-haired babies in tow, all headed in the same direction: Washington.

It caught the attention of the nation in a way that the Bonus Bill itself had never been able to: an army of down-on-their-luck doughboys, congregating hopefully at the very seat of government. The press dubbed it the Bonus Expeditionary Force, the bastard child of the AEF – the American Expeditionary Force – that had shipped out so dashingly to war in 1917. Housewives baked pies and cakes for these Bonus boys, handing them out as the veterans passed through their little towns. At countryside sidings, farmers drew up horse carts loaded with whatever they could offer: sacks of potatoes with field soil still clumped to the burlap, crates of turnips, bread, freshly laid eggs and pats of butter.

Madeleine was especially moved by the individual stories that increasingly peppered the newspapers. She took to reading out to Jim the accounts of hardship and years of desperate poverty, the tales of newfound optimism, as veterans talked equally of their struggles, and the windfall the Bonus Bill would bring once it came to pass. Jim never said anything in response, she noticed, but neither did he stop her, listening without comment as she read aloud to him.

It was the middle of May when the Lindbergh child was finally found, or what was left of him. The boy had been killed, his tiny body abandoned in the woods.

'I'm sorry, Madeleine,' the Major said gruffly when she visited the morning after the discovery. 'The Lindberghs – their poor son. Nobody deserves what happened to them.'

'I know,' she said simply. She hesitated. 'I've been thinking about your editorial,' she said, the words tumbling out in a rush. 'If the newspapers won't publish it, why don't you simply write to Washington? President Hoover, the Senate, send it to them all.'

The Major frowned.

'She knows someone there,' Jim stepped in to elaborate. 'Madeleine has a friend from university who works in Capitol Hill. He might be able to get it to a couple of congressmen.'

They sent the Major's article. 'Nothing will come of it,' the Major said to himself. 'Damn fool's errand.' But nonetheless, his spirits were buoyed. He watched hopefully for the mail, sifting through the catalogues for word from Washington as the flowers began to fall from the apple trees, carpeting the orchard in drifts of white petals that hopped and swirled in the afternoon breeze and caught in the manes of the horses.

The month progressed, and with it came black flies, nicking and biting. The Major, much to Madeleine's amusement, stuck a tall fern into the band of his hat as he worked among his plants. 'It draws away the flies,' he solemnly maintained. Jim began to whistle the opening bars of Yankee Doodle, poker-faced. The Major's eyes twinkled and he began to sing along, in a deep, rich baritone.

'Yankee Doodle went to town, riding on his pony, stuck a feather in his cap and called it macaroni.'

He drew his arms akimbo and performed a lopsided little jig, the fern on his hat bobbing in time to the tune. Madeleine laughed so hard that Ellie came out to see what was the matter and stood watching from the doorway, hands on her hips, smiling broadly at this bit of noonday nonsense.

Madeleine's mother called at the Garland place and in an unusual display of firmness, insisted that her daughter stop testing the bounds of propriety and return to Boston. Jim and she spent as much time together as they could in the days leading up to her departure, neither willing to be the first to address exactly where her leaving left them, both filled nonetheless with a silent, unaccustomed ache at the prospect. It manifested itself in other, wordless ways – in her reaching repeatedly to caress his arm as he drove, in the amplified intensity between them as they kissed. Jim had been taken aback and touched by her confession that despite that worldly, sophisticated air that drove him so wild, Madeleine hadn't gone much further than some heavy petting with any of her previous boyfriends. He was the one to pull back, time and again, gently staying her hands as they strayed hungrily down his body, his breathing heavy as he stared into her eyes.

He took her hiking as he'd promised, to the tall ridge that overlooked the sinkhole, an emerald pool that lay to one side of the river. 'Local legend has it there's treasure buried down there,' he told her. 'And that if a man jumps in there at a woman's behest, it's a sign of true love.'

She stared at the deep green water so far below. 'So have you? Jumped in there before?'

'Sure,' he said laconically. 'As kids, some of us would come up here after school, dare each other to dive in.'

She smiled. 'And if I asked you to?'

They stood there, facing one another. 'No.' He waited a beat before continuing: 'Although, I might go in unasked.'

He began to unbutton his shirt, taking it off and now his corduroys, holding her gaze all the while. Stripping to his boxers, he took a step backwards.

'No!' she exclaimed, reaching for him at the last moment. He stepped away, silhouetted for an instant against the lip of gentian sky and sun-warmed rock. Then he was gone, and she ran to the edge, watching, his body a thing of beauty and grace as it fell. The muted sound as he sliced through the water. He was lost from sight for an instant and then there he was, pushing the hair back from his forehead, grinning as he shouted for her to come in too.

She stood laughing at the edge of the ridge, and began to undo the buttons on her dress. He watched, treading water, as her clothes came off, one by one – the slip, the stockings, the garter belt. A brief hesitation and then her hands moving behind her back as she unfastened the last wisps of silk and lace beneath.

Venus Anadyomene.

Madeleine lifted her arms above her head, raising her face briefly to the sun, then launched herself with a dancer's pliancy from the edge of the rock. He watched, his heart suddenly in his mouth as she arrowed through the air, the wild, auburn tumble of her hair about her naked shoulders like the outstretched wings of a bird.

Not long after she left, the Major received a response to his letter. A short reply, typeset. It thanked him for the missive, assuring him that his sentiments would be taken into consideration as appropriate. If he were ever in Washington, it offered, the Senator would be pleased to try and schedule a quarter-hour to discuss his ideas in detail.

The Major slowly reread the letter, the rancid taste of disappointment in his throat. 'I thought as much. Damn fool's errand,' he said tightly.

'It's a response at least,' Jim pointed out. 'Maybe you should press further.'

The Major crumpled the letter into a ball. 'Fool's errand,' he repeated, the left eye beginning its telltale switch. 'None of them gives a—'

'So that's it?' Still on edge after Madeleine's leaving, Jim impatiently cut his father off mid-sentence, surprising the Major into silence. 'So you just give up, maybe write yet another article that the damn *Gazette* has no intention of ever publishing? For God's sake.' Jim jabbed a finger at the newspaper lying on the side table, pointing at the collage of Bonus marchers saluting and grinning into the cameras. 'This obviously matters to you, so call those congressmen's bluff. Go to Washington. Meet with this damn senator. There's more you can do than just sit here writing those letters. Major, you—'

Jim paused, trying to find the right words, frustration built over years coming all at once to a boil. Years of trying to come to terms with the aloof distance that the Major maintained with those around him, surrounded by invisible boundaries that nobody was permitted to breach. Years of trying to understand just why the Bonus Bill, an issue that held no consequence for them at all whether it was passed or not – a cause that concerned men the Major did not even know – seemed to hold so much more importance to him than his only son. And why, if it mattered so much, he didn't do more.

Their eyes met and held in the mirror, the Major's left eyelid drooping. Jim turned away. 'It matters to you,' he repeated flatly as he left the room. 'So do something about it, do more.'

The Major sat there, staring at the newspaper, Jim's uncharacteristic outburst still echoing in his ears. 'A steady trickle growing rapidly in volume, more joining each day until all roads it seems, lead to Capitol Hill,' the caption beneath the collage read.

The faces of the veterans in the grainy black-and-white photographs were tired and lined, marked by the disappointments endured by the moneyless each day. Nonetheless, there was something infinitely touching about their expressions, the eager hope that burned so brightly in their eyes. The Major took in those photographs, playing Jim's words in his mind, and something began to unfurl deep inside him, a memory of his former self perhaps.

He smoothed out the letter from Washington, filled again with anger as he reread the brief, dismissive paragraph. He glanced at the black mirror, unconsciously squaring his shoulders and holding himself straighter in the armchair as he arrived at a decision.

'Jim!' he called after his son. He cleared his throat. 'James William!' he called again, louder, the firm tone of his voice ringing unexpectedly about the room.

Word spread around Raydon like it always did, without anyone quite knowing who it was that had first announced it, but everyone somehow knowing all there was to know about Jim and the Major's upcoming visit to Washington. A mountain of goods began to be dropped off at the general store, with a muttered 'for when the Stonebridge boy comes by'. Barrels of apples, a massive smoked ham, cuts of salted pork, farmhouse eggs, canned beans, bottles of all shapes and sizes filled with cider – both kinds, hard as well as sweet – maple syrup, apple butter, a myriad assortment of home-made jams and fruit preserves: all these were left without much fuss or nattering by folk who'd heard about the Bonus Army and wanted to do their bit for 'them hard-luck doughboys'.

When Black Pete emerged from deep in the woods on his seasonal trip into town 'for victuals and stuff', he too heard about the upcoming trip. He rubbed his beard, dislodging a gentle shower of the soot from his ancient stove that stuck to every part of his clothes and skin, thus earning him his moniker. 'Bonus Army? These the same boys who fought in 1917?' he enquired at the general store.

Yes, he was told, the same, except they were no longer boys, most pushing forty by now.

'Wasn't you in the army too, Black Pete?' old Asaph asked, crinkling his eyes as he tried to remember. 'He was too,' Jeremiah concurred. 'Spanish American War, back in 1898, ain't that right?'

Black Pete rubbed his beard again, sending another sprinkling of soot down to the floor. 'Ayuh, that be right,' he confirmed. He said no more as he handed over his load of trapped skins and fur, but later that afternoon, he was spotted on the road that led to the Stonebridge place, bent nearly double under the weight of the sack he carried on his shoulder, his old husky walking stiffly by his side.

'I'd have left it in town,' he explained to Jim, 'except they telled me that you'd already been and I'd not been certain when exactly you and your pa were off to see them Bonus soldiers.'

'Tuesday,' Jim said, scratching the dog behind her ears. 'The Major will be glad you came.'

He was, shaking Pete's hand and dislodging yet another smattering of soot. 'It's good to see you, Pete. It's a hot day, come on in and have something for your thirst.'

Ellie spread newspapers on a chair in the kitchen, their guest not taking offence in the least, even gallantly lending her a hand before he sat himself down.

The old dog was hesitant to enter, and stood at the door gently wagging her tail. Jim stroked her greying head and she licked his hand. He brought her a piece of chicken from the pantry and she grabbed it in her mouth, settling down on the stairs with a sigh. Black Pete jerked a thumb in her direction and chuckled, revealing the gaping holes between his teeth. 'She and I, we're of a kind,' he grinned. 'Don't take to being indoors none too much.'

'Well you stink ripe enough,' Ellie observed matter-of-factly. 'Isn't it time for one of your baths?'

'Ayuh, that it is,' he agreed. 'Got held up a bit this year, I have. Still, twice a year's enough for a man, I reckon, once in the spring after ice out, once in the fall before ice up.'

He stayed a while, discussing traps and other matters with the men. He'd seen the bobcat earlier in the spring, but it was a canny one and had got away before he could slug it; he'd seen young Jim too, with his girl, riding down one of the old paths not so long ago. He drank deeply of the Major's whisky, refusing, however, to accept the remainder of the bottle as a gift. Ellie pressed a pie into his hands as he was leaving and would brook no argument. Again, that slow, gap-toothed grin. 'Now this here's a real treat, Miss Eleanor.' Clicking his heels together, he saluted the Major. 'You do right by those fellas, James,' he said. 'Tell them too, that if any of them soldiers fancies living in these here woods, Pete's prepared to be a right good neighbour.'

He turned at the corner of the drive to wave at them. Hawking his throat, he spat generously into the bushes. 'Damn politicians!' he called.

'Goddamned politicians!' the Major shouted back in robust agreement. Jim looked at his father, amused.

Black Pete waved a final time, shuffling off around the bend with his dog. When they opened his sack, they found it stuffed to the brim with tobacco for the veterans in Washington. Ellie was so touched by his beneficence that she didn't grumble, not one word, as she stripped the sooty sheets of newspaper from the chair and threw them in the grate.

THE AISNE

France • Winter 1914

FROM THE JOURNAL OF

James Arthur Stonebridge

3 November 1914

We're shadows upon a quiet road. We march single file: weapons at hand, eyes on the man in front of us.

We lost three more this afternoon. A beat earlier, there were four. Then a shell, falling precisely through the entrance of the dugout. Three gone, exploded into nothing. Leaving just the fourth untouched and shaking like a leaf.

I try to grasp the odds of it, the stark elegance of the maths that must precede the specific arc of a shell, angling it over parapet and just short of parados, into the slender entrance of a dugout where once four stood, safe.

Gaillard and I cleared the debris, using the mess kit that had belonged to one of the men to scrape his brains from the clay walls.

Eyes forward, fixed on the boots just ahead. Now clearly visible, every creased, hobnailed detail in this striated light of the stars. Now but a silhouette in the dark. Now a man stands, flush with thought and word and memory, and just like that, he is gone, and what is left of him fits tidily into his spoon.

We press forward, along these roads of muffled sound. Just another patrol, on another night-trodden way. Somewhere a mirror must lie tilted, pitching us into this underbelly, nightmare world. Where the sun still rises and sets, and the moon steps out pale and gleaming, but nothing else remains the same. Storm clouds of dust and earth, spliced by the lightning flashes of the guns. Shrapnel like steel-winged birds, and then the rain, a terrible rain of shredded uniforms and glowing metal, of cartridge casings and wet, human flesh. On the horizon, the blackened silhouettes of tree stumps stand in mute and damning judgment.

What valour in this? What glory, what rationality to sitting about in trenches at the mercy of the shells, firing blindly at an enemy we cannot see?

The patrols are almost a relief. Almost.

We went on one yesterday, through the countryside that adjoins our sector. Inching across unknown ground, through what grass and cover we can find, nerves on fire from the peculiar strain of listening for the slightest rasp, the smallest of movements that would give away a Boche patrol, similarly advancing from the other side of the wire. We hear a rustling up ahead and freeze mid-crawl. I press my chin closer into the earth, trying desperately to see ahead. I kick myself for not using more of the charcoal that was passed around before we left, Obadaiah grinning as I administered it to neck and pasty face.

'Lord, but I thank mah mammy and pappy,' he said, exaggerating both diction and piousness, 'for this here coloured skin.'

Jackass. I start to smile at the memory, but it is a small and temporary rictus, my mind jerking back to the present, every ounce of concentration on the soft but unmistakable rustling of something moving towards us. My hands are slippery; I wipe them on the grass.

Gaillard appears to my right, crawling carefully backwards. 'Wait for the signal,' he whispers, and is gone, inching towards the next man.

The sound grows louder. I lift my head and now I see them, can actually make out shapes moving through the darkness towards us. 'Why aren't they taking cover—' but before I can fully formulate the thought, '*Feu a volonté*!' It's the signal we're waiting for. A surge of adrenaline as brute instinct takes over. Fire at will, and I squeeze off shot after shot, everything seeming to melt away until the only thing left is the rage pulsing through every inch of my skin, get the enemy, get them, get that bastard Boche before he can get me.

The shapes scatter, and now I hear it, a bewildered crying.

'Stop your firing, stop. Halt!'

The sound, I recognise it, it isn't crying, but *lowing*. I crawl towards a shape lying crumpled on the ground, a darker black than the shadows around it. I know already, even before I reach it: it's a cow. Only a damn cow, part of some small, abandoned herd that has wandered in between the lines.

Hark, glorious warrior. Hail, valiant soldier. I thought I had felled a man, but instead have shot up a cow. I don't know whether to feel relief, or disgust, or marvel at the absurdity.

Gaillard wants to haul the carcass back to the trenches – it's petite enough he says that he can manage it. For an instant I almost think he can, Brother Strong Heart Mighty Oak, but we're ordered to return at once – machine gunfire has started to come our way, and it won't be long before this spot becomes a hellhole.

All the way, the memory sticks in my throat, sharp and bitter, of the killing rage that took a hold as I squeezed the trigger, the cold-blooded satisfaction as my bullets struck home.

We make it back to our trenches. 'We could've feasted on steak frites tomorrow,' Gaillard says bitterly. 'Imagine – fresh beef for once, not from a can.'

The clouds lift. The road glints, white as bone. Eyes forward, itchy finger, trigger-happy. Shadow, mirror-image world, where in one instant a man stands whole and in the next, a grease of pink mist is all that remains.

In the end, perhaps this is all there is, the thin, dark spaces between tendon and sinew, this emptiness through which we march as if in a dream. The tread of our boots rousing the beast, luring it from its lair. Sprung from the madness that lies within each of us, it waits beyond an unseen corner, swinging its steel-tipped tail. We march forward, along these ghosted roads, like ants along the gleaming white of its ribs.

FOURTEEN

November 1914

We been sittin' in cold water so long, my buttocks been turned to ice. Still, it do some good. The cold seems to slow down the cooties, or maybe it just that my skin so ashy and frozen, they can't get none of their devil-spawn teeth into it. My legs feel heavy as iron. I stretch, tryin' to ease the kinks from them, and my shiftin' 'bout in the slush make a cracklin' sound, like a spoon breakin' through a snowball cone. James jerks awake. The white of an eye as he stare at the parapet but ain't nothin' more to hear or see and he relax once more. A few others cuss sleepily at being woken. Karan pull that dressin' robe of his tighter 'bout hisself, fussin' with the ties.

A right grand thing, that robe – all reds and golds, sunset-coloured. Come in a care package for him from London. Karan, he gone and found a bunch of rich old ladies in the newspapers, the sort who been placin' advertisements ever since the war begun, 'bout wantin' to sponsor a soldier. They were a little alarmed at first to find he ain't a Christian, never mind English or French, but they find an excitement in it, writin' to this dark-skinned foreigner so bravely fightin' in France. Karan, he send them long letters 'bout life in the Legion, 'bout tiger hunts and the rains back home in India. He ask after their health, how their rose bushes are doin' and the latest gossip from their parish. They reply with fat care packages, filled with chocolate and sherry and such, that he then share with us all.

'You should try it,' he tell me, seein', I guess, that I been 'bout the only *jeune* here who never get no mail.

Seein' that robe, the notion sure did cross my mind for a minute, but only a minute – I ain't got it in me to be writin' no long, word-filled letters to nobody.

James, he gone right back to sleepin', if it can be called that, this half-sittin', half-dozin' thing we got goin' on here in the freeze. It 'bout all a body can get around here, and it ain't never enough. There's a draught tonight, ripplin' the water that be lyin' always at the bottom of the trenches. I hold my jaws tight so my teeth don't go chatterin'. The *anciens*, they don't take none too kindly to no snorin' or chatterin' teeth. Gaillard be roarin' with laughter as he tell how plenty *jeunes* been cured of that habit. The snorer's lips be gently coated with varnish as he sleep, and his mouth closed shut. Come mornin', when he open his mouth to yawn, his lips part, tearin' off paper-thin bits of skin and flesh. Happen once or twice, every snorer be proper cured, even if – Gaillard grin broadly, pointin' at the bandana around his chin – even if a man got to bind his jaws shut hisself every night since.

The barracks and trenches of the Legion lie mostly silent as a result, causin' my stretchin' to sound powerful loud in my ears. I'm surprised there ain't no response from the Boche. No grenade tossed from their trenches, no quick burst of rifle fire, none of the how-dee-dos they be sendin' our way at the smallest movement. We be doin' the same. It's the way of the Front – just sort of remindin' the other side that you here, awake and listenin'.

The more I think on it, the more it start to nag and niggle at me just why they been so quiet tonight. I got half a mind to get on the fire step and take a look across No Man's Land, but damn, it cold.

Karan's bathrobe catches my eye again. Its colours are of fire. When he first pulled it on, how we laughed. The sight of him, hunched over in that great woollen thing!

'This robe,' he say then cheerfully, 'is the one civilised thing I have on me. It brings to mind my favourite chair, of sitting before the fire at Cambridge, a bottle of port by my side and a decent pipe in my mouth. Here I am now instead, camped in this goddamned mud like an animal. I'm putting on my robe, and you can all go to hell.' That robe 'bout the only thing that Karan refuse to share. Fallen in love with it he has, and taken to wearin' it all nights now, wrapped over his uniform.

Lookin' at him now, I disremember why we found it funny. Karan in his fire-coloured robe seem to me no more strange than this crazy-makin', upside-down war. Shootin' at the enemy from holes in the ground, livin' among rats and toadfrogs, with the stink of the dead comin' from above our heads, not buried six feet below. If anythin', that warm robe, it look real good to me right now. I eye it with wantin', picturin' it over my own shoulders, easin' some of the stiffness from them.

This devil-spawn cold. When was the last time I got a decent night's sleep? What I'd give to lie in a proper bed. To lie down flat, with enough room to stretch in any direction I want. Pull these boots from my feet, remove the pack, all the gear, till there ain't nothin' on my skin but the hair the good Lord given. Lyin' naked as a newborn babe, in clean white sheets, soft as can be, and scented of perfumed soap.

I'm goin' to get myself a bed, I decide. First thing I do, soon as I'm out of here. A real special one, brass, the sort that so high most folks be needin' a foot stool to get in it. With pillows that plump up nice, and covers soft as butter, and one of those *ciel-de-lit* things draped over the top, like I seen in the window of an antique shop back home once. All white and blue silk, like starin' into clouds when you lie down.

And the cher I'm goin' to have in there with me! Eyes so brown and lips like candy. Buttocks that spill from my hands. I wait a moment, but ain't no pleasure in the thought. Bubbies real firm, with nipples like . . . Ain't no use. It so cold ain't nothin' stirrin' inside me tonight, not so much as a hair liftin' at the notion.

I ain't lettin' nobody in that big, soft bed, I decide. Nobody next to me, nobody in the same room, or the next room even, not like here where day or night, a man ain't never by hisself.

Not like here. That snap my attention right back to the Boche. Why is it so quiet? I imagine a party of Boche, crawlin' quiet as can be across No Man's Land. Obadaiah, you a fool, is what. Dreamin' 'bout beds and such when a night raid might be just minutes away. The moon, she sail above our lines, turnin' the water we sittin' in to ink. There's a line of frost along the lip of the trench, and it shine.

There's men out there, I'm sure of it, men with bayonets and grenades, crawlin' closer every second. Never mind no bed, ain't goin' to be so much as a coffin to bury me in, just this foul and stinkin' mud by the time they done with us.

Cold as it is, the sweat break out on my head.

I tighten my fingers 'bout my rifle. 'James,' I hiss.

He groan as he open his eyes. 'The Boche . . .' I begin. He shake his head, cuttin' me off as he point a finger at the sky, and then damned if the Yankee don't go right back to sleep.

I look up, confused. Ain't no clouds, not a single one, just the moon, hangin' low and fat as a cantaloupe.

The moon.

The *moon*.

I'm a fool, is what. With the moon that big, ain't no chance of cover. Lookout sentries goin' to be seein' from here to Paris and Berlin, the light so damn bright. Ain't goin' to be no raids, not tonight. I feel so relieved and so foolish both at once, 'bout all I can do not to laugh out loud.

My teeth start to chatter. I hold my jaw tight, but I feel them still, buckin' 'bout inside. I try to find the rhythm in it, but it just too cold. I rub my hands together, tuck them under my armpits to find what warmth they can. Leanin' my head against the wet walls of the trench, I try and get some sleep.

The moon, she rise higher, dancin' on my eyelids all the while.

Three months, we'd given it, three months to this war, to give the Boche a right sound thrashin' and send the Kaiser whimperin' back to his hole. No such thing. Thanksgivin' just 'bout upon us. Christmas and the new year around the corner and we still here. The Boche be givin' good as they get, and oftentimes better.

A real lickin' they given us yesterday. It started slow. Two shells they send our way at first. One fall wide, the other just miss our trench. It land to the back, right on the parados, sendin' a mess of shrapnel and sandbags fallin' all over us. When the blast settle, we sit up shakily and look 'bout, everybody nervy, jumpy like, over how damn lucky we just been, and tryin' not to show it. Our ears still ringin' from the blast as we listen for the screams that be followin' a shellin'. There's none, not this time, and we dust off our jackets, tryin' for our hands not to shake, lookin' with relief at each other from the corners of our eyes, and actin' all the while like it ain't no big deal at all.

Danny, he make a big show of brushin' off the letter he been writin' before the shell hit. 'Hey James,' he ask, pickin' up his pen, 'how do you spell "delightful"?'

We laughin', our voices comin' higher and louder from relief, when the real shellin' start.

Minnies. Potato mashers. Coal boxes. Shells of all shapes and sizes; everythin' that the Boche got, they send our way. Whizz bangs that sound just like their name – whizz, then bang! and only pink mist where a livin', breathin' man been a second ago. Jack Johnsons, yes, named for the champ, so big and beefy, they leave sinkholes where they land, takin' out chunks of ground and everythin' livin' on it, nothin' left but a cloud of black smoke.

And the racket. Such a racket. The shells come screamin', roarin' towards us, blottin' out the day with their noise. They fall hard and fast, blowin' the ground right from under us. Louder and louder, rattlin' my ears and fillin' my lungs, so big and angry that sound, it got a shadow all of its own. The dark centre of it, filled with a killin' rage. I feel its evil, its pressure, its hard weight pressin' down.

My gut and every inch of my bumfuzzled brain's yellin' at me to get up and run, get away fast as I can. Only, ain't nowhere to run to, nothin' we can do but lie here as the sound of the shells rip through our heads.

My breath come in bursts and each breath I take, it fill me with surprise 'cause all around me, men are dyin'. Torn and thrown apart like ragdolls with the stuffin' spilled from them, while I'm still breathin', in, out, in, out. I dig my hands into the earth, huggin' her close as she buck and shudder like a live, breathin' thing. I don't know no more where I begin, where I end. It's like I been stripped clean of skin, of muscle, and all that left is smoke. The shells, they still roarin', and I don't know no more if I'm alive, don't know where I am, I can't think, I can't think with this noise, this roarin' that fill my ears.

Still the shells fall, suckin' the light from the hour, nothin' to see no more but clouds of dust and earth. I'm breathin' in smoke and the drowned-out cries of the dyin'. I can feel each of their wounds, their screamin' agony, and still they fall, them shells, till I can't take it no more, can't take their roaring. The roarin', the smoke spillin' from my mouth back into the cold takes me with it, wingin' me away from here, please, away, anyplace but here, far, on a thin peel of grey.

A warm day in Louisiana, the water flowin' like silk beneath the pirogue. I glance at Pappy's back to make sure he turned the other way and trail my fingers through the water, drawin' shine through the brown. It loggin' season, and I'm headed with Pappy and some of the others down to the swamp. A right big cypress goin' to be cut down today and I'm happy as a pup with two tails at being allowed along.

She big, that tree, the fattest I ever seen. Right by the edge of the swamp she stand, towerin' over the others. Branches thick with moss, spreadin' long and wide over the brown water, throwin' shadow stripes on Pappy's arms as he guide our pirogue closer. Big, real big. When I stand at the bottom of her and look up, that trunk, it seem to go on forever. So thick that two of me could have tried to circle her waist where the girdlin' been done and the bark removed, and even then, it wouldn't have been enough.

They start sawin' at her and I stand close as I can, unmindin' of the chips that fly out. 'Stay clear,' Pappy remind me, and I move away for a few minutes before workin' my way back again. She just so big. Make a grown man look no bigger than an ant, she do, and it fill me with a strange thrill, the thought that we can bring her down all the same.

Pappy yell at me, real annoyed, and I can tell he mean business. 'Alright, alright,' I say, and slip off to the other side of the tree when he turned the other way.

I stand in the heart of her shadow, stretchin' my neck far as it will go but I still can't see the top of her. Just branches, so many, with its and bits of blue showin' through. A boy, he could climb those branches, up, up, all the way to the sky. She tilt a little as I stand there. Tilt some more, just a bit, and the men back off. I mean to as well, I do, but somehow I just stand there starin' as she tilt again real slow, and that tree, she begin to fall.

'Obadaiah!' Pappy yellin' at me to move, run boy, hard as you can, get outta the way. All those branches swayin' like there's a wind; a creakin', groanin' *sound, so loud, and it seem like that sound, it come from below the ground and above my head all at the same time.*

'RUN!'

Now I run, fast as I can, but I'm right in the drop zone. That tree, she headed straight for me as she fall, as if mockin' what I was thinkin' earlier, 'bout how easily we cuttin' her down. The thunder *she make, crackin' and breakin' through the other trees. Such a terrible, angry sound.*

I run fast as I can, but that roar, it get louder and louder and I'm screamin' now, but all I hear is that sound. The shadow of it over me, blockin' out the sun as I splash into the water – please Lord, stay the 'gators – and there ain't noplace to go, no way to outrun that roarin'. I take a deep breath and dive for the bottom. Bubbles through muddy water, my heart fit to burst as the tree, she crash into the water above me, the tips of her branches brushin' against my neck.

Pappy yanks me ashore. His face white as a ghost. The men shake their heads; they laugh and slap my back, and I cough up water. My ears ringin', my legs got the shakes real bad, mind swimmin' with the memory of that roarin' and the way it filled my lungs.

All afternoon long the Boche shell us, our artillery firin' in return. When the guns finally go quiet, it the turn of the wounded. It's only now we can hear them.

'*Brancardiers*! *Brancardiers*!' Cries for stretchers, for the medic, for water.

I sit up, and the earth feel like she still movin'. Take a while for my eyes to focus, to make sense of the shapes movin' through the dust. Men stiffly gettin' to their feet, coughin', weakly cussin', as we take count of hands and arms and legs, pickin' ourselves up again.

I breathe in. Out. There a firework smell to the air. On account of it still being early in the war, on account I ain't yet gotten bone-sick of it all, I breathe, giddy with relief that I made it through.

Danny, he didn't. I find that letter he was writin'. I dust it off, and 'delightful' – the word swim up between my hands.

Nightfall be quieter than usual, touched still by blood smell. James hand me a plug of chaw. I place it in my jaw, feel the juice beginnin' to take. The air still bangin' 'bout in my chest, like wind in a hollow. I think again 'bout that long-ago cypress. Later, after he cooled down, Pappy showed me the stump. It had more rings than any tree I ever seen.

'A thousand-year cypress,' Pappy had called it then, half in jest, watchin' as I touched those rings.

'I seen a thousand-year-old cypress once,' I hear myself say now, as if from very far away. 'Seen it up close, heard it roar as it fell.'

James shift the chaw 'bout in his cheek as he stare straight ahead, at the wall of the trench. There a cut on his head; the blood shine wetly red, as if still new.

'Trees have words,' he say then, as if in a dream. 'You go to the heart of the sugarbush and listen long enough, you start to hear it, their maple song.'

FIFTEEN

I stay my shovellin' to stamp my feet, shakin' the frost from them boots. The mornin' sun been slowly thawin' them out. Weather's turned so cold now, our boots freeze at night, the leather cuttin' into our feet like blades. I stamp 'bout again, and the water inside them boots go sloshin' back and forth.

So much wetness be collectin' inside there that I can't hardly feel my toes no more. I try and curl them, cussin' at the pain. These past weeks, Karan, he been hackin' at that precious robe of his with his bayonet, handin' out make-do System D socks for us that ain't got better. We make Russian socks with the strips, tyin' them 'bout our feet and ankles. The warmth of the wool help, but it ain't enough. Newspaper then, plugged into the gaps between leather and wrapped foot. The mornin' melt soak the paper and our feet through and through. Our orders be to keep our boots on at all times in the trenches. I don't want to be takin' off those boots no how. Once they come off, I ain't sure if I'm goin' to be able to get them back on again.

This young *jeune*, he couldn't stand it no more and pulled off his boots against the order. I seen his feet then. A mess of blisters and shiny red skin, raw as meat and stinkin'. Gaillard, after he yell at him somethin' fierce, shown him how to grease a thread in candle wax and pass it through the blisters to slice them off. The kid suck it up, but when it come time to put on them boots again, the pain was so bad he pass right out and mess his pants. James and I, we got them boots back on for him; ain't nobody made no jokes 'bout his pants either when he woke.

My belly rumble as I pick up my shovel again. Shellin' turned so bad, ain't no way for the supplies to reach the Front. We got bread rations, once we got a thin soup that George the cook manage to get through to the trenches. We hole up in the dugouts and listen to the shells, and each day, there more of the dead and wounded.

Worst are the horses from the wagon trains. They scream all night in pain.

I start shovellin' again, workin' through the muck. Been so much shellin', the trenches keep fallin' in. We be steady diggin' new ones and re-diggin' the old; I done so much shovellin' that I ain't sure no more if I'm legionnaire or ditch digger, first-class. We supposed to dig the trenches in this part of the line eight to ten feet deep – there's plenty snipers watchin', just waitin' for a chance to aim at a legionnaire's cap. The trenches, they supposed to have all sorts of twists and turns in them too – smaller chance that way of Boche bullets makin' it down the line.

'Fuck.' James leans on his shovel, wipin' the sweat from his forehead. He ain't said a word 'bout his feet, but I can tell they been botherin' him too, the way he been settin' them boots down real careful like.

'At least we only got to dig narrow,' I say. From two and a half to three feet wide, the trenches got to be. Narrower the better – less space for the Boche shells to drop inside.

He look at me, the breath hangin' like white cotton 'bout his beard. He point his shovel down the zigzag shape of the trench. 'Only here,' he say, 'are narrowness and crookedness virtues.'

We keep workin'. There's messes left from the shells; when we raise the duckboards from the stinkin' slush at the bottom of the trenches to dry them out in the sun, sometimes among the rats that been growin' fat as cats, we find its and bits of what once been men.

It a picnic alright, just as that soldier said at Noisy Le Sec.

This one time, James and I been assigned clean-up duty alongside Chevalier, one of the largest legionnaires we got. Chevalier, he got the face of a child, all smooth, with eyes that remind me of Pappy's. Quiet he be, and boo coo crazy 'bout his wife; when he talk of her, how she be such an angel and all, Chevalier's voice go real soft. His eyes shine then, and he looks like he should be in a choir someplace, singin' praises to the Lord. A right good legionnaire he be, always among the first to volunteer, doin' whatever need to be done with no fuss or whinin'.

We been muckin' out a section of the trench with him, when he asks what we been doin' before we came down here. I tell him 'bout Louisiana and James talk of his apple orchard. Chevalier nod.

'And you?' James ask.

Chevalier raise an awful smellin' plank to his shoulders. There a gentle smile on his face. 'Me? I'm an artist.'

The sector gone quiet for a few blessed hours when a shot ring out from one of our outposts. Gaillard take me and James along to investigate. We go fast as we can through the slippery trench, splashin' 'bout in them puddles we got in our boots. When we get to the outpost, we find the young *jeune*, the same one who gone and taken off his boots, shot through the arm. He's tryin' to tie a bandage around the wound.

'Clean through the arm.' Gaillard's voice, it got an odd tone to it.

The *jeune* will not look at us. '*Oui*.'

'How many were there?'

'Don't know.'

'A patrol, or a sniper?'

'Didn't see.'

'*Merde*! What did you fire at then?'

'I didn't. They – he – shot me before I could do anythin'.'

Now I'm puzzled. Could have sworn it was the low roar of the French issue Lebel I heard, not the crack of a Boche Mauser. From the look on his face, I know James thinkin' along the same lines.

The *jeune*, he keep fiddlin' with the bandage. Lookin' real hang-dog, lips all white as he keep windin' that bandage, way too much of it, 'bout his wounded arm.

James bend frownin', pick up the rifle lyin' on the ground. He open the breech and an empty cartridge roll on to the mud.

The *jeune* look at us then. Tears come into his eyes. 'I want to go home,' he say. Gaillard say nothin', but he look awful grim. He search among the sandbags and find the length of bandage that been bunched up and hidden clumsily away. It's wet, with burn marks around the centre, and stained with blood.

'Send me home,' the *jeune* say again, his voice higher as he look at us pleadin' like, eyes goin' from face to face.

I ask James later 'bout that wet bandage. He quiet a while. 'If, before you fire,' he say then, voice flat, 'you press a wet cloth against your skin, it prevents the gunpowder markings of a self-inflicted shot.'

The *jeune* is taken away from the trenches. I don't ask, not James, not Gaillard, what goin' to happen to him, and nobody say. 'They done sent him back to his mammy,' I tell myself, but I dream of him that week.

A cold mornin', thick with fog. The firin' squad linin' up in a quiet courtyard; a young, milk-faced *jeune*, shiverin' against the far wall.

We been in the trenches so many weeks, been shelled so long, that I just 'bout had it. It a relief to be put on patrol duty. We set off to the far right. The ground is uneven, with shrubs and such that offer cover as we crawl. A small bunch of trees up ahead in a dip where the shells ain't reached yet. We all thinkin' the same, and when we reach them trees, the Corporal barely given the signal when we rise to our feet, silent as the night. Sure feel good, to walk like men for awhile, on two legs and our backs upright.

It real quiet tonight, ain't nothin' to see and we almost at the far end of the tree cover when a Verey light go off on the horizon. We stay where we are, huggin' the shadows and wait as it flare upward, die. Things go dark and quiet again though, and our breathin' ease up. The Corporal signal for us to turn back when the Boche, they send up another Verey light, and two more come shootin' into the air after it.

It's so bright, I can make out the stones in the earth. A knot in the tree nearby, shaped like a woman's hairpiece. The faces of the men around me, eyes starin' out from under the streaks of camouflage black. I blink, and all I just seen presses white behind my eyes. We still standin' there, frozen, as the flares die away and the first shells go openin' up the dark.

James and the others, they hit the ground, shelterin' behind whatever dip and bend they find. Me myself, I stay where I am. Somethin' snap inside me and I just keep standin' there as the shells, they come roarin' towards us. I'm done. Done with the stink of the trenches, sick of sittin' 'bout like pigs in a slaughterhouse, helpless and waitin' for them shells. I'm tired of being so brim-filled with fear and anger that I want to hurl my guts out. Tired of kneelin' in the mud, tired of lyin' in the ground helpless as a babychild while I listen for them shells and wait for their train-weight to crush my bones.

Legionnaire Obadaiah Nelson ain't goin' to hide and huddle no more. If I'm goin', I'm goin' to go lookin' the damn thing in the face. My hands got the shakes so bad, I can't even reach for my gris-gris;

the butt of my rifle keeps knockin' against a tree. A shell explode behind us someplace and I see James' face near my feet. Can't hear no words, but I know he yellin' at me to get down, get down, jackass!

Roaring's awful loud now, that devil-spawn train rattlin' towards us all, and ain't nothin' to do but stand there and greet it head on. That cypress, she come floatin' up from the bayou and I think of her as I stand there, that thousand-year-old cypress, and how trees got songs, ain't that what James said? The shells, they keep singin' overhead, and in that crash and roar of sound, I *finally* begin to make them out.

The *songs*. The shells got *songs*.

'Get down!' I make out the words by the way James' mouth moves.

My hands they still shakin', the knock-knock rhythm of the rifle against the bark, but I stand there and listen to the singin', the low note of the shells as they begin their flight, the climb to the high note, the slow fall as they come down, away to the back of our patrol. The trees still standin', and so am I.

Next thing I know, James come crashin' into me, two hundred pounds of Yankee anger throwin' me flat on the ground. 'Fool!' he yell in my ear. 'You goddamned, fucking jackass,' he shout furiously, and I start to laugh.

I laugh like I gone boo coo crazy, belly upwards, into my head. I laugh 'cause only a madman would think to jump up durin' an artillery attack, 'cause only this damn fool Yankee would think to save my hide while riskin' his own. I laugh 'cause the shells, they're still fallin', but finally I've learned their song.

I laugh 'cause of James, on account that in this here hellhole pit of the worst kind of madness, I gone and found myself a friend.

I explain after we make it back, to the entire patrol, and James, cooled down enough that the smoke stop comin' from his ears.

'They got their own music. Each kind of shell, it got a song, different soundin' from the others. It start low, hittin' high at the last point of climb, goin' low again on the fall.'

Gaillard, Karan and the others lookin' at me like I gone and hit my head on somethin' hard, but James frown as he start to get it. 'So depending on where the high note sounds—'

I grin. 'Dependin' on how far or near that high note sounds, you can tell if a shell's goin' to fall in front of us, behind, or right on our sorry asses.'

They don't fully believe me at first. They can't tell no difference in the sound they say, it all the same banshee cry. I know I'm right though, and when I'm proved as much a couple times, they look to me the next time the Boche let a few loose.

It feel good, this small victory. Feel real good, to be able to stand tall while death sings in the air, to control at least this much: to know if that roarin', it comin' for you today or not.

Thanksgivin' come around and we give thanks alright, seein' as we being sent to the back of the lines for a bit of rest. There's no turkeys, no cranberries, and there sure as hell ain't no pie, but we get it in our heads to have ourselves a Thanksgivin' feast all the same. Only thing, our pay and the mail both be late comin' in once more. Ain't no packages come through in weeks, not even one for Karan. We pool our sous and francs together but we ain't got enough among the lot of us for a proper dinner out. So many soldiers be passin' through here these days that the cafés in the village gone and raised their prices. 'We must eat too, Monsieur,' a proprietor tell us, spreadin' his hands. By the look of him, he sure been eatin' more than enough thanks to the war.

Et voilà, System D. We break into the back of that fat proprietor's café. We help ourselves to what we find – plenty of wine, more than enough to go around, but other than eggs, two loafs of bread and a couple of meat pies, we still ain't got enough food for a proper Thanksgivin' dinner.

We discuss the problem while sittin' in the baths that be rigged up for us in an old barn. The water sloshin' 'bout in the feed troughs don't stay hot too long, but it feel mighty good all the same. When we done washin' off the mud from our hair and skin, we be gettin' right into the troughs, pleasurin' in what water still be left.

'How 'bout we cook our own dinner?' I take a deep drag of the one cigarette we got between us and pass it along to James. 'The fields outside the village. I could find some potatoes I bet.'

He take a long, slow drag, eyes half shut. 'There's still the matter of the main course.'

'Maybe we go on a hunt, then?' My words got an empty ring to them though. Ain't much to hunt around here. Other sectors, we seen rabbits and such, come runnin' out from their burrows after a shellin', but not in this part of the Front. Ain't nothin' but us men and critters that live in the mud, and I know we are in France and all, but I ain't 'bout to start eatin' no snails or toadfrog legs, I ain't.

James takes another drag, blowin' the smoke into a long 'O' that shivers in the steam-filled air. 'There's the woods we passed, on our way from Verzy to the Front. They aren't too far from here. Maybe there are deer,' he says thoughtfully. His face brighten. 'It's far enough from the shellin' that there still might be pheasants, in the beech trees.'

I chat up one of the nurses at the dressin' station and the cher go and arrange a ride for us on a medic wagon bound for Paris. It diabolic early and miserable cold when James and I set out. There a wetness in the air, the sun workin' up the nerve to rise from behind a mess of blue-black clouds.

James meanwhile, he look right comfortable, even nearabout smilin' as he takes in the weather. 'A lowery, New England sort of morning,' he comment, pleased.

Crazy fool Yankee. I'm too cold to even ask what 'lowery' mean. I stamp my feet on the floor of the wagon tryin' to get some feelin' into them. Blowin' into my frozen hands, I make a note never to set foot nowhere near New England in November.

They drop us off near the turnin' to the woods. I call out thanks and stand awhile watchin' as the wagon drive away, the shift of the gears echoin' down the road. After it gone, silence press down like a glove. James already stridin' towards the tree line and I hurry after him. Frost lie thick on the ground and I turn around to look at the footprints we leave as we climb a bank. Two pairs of boots, just two, clear as can be in the frost. Not like the trenches, with the trampin' of hundreds of boots, forward and back, this way and that in the mud, toe over heel over toe till there ain't no tellin' one man from another no more.

It strike me that this here's the most I've been alone since we gotten to the Front. There's pleasure in the notion. I figure James, he feel the same way – when I look over at him, I see the way the lines 'bout his jaw begin to ease up as we walk on.

A white mist come rollin' in from the east, like wet, fine-spun cotton. It drape the trees that back here, still untouched by the shells. Now that I notice, powerful strange they look too, the trees, nothin' like I've ever seen before. They look to me like beech, 'cept they stand no more than four, maybe five feet off the ground.

'Les Faux,' James say quietly. 'that's what they're called. *Fagus sylvatica,* variety *tortuosa.'*

'Tortuosa' – the word stay in my head. It mean tortuous, James say, when I ask, all crooked. I take in the branches stickin' out through the mist. They crazy twisted, all knotted and bent over themselves.

James pass a slow hand over his beard, gatherin' the wetness from it. 'Legend has it that the disbelievers of the Church were cursed. That their souls are trapped in these trees, held here for ever.' He shake the moist from his fingers; the droplets disappear into the fog.

How do the Yankee know all these things? I look 'bout me and it give me a turn as I start to make out shapes. Shapes both animal and human, in those strange, gnarly branches.

The mist rollin' in thicker, mufflin' all sound. The deeper we go into the woods, the quieter it get, until I can't hardly hear the batteries no more. Only a few of our footprints that I can make out now in the grass behind, before the mist settle on them like a soft white duvet. Them crooked, *tortuosa* trees reach towards us. Faces, open-mouthed, with starin' eyes. Now and again there's a faint flash of shellin' from the Front. It colour the mist, a low light that make the branches glow blackly, pointin' with torn and hollow fingers at James and me as we pass.

Still the fog roll in, pressin' cotton-soft. White on my hands, in my nose and ears, wet against my skin. I feel the cold reach down my throat, up into my head. We lower our guns as we walk; ain't a sound now between the two of us. It start to feel like we the only livin' things left in the world. Feel like a man might roam this strange cloud garden, this forest of the crooked, and if he walk long enough, the mist might swim right through his bones. Walk long enough, far enough, and a man might slowly learn to forget all that he seen. Filled with this white quiet, no more of this crazy war, leave the dead behind with their fixed, empty eyes.

The roe fawn pop out so sudden that we come to a dead stop and just gawp. There's two of them, 'bout six months old I figure, although it hard to tell – these here French deer run pretty small. Not even a couple of feet tall these two, and right lively, jumpin' 'bout the underbrush, stoppin' now and then to twitch their noses in the air. James and I, it like we been turned to stone. There's somethin' so easy and carefree 'bout them. Somethin' so natural, somethin' we half 'member from before we got to the Front, somethin' we ain't seen nothin' of for too long. Ain't no *fear*, there just no fear in them.

We stand there and watch, how long I couldn't say, as those deer babies play. This is beauty at its clearest, a perfect harmony which I ain't never goin' to figure out the chords to, but it's okay, 'cause just knowin' it's there is enough. I likely been all kinds of lightheaded from the cold 'cause I blink and find there tears in my eyes. Them critters, they ain't just fawns no more, but things of song and grace. In their dance lie all the dances of the world, that of dandelions through an open field, of a cypress tiltin' into a flowin' river and of a champion boxer sidesteppin', cat-footin' round a ring. We stand to one side and watch, and it feel like it's there, right there, within reachin' distance, the answer to all the questions ever wondered by anyone in the world.

The wind turns, a slight shift. The fawns stop, look 'bout and start to jump away, liftin' their short tails. We raise our rifles, automatically, two shots goin' off at the same time.

It's James who go over to the carcasses. They small enough that he can carry them both in his arms. We walk back in silence. The gun batteries have become louder, or maybe it just that I notice them once more, the flash of their explosions pushin' against the mist all the way.

When we get back, I go searchin' around and dig up some old potatoes. I find a forgotten vegetable patch, damp and rottin', but some of the beets don't look too bad. Karan be workin' his magic on good King George and he come through with a big pat of butter.

I get up a stew later that day, with the potatoes and beet greens, and boil up the eggs. The deer I roast under bricks, with some wild sage and butter. It missin' garlic and there ain't too much meat besides, but we act as if it a feast set for the Gods. Well, most of us anyhow. James don't eat much at all, swiggin' away instead at the wine, and the rum we been rationed. I pick at the meat; it seem to stick in my throat.

*

'Rabbits, rabbits, rabbits,' James say to me a few days later. For a minute, I think he talkin' 'bout another hunt. The corner of his mouth lift, but there a worn look 'bout his face. 'Don't they do this down South? For luck,' he explain. 'If on the first of the month, "rabbits" is the first word you say, good luck is sure to follow.'

It is 1 December 1914. That afternoon, we ordered back to the Front.

It snow that night. Just flurries at first that stick to our canteens and the wood and wattle roofs of the dugouts, then it come down heavier and heavier, and I ain't sure if it the snow that done it, or the generals sittin' cosy, but firin' from both our side and theirs drop off. The night goes blessedly silent. The snow get in our hair, our eyes, and we got to keep brushin' it from the barrels of our rifles.

Still, ain't one cuss or gripe to be heard up and down the line. We just sit there, nobody sayin' a word, just leanin' back and watchin' the snow come down.

It's only the next mornin' that it occur to us. 'Looks like we'll have ourselves a white Christmas after all,' say James.

The fightin' ease off in the days that lead up to Christmas. It so cold I 'bout freeze my tail off, but I just been so thankful for the break in the gunfire, I don't care if I freeze from head to foot and start pissin' ice and shittin' snowballs.

Finally supplies can come up through the lines, with the mail. Everybody pounce on parcels and letters. There's care parcel after care parcel for Karan; Chevalier get nine letters from his wife and he drink them straight up like hot buttered rum. James look at me, quick like, and I know what he thinkin'. He wonderin' how come there ain't never no mail for me, but who gonna be writin'? Pappy's long gone and it just been the two of us before that.

It never bothered me none before, but sittin' here with only a canteen in my hands as folks call out news from their letters – someone's woman gone and won the church bake contest, somebody's kid had a birthday, someone else's brother was right there at Fenway Park for Johnny Evers' tie-breakin', two-out, two-run single in the bottom of the fifth – I start to feel sorrier than a broke-tail dog.

James start to fuss 'bout in his parcels. 'Catch,' he say, and toss a tin of Fatimas at me. I ain't in no mood for no charity, but before

I can throw it back to him: 'It's from my wife,' he say quickly. He tap the letter in his hand. 'I'd written about you and your damn fool ways.' He shrug, as if there ain't no accountin' for the ways of women. 'She wanted to send you something for your Christmas stocking, I suppose.'

I'm only half convinced, so James, to show he tellin' the truth, start to read aloud from his letter. "Jim says his prayers every night, without need of prompting. How I wish you could see him, the way his little rear sticks up in the air as he kneels beside his bed. He has two things that he prays for. The first is a magic carpet. The second, for his father to be home for Christmas."

James go silent for a moment as he read the rest of the paragraph in his head. He clear his throat. 'Here it is – "I'm sending a few things that may be of use, and a tin of cigarettes, a woollen cap and two pairs of socks for your friend Obadaiah."' He look at me and shrug again. 'She sent them.'

I turn the tin of Fatimas in my hands, tryin' not to show how damn heart-pleased I am, as if it be a regular thing, like I got plenty folks out there to send me gifts all the way to France. I open the lid. The baseball card inside is of 'Three Finger' Mordecai Brown. I pass it round the others. Feel real good to have somethin' of my own to show around.

It only when I look closer at the cap and socks that I see the initials, 'J.A.S.' stitched into the linin' and over the toes. I grow real still as it hit me – his wife never sent me nothin'. These here things, they meant for James. The Yankee, he awful smart, I always known that. All that stuff he just read aloud from the letter, those words 'bout me were made up, those lines never written at all. James ain't said nothin' to his family 'bout me. The thought, it cuts deep. Here I am, figurin' we be buddies, but I'm a fool is what, to think our friendship matter to him.

I bunch the cap, them socks, in my fist, all angry and fixin' to return everythin', but the look on James' face stop me. He sit all hunched over his letters, rereadin' them line by line.

They still gifts, aren't they? Real gifts that someone thought to give me, gifts from this damn fool Yankee. *System D,* I tell myself. *System D. Now don't you be no ninny, Obadaiah Nelson – powerful useful these goin' to be in this devil-spawn cold.* I stuff the cap and socks into my sack. The anger go quickly as it come. Although it still bother me, like a thorn pressin' deep inside, the notion that he ain't said nothin' 'bout me to his folks back home.

It strike me then, sudden like. 'How come you ain't never talked 'bout your son before?'

He hesitate, then pull a photograph from between the pages of his journal. The little boy in the picture, he 'bout four or five years old. Barely knee high to a duck he look, sittin' in a chair so big, so carved and grand, it just 'bout swallow him whole. His hair's flip-floppin' over his forehead as he looks into the camera, with a face the spittin' image of his pappy's.

'Jim,' the Yankee say, by way of introduction.

He don't say nothin' when I point out how much the boy look like him, but he smilin' as he take the photograph back. I see the way his eyes soften too, as he rub a thumb along its edge, gentle like, back and forth.

SIXTEEN

December 1914

Christmas Eve, and the snipers on both sides gone silent. The rain of all mornin' slowed at last to a drizzle, and come evenin', even that small, drip-drip sound against the roofs of the dugouts stopped. The stars out early tonight; one, another, then some more all at once. Their light lie on the ground, blue and shinin'.

I'm in a dugout with James and some others, everybody of us huddled together in balaclavas and such. Rats be scratchin' in the corners but we don't pay them no mind. We just glad 'cause for a little while after it rains, the stink of the trenches die away. There's a wet-clay smell, pleasant, like river-earth by the bayou. The branches roofin' the dugouts, they still wet; they smell of pine.

We hear a sudden whisperin' and hustlin' over by the lookout post. The feel of the dugout change at once. Nobody say nothin', but muscles go tight, ears strainin' to tell from the sounds outside just what it is that headed our way. Night raid? Full-on attack?

'Boche comin' over to fill our Christmas stockings,' I jest, to break the tension.

James spit a mouthful of chaw juice into the corner. All the anger coiled up inside of him, it right there in that stream, the juice comin' out with such force that any rats caught in the way surely struck blind. I'm listenin' hard for what goin' on outside, but the joke come into my head anyway: Christmas Spectacular! Special show by Yankee James Stonebridge: *Three! Blind! Mice!*

I know how the Yankee feel though. One night, just tonight, would've been good to have some peace. I can hear men rushin' 'bout outside. We stay where we are, holdin' on to the few moments we got in the dugout before the *alarme* sounds.

Karan burst through the entrance. 'You've got to come see this!' The tie of his precious robe is draggin' loose in the mud but he don't even notice. 'The Boche . . . you have to see this,' and he disappear outside.

That shake us up proper. There's a right scramble as we rush to the lookouts. Sure bright tonight. I can see the rolls of bobwire real clear, the cemetery-quiet of No Man's Land, all the way to the Boche trenches, and their parapets all done up with lights.

Wait – lights?

'What the . . .!' someone whispers.

Them lights, there so many, it look like a street from Storyville, the bar at Tom Anderson's, all lit up and stretchin' for half a block. I push closer to the gap in the sandbags. There's *candles* strung all along the Boche parapets. Rows and heights of them, all lit and shinin'. I start to make out branches, and trunks, and I realise just what it is I'm seein'.

James breathe out sharply. 'I'll be damned. *Tannenbaums?*'

'Tannenbaums,' echoes Karan. 'Looks like the mail came in on that side of the trenches as well – the Boche have got themselves a holiday delivery.'

Christmas trees. The Boche have gone and put out little Christmas trees all along their parapets.

Chevalier look like he been struck by thunder and lightnin', as if he seen the Christmas miracle itself. James brush absent like at the bits of straw from the dugout floor stuck to his coat, eyes fixed all the while on those twinklin', golden lights.

'I almost raised the alarm,' Karan tell. 'Couldn't for the life of me figure out what they were when the Boche first lit them up. Thought they were some diabolical new version of Verey lights.' There was a dreamy, faraway look in his eyes. 'Then I was afraid that I'd fallen asleep at my post and was dreaming of Diwali back home, when all the state is lit, with mud lamps. And I stand on the ramparts of the fort and look down on to a sea of lights, twinkling under the stars.' He shake his head. '*Tannenbaums*! Blinking Christmas trees at the blooming Front!'

'Christmas trees,' James repeat slowly. He grins, and that grin, it grow bigger and bigger, and now I'm grinnin' too, we all are.

'Christmas trees!'

Not everybody been as pleased by the *tannenbaums.* To many of the *anciens,* them trees an insult. They cuss out the Boche for all those villages of France under enemy occupation this winter, cussin' at this fake, wartime Christmas show.

'*Cochons*!' Gaillard shake his fist at their lines. He turn angrily away and we watch him go, guilty, but not so much that we follow.

We stay here instead, by the lookouts. Just for a while, we want to forget. Forget where we are, forget these torn-up, beat-down fields, leave behind the blood-stink mud. Tonight the air smell of pine and them Christmas candles, they dance, shinin' and golden. We take them in hungrily, fillin' eyes and hearts, 'memberin' past Christmases and filled with thoughts of home.

Ain't nobody say nothin', but we all wonderin' the same thing: if the *salaud* enemy can get their trenches all lit up for Christmas, if they can line them parapets with candles, fill them with such beauty, then maybe, just maybe, them Boche, they ain't so much *salaud* after all?

Soon after, the singin' start. Only snatches at first, comin' from the back trenches of the Boche. It start to move forward, that singin', from trench to forward trench, with more and more voices joinin' in. They sing in German and I don't know none of the words, but I recognise the carol all the same.

'Silent Night', the Boche, they singin' 'Silent Night'.

Their voices rise and fall from behind them golden Christmas trees. Ain't a man movin' in our part of the trenches. We struck dumb as we listen, melody and rhythm washin' over us. The night is cold, but filled with stars and music. Music, fillin' in the empty spaces: the gaps in the wire, in this shell-hole earth, in all the terrible things we seen but ain't got no words to describe, in the ache steady growin' inside of us, the darkness we try so hard to hide.

A hardenin' frost sweep in overnight. The next mornin', we have ourselves a white Christmas, just like James said we would. The rain-slick belts of bobwire all frosted over, shinin' white in the early sun. There's bits of ice in the straw all along the floor of the trenches, like beads of glass. These too catch the sun, turnin' many-coloured in the light that be sweepin' in from one end of the trenches to the other.

Ain't no firin' all mornin', not from our side or theirs. It awful peaceful and the birds start to fly in. All kinds, so many – red-tailed, sunflower-sided, hook-beaked, all the callin', singin' birds we ain't hardly seen these past months, they suddenly back, the sky thick with their wings.

It's Christmas mornin', and I know, I just know that those birds, they know it's Christmas too.

'Christmas caroling,' James say, pointin' at the birds.

All that mornin' they there, our visitors, hoppin' on the parapets, singin' from the bobwire, flyin' both to our side and to the Boche trenches. James pull out a tin of nuts from his holiday packages and pass it around. We hold out the nuts and the birds so tame – or hungry – they hop on our fingers and peck from our palms. One – a finch, James say – even allow a stroke or two of my finger across his wings before he fly away, chirp-chirpin' all the while.

Chevalier, he got that look in his eyes, the same one he get when he talk 'bout his wife. He pull out sheets of notepaper from his sack, and with that Sunday-church look still on his face, sit down to draw.

'*Bon camarade*! *Bon camarade*!' The Boche start to call out to us. The French words sound thicker, more rough, in the German accent.

'*Salauds*!' Gaillard yell back.

They try again. 'Let's all go drink champagne in Paris,' one of them call in French. This don't sound too bad a plan to me, but that's not how the Captain sees it.

'Not if we get to Berlin first!' he roar in reply.

'How about a drink here?' the Boche try then. 'Did you like our singin' last night?' he continue, without waitin' for an answer. 'Why didn't you sing with us?'

'We'd rather die than sing with you,' Gaillard shout.

'Well,' the voice cheerfully reply, 'your singin' would probably be the death of us anyway.'

Gaillard chuckle at this and we grinnin' too. The Captain's mouth twitches – he as fond of a good joke as anyone – as he draw hisself to his full height and spit on the floor of the trench.

'*Salauds*!' he exclaim, but we can see it more for show than anythin' else.

The Boche ain't done yet. 'Bout an hour later, they tie a white cloth to a rifle and wave it above their parapet. At first, we think it a bird. That cloth, it rise higher, above the *tannenbaums*, high enough that there ain't no mistakin' the signal now for anythin' but a truce.

As we watch, a Boche climb out over the parapet, wavin' that flag.

We watch as he make his way through the Boche wire and across No Man's Land. The birds fly up a bit as he come close to them, then settle back down as he pass.

Gaillard speak German and is sent to meet the Boche halfway, at the wire. We got rifles trained on that Boche and at their trenches, ready for the first sign of a trap.

The two stand there talkin' a right long time. The Boche reach inside his coat and the Captain's shoulders go stiff with alarm. All the Boche do though, is hand over a package. They talk some more, Gaillard and he, and then each make his way back, pushin' through the birds.

'*Alors?*' demand the Captain as Gaillard get back in. 'What did they want?'

'To wish us a happy Christmas,' Gaillard shake his head and hand over the package. 'They wish us a merry Christmas, with two bottles of their best *Liebfraumilch.*

'They also want a truce for all of today,' he continue, 'so that we can bury the dead from the past months that are still lying out there. A truce,' he repeat to the Captain, spreadin' his paws.

Urgent communiqués are sent to headquarters, and orders come back just as fast: we to go ahead with the truce, so that the dead can be attended to. We to remain on our guard and 'exercise full caution at all times'.

Sure feel odd, to climb up the ladder on to open ground. James, he stumble, right hisself. I know it ain't from the ice on the frozen field, but from our legs that feel like jelly, off balance from the strangeness of it all. The shell holes trimmed in white, like the edges of an ice rink, or salt along the rim of some frou-frou, dolled-up drink. The birds fly around us as we walk, so close that their wings brush our hands. Here now, the dead. So many together, thick as driftwood on a beach. I reach for my gris-gris.

'You don't need that,' James say quietly.

How he know 'bout my lucky charm, I can't say. He ain't never said nothin' 'bout it before. I snatch my hand from my pocket, embarrassed.

'There's nothing left of these men,' he go on, almost to hisself. 'Not the good, nor bad, nor anythin' to fear.' There's a look on his face I can't figure out as he work his shovel into the frozen ground. 'Nothing left of them here,' he repeat. 'They're long gone.'

It shame me that the Yankee thinks me 'fraid. I dig the blade of my shovel hard into the ground, hard as I can, harder than him, as if to show him he got it all wrong. I wrassle with the frozen earth, and as I dig and push, I look, really look, at the dead all around. I see their broken bodies, so still, so empty and somethin' catch in my chest at the waste of it all.

James is right. Ain't nothin' here of men, just bodies starin' with cold glass eyes.

The sound of shovels against the icy earth, and song, so much birdsong. Ain't nothin' left of these men. Now there only this – white ice and blue sky, and singin' fire-winged birds.

We collect tags and boots, sortin' through the dead. The ammunition, each side has agreed, gotta stay in the sector where it found. The Captain right pleased with the arrangement, the Boche being better supplied than us.

We slowly comin' up on the Boche as we move across the field; they close enough now that we can make out their faces. This is the first of the enemy we've actually seen. In this part of the sector, our trenches lie close enough that we hear the sounds of their reveille each mornin', near enough that we can smell their breakfast cookin'. We hear them shufflin' 'bout, listenin' for the smallest movement from their side, weapons ready. Still, even after all these months at the Front, most of us ain't never seen a livin', breathin' Boche up close. Just one more thing 'bout this crazy, mixed-up war.

Six-foot tall giants, they been sayin' of them in our trenches. Fierce, real fierce. Blonde, with arms thick as tree trunks.

The men we see ain't no giants. They thin, and some wearin' glasses, the sort you see on bankers and accountants and such back home. The same half-nervous, half-curious looks on their faces, as I figure there must be on our own. We look at each other, look away, keep diggin', look again. We keep on workin', gettin' closer and closer, and now there a Boche right by me.

'*Camarade*,' he say, shy like.

I ain't want to be talkin' to no bastard Boche, so I act like I ain't heard. Then, seein' as it Christmas and all, I figure I should at least nod in reply.

'*Sénégalais?*' he ask.

'Senegalese? I ain't no Senegalese,' I say hotly. 'I'm a Yank! America,' I say to him, 'America!'

His eyes go wide at that, and he stare at me as if I just say that I'm straight from kingdom come. He grin, and then damned if he don't say: 'Jack Johnson.'

Jack Johnson! My mouth just 'bout fallen wide open at that. *Jack Johnson,* the Boche just said! He got his fists up now, as if he in a boxing ring. 'America,' he say again. 'Jack Johnson!'

We get to talkin' after that, whatever little we can, given he only know a few words of French, and I ain't speak no German at all.

'Hans Fitschen,' he introduce hisself.

He shows me a picture of his home, near Munich, he say. I tell him I come from the bayou, but he has trouble sayin' the word Louisiana.

'America!' he say once more.

To our surprise, the other side, they ain't that different from us at all. We been tryin' our best to kill them. Now here we are, face to face, and findin' that they just men, men like us, tired of the mud and the wet, grumblin' 'bout the food, cussin' them fat-cat generals who don't seem to know much of anythin' at all.

Just regular men, with mothers and homes, heart-sickened by these killin' fields and the war.

Chevalier pull out his drawings from that mornin', of us feedin' the birds. The Boche crowd around, exclaimin' and pointin'. One of them start to clap. Chevalier smile shy like, offer him one of the drawings. The Boche, he don't understand at first. Chevalier push the sheet of paper at him, and he take it then, grinnin' and noddin', and reachin' into his coat, he hand over a pack of precious cigarettes.

Suddenly men rushin', slippin' in both directions across No Man's Land, hurryin' back to their trenches for what gifts they can find. Cigars, tobacco, a couple of *tannenbaums,* bread, wine, all these pass hands; when there ain't nothin' left to give, men exchange buttons from their coats.

All afternoon it last, this Christmas back and forth. When all the dead taken care of, orders come for the truce to end. Hans Fitschen, he seek me out, bringin' a buddy along. The other Boche, he speak a bit of English, and translate for Hans: 'When the war is done, Hans will be comin' to America.'

Hans push his glasses up his nose and beams. 'America!' he say, and hold out his hand.

'You do that,' I reply, shakin' his hand. 'You do that, and tell you what, maybe we'll go watch the Champ together.'

The evenin' sun be blood red. The birds, they all flown away, sudden as they came, but the Boche gone and lit their *tannenbaums* for another night. Our trenches still buzzin' from all the goin's-on of today. I look at them lit-up parapets of the Boche from the fire step and wonder if it the same there, with them.

'Not so bad, are they, up close?' I say to James.

'No,' he say slowly, 'they're not. One of them said to me that they've been scared witless by the Legion all this while. Six feet tall, they heard the legionnaires were. Tempers of madmen, and legs thick as tree trunks.'

I grin. 'Hans Fitschen movin' to America,' I inform him. 'After the war. We goin' to watch some great boxin' together. Do you think . . .' I ask. 'The war – it can't . . .' It feel unlucky to say the words out loud, so I don't.

He know though, what I'm thinkin'. Everybody of us thinkin' the same. Those Boche we met today, they just like us, keen to be done with this crazy war, to wrap it up so we can all go home.

James and I, we stand there in the cold, starin' at those golden *tannenbaums*. Both thinkin', hopin', that maybe, just maybe, the war, it ain't goin' to last much longer after all.

Word come from headquarters later that evenin'. A French artillery attack planned for tonight. Seein' as it Christmas though, the attack gonna begin late, at 23:00 hours, which be midnight in Berlin, and so, 26 December there.

James frown. 'It will still be Christmas *here*,' he point out, but this fact, the brass, in their wisdom, gone and forgot.

WASHINGTON DC

1932

SEVENTEEN

July 1932

Jim rolled down the window as far as it would go, letting what little breeze there was into the cab of the truck. The Major and he had set off early that morning, the trees still dark silhouettes along the side of the road, the cool wash of air over the hills pristine. It had got progressively hotter as the hours went by, the highway steadily more crowded, until, by the time they were on the turn-off that led to Washington DC, their progress had slowed to a crawl.

The road ahead was crowded with veterans and their families. Most carried all that they owned. Despite the heat, many of the men were dressed in what remained of their doughboy uniforms, tatty overcoats with lapels missing and mismatched buttons. Some wore medals on their chests. They carried knapsacks and old suitcases, sometimes little more than a worn-out grocery bag stuffed with all their belongings. Bedrolls and bits and pieces of mess kits were slung upon their backs, with tin cups, obviously of army issue, dangling from belts here and there. A family of six, packed into a car with a cracked windshield and battered fenders, the paint long scraped off the back. Jim spotted clothes piled up on the back seat, a crate of potatoes, a rocking chair and an old radio tied to the roof. From an open window, the American flag fluttered in the breeze.

Jim glanced at his father, still marvelling at the fact that they were undertaking this journey at all, knowing how crowds upset him. To his surprise, the Major was leaning his head eagerly outside, one arm along the window as he drank it all in.

'Pull up,' he said to his son as they inched abreast of a merry crowd of about fifteen men. They were singing as they marched, waving rough, home-made placards at the oncoming traffic.

'Bonus or Bust! Cheered in '17, jeered in '32!'

'Headed to Washington, boys?' the Major called. 'Come along, we'll give you a ride.'

At first, the men refused. 'We've made it this far on pretty much a prayer and shoe leather,' they said cheerfully, pointing at the old puttees and hobnailed boots they wore, telltale wads of newspaper sticking out from the sides where the leather had given way. 'We're going to walk all the way there, show those fat-cat senators what it takes to be a true doughboy,' they declared.

He'd been a doughboy too, the Major retorted. Damned if he was about to let any man who'd tramped about in the mud of France go walking to Washington, not when he was headed there himself with a pair of wheels under him. 'I'm Major Stonebridge. Get your damn fool selves in here, and that's an order,' he said, in a tone that brooked no interference, and they sent up a cheer that made Jim grin.

'AEF! AEF! Three cheers for the Bonus Army!!'

They scrambled in among the sacks and crates of provisions stacked in the bed, and when all of that space was used, lined up on the running boards on either side of the truck. 'Say Major!' one of the men called. 'Whereabouts did you serve?'

Major Stonebridge hesitated. 'A desk job, mostly,' he said. 'Translating.'

'He enlisted with the French Foreign Legion,' Jim interjected. He looked in the overhead mirror at the men. 'Went over in 1914, soon as the war began.'

The Major said nothing, continuing to look out the window, but surprised and touched that his son remembered.

'1914, huh?' the man said soberly. 'You spent more time over there than all of us combined, I figure.'

The Major was silent for a moment. 'It isn't so much the time one spends fighting, as how well one fights,' he said then, and they sent up another ear-splitting cheer. 'I reckon every last one of you boys fought like a hellcat in hot water.'

They rolled onwards towards Washington, and the men started to sing once more, in merry, discordant chorus.

'My bonus lies over the ocean, My bonus lies over the sea . . .'

They hollered greetings to every other group of veterans they passed, waving their placards and flags, and banging on the sides of the truck.

'My bonus lies over the ocean, O bring back my bonus to me!'

Jim noticed the twitch of amusement in his father's face. There was something else as well, something that he hadn't seen in that worn cast of features for a very long time – a firm-jawed sense of purpose, and of pride.

Their progress was so slow that it was evening by the time they approached the city. The Washington Monument towered above the tree line on the horizon, the shaft of the obelisk pointing straight up, like some immutable beacon of hope.

The men fell momentarily silent as they caught sight of it. Someone whistled, low and long. 'Would you look at that? Washington DC. We're here, buddies.'

'That thing's huge!'

'Ah, it ain't so big. You should see mine when I got the missus with me.' They fell about laughing, revelling in the camaraderie they'd missed for years, converted again to the mere boys they'd been when they'd shipped out to France all those decades ago, nervous, excited and wisecracking all the way.

Unsure where exactly to head next, they polled some of the groups that they passed. Most said they were headed to the Anacostia Flats, where a large veteran camp had been set up. There was little need to ask for directions – Jim simply followed the long, slow line of trucks and cars with 'B.E.F' and 'BONUS ARMY!' emblazoned on their sides. Balding men with signs strapped to their backs: 'Imagine if the Kaiser had won!' Riders on motorcycles with the Stars and Stripes fluttering from the handlebars: 'We done right in France, now do right by us, America!' A baby, sound asleep in a pushcart.

Jim wondered again what Madeleine would have made of it all. An eager sense of anticipation hung over the crowd. This was no motley gathering of down-on-their-luck folks, tramping aimlessly about the country as so many others were. The men of the Bonus Army may have been thin and shabbily dressed, but they held themselves tall, filled with a touching faith in the justness of their cause. So affecting was their demeanour that local pedestrians stopped to watch, the younger among them breaking into spontaneous whoops of applause.

Through the city they went, towards the river and the 11th Street Bridge, the motley procession of vehicles and people crossing over reflected in the river's water as it lapped gently against the draw spans.

Jim was reminded of an illustration in one of his grandfather's books, of an ancient pioneer caravan pressing forward, the images shimmering in the water like a mirage.

He pulled up outside the entrance to the camp. The men jumped eagerly from the back and began to gather their meagre belongings. Jim stretched and got down, looking curiously about him.

It was a crescent-shaped piece of land, no more than ten acres across, and identified by the city as a park development. The 'park' was very much a project in progress: demarcated at one end by the white lines of a baseball diamond and a desultory attempt at a tennis court, it was bounded at the other end by the river, thick with sludge and debris from an open sewer, and a city dump scattered over a small hill.

In the few weeks that the veterans had taken over the land, it had been transformed, virtually overnight, from a barren mudflat into a thriving shanty town. Hoovervilles, they were called, these shanty towns of the poor and transient, named after President Hoover whom they blamed for their suffering. Hundreds had sprouted all across America during the grind of the Depression, and the Anacostia Flats, with its view of the Capitol Building, now boasted the largest Hooverville of them all, startling both for the speed of its manifestation as well as the eccentricity of its architecture.

Jim took in the shabby tents, the shelters built from tar paper and scrap lumber that stretched in precise, military rows. Here was a lean-to with the rusted bonnet of a car for a roof, there, a structure conjured out of fence posting and a wooden advertisement for shoes. Men had scoured the junk pile on the hill, requisitioning every bit of scrap that could conceivably be put to use. Rusted bed-springs, egg crates, newspapers, strips of wallpaper, cardboard boxes, tin cans that they hammered flat and nailed together, whorls of barbed wire, pieces of corrugated iron, ripped car seats with the stuffing spilling out – every discarded, forgotten piece of rubbish had been repurposed and brought back to life here in Anacostia.

'Bonus Inn', a sign on a shack made from wooden shutters, half its slats long missing, proclaimed; pebbles had been painted white and arranged in starfish patterns around the front. A rudimentary shelter, no larger than a chicken coop, was propped up at the back with a child's chalkboard. 'Stay Till They Pay!' someone had scrawled defiantly across it. One man had simply claimed a barrel set on its side and lined it with grass for his home; another, a casket set on trestles. A third had appropriated a piano box – 'Castle of Music,' he'd painted along the side.

Despite its ramshackle construction, a distinct orderliness permeated the camp, with many of the shelters proudly sporting the American flag. Dozens, maybe hundreds of flags, the collective mascot of this grizzled, rag-tag army, planted firmly in the mud and fastened to rickety roofs; the red, white and blue of the Stars and Stripes visible everywhere he looked.

The sun sank lower into the horizon, shards of metal and glass gleaming from among the shanties in this last light of day.

The Major got down awkwardly from the truck, his damaged leg cramping after the long ride. 'There's no need for any of that,' he said gruffly when their passengers thanked him, leaning on his cane as he shook their hands.

Jim dropped off a load of provisions at the registration tent, where despite the late hour, a long line of men snaked outside the entrance.

'There this many every day?' Jim asked the stocky veteran behind the desk.

'More,' the man replied happily, removing his glasses and rubbing his eyes. He tightened the knot of string that held the glasses together at one end and pointed at the stack of papers beside him. 'We got each one in here, y'know,' he said proudly. 'Name, rank, company served in during the war. Everyone's got to sign up before they're allowed to stay. This here's an honest-to-God doughboy camp, no bums or troublemakers allowed.'

He nodded appreciatively towards the crates that Jim set down. 'The men will thank you kindly for that. Easy it ain't, feeding so many.'

'There's more in our truck.'

'Then we gotta help you unload.' He rose to his feet. 'Mike Connor,' he said, holding out his hand.

Placing his glasses back on his nose and hollering for volunteers, Connor walked with Jim back to the truck, talking all the way.

Lights were starting to come on in the city across the river, while an inky darkness spread about the Anacostia Flats, spurred on by the lack of electricity and broken now and again by the fitful light of a lantern.

Connor shook the Major's hand. 'Real square of you and your

townfolk, Major. The cigarettes 'specially – never have enough around here.'

'How many men in all?' the Major asked.

'Twenty thousand or thereabouts. Our camp here's the largest, but there's more, about nineteen, twenty, I reckon. The city's got some of us housed in a group of buildings downtown that are going to be demolished soon. Not much more than brick shells and some with fallen-down roofs, but still, it's a place for a man to rest his head.

'We got men from all over the country here,' Connor continued, 'from just about every corner of every state. There's fruit pickers from Florida, miners from Pennsylvania, factory workers from Ohio . . . men who've been trying to make it just about anywhere in the country. About seven hundred wives and kids too.' His eyes twinkled. 'Just today, we took in the O'Brien six, all red-headed and scrappy as hell. It's been a struggle, getting enough food to go around, but we been managing so far. Slum, mostly.

'Slumgullion,' he explained to Jim as he lifted a crate from the bed of the truck. 'Doughboy speciality – a bit of meat, whatever vegetables you've got, boil the lot together. There's coffee in the morning, a bit of bread, and potatoes. It ain't much, but we make do.'

A rooster came squawking over, flapping its wings. It looked them over with beady eyes and started to peck at the burlap sacks. Connor laughed, the headlights of the truck revealing a set of alarmingly rotted teeth. 'Get on with you,' he said amiably, shooing the bird away. 'This here's Rooster Curtis,' he informed them. 'Belongs to one of the families in the camp, and there ain't nothing that Curtis won't eat, ain't that right, Curtis? He's been having the time of his life here alright. Roaming in and out of the shacks, helping himself to a bit of wire here, a bottle cap there. Become sort of a pet for the whole camp, he has.

'Ain't it time for you to get some sleep?' he demanded, as the rooster sidled towards the sacks again. It cocked its head and looked expectantly at Connor as he fished in his pocket and tossed it a bit of bread. The rooster pounced on it triumphantly and strutted away.

'Folks been helping as best they can,' he continued chattily as he unloaded another crate. 'Chief Glassford – he's the Chief of Police in DC – comes around often as he can. Given out of his own pocket more than a couple of times. Money to buy meat, potatoes, coffee . . . That tells you something, doesn't it? Folks care. They ain't forgotten what we done for them in France. Some folks at least, they still remember. You staying in DC long, Major?' he asked.

The Major slapped away the mosquitoes that had begun to whine around them. From somewhere within the camp, a band was playing; a chorus of voices, lifted in song.

'Trying to get to one of the senators. We'll see.'

'Well, I surely hope he hears what you have to say. We need more of the Government listening. We ain't asking for no handout, only what was promised.'

'The men here . . .' The Major cleared his throat, tapping his cane against the truck. 'Anyone here from the French Legion?'

'The Legion?' Connor shouldered a final crate, lofting a sack on to his back. 'There's a few from the AEF divisions that fought under the French flag, if that's what you mean. You'll find them about the camp. Anyhow, I hope you'll come by in the morning sometime,' he called over his shoulder as he staggered away. 'We try and have ourselves some fun around here. Boxing matches, drills . . . just like the old days.'

'Like the old days,' the Major echoed, a strange tone, one that Jim couldn't quite identify, in his voice as he scanned the darkened camp.

EIGHTEEN

14 July 1932

It was nearly ninety degrees in what little shade there was in the overhang of the Capitol. The air felt dense and sticky, a mugginess exacerbated by the rivers bordering the city. Jim thought longingly of the Connecticut back home. She too flowed sluggishly on days like this, but there were pockets of respite to be found along her length, cool green shoals and shadowed rocks, covered with moss. He mopped the back of his neck. The oaks that lined Pennsylvania Avenue stood wilting in the humidity. Even the grass around the buildings seemed to droop: the sprinklers had not been turned on last evening, in deference to the veterans who had camped en masse on the lawns of the Capitol that night. The cordon of policemen assigned to watch over them leaned about listlessly at the foot of the Hill in a damp rim of blue. There were no birds, none of the small insects of summer; nothing seemed to move in the torpid morning except for the stumbling procession of men circling Capitol Hill.

The veterans had been informed early that morning that they were no longer permitted to camp on the grounds of the Capitol. The police were sympathetic but firm as they delivered their orders – the men had to keep moving if they wanted to visit the Hill.

If that's what it would take, the veterans replied, then move they would. They'd march without pause around the Capitol until the Senate took action on the Bonus Bill. The Death March, they called it as they began to file around the buildings, led by a disabled veteran in a steel brace that enveloped his back and neck like a cage. Jim watched as a veteran shook the American flag that he was carrying, trying to restore some snap to it. It rustled briefly before drooping on its staff once more.

How long could they keep it up, Jim wondered, as he mopped his neck again. They'd already been marching when the Major and he had arrived at the Hill early that morning. The young aide was polite as he invited them in. With only a few days to go before the Senate was adjourned for the summer, the Senator's calendar was especially busy, he said, but he'd see what he could do. He gestured towards the chairs in his office, but Jim, uncomfortable amidst all that officious marble and dark wood panelling, had opted to wait outside.

They should do it in groups, he mused to himself. Keep one group marching while the others got some rest . . . The men had attempted to shave and clean up in the washrooms about the plaza, but nonetheless they looked worn, lack of sleep accentuating the hollows under their eyes. Their trousers hung wrinkled and grass-stained, sweat mushrooming in patches of pale yellow on their shirts as the day dragged on.

Slowly but surely, the Death March began to make its presence felt within the building. Jim noted with amusement and not a little satisfaction the faces that started to appear at the open windows as the senators looked out at the veterans on the lawns. Puffing agitatedly on their cigars, they asked one another what it all meant; Jim grinned at the consternation that carried clearly in their voices as they wondered if they were under siege.

Word of the march began to spread around the city. More veterans arrived, from Anacostia and the other camps downtown. Local Washingtonians, drawn by the spectacle of these resolutely marching men, came to watch, despite the oppressive heat. Reporters followed in their wake, armed with notepads and cameras as they scouted for news.

'Look here, over here, buddy!'

The Major was still holed away in the aide's office as evening came around. It brought with it little relief. Heat pressed down on the city, the air heavy with a brewing storm. Jolted into alertness by the ever expanding crowd, the police had started to patrol, separating veterans from onlookers, ordering reporters to move along, and keeping a sharp watch for trouble.

The floodlights around the Capitol came on, just as the first strains of 'The Star Spangled Banner' carried over the buildings; the Marine Band was playing at a concert nearby.

'Turn off all those damn floodlights for a week and use the money to pay us our bonus instead,' a veteran called hoarsely, and a cheer went up through the crowd.

A couple of onlookers tried to kick over a floodlight and were promptly hauled away by the police. Still more people came, abandoning the concert to watch the drama unfolding here instead. Tempers were increasingly on edge. A woman shrilly accused a policeman of pushing her, nearly setting off a free for all. Newshounds came rushing over. Camera flashbulbs went off all around and a veteran fell writhing to the ground.

'Shell shock, the poor bastard,' Jim heard someone mutter.

When the Major finally emerged, still not having been able to meet with the Senator, he stood on the stairs, stunned by the carnival that had erupted over the grounds. People were shouting, jostling, jeering; the sharp blast of police whistles sounded all across the Plaza. There were so many people crowding on to the Hill that eventually the Capitol was ordered closed.

Jim wondered what to say as the Major and he headed back to the rooms they had rented. Jim hadn't cared for the landlord, but the lodging was well priced and conveniently located, right above the latter's grocery store in a neighbourhood that adjoined the Anacostia camp.

'We can try again tomorrow,' he said carefully.

The Major massaged his knee tiredly. 'We will,' he agreed simply.

The next day began in much the same way, except, Jim noticed with satisfaction, that the marchers now divided themselves into two groups. While one group kept the Death March going, the other caught a couple hours of sleep in a vacant lot that fell outside of congressional jurisdiction, and from where they couldn't be evicted.

'Jim!' someone called cheerfully. Connor, from the registration tent at Anacostia, was striding smiling towards him, fanning himself with a rolled-up newspaper. He introduced his companion, a slight, stooped figure, puffing on a cigarette. 'Joe Angelo, from Camden, New Jersey.' Jim shook Angelo's hand, taking in the Distinguished Service Cross pinned to the concave chest.

'The Major in there?'

Jim nodded. 'Waited all day yesterday too.'

'Politicians!' Connor shook his head. 'Here, you seen this?' he asked, shaking out the newspaper. 'The *BEF News* – we've even got our own paper.'

The cartoon on the front page was that of a long line of men and women. On the horizon, the figure of a veteran loomed, in full dress kit and with 'BEF' inscribed on his cap. He stood erect, a half-smile on his face, as with a raised arm, he pointed the way towards Washington.

'You gotta read this.' Connor chuckled as he jabbed at an article.

'A Tough Old Bird,' Jim read. Rooster Curtis from the camp had apparently contracted such a severe case of indigestion the previous week that an operation had been necessary to save his life. In the rooster's maw were found: four honourable discharges (not masticated), one set of false teeth, one unopened package of B.D. tobacco, a yard of barbed wire, and various other odds and ends too numerous to mention. The correspondent was happy to report that after a few days spent in recovery and repenting his sins, Curtis was now back to form, thriving on a daily diet of tent pegs, soap, cigarette butts and rival newspapers.

Jim grinned. 'He seemed hungry enough to me the other night. "Tough Old Bird" alright.'

'Well, he's a member of the BEF now, isn't he? He's gotta be tough.' Connor laughed. 'Come grab a sandwich with us,' he invited.

Jim hesitated, glancing towards the building.

'They're going to make him wait most of today too, y'know. Come on,' Connor urged, 'we won't be long.'

As they walked, Connor said: 'Joe here testified last year.'

Angelo nodded. 'House Ways and Means Committee. Walked all the way from Camden, I did, in the middle of February. Got here with my shoes soaked through from the snow and my feet all swollen. Wanted to show them we *needed* the bonus; we wouldn't be asking for it if we didn't need it bad.

'The congressman asks what sort of work I do. "Nothing," I answer, "I'm nothing but a bum now."

'"Mr Angelo," he says, "with your marvellous record of heroism and service, how is it that you have been unable to find employment?"

'"I've been looking for two years," I tell him, "but there ain't no point to my searching, not when there's nobody hiring in Camden." I tell him how I went to the Fire Department soon as I came home from France. You know what they said to me? That I was too light.

Too light! I weighed a hundred and seven pounds when I went on the scales in Uncle Sam's Army. Pound for pound, I given those Boche good as any man out there, and better than many. I seen shells, I seen bullets, I been through all kinds of hell and back, only to be called "too light" back home. Give me two years, I told them at the Fire Department, just two years and I'd weigh as heavy as any of them. Why? Because of all the sitting around on their asses they did.'

Angelo puffed on his cigarette, thin shoulders hunched. 'I tell this story in the House, and they're not sure what to make of it. Some nod, as if they understand. A few start to laugh, then cough, embarrassed.

'"You have not been treated right," a congressman says to me.

'"No, I haven't," I agree. "I've not had a square deal."

'I can make money in New Jersey, I tell them. Bootlegging, other "businesses", but that ain't what I want to do, going against the laws of the United States. An honest job is all I'm asking for, and if that ain't available, then at least give me my bonus.'

Taking a last puff of his cigarette, he flicked the stub away. 'That hearing was more than a year ago. What have they done for us since then? Nothing. And now, when we march outside Congress, they get all shook up and tell us we ain't got no business being here. I tell you, we got just as much right to be here as anybody else, more, after all we done for this country.'

'They ain't all bad,' Connor protested. He jerked a thumb towards the buildings of the Capitol. 'There's many in there trying to help us. They ain't *all* bad,' he repeated, as if trying to convince himself. 'It's a smart thing we've done, coming here to Washington. Show them we're no bums but the same doughboys they cheered on. They'll do right by us. They will.'

He turned eagerly to Jim. 'The camp at Anacostia? You know the name of the road that leads to it, coming up from Maryland?' He grinned. 'Good Hope Road. If that ain't a lucky omen, I don't know what is. Good. Hope. Road. You couldn't make this stuff up if you tried.'

The Major shifted uncomfortably in his chair. His leg had started to spasm again. He stretched it, trying not to wince as the taut muscles reluctantly gave. The headache that he'd been ignoring had worsened and it hurt his throat to swallow. He shifted position once more, mind wandering to the farm. The fruit had been coming out nicely on the apple trees when they'd left. Ellie's boy had promised to water them, and he knew Ellie would be breathing down that young man's neck to see that it was a job well done. Still, a few of those trees were downright fussy . . . He touched a hand to his throat, trying to ease the soreness.

'Coffee,' Jim said, holding out a cup. He looked at his father with concern, noting the pallor of his cheeks.

The Major took the coffee, grateful for its warmth. 'Things still busy outside from the sounds of it?'

'They're still marching. How're things in here?'

The Major grimaced. 'There's a few of us waiting. This evening, the aide said, but we'll see.'

Jim saw the way his father's hand trembled ever so slightly as he raised the coffee to his lips. 'Connor sent this for you.' He handed over the copy of the *BEF News*. 'There's an article about a certain rooster that you might find amusing.'

The Major opened the newspaper, smiling wanly over Rooster Curtis' antics. He pressed the cup of coffee against his throat, trying to dull the ache as an adjoining article caught his eye.

'Veteran's wife writes story of her life in BEF', it began.

EASTWARD HO!

Marion I. Anderson

The sun shines, the rain descends, and history repeats itself. Sturdy, lion-hearted pioneers, who blazed the trail 'Westward Ho' now look down to see their descendants blazing a trail back to the east . . . to the foot of the United States Capitol. They are here in defence of a just cause. Patriots, everyone – and Americans.

The railroads and bankers are not going to save this country from anything that overtakes it. The seasoned veterans – the men who are marching now – are the boys who are going to stand by and fight! The farmers in their sad predicament say one to another, 'That's what we ought to do.' The great army of the unemployed say one to another, 'That's what we ought to do.'

> The veterans have the advantage: they know how to organise. And they don't know what getting licked means. They are marching on Washington, asking for that which is theirs . . . and back out there the country awaits their destiny.

The veterans marched all day. So vexed were the senators by the steadily increasing numbers trudging past their windows that someone, Vice President Curtis included, some said later, picked up the 'phone and dialled Navy Yard. A contingent of Marines was to be sent at once to clear the veterans from the grounds.

Two companies of Marines were duly dispatched, in full battle gear and with fixed bayonets. They assembled in formation on the Hill, eyes filled with shame over the task they had been assigned.

Mistakenly believing that the Marines were there as a token of support for their cause, the veterans started to cheer. They surged about the troops, shaking hands and slapping backs, a few among them even recognising acquaintances dating back to the war years and beyond.

A vein of doubt rippled through Jim as he stood watching from the sidelines. Something wasn't right, a suspicion confirmed when the Major came limping out of the building, his face drawn.

'Those Marines—' Jim began.

'Those Marines aren't here for show,' the Major said tersely.

Realisation was slowly beginning to dawn upon the veterans as well. The Marines had been ordered to the Hill not in support but to remove them with force. The cheering of a minute ago gave way to an ominous buzz of disbelief and anger.

Things were poised to turn ugly had it not been for Chief of Police Pelham Glassford. He demanded an immediate recall of the Marines. They left, bayonets lowered, as the floodlights came on around the Capitol, highlighting the distaste, and the relief, etched in equal measure upon their faces.

Behind them, hooting in derision at the dazzlingly lit Capitol, clanking their battered tin cups and canteens and waving the Stars and Stripes, the veterans resumed the Death March, singing.

'Oh, Mellon pulled the whistle boys; And Hoover rang the bell. Wall Street gave the signal; And the country went to hell!'

The Major stood on the stairs, watching in silence. It was going to come to nothing; all of this was going to amount to nothing. How would the Bill ever be passed when there was so much resistance to it from within the hallowed portals of the Hill?

That old feeling of helplessness, of being adrift, of being unable to connect with anything of meaning . . . the Major wearily rubbed his forehead. Suddenly aware of Jim's gaze upon him, he straightened, trying to gather himself. He looked then, at his son, and knew he'd come to the same realisation: the Bill was unlikely to be passed.

There was something more that the Major saw in his son's eyes though, a steady, reassuring fortitude that seemed to reach out to the older man without need of words or explanation, an invisible supporting hand spanning across the few feet that separated them, father and son.

Jim bent down and lifted two hand-drawn signs at random from the small pile left scattered by the stairs during the earlier excitement over the Marines: 'Give Us Our Bonus Now!' and 'Asking Only For What *You* Promised!'

He handed one to his father, a small, wry smile on his lips. Holding the other high, Jim turned around and, without a word, began walking towards the veterans. The Major swallowed past the lump in his throat, which had very little to do with the soreness that had been plaguing him all day.

'Damn fool boy,' he muttered, as he gripped the placard closer and limped down the stairs, to join Jim and that ragged, tattooed, doggedly marching brigade.

NINETEEN

16 July 1932

Jim glanced curiously at the Distinguished Service Cross medal pinned to Joe Angelo's chest. Still, he didn't want to ask. His father had not once in all the years that he'd been back spoken about his own medals. Jim might not even have known about them had it not been for Ellie. She'd taken him by the hand one day, not long after his mother passed, and shown him where they were hidden, inside a pewter vase. Anywhere else, Ellie had explained gently, and the Major would keep finding them and throwing them into the garbage.

Angelo seemed to share no such reticence. 'You know how I got this?' he asked, gesturing at the medal. 'In the Meuse Argonne, with the 304th.'

He'd been assigned as an orderly to a lieutenant colonel. A real daredevil officer he was too, walking about the Front to reconnoitre the terrain, even slipping into No Man's Land to make sure that the ground was solid enough to support the weight of the tanks. Angelo grinned. 'Drove the senior officers crazy, but he did it anyway.'

The day of the attack had started with the usual barrage of artillery fire; American tanks starting for the enemy lines just before dawn. 'I can hardly see my fingers, the fog's so thick on the ground. We hear the guns ahead but can't see a thing. We've no idea where our tanks are. So the Colonel decides to leave the observation post and go find them. We follow in the general direction of the shelling and come upon five of our tanks stuck in the mud. The shelling's been too heavy for anyone to dig them out again. Well, damned if the Colonel doesn't run on up to one of the tanks and, grabbing a shovel that's tied to the side, start to dig. We step up right beside him, and keep at it all through some real heavy firing from the Boche. We free each one of those iron horses and they start to move forward once more, but there's no time no cheer, what with the Boche still slinging bullets every which way. Besides, the Colonel's already sprinting ahead like a jackrabbit, yelling for us to follow.

'We're racing forward,' Angelo continued, 'just running hell for leather, and get all the way to the top of a rise when we realise we've run right into the sights of a Boche nest. The machine guns swing our way. "Who's with me?" the Colonel shouts, waving his baton.

'There's five of us who keep him company. I run as hard and fast as I can – when I look back for just a second, I see that all the other boys who came with us are down. It's just me and the Colonel now.

'Now, I ain't got no idea where exactly we're running *to*. Any further, I reckon, and the Colonel and I going to be jumping right into the laps of those Boche. Lucky for both of us, it don't come to that – a bullet gets the Colonel. He keeps going another forty feet or so before he falls. I drag him into a shell hole. The bullet's gone in high through his thigh and come clean out the other side, right through the ass. He's bleeding pretty bad, and I rip up his trousers and bandage the wound the best I can. Nothing to do now but wait for reinforcements. When we see our tanks come up over the rise, I run to them in rushes, staying real low to the ground, and point out where the machine-gun nests are. Then I run back to the shell hole to stay with the Colonel. More tanks come around. I go back out again to point out the nests, come back once more to the shell hole. I tell you, it's a blessing I'm little because those bullets, they keep falling all around, but not one of them gets me.

'Our boys finally take out those Boche guns and get us the hell out of there. The Colonel gets a DSC for digging out those iron horses and they give one to me,' he waited for a beat, eyes crinkling, 'for saving the Colonel's ass.'

Angelo's brow furrowed as he looked at the men doggedly marching around the buildings. 'Them fat-cat politicians, they done all kinds of nonsense to the likes of the Colonel too. He was promoted three times during the war. Why? Because he fought like hell, that's why. And what do they do after we win and the war's over? Cancel all battlefield promotions and demote him back to captain.' He shook his head at the craziness of it all.

'He's still in the army, been promoted to Major now, but for me he'll always be the Colonel. He's stationed right here, across the river at Fort Myer. Any time I wanted, I could've gone to him, asked for a loan to tide me over. I ain't done that though,' he said proudly, 'and I ain't about to. He's been down to Camden to see me. Caused quite a stir in the neighbourhood, rolling up in a shiny Pierce Arrow. He and his wife, they given me gifts – a gold watch, a bowl, a tie pin . . .' He patted the medal on his chest. 'They know alright, just how much I done in France.'

He slowly stubbed out his cigarette as he looked up at Connor. 'You're right,' he acknowledged. 'What you said the other day. They're not all bad. There's some real good men standing up for us, and Colonel George S. Patton, he's one of the very best.'

The Major finally managed to meet with the Senator, who apologised for the long wait, but: 'The Senate is due to adjourn tomorrow,' he pointed out. 'There's a great deal still on the agenda, and it doesn't appear as if anything can be done about the Bonus Bill in this session.'

'And yet the House found the resources to pass a two-billion-dollar relief bill yesterday.'

'Indeed,' the Senator agreed sharply. 'Relief for the unemployed, home owners and a host of other pressing matters.'

'The veterans outside your offices, they're unemployed too, Senator. Why aren't their needs seen as pressing? Read this,' the Major said, pushing the *BEF News* across the desk. 'No, I must insist. This article, by the wife of one the veterans in the camps.'

'They're going to "march on Washington and fight"?' the Senator quoted incredulously as he scanned through the article. 'Fight against their own Government, "elected by none other than the people themselves"? Come, Major, you're a thinking man,' he scoffed. 'Many of these so-called "veterans" are no more than a bunch of communist radicals.'

The Senator gestured towards the window. 'These shenanigans outside – they're just a wind-up job by political factions with an eye on the presidential elections this year. I ask you, is this the face that we want to present to the world? The very seat of our Government being overrun by these . . . these . . .'

'These?' the Major prodded coldly. 'These men who've shed blood for their country? Come, Senator, as a thinking man, let me remind you that the men out there have a genuine and pressing cause. Wind-up job? There's no wind-up job. These men are here of their own accord, and they have just as much say in the governance of this country as anyone else. More, if you ask me, than most of the men sitting in this building, the likes of whom have never so much as set foot upon a battlefield or sacrificed anything for the good of this country.'

The Major limped from the Senator's office without a second glance, his face dark with anger.

It finally rained, a massive outpouring of the brooding, pent-up force that had been amassing all that week. An electrical storm hit the city, arcs of lightning crackling across the Hill, bucking and zigzagging over the river and highlighting the bridges in stark relief. The veterans on the Hill ran for cover, as did the policemen assigned to monitor them, demonstrator and lawman alike sheltering on the steps and against the stone balustrades of the Capitol as the storm lashed out overhead. Rainwater poured down the streets, overwhelming the sewers and flooding the pavements, washing into parked cars and choking their engines silent. Many outlying neighbourhoods lost power. A number of the residents didn't bother with candles, but stared transfixed from their windows instead at the savage, unsettling beauty of the night.

Jim and the Major were caught in the storm as they headed back to Anacostia. By the time they reached their rooms, father and son were both drenched to the bone.

It poured all night, finally petering out towards daybreak. A light steam was rising from the sidewalks when Jim finally woke the Major. The Major groaned and turned over. 'Breakfast,' a concerned Jim said. 'You need to eat something.'

The Major muttered incoherently and was drifting off to sleep again when he remembered. He sat up in bed, looking at Jim with bloodshot eyes. 'The Capitol. What time is it?'

It was already crowded by the time they got there, but somehow the indefatigable Connor managed to track them down. 'They stopped the Death March at dawn,' he cheerfully filled them in. 'There's going to be thousands of us here today anyhow, waiting to hear what Congress decides.'

Today, 16 July, was the last day that Congress would be in session for the year. If they adjourned without revisiting the Bonus issue, all legislation on the Bill would officially be shelved until further notice.

Alarmed by the ever increasing numbers pressing upon the Hill, the police had organised themselves into cordons. More veterans kept arriving by the minute. A huge contingent from Anacostia showed up, banging on drums to sound their advance. The crowd rushed forward, galvanised by the gusto of the newcomers as the police blew furiously on their whistles and tried to maintain order.

The Major staggered, carried forward by the momentum of the crowd. Jim grabbed hold of his arm, steadying him. Despite the balmy temperatures and the press of bodies around them, the Major was shivering. He clasped his arm protectively about his father's shoulders, buffering him from the crowd. 'We should leave,' he yelled. 'You need to see a doctor.'

The Major shook his head.

The crowd appeared to have doubled in just over an hour and was turning increasingly rebellious. There was another collective surge forward as they pressed against the cordon. For a few tense moments, it seemed as though there was a full-blown riot in the making, when a volunteer nurse grabbed a megaphone.

'Come on, boys!' she cried. 'Who's singing "America" with me?'

Connor let out a whoop. 'The Flower of Saint Theresa, we call her,' he shouted in Jim's ear. 'She had a flower shop in New York, but when those damn Wall Street bankers closed her down, she decided to dedicate her life to service instead.'

'Come on,' the Flower urged in her nurse's uniform, blond hair shining. 'Come on, boys, together – "America"!'

'You heard the lady,' the leaders of the march yelled, following her example. 'Let's not have any trouble now, not after all we've been through. Let's sing, boys, let's give Congress a show like they've never seen before.'

The crowd fell still, a great calm descending upon the Hill. 'Sing!' she urged again, and they did. All the veterans gathered there, thousands now, their voices lifting together in song.

'My country, 'tis of thee,
Sweet land of liberty,
Of thee I sing;
Land where my fathers died,

Land of the pilgrims' pride,
From ev'ry mountainside
Let freedom ring!'

The powerful beauty of the anthem, of so many voices singing in perfect unison, raised the gooseflesh on Jim's arms. Beside him, his father was mouthing the words; when he looked over at the police cordon, many of them were standing to attention as they too, sang along.

'My native country, thee,
Land of the noble free,
Thy name I love.'

The sound of close to ten thousand voices raised together in song was so profoundly affecting that orders were issued from within the Capitol – the police cordons were to be disbanded. The Bonus Army would be permitted to occupy all of the steps of the Capitol provided they left a walkway for members of Congress. Furthermore, the veterans could send a delegation to the Speaker of the House, to present their case.

The leaders huddled, putting together the delegation, with Connor immediately nominating the Major. They presented the Speaker with a petition not to adjourn Congress, but merely to recess and reconvene, so that the Bonus Bill might be reconsidered. The Speaker accepted the petition without comment.

There was nothing to do now but wait.

When he returned outside with the rest of the delegation, the Major looked even more pale than before. By sheer force of will, he'd controlled his shivering while in the meeting, but he felt cold, so cold, as if he'd been swimming in snowmelt. He sat down heavily next to Jim, avoiding his son's worried gaze.

Connor looked delightedly about him. 'Have you ever seen anything like this? What a show our boys are putting on today. I ain't much of a betting man, but something will come of this, it's gotta. Good Hope Road,' he said exultantly to Jim. 'I told you, didn't I? The road of good hope.

'Say!' he exclaimed. 'The Major all right?'

*

The resourceful Connor found a doctor nearby and they rushed the Major over. 'Bronchitis leading to pneumonia,' he pronounced. 'He fainted, you said?'

The veterans, meanwhile, continued their vigil. There were so many men amassed along Pennsylvania Avenue that finally at 10:30 p.m., an anxious White House announced that President Hoover would not after all be making the traditional trip to Capitol Hill to oversee the adjournment of Congress. Just under an hour later, at 11:26 p.m., the seventy-second Congress of the United States adjourned. Many Congressmen left stealthily through back doors and the underground passages of the Capitol to avoid encountering the men still waiting hopefully outside.

It was a while before the Bonus marchers began to realise that the Capitol lay empty. There was nobody inside; Congress had adjourned without taking any action on the Bonus Bill. A crushed stillness fell over that vast crowd. Slowly, in twos and threes, the veterans began their disappointed exodus back to the camps. Behind them, the Capitol loomed over the skyline, the dome of its cupola glittering against the inky, starless night.

TWENTY

19 July 1932

MAJOR GENERAL BUTLER GIVES FIERY ADDRESS TO BONUS ARMY; URGES THEM TO STAND THEIR GROUND

WASHINGTON, 19 JULY.

With the Anacostia River and a summer sunset for a background, Major General Smedley D. Butler, retired officer of the Marine Corps, called on the Bonus Army tonight to stand firm. Thousands of Bonus marchers remain hunkered down in the camps even after the adjournment of Congress a few days ago.

'If you want to go home and haven't the courage to stick it out here, then go on home,' Butler shouted. 'But the rest of you, hang on. As soon as you pull down your camp flags, this thing will evaporate into thin air.'

Butler, who some months ago was shut off the radio for profanity during the course of a speech, took full advantage of the fact that there were no censors here tonight. With a 'damn' or a 'hell' in every few words, he evoked rousing applause as he addressed the veterans. Blue shirtsleeves rolled up, white collar opened, and dripping with perspiration in the evening heat, Butler exhorted and berated. Men hung on to his every word, with even the camp mascot, Rooster Curtis, pausing in his pecking at the base of the podium as if to hear what the General had to say.

'It makes me so damned mad to hear some people speak of you boys as tramps. There isn't as well-behaved a group of citizens anywhere as you are. They didn't call you that in '17 and '18. I never saw such fine soldiers. I never saw such discipline.

> 'You've got a great issue. This is the greatest movement of any kind in the history of the United States. This is the greatest demonstration of Americanism this country has ever seen.'

'I'm coming to DC,' Madeleine declared. 'It's been far too long as it is, and now you say that you might be there another week or more! I'm coming, and that's all there is to it.' Her voice lowered throatily. 'I miss you.'

He rested his forehead against the wall, filled with longing.

'Are you going to say anything?'

The memory of her face swam into sharp focus. The silk of her skin against his own, that day in the water.

'Jim? Are you there?'

'Yep.'

'Well, say something!'

'It's awfully hot here,' he offered.

'James William Stonebridge!' The indignation in her voice carried clearly over the wires. 'Is it too much to ask that you say you miss me too?'

He grinned. 'I'll see you soon.'

It was now 23 July, exactly a week since the Major had collapsed on the steps of the Capitol. He'd burned with fever for days, hacking and coughing, even in his sleep. Finally, he'd broken into a sweat, rambling in delirium as he tried to throw off the covers. At one point during that night, he'd woken. He muttered something.

'What?' Jim asked, startled.

The whites of the Major's eyes showed as he cast about. 'Henry,' he mumbled.

Jim bent closer. 'Who?'

The Major burst into an agitated stream of French. Flinging the covers aside, he tried to rise. Jim held him back, but he struggled with surprising strength, the veins in his neck blue against the mottled skin as he strained. He groaned as he fell back against the pillows. Another unintelligible stream issued forth from his lips. He moaned again, and fell into a deep sleep.

That had been the turning point, after which his condition had steadily improved. The doctor pronounced his patient well on the path to recovery. Still, given his weakened condition, there was danger of a relapse. It was advisable that he rest for at least another week, he cautioned; travel was not recommended.

Jim had expected his father to chafe at this, but to his astonishment, the Major nodded resignedly. 'Connor and the boys,' he asked weakly. 'How're they holding up?'

'Holding on. Here,' Jim said, handing him the latest copy of the *BEF News*, 'thought you'd like to read this. Butler's address at Anacostia.'

'He's a good man,' the Major muttered, scanning the article. He wanted to leave right away for the Anacostia camp, and frowned when Jim said he couldn't, not yet. 'Stop playing nursemaid, boy,' he rasped irritably.

Jim stood his ground. 'I suppose this means you're getting better,' he said unperturbed. 'That's what Ellie says anyhow – that if someone ill starts to get mad, it means they're on the mend.'

The Major snorted. 'Ellie also once told me to wash my head in sage tea. It would make the hair grow back again, she promised.'

'Sage advice.' Jim grinned. 'She sent you a message, to get well soon. Suggested I get my hands on a bit of raw goose fat. You're to rub it into your chest every night, she says it will get the chills out in no time.'

The Major shuddered at the prospect, the movement bringing on a fresh bout of coughing. He leaned back against the pillows, suddenly tired.

'Stop staring like a jackass, boy,' he said hoarsely. 'It's just a damn cough.' He looked up at his son. 'I'm fine,' he said, his tone gentler. 'You've had to follow your old man for days around the Capitol as it is. I'm fine,' he repeated. 'Go on, get out there and enjoy the day. We're going to Anacostia tomorrow,' he added as Jim was at the door. '*Tomorrow*, and I'll have no arguments about that.'

'Yes, Sir, Major Sir!' Jim said, grinning as he mock saluted his father. He was shutting the door behind him when he paused. 'Wasn't too bad, you know.'

The Major looked up enquiringly.

Jim fiddled with the doorknob. 'Wasn't too bad at all, following my old man about,' he said, the words coming out in a rush.

*

'Oh, I'm right glad to see you doing better, Major!' the landlady exclaimed the following morning. 'You've been so ill.'

'It was just a cold,' the Major muttered, embarrassed by the attention.

'Yes, a cold *and* a fever *and* the chills like you would not believe,' she said. 'Be sure you bundle up now,' she fussed. 'Don't pay the sun no mind, you need to keep your chest nice and warm.'

'Yes, yes,' the Major mumbled. 'Thank you for your concern, it's very kind.' Raising his hat to her, he edged quickly out the door and stood blinking in the sunlight. 'Women!'

'Nursemaids, the lot of them.' Jim solemnly agreed.

The Major glared at him and then his lips twitched. 'You know,' he said, 'our Ellie advised me once that I should wear my socks – ones that I'd worn all day long, mind you – around my neck as I slept.' He chuckled. 'Said it would help if I felt a sore throat coming on. The socks needed to be flush against my windpipe, or else it wouldn't work.'

The unexpected and easy banter between them, coupled with the prospect of Madeleine's visit, made Jim light-hearted enough that he whistled all the way to the flats. The Major glanced at his son, amused, but made no comment.

The camp showed little evidence of attrition. The rows of ramshackle shelters still stretched in every direction. Heat rose sharply from the sun-baked flats, dust devils in the wake of the rusty, beat-up cars that sputtered in and out. A veteran wearing a pair of overalls fashioned out of an oilcloth advertisement for hot dogs was patching up his lean-to; his neighbour sat hunched over a fistful of crooked nails, patiently hammering them straight with the aid of a rock. Long lines snaked outside the makeshift post office and the green flaps of the Salvation Army tent were pinned open to reveal a lending library set up for the men. The strains of a ragtime band sounded from somewhere among the shacks. They stopped by the registration tent where the ever ebullient Connor bounded up to greet them.

'Major!' A wide grin split his face. 'Boy, am I glad to see you're doing fine.'

'It was just a cold, Connor,' the Major said, a touch of asperity in his voice. He hesitated, tapping the end of his cane on the ground. 'How are things around here? Morale?'

'Good, real good. Some days being better than others. Folks have been mighty decent about sending us supplies and stuff, but sometimes it's just bread and coffee the whole day.' A shadow crossed his face. 'Rooster Curtis is missing though. Disappeared some time yesterday and ain't nobody seen him since.'

Jim and the Major both glanced involuntarily at the mess kitchen and the large, wood-fired stove.

The Major cleared his throat. 'How long do you boys intend staying?'

'Till they pay us our bonus, I reckon,' Connor said simply. 'In a lot of ways, it's like being back in the army. The goddamned reveille in the morning, same bad chow, and ain't enough of it either. Some old timers gotten so settled in, they think they're back in uniform – keep stopping by the registration tent for passes to leave the camp and asking where they should register for furlough.' He laughed and shook his head. 'This is home now. The boys around here, we . . .' He dug his hands in his pockets, looking almost boyish as he searched for the words. 'We're buddies,' he said finally. 'We just sort of fit together, and we ain't been fitting in too much, not since we been back.'

'Yes, well, combat has a way of doing that, doesn't it,' the Major said flatly. 'Once you've served together, dodged your share of bullets – it's hard to figure out civilians after that.'

Jim glanced at his father in surprise.

'Angelo?' the Major asked. 'He still around too?'

'He sure is. Come on and I'll show you what he's been up to.' Connor led them through the camp, talking all the way.

Jim followed, listening with only half an ear. *It's hard to figure out civilians.* It had never before occurred to Jim to think of his father and the other veterans as being somehow altered by their experience into a breed apart. He looked about the camp, trying to picture it through his father's eyes. A group of veterans, in threadbare trousers and BVD undershirts, were huddled around a hand-crank gramophone, listening to 'Cohen on the Telephone'.

'Hello, I'm Cohen . . . COHEN . . . I'M COHEN . . . No, I ain't *goin'*, I'm sitting here! Hello!'

They were mouthing the words aloud, obviously knowing the entire routine by heart, but cracking up all the same over each farcical mix up.

'This is your tenant COHEN . . . YOUR TENANT COHEN . . . No, not LIEUTENANT Cohen!'

Did these men, his father, Connor, all see themselves as irrevocably changed, marked in some invisible way by the war?

The Major paused beside a sapling that someone had planted. Next to it was a sign: 'If Congress has its way, we'll get shade before we get our bonus.' Talking all the while with Connor, he brushed the dried leaves away from the sapling, crumbling them absently between his fingers before dropping them to the ground.

An image rose in Jim's mind, of his father pottering about in the apple orchard back home, happiest when he was alone with his trees. He recalled how anxious the Major became at the prospect of meeting anyone unfamiliar. That curmudgeonly reticence, he realised with a jolt, had been nowhere in evidence all the days they had been in Washington.

It all began to make sense – his father's equanimity over having to stay an extra week in Washington, his eagerness to get to the camp as soon as he was well. Jim examined the limping figure ahead, a pang of jealousy going through him at the effortlessness with which his father was conversing with Connor.

As if on cue, the Major looked back. A small, quick smile as he gestured for Jim to catch up, before turning back to his conversation. The brief flare of resentment melted away. Jim's expression softened as he took in the relaxed way his father seemed to hold himself here, the easy command of his bearing, the animation in his face was that of a man at last back among his own.

They walked to a small clearing in the middle of the camp where a coffin lay on the ground, roomy enough that a small-boned man could sit up inside. 'Tombstone Bonus' it said on the side. In smaller script, an explanation below: 'The Government says they will pay our bonus in 1945. By then, most of us will be dead.' There was a stovepipe affixed to the top of the coffin and a gaggle of tourists were lining up to deposit twenty-five cents each for the privilege of peering down at the 'entombed' doughboy.

Connor banged on the side of the coffin. 'Hey, Angelo! Look who's here to see you!'

A sepulchral voice floated towards them. 'Colonel Patton?'

'No, but I've got a Major with me,' Jim said, amused, as Angelo flung open the lid.

Connor pointed out the small patch of land off to one side, where wooden crosses had been painted white and staked into the ground. On each hung a rough hewn RIP, addressed to those congressmen especially opposed to the Bonus Bill. Knots of tourists wandered about, gawking at the names.

'There's fewer tourists now than there were in June and earlier this year,' Connor admitted. A group of veterans kitted out in the tatty remnants of army coats and boots and with stomachs sucked in as best they could, marched before another small crowd. 'The men do mock drills for a bit of cash, we've got five rodeo riders that came up with the Texas outfit . . .' Connor's voice trailed away, a sudden look of doubt upon his face.

'They're all ways to earn money, and there's no shame in that,' the Major said quietly.

'No. No, there isn't,' Connor echoed, his eyes fixed on the men. His face brightened. 'Some folks been selling subscriptions to the *BEF News*. A dollar for every twenty subscriptions, and *twenty-five thousand* copies being sold daily, can you believe it? There's other things too – a baseball match, us against Chief Glassford's police force, an "all camps" boxing exhibition – that last one netted us three thousand dollars.'

The Major nodded. He pointed with his cane towards the street signs planted in the alleyways, each named after a state. Pennsylvania for the men from Philly and the steel towns, New Jersey, Ohio, Arkansas, New York . . . He cleared his throat, tapping his cane on the ground.

'That sign over there, for Louisiana. Anyone here from the French Legion?'

'You already asked me about the French Legion, remember, Major? When you first got here.'

A group of children came rollicking around the corner. 'Hey, watch where you're going!' Connor yelled good-naturedly as they all but slammed into the three of them. The children disappeared down an alley, whooping as they chased after a ball, their little brown-haired mutt barking excitedly alongside.

*

'So who do you know from Louisiana anyway?' Jim asked as they headed back to their rooms.

The Major looked out over the river. 'Someone I knew a long while ago,' he said, his voice distant. 'It's not important.'

All at once, Jim remembered the name his father had called out in his fever. 'Who's Henry, by the way?'

The Major stumbled, righting himself with his cane. 'What did you say?'

'Henry?' Jim said doubtfully. 'It sounded like that anyway. You said the name in your sleep.'

'I don't know what you're talking about,' the Major said stonily.

They walked on in silence, the easy camaraderie between them turned cold and gelid in an instant.

'For fuck's sake!' Pulling out his pocket square, the Major pressed it against his suddenly twitching, watering eye.

TWENTY-ONE

27 July 1932

'Remarkable,' Madeleine murmured, as she walked beside Jim.

He glanced surreptitiously at her yet again, taking in the smattering of freckles across the pale skin, the upward tilt at the corners of her bow-shaped mouth. The separation of the past weeks made the magnitude of his attraction to her all the more unsettling. 'You should see the dugouts further in. Some of the men didn't bother with fixing themselves shacks, just tunnelled dugouts for themselves like they did in France.'

'No, that's not it.' Her eyes travelled over the rows of washing that hung behind the shacks. The items were unfailingly modest – a tattered towel, a shirt or two, a pair of trousers, the sun picking out patches of shine on the faded fabric, but she noticed how neatly they were hung. 'It's the men themselves.'

Madeleine had demanded to be taken to the camp as soon as she'd arrived in DC. Her mother, having fallen victim to a monstrous headache after the journey, was only too relieved to be able to draw the curtains and sleep.

She'd pressed her lips to his impetuously in the elevator of the hotel as the operator coughed into his white glove. Jim grinned, half embarrassed. 'This might not be the sort of place to do that.'

She held his face in her hands. '*Every* place is the sort of place to do this,' she declared. She'd kissed him again, and he'd felt himself hardening in response.

She'd chattered all the way to Anacostia, her face resting against his arm. When he stopped the truck, she looked about her in surprise. 'So, where's the camp?'

'Close. Come on.' He took her upstairs to their rooms, secure in the knowledge that the landlady and her brother were in their grocery store downstairs, and that the Major was already at the camp.

He held the door open and she brushed against him as she entered. She tossed her hat on the bed, hands on her hips as she looked around. 'So where . . .' she began when he pulled her towards him.

'*This* is the sort of place,' he said, and staring deep into her eyes all the while, he kissed her, pushing his tongue into her mouth with a passion so naked and heartfelt it took her breath away.

They were there a while. Keen as he was to show her the camp, Jim was content to lie there, head on her breasts, breathing in the musk of her skin. She stretched languorously beneath him. He opened his eyes, watching as she flexed her feet. It was a three-step routine, he knew. First the toes pulled in towards the rest of her body. They held for a couple of seconds before straightening to point at the ceiling. Then the outward tilt, ankles dropped low, the toes curling inward again. 'Genie shoes,' she called it, this in and out flex. Hold the genie shoes, for one beat, another, and then the toes turning outward, pulling as far as they could go.

She trailed a hand down his bare back. 'God, I missed you,' she repeated softly.

He raised himself on an elbow. Lifting a damp curl of hair away from her cheek, he tucked it behind her ear. 'Me too.'

They kissed, tenderly. She trailed her fingers lower down his back, the puppet strings inside him that she so effortlessly controlled tightening at once in response, a stiffness beginning to return. He cupped her bottom, and she giggled. Wriggling out from under him, she rolled over and got out of bed.

'The camp,' she said, sweeping back her hair. 'Come on.'

They walked the short distance there. The sun was bright over the slow-rolling river, erupting in shards of shine. She slipped her hand through his, resting her cheek now and then against his arm.

'They're close,' she had observed almost instantly of the veterans. 'They seem banded together, in a way that doesn't . . . well you don't see it too often in the outside world.'

'Look,' she said now, gesturing discreetly at a sign in the ground. 'BARBER SHOP,' it announced. In a worn but still serviceable barber's chair, complete with reclining back and slatted footrests, a man was getting a shave.

Jim shrugged. 'They're not just veterans, you know. They've also been farmers and steelworkers and barbers – so what?'

'You don't see it? You don't even see it! Jim! Look around – *there's no segregation here.*'

Jim blinked. She was right. He hadn't even noticed – the barber was black, his patron, white. He looked about him, seeing with new eyes what she'd picked up at once. The group there, over by the camp piano: mixed. The piano was being alternately pounded by a veteran with a Harlem accent, and a ginger-haired Bostonian. Three men housing together, in that shanty over there: again, of mixed colour.

What made it all the more remarkable, Jim knew, was that outside the confines of the camp, Washington was still very much a colour-conscious city. Schools, restaurants, movie theatres – all were segregated. The buses too, including those that plied between the city and the veteran camps, whites travelling separately from blacks.

Here on the Anacostia Flats however, the colour line had vanished. In this crazy-quilt shanty town, where every last piece of junk was picked over, refurbished and put to use, the colour divide was the one thing that had been cast aside as worthless. Black or white, it didn't matter here. Men eating, walking, marching together with little thought of race or background, recognising a deeper fraternity in all they had gone through together, in the scars, both exposed and hidden, that they bore.

They caught up with the Major at the registration tent. 'My dear!' he exclaimed, as Madeleine kissed him on his cheek. 'Is it possible that you grow more fetching each time this old man lays eyes on you?'

'It's the Major who grows more charming each time I lay eyes on *him*,' she countered, laughing.

'Well, well, and who is the little lady?' Connor wanted to know.

'Madeleine Scott,' she introduced herself as he vigorously pumped her hand.

'Michael Connor, and it sure is a pleasure. Say, you folks staying on for the match, I hope? You gotta see these kids. Twins, not more than seven or eight years old I reckon, but scrappy as hell. Their dad organises boxing matches between the two of them and half the camp shows up to watch. There's one right about now, you gotta come.'

'Oh, don't you worry now,' he assured Madeleine, seeing the dubious expression on her face. 'Neither of them gets hurt, well, not too badly anyhow,' he amended. Connor laughed. 'Those little devils, they've been having the time of their lives around here. We even got a school here, y'know,' he said to her with obvious pride. 'Some of the wives got together and set it up . . .' He was still talking as they headed into the camp, to pick up Angelo from his coffin.

A crowd was already milling about the boxing ring. An impromptu band, consisting of a veteran on a harmonica, and a couple more on the drums and the trumpet, were setting up. The band too, was of mixed colour, Jim noticed ruefully. Ever since Madeleine had pointed it out, he seemed to find fresh evidence of assimilation everywhere.

Connor looked hopefully around for Rooster Curtis, who it seemed was still missing. 'Wherever is that darn bird?' He pointed at the ropes. 'He's usually the first to get on there, likes to get right up close and watch. Doesn't get fazed one bit by all the yelling and cheering that goes on.' He shook his head fondly. 'Crazy old Curtis.

'That ring there was one of the first things to come up around here.' He grinned. 'The boys that built it had it up before some of them had even figured out where they were going to sleep.'

'Speaking of sleep,' Madeleine turned to Angelo. 'You don't actually *live* in the coffin, do you?'

'Nah,' Angelo scoffed. 'Got myself a pup tent.'

'That's right,' Connor said, grinning. 'Angelo here's got a tent, I got myself a chicken-wire shack. There's plenty real estate about, all rent-free. Folks can choose from mountain views,' – he gestured at the dump that loomed to the rear of the camp – 'or a plot overlooking a river bank.' Cue the sewer-filled river. 'All on swampland generously donated by our grateful Government.'

'But what about your own homes?' she pressed, bemused. 'Don't you want to get back?'

It was their turn to look surprised. 'Well, that's just it,' Connor said slowly. 'Most of us don't have homes to get back to.'

'Oh, I'm sorry,' Madeleine stammered, turning scarlet. 'How naïve of me, I meant no—'

'I take it these are our little champions?' The Major gestured at the two mop-headed boys climbing into the ring, in an attempt to change the subject.

Connor nodded, but his mind was elsewhere. 'Oh don't be sorry,' he said to Madeleine. 'No, most of us ain't got much to go back to. Before I got here, to Washington, I'd just put a down payment against a house for my wife and myself. It wasn't much of a house, and I put in all the dollars I had, but it weren't enough. When I heard about the BEF and the march to Washington, I told the banker to hang on to that house for me. I'd be returning with my bonus, I said, and he believed me.' He laughed, but for once, it sounded strained. 'I believed me too. I reckoned they'd pay our bonus for sure this time. Well, wouldn't you know it, they didn't.'

A gong sounded, and the match began.

The two boys were fast and lithe. 'Come on Nick! Get him, Joe!' the crowd yelled as they ducked and swung with gusto. Both were determined to win, both equally well matched. They landed punch after punch with their kid-sized gloves, dancing about in their laced shoes, the sweat dripping off their backs. 'Come on, boys,' Connor roared, spirits restored.

Half-time was called and the band struck up a lively tune. Connor jumped up to talk with the boys' father and Jim leaned over to Madeleine. 'You doing okay?'

She nodded, slipping her fingers into his, watching as a hat was passed around the audience, who tossed in pennies and nickels.

'How much must they make?'

'The boys?' Jim rubbed a thumb against her fingers, struck again by their slenderness. 'A dollar, maybe two. There's not much to go around here.'

'I wish there was more we could do . . .' She sat up straight and looked at him, her eyes bright. 'I know. I could dance.'

'What?'

'Dance!' she yelled in his ear. 'Up there, in the ring. A small piece; the band could play something, and we could pass a hat around.'

'Don't be silly,' he said, startled to see that she was serious.

She started to bristle. 'What's so silly about it?'

'I'm not having you go up there and dance in front of all these men.'

The gong sounded for the second half and she subsided, a mutinous cast to her lip. Jim glanced at her, figuring he ought to say something to mollify her, but she pulled her fingers from his grasp.

The two boys sparred and punched, spurred on by the encouragement of the crowd, until the bout finally ended – as all of them tended to do, Connor admitted – in a draw. The audience broke into a cacophony of clapping and cheering. Jim set his fingers to his mouth in a piercing wolf whistle. Grinning, he idly scanned the crowd, noticing anew the number of faces of colour, when one man in particular caught his eye.

He was standing next to the ring, facing them. He seemed older than most of the veterans here, about the Major's age, and dressed in a crisp white suit that was all the more striking against his dark skin. One hand rested lightly on the ropes, the other was in his pocket as he stared at their group. Jim frowned, assuming at first that he was staring at Madeleine. When he turned protectively towards her, however, he saw that she'd moved away to speak with Connor. When he looked at the stranger again, he realised it wasn't Madeleine at all, but the Major who was the focus of his attention.

The Major had seen him too. He leaned heavily on his cane as he stared at the man, face as white as a ghost.

'Madeleine here says she wants to dance,' Connor cheerfully butted in just then.

'What? No. Madeleine—'

Distracted by her wilfulness and preoccupied with dissuading her from dancing on the stage, Jim forgot about the stranger. When he did look back, the man was no longer there. His father, too, was nowhere to be seen.

TWENTY-TWO

28 July 1932

Traffic was at a standstill all along Constitution Avenue. People started to step from their vehicles, shading their eyes against the sun as they wondered about the delay. All the way up front, a line of policemen moved about the cars.

He should have stayed with his father, Jim thought again. The outing had been Madeleine's idea. They'd got into an ugly argument the previous evening at the camp. He couldn't believe she would entertain the idea of dancing up there on the stage; he was controlling and narrow-minded, she accused. The upshot of it all had been her hailing a cab and storming back to her hotel. Angrily, he'd refused to follow. Someone remembered seeing the Major leave the camp a fair while earlier and Jim had stayed on late into the night with Connor and his buddies. When he'd returned to the rooms, his father was already in bed. There were two messages from her, which he ignored.

He awoke this morning to find his father seated in the chair by the window, staring into space.

'Morning,' Jim had said, and repeated it twice before the Major heard. The Major turned towards his son and there was something about the unfocused expression and faraway eyes that was deeply troubling. It had something to do with the man by the boxing ring, Jim thought suddenly to himself, although he had nothing to base that conviction on. Just then, the telephone had started to ring downstairs. It was Madeleine again.

'You didn't call me back.'

'Wasn't anything to say.'

'Are you always this stubborn? Wait, what am I saying? You're *always* this stubborn.'

He was silent.

'Mama agrees with you, by the way. She says it would be a bad idea to dance in the camp – I believe "tasteless" was the exact word she used. Normally, I'd have pooh-poohed her, but since you feel the same way, maybe she has a point.' She waited for a response. 'Come on, stubborn, let's not argue,' she'd cajoled, laughing. 'Meet me at the hotel at eleven, I have a surprise for you,' she said, and hung up.

The Major was still in the chair, lost in his reverie. 'Come with us,' Jim had offered, but his father shook his head.

'The camp.'

When he drove his father over, they had found the camp abuzz with news. The veteran camps in downtown Washington had been notified by the police early that morning of a planned partial evacuation.

'Those camps must've gotten awful crowded, I'm guessing. The folks moved from there will be set up some place else, somewhere outside the city, they're saying,' Connor filled them in. Although the evacuation was to be a peaceful exercise, veterans from all the other camps were heading over in a show of solidarity with the evacuees.

'You both coming?'

'I will,' the Major decided. He glanced at his son, a tired spark of humour in his eyes. 'Jim here has his lady to tend to,' he said dryly.

The men had guffawed, and Jim grinned, relieved to see his father brightening after his earlier apathy.

He'd offered to drop the lot of them over at Pennsylvania Avenue. When they reached the place, they found a swarm of policemen surrounding the cordoned-off camp while a crowd milled about restlessly on the periphery.

'All going well so far?' the Major asked a veteran.

The man spat into the mud in response. The official directive had changed, he told them disgustedly. Instead of a partial evacuation, *all* the veterans in the buildings downtown were to be removed, effective immediately. To add insult to injury, they'd just been informed that the promised alternative campsite was not quite ready: they were being turned out with nowhere to go.

The Major's lips had tightened.

Connor was taken aback by the news. 'It must only be for a while, till the other place is ready,' he reasoned. 'Until then, we'll make room for every last one of them in Anacostia.'

'Maybe I should stay,' Jim said, worried in spite of himself.

The Major shook his head. 'There's nothing any of us can do about it,' he pointed out. 'It'll all be over in a couple of hours. Go. Madeleine's expecting you.'

He was still preoccupied with the evacuation as he turned into the parking lot of the hotel. She came running out of the foyer and was climbing in, almost before he'd brought the truck to a complete stop. Winding her arms about his waist, she kissed him, driving all thoughts of the camps temporarily from his mind.

'I missed you,' she said. She leaned back, equal parts amused and exasperated when he said nothing. 'Why Madeleine,' she said for him. 'I missed you too.'

'I saw you just yesterday, didn't I?'

'Oh, never mind!' She was smiling as he kissed her neck. 'Here.' She handed him a brochure.

The leaflet was an advertisement for a pleasure flight. 'See Washington as Never Before!' was written around the image of an aeroplane, its propellers in full whirl as it soared high above the Lincoln Memorial.

'Come on, it'll be fun,' she urged.

They drove over the Memorial Bridge to the far shore of the Potomac River. Hoover Washington airfield was packed. Men in suits, newspapers tucked under their arms; women herding children, the click-clacking of their heels echoing off the walls as they hurried to catch their flights to Chicago and New York; and tourists, so many, gawking at the newly constructed building and posing for pictures against the backdrop of the gleaming planes parked outside.

It ought not to have taken him aback, the press of the crowd, not after the congestion of the Anacostia camp, Jim thought to himself, but it did. A pair of pilots swaggered by to the admiring glances of the crowd. He frowned. Who knew if those jackasses could truly even fly?

'Let's forget this,' he almost said to Madeleine, his mind going back yet again to the Major, 'how about we go back downtown instead?' She was smiling up at him though, eyes so wide with excitement and anticipation that he held his tongue. Spotting a vendor selling hot dogs, he steered her over, relieved to get out of the way of the jostling throng.

A group of men sauntered up behind them. Jim listened to their chatter at first with only half an ear, then with growing incredulity. To listen to them yarn, each man was evidently a supremely accomplished pilot. Awe-inspiring were their flight records, every last one among them, a bonafide hero.

Jim looked at Madeleine in disbelief. 'Did you hear . . .?'

'Excuse me, gentlemen,' she called out, to his consternation. She waved the brochure at them. 'Would any of you be available to take us up for a spin?'

One of the pilots stepped forward. 'Any member of the Flying Bologna Club would be honoured,' he said cockily, 'but allow me to be the first to offer my services.'

Jim eyed the man with suspicion, taking in the aviator glasses tucked into the pocket of his shirt, the raffish tilt of his hat.

Madeleine cocked her head. 'The *what* club?'

'The Flying Bologna Club. Dedicated to the promotion of the inaccurate principles of flight.' He pointed solemnly to the badge on his shirt, shaped like a sausage with two wings attached. 'Don't get taken in, though, by our gas,' the pilot assured them. 'We *can* fly, you know.' He quoted them five dollars for a trip above the Lincoln Memorial, the Monument and the Potomac.

Jim nearly choked. 'It's the Depression, or haven't you heard? Fifty cents,' he countered, 'and that's only because my girl is keen.'

They settled for two fifty, not that Jim was too pleased by the price, and walked out to the Curtiss Robin. She was a trim little three-seater with a closed cockpit. Jim ran a hand over the sunset-orange body, taking in the proud jet of the wings, painted a cheerful yellow.

'Nervous?' Madeleine whispered.

'No,' he said flatly, although he was, a little. He nodded towards the pilot who was walking jauntily around his plane, checking the undercarriage. 'I should be though, what with Bologna Boy at the wheel.'

She giggled as they settled themselves into their seats.

'Have you two flown before?' the pilot called.

'We should get a move on,' Jim said tersely. He kept his face impassive as the plane taxied into position, although his stomach was starting to tie itself in knots.

Madeleine leaned into him. 'Excited?'

'Sure.'

He turned to the window, so she wouldn't see the apprehension in his eyes. The plane began to move down the runway, gathering what seemed to him an inordinate amount of speed. He shouldn't have agreed to this, definitely not with Bologna Buck at the controls. With a stomach-lurching lift, they rose into the air. A steady momentum upwards, gravity pulling his head back, when thankfully, they levelled. Jim caught his breath.

The sky stretched above them, to the side and up ahead, a canopy of blue reaching in every direction. 'Look,' Madeleine called, above the noise of the engines. Cautiously, he leaned forward to peer from the windows, eyes growing wide with wonder at the sight of the Potomac far below.

An image flashed in his mind, from years ago, of a magic carpet in one of the books back home. He remembered the illustration in precise detail. A boy, his pet monkey perched beside him. The fraying edges of the carpet that was winging them through the sky. He remembered, too, the boy lying on the rug of the library, completely absorbed in that story. Filled with yearning as he studied that magic carpet, wondering what it must feel like, to soar so far above the earth.

A great sense of disbelief, then exultation stole over Jim as he watched now from the windows of the Robin. He was *flying*. The world dropped away beneath them, the edges of maps rendered at once meaningless and obsolete.

He laughed out loud. Madeleine's hair lay wild about her shoulders as she turned to him in delight. 'Do you like it? I knew you would!'

He laughed again, kissing her fiercely on the forehead. 'The Connecticut,' he yelled, pointing at the river below. 'That time when you flew over it, did she look the same?'

It was the pilot who spotted the cavalry. 'Do you see them?' he called over his shoulder, puzzled. 'The riders?'

He flew lower, banking over the Arlington National Cemetery. A stream of horses and men galloped through the park, now hidden, now coming into view from under the trees. The smile was wiped from Jim's face as he filled with a sense of foreboding.

'Where are they headed?' Madeleine wondered.

He said nothing, watching grimly as the horses raced forward.

From this vantage point, their manes streamed about their heads like the fronds of some richly coloured, underwater fern.

The terminal was abuzz with rumours when they landed. People had seen the troops thundering over the bridge towards the Capitol. They were amassed at the Ellipse, just south of the White House, some had heard.

'We have to leave,' Jim snapped, rushing Madeleine along as she thanked their pilot for the ride.

She hurried beside him, trying to keep apace. 'Whatever is the matter with you?'

'They're going after the veteran camps downtown. The Major,' he said tightly. 'He's there.'

TWENTY-THREE

28 July 1932

Major George S. Patton cantered along Pennsylvania Avenue in full dress uniform, oblivious to the stares of passers-by as he reconnoitred the terrain. His riding boots shone as he gently pressed his spurs into the flanks of his mount. The avenue, he noted with satisfaction, was akin to a broad, flat plain; the tanks should have no difficulty in traversing it. Assuming it was executed to plan, the entire operation could be completed with minimal fuss.

A pall of tension had hung over the barracks at Fort Myer this past month. It reflected the unease rippling through official circles as the impasse with the Bonus Army had dragged on. Congress had adjourned, so why, senior officials had questioned, were the veterans still in Washington, crowding the parks and the restrooms at gas stations around the city? The Bonus Army had thousands of mouths to feed, with hardly enough to go around. Things had been kept under control thus far, but with thousands of hungry, increasingly restless men still camped around the city, officials feared that Washington was sitting on a powder keg.

Today was the culmination of weeks of preparation. For many days now, Fort Myer had been on high alert. Everyone, regardless of rank, had been restricted to the confines of the post – they could leave the Fort only with special permission, and only for short periods of time. War belts had been kept polished and ready and sabres placed within easy reach, with troops and officers alike put through anti-riot and anti-mob training.

Orders had finally been received earlier that afternoon. The 2nd Squadron of the 3rd Cavalry was to report to the Capitol at once. A band of over two hundred soldiers had pounded through Arlington National Cemetery, racing over Memorial Bridge to group on the Ellipse across from the Treasury Building. The infantry had followed suit in trucks, with an additional two hundred and fifty soldiers dispatched from nearby Fort Washington on a steamer along the Potomac. The old FT17 tanks that had last seen active duty on the battlefields of France had been pressed into service once more, loaded on to flatbed trucks that were even now trundling into the city.

Major Patton pulled on the reins as he approached Third Street Northwest, and his horse tossed its mane and whickered. He patted its neck as he observed the camp ahead, his mind running once more over the facts from the official briefing:

- Earlier that morning, the police had attempted to evacuate the premises. The proceedings, however, had quickly turned ugly;
- A riot had broken out between the veterans and the police. By the time the uprising was quelled, one veteran lay dead, and two others wounded;
- Since the police no longer had the situation under control, the administration had called on the army. They were to rid the area of the Bonus Army and defuse the threat that they posed to peacetime Washington at once.

Major Patton touched the sabre by his side, registering the familiar nub of the olive drab canvas cover, the solidity of the rawhide and hickory base. Model 1913. The sabre was one that he'd designed, the most recent one to have been issued to the US Army. 'Sabre George' they'd called him, in the barracks . . .

He patted his horse's neck again. Evidently not much had been accomplished during the scheduled evacuation of the morning – the camp still teemed with occupants. A demolition crane stood stationary to one side of the buildings, surrounded by a crowd of spectators – veterans from the other camps, people with pushcarts, women with toddlers, workers from the nearby government offices, passers-by and tourists. Despite the number of people, a quiet hung over the crowd, there was a palpable sense of tragedy, ever since the unwonted casualties of the morning.

Nobody knew quite what to make of the sudden appearance of a mounted cavalry officer. At first, they watched in silence as Major Patton turned his horse around and cantered back towards the White House. Someone, it wasn't clear whether veteran or spectator, suddenly hooted in his wake. This call was picked up by the crowd, following him all the way to the Ellipse, amplifying and changing as it passed from mouth to mouth, so that it was hard to tell if the din echoing along Pennsylvania Avenue was jeering or wild cheering.

It was almost 4 p.m. when Jim was finally able to get off Constitution Avenue and find a parking spot on one of the side streets. 'I'll walk you to your hotel,' he said tersely to Madeleine.

'It's only a few blocks from the Capitol,' she pointed out. 'We're headed in the same direction; let's collect the Major and you can both walk me over.'

A newsboy came rushing down the street, waving the evening edition. 'The army on Pennsylvania Avenue! Read all about it right here – troops on Pennsylvania Avenue!'

Jim grabbed a copy. 'TROOPS ORDERED TO OUST MARCHERS' the headline said in a bold, eight-inch typeface. They quickly read through the article.

'Dead?' Madeleine said shocked. 'They shot a *US veteran* dead?'

Jim's lips tightened. Tossing the newspaper aside, he grabbed her hand and began to run.

Despite the earlier din, the Ellipse was shrouded once again in an eerie, watchful silence. It sent a chill down Jim's spine to see the troops arrayed on the grounds. The cavalry first, steel-helmeted. Row upon row of infantry behind them, in battle gear. Massive flatbed army trucks, bringing up the rear.

'Tanks,' someone muttered, 'there's tanks in them trucks.'

A small, wire-haired dog began to bark uneasily and its owner gathered it into his arms.

Major Patton sat ramrod straight, looking over the avenue. Although the cavalry had been primed and ready for a couple of hours now, it had taken an inordinately long time for the infantry to arrive. All the requisitioned soldiers had finally been accounted for, and were at last assembled on the grounds.

He glanced towards the gleaming black staff car that stood parked to one side, still intrigued by the fact that the Chief of Army Staff, General Douglas MacArthur, had thought this operation important enough to supervise it in the field. The General had alighted from the car when it pulled up a half-hour ago, impressively arrayed in full dress uniform. Eight rows of medals shone on his chest as his aide,

Major Dwight D. Eisenhower, briefed him on the proceedings, after which final orders were issued to the officers of the cavalry, infantry and tank platoons. The troops were to use such force as was deemed necessary to accomplish the mission. Women and children found in the affected areas, however, would be accorded every consideration.

Major Patton looked at his watch. He went over the terrain yet again in his mind, visualising the broad, straight lines of the avenue all the way to the evacuation sites. A horse behind him stamped its foot, and his own mount, picking up on its tension, tossed its mane in response. He stroked the warm, muscled neck, and a movement in the crowd caught his eye. He tracked the deep russet of the young woman's hair as she hurried through the crowd. Deep auburn red, her hair, a burnished, fox colour.

For a split second, his attention wandered. He'd recently been appointed Master of the Foxhounds at his riding club. The privilege of leading the hunt had come at the hefty price of two thousand dollars, but it was worth it. *Someone* had to keep up tradition, as he'd written to his wife. Particularly in periods like these, of economic depression – the nouveau riche who appeared so sporty when times were good, scuttled for cover when they lost so much as a nickel . . .

The young lady hurried along, that mane of hair appearing and disappearing in the throng, headed in the general direction of the camps.

The camps. Major Patton frowned, his attention snapping back to the task at hand. Raking his eyes over the avenue, he took in the ever increasing numbers of onlookers pressing along the sidewalks, and looked at his watch once more.

Finally, at 4:30 p.m., the troops began their advance. The crowd had grown all day and was so dense that Jim and Madeleine were yet to reach the downtown camps.

Madeleine looked over her shoulder as the iron click of the horses' hooves sounded down the avenue. There was something at once magnificent and unsettling about the sight. Troops advancing thirty abreast, in perfect, practised synchronicity. Behind them came the trucks, followed by four companies of infantry. The soldiers marched like automatons, their faces unreadable.

'Faster,' Jim urged, pulling her along.

The troops halted a block from the camp. They shifted position so that the foot soldiers now held the point and forward flanks. A command was given. As one, bayonets were affixed to rifles and sabres drawn, a sudden armament of steel appearing smooth and glittering in the summer evening.

Unbelievably, a smattering of applause broke out among the crowd. Civilians mostly, people uncertain of what they were witnessing, thinking that they were privy to a ceremonial display of some sort, a show, perhaps, of military prowess.

'Wait . . . Jim . . .' Madeleine gasped. She tugged her hand from his grasp. 'I need . . .' She bent forward, placing her hands on her hips as she tried to catch her breath. 'I need a minute.'

'It's all rather grand, don't you think, dear?' a sweet, blue-haired old lady asked Madeleine.

'You'd best be going on home,' Jim advised tersely.

'And miss the parade?' she exclaimed indignantly.

They were close enough to the camp now that the silhouette of gaping, derelict buildings had come into view. Jim looked about him, his eyes filled with worry. Where was his father?

'We need to hurry,' he urged Madeleine. And as if to underscore his point, the trucks let down their ramps. Five tanks rolled in unison out on to the avenue, with a laboured creaking and clanking of gears, as a few yards away, two soldiers began deftly to mount a .30 calibre machine gun on to an armoured carrier. A collective gasp went through the crowd.

Jim desperately searched the sea of faces around him, looking for the Major, for Connor, for any of the men from Anacostia. He'd been foolish to drag Madeleine into this. *Why weren't these people leaving?* He could understand the veterans standing their ground, unwilling on principle to give even an inch before they absolutely had to. It was what his father would do. But these others . . . standing about like lemmings, shifting from foot to foot as they glanced uneasily at the soldiers and then at one another, wondering what to do.

Jim tried to gauge the time it would take him to work his way through the throng and get Madeleine away from here. Far too long, they'd never make it in time. He turned towards the veteran camp. The only path that made sense lay forward, to somehow skirt the camp and the police cordon that surrounded it.

He took such a firm hold of Madeleine's hand that she winced.

'Don't let go,' he instructed, and plunged forward through the crowd.

Another order was given. The soldiers pulled on their gas masks. Someone in the crowd cried out in astonishment. Jim went faster, using his shoulders to barrel forward through the crowd. *Why weren't these fools leaving?*

The tanks began to crank forward, belching thick, black exhaust. That was the catalyst the crowd needed. With cries of panic, people started to scatter. The impenetrable mass of just a moment ago collapsed into its soft-bellied centre, people running this way and that, spilling into the avenue only to be pushed back by the advancing troops, shoving and tripping over one another in a belated attempt to put as much distance between themselves and the besieged veteran camp as possible.

'Jim, slow down, I can't . . .' Madeleine panted, but Jim simply took a tighter hold of her hand.

The camp was only a few paces away now. He could make out the groups of veterans standing in the crumbling doorways and amidst the broken-down walls, their wives shading their eyes against the sun as they peered anxiously towards the avenue. The police cordon that girded the camp still held despite the press of the men jammed up against it. Here, so close to the camp, the crowd was mostly veterans. Just veterans, Jim saw, given away by their bedraggled ties and thin faces, and the way they stood their ground, defiantly facing the advancing troops head on.

Most of them had stood there all day. They'd remained peaceable as the police had begun the evacuations that morning, done no more than shouted slogans and waved their flags. Even when the scuffle had broken out inside the camp, resulting in the fatal shooting that afternoon, they had not resorted to violence. They'd stood and watched in shocked silence, deeply shaken as the body of their compatriot was removed. Quietly, they had continued their vigil.

Now, finally, they had reached breaking point, seething with rage over this last, unfathomable betrayal. The *army* had been called out against them. The army, the same one they had fought in, the army that they had burrowed in trenches for, been bullet fodder and shell bait for, that very army was now riding down its own.

'The last time I saw bayonets raised against me, I was in France!' a veteran called contemptuously to the advancing troops.

'If only we had guns,' another shouted, red-faced with anger.

'I was shooting down Boche when you was still in half pants!' yelled a third.

The troops continued their measured, purposeful advance along the avenue. A few of the veterans scrabbled in the dust for stones and pieces of brick, anything with which to arm themselves. They flung these pathetic pieces of rubble at the steadily advancing troops; these too, were disregarded. Another command was given, and the contingent halted. A deep silence pressed down on the block, so intense that Jim stopped in his tracks.

A trio of pigeons burst squawking from an oak. Automatically, he followed their flight. The birds soared higher and as they whirred upwards, something followed in their wake. A cluster of grey metal canisters, arcing gracefully and trailing plumes of gas.

Without warning, giving the unarmed veterans neither any notice nor the time to disperse, the army had unleashed tear gas upon them.

Jim yanked Madeleine towards him, shielding her head with his arms. The canisters burst open upon the sidewalks and inside the periphery of the camp, enveloping everything in a pall of dense, stinging smoke. He held her tight against his chest, as she coughed and gasped for air. Men were bent double all around them, veterans hacking and coughing, staggering about like drunkards as they reeled from the acrid gas. 'Close your eyes,' Jim shouted to Madeleine, his own throat seizing. 'Your eyes, don't let it get in your eyes.'

His throat was on fire, raw and inflamed. He started to cough, inhaling even more of the gas and worsening the burn. The masked troops were sweeping the sidewalks now, using their bayonets to urge the veterans along.

'Arm us, just arm us damn you, so we can have a fair fight!' a veteran shouted hoarsely, collapsing at the end of his challenge into a fit of laboured wheezing.

'We have to move,' Jim gasped over the smoke.

Madeleine squinted up at him, eyes streaming. 'I can't see.'

A fresh canister landed right at their feet, rocking slowly as it spewed out its load. Jim bent, and uncaring of the heat that burned through his palm, picked up the canister and flung it as hard as he could at the troops. Lifting Madeleine into his arms, he began to sprint, filled with the sole aim of getting her as far away from the soldiers, from the gas, as he could.

The police cordon had broken. He charged past it, lungs burning, and raced into the veteran camp. Images loomed from the smoke like some twisted nightmare. A man scrambling towards a jalopy, two little boys tucked like sacks of potatoes under his arms. Behind him, a woman, crying aloud in panic, carting a black cat and an armful of clothes. The high-pitched sound of a child crying. Soldiers marching methodically through the rubble, clearing out the buildings one by one.

An officer barked a command, and here now was the cavalry, galloping across the broken ground. Veterans scattered this way and that, trying desperately to shelter their families. Women shrieking, people stumbling blindly into excavation pits as they fled the flailing hooves and sabres. The muzzle of a horse, directly in his path, its rider's face distorted by the gas mask into a featureless, subhuman form. He gestured with his sabre towards Jim, a wide, sweeping motion, the metal agleam as it looped through the smoke. Jim swerved to the right and continued to run.

'The flags, not the flags!' someone shouted, but it was too late. The soldiers had begun to torch the tenements. They burned like kindling, sparks catching the flags perched proudly atop the ramshackle roofs. The Stars and Stripes, beautiful Old Glory, swallowed whole by the flames.

Jim raced on, holding Madeleine close, through the chaos of the camp, to the far perimeter and beyond, and still he ran, down one side street and yet another, to the top of a grassy bank. His legs were trembling when finally he stopped. 'Are you alright?' he rasped as he set her down.

She nodded shakily.

'Jim!' she whispered, horrified. She took his hand in hers, and it was only then that he realised he'd burned himself, handling the canister of tear gas.

He shook his head, wanting to say it was nothing, but unable to voice the words. Already sick with worry over his father, his mind flooded now with all he'd witnessed, the relentless targeting of the poor and the needy by those far more powerful than they. To his shame, there was the prick of tears behind his eyes. 'It's nothing,' he said, trying to pull his hand away. She wouldn't let go, her fingers intertwined tightly with his, her own eyes filling with tears.

They turned to look at the Capitol. Flames were leaping from the burning camps. A savage, upside-down sunset, lit from below, staining the pristine stucco of the buildings.

The forced evacuation of all the camps in downtown Washington continued through the evening, supervised by the immaculate figure of General MacArthur himself.

'The American flag means nothing to me after this!' an onlooker called in disgust.

The General turned to the soldiers nearby. 'Arrest that man if he opens his mouth again,' he ordered.

TWENTY-FOUR

Anacostia • 28 July 1932

The areas around the Capitol remained thick with troops and police even after all the camps downtown had been cleared. So many of the side streets and so much of the avenue had been cordoned off that it took Jim and Madeleine hours to return to where the truck was parked.

Getting Madeleine back to her mother at the hotel would have been a marathon undertaking that evening. 'I'm coming with you to Anacostia,' she insisted. 'I'll call Mama from there.' Jim did not argue, loath as he was to let her out of his sight and deeply anxious to get back to Anacostia and find his father.

Yet again, the 11th Street Bridge was thick with men, women and children making their way across to the Anacostia Flats. Unlike the jaunty, upbeat throngs that Jim recalled from not a month ago, however, these crowds presented a grim spectacle. The bright note of hope that had so singled out the Bonus marchers was replaced with a weary, worn-out defeat. Gone were the rough hewn 'Bonus or Bust!' banners. Gone, the hand-painted signs exhorting the country to do right by their doughboys. Even the flags, once so proudly brandished, were missing, reduced to ashes along with the rest of the downtown camps.

Men trudged with bowed heads, carting what remained of their meagre belongings as they led their families away, towards what, they no longer knew. Nobody spoke, not even the children, their tear-stained cheeks streaked with dirt and soot. They made virtually no sound as they walked, a silent, beaten-down procession retreating into the dusk.

'I wish we could offer more of them a ride,' Madeleine said tearfully. The truck was already filled with as many of the evacuees as they could fit. Two men were squeezed into the cab, one practically sitting atop the other. The bed of the truck was packed with men and their families, with more veterans cloistered silently on the running boards at either side.

'Like dogs, the Government treated us,' one of the veterans in the cab said bitterly. 'Like a dog that you feel sorry for and take in for a while. You pet it for a bit and feed it table scraps, but it just ain't prettied enough, what with its fleas and all. So you throw it out into the streets once more.'

They stopped first at the rooms where Jim and the Major were staying. The landlady was pale as she let them in. 'You poor dears,' she said, as she took in their smoky, dishevelled countenances. 'We heard about it on the radio. You poor dears,' she said again, and her lips trembled.

'Has my father been by?'

To Jim's profound relief, she nodded. 'He came in a while ago. Asked for you soon as I opened the door. Limping something bad he was and the eye . . .' She gestured at her left eye. 'Still, he insisted on leaving at once for the camp. Said to tell you if you came in that he'd be at the registration tent.'

Madeleine placed a call to her mother to assure her she was fine. The taciturn landlord stopped them as they left. 'I've got some fruit you can take with you,' he said gruffly. 'There'll be hungry children in the camp.' He loaded them up with apples, a crate of oranges and all the milk he had in the grocery downstairs.

A gibbous moon was rising as they set out once more into the night. As she took in its spare, apathetic shine, Madeleine was reminded for an instant of looking at a reflection in the Major's mirror. She raised her face to it, feeling suddenly drained, letting its cool light sift over her skin. She wondered at its beauty, at the nonchalant elegance it cast over the affairs of men and the pathos so far below. There was a sudden stinging at the back of her eyes, a lump in her throat at the unfairness, at the cruel beauty of the world.

She reached for Jim's hand, glad of the warmth of his fingers as they closed over her own.

The Major glanced anxiously again towards the entrance of the registration tent. Jim ought to have been here by now. At least there'd been no word of additional casualties since the afternoon, neither among the veterans nor the civilian onlookers.

A pall of despondency hung over the crowded tent, lines of

veterans with deadened eyes waiting quietly to be registered. A sharp taste rose in the back of the Major's throat as he took in their slack, defeated faces, his mind filling anew with images from that afternoon. His eye began to twitch again. He pressed his pocket square against it, willing himself to concentrate on the task at hand.

He continued with the registration of the family clustered about the table, having volunteered his services at the tent as the first of the evacuated veterans had begun to arrive in Anacostia. The little daughter of the family stood silently watching as he completed the forms and handed back the discharge papers to her father. The Major wished he had something to offer the child, an apple, candy, something. He smiled tentatively at her and she looked away, down at the floor, clutching a small, hand-me-down doll in her arms. Her father wearily lifted her up, and placing an arm around his wife's shoulders, led them from the tent.

The Major looked towards the entrance again, and there, at last was his jackass son, striding through the tent flaps, Madeleine following behind. A flood of relief washed over the Major, so strong that his hands started to tremble. He masked it at once, capping his pen with more force than was necessary and demanding to know just where they'd been all this while and why the devil they'd taken so long.

Connor came over to slap Jim on the shoulder. 'You come to help us out too? The Major's been signing in folks all evening.'

'Is there room for everyone? What about food?' Madeleine asked.

Connor removed his glasses and rubbed the bridge of his nose. 'We'll make do.' He gestured at the provisions they'd brought. 'That'll help, a bit.' He tried to smile, but it was a poor attempt. 'We've made do in the past, we'll do so again.'

Jim and the Major glanced at the lines of veterans and their families snaking out the tent, but said nothing in response.

On the other side of the 11th Street Bridge, General Douglas MacArthur had just called a debriefing meeting. The troops had taken a well-deserved rest after the evacuation, and he'd waited until all the horses were taken care of, and the men fed, before summoning the officers on duty.

He stood before them now and calmly revealed that the operation was not yet complete. Contrary to what they'd been led to believe, the troops would not be returning to base just yet. *All* the camps in the Washington area were to be evacuated that night, the city rid of every last one of the Bonus marchers.

They were to move across the bridge to Anacostia.

If Major Patton was surprised to hear the order, he gave no sign. In less than ten minutes, the cavalry had saddled up and was on the march again, the infantry following closely behind.

It was after 9 p.m. when they crossed. The veterans sharing a weary smoke near the stanchions froze as they saw them approach, then, galvanised into action, they flung their cigarettes to the ground and raced to the camp.

'The soldiers are coming! They're coming!'

Here too? Heads whipped around in shock, necks craning fearfully in the dark towards the direction of the bridge. A woman started to cry, quietly at first and then with increasingly hysterical sobs as her husband tried to comfort her.

'They're going to clear out Anacostia as well,' the Major said, as the realisation dawned on him. He rose to his feet, filled with a hollow, impotent anger. 'They're going to clear out all the veterans from Washington.'

'They want us out of Anacostia?' Connor asked disbelievingly. 'But . . .' He took off his hat, looking around the tent in bewilderment as he raked a hand through his thinning hair. 'Why? There's no buildings here to evacuate, there was nothing and nobody here but mud and mosquitoes when we first came. They want us gone from here too?'

Slowly, he shook his head from side to side, as if to clear it. 'Well,' he said bitterly, his face turning red, 'if it's a fight they're after, they'll get one alright. We'll fight!' Connor roared suddenly. 'We'll stay right here and fight! Let's show them some of what we showed the Boche back in '18!'

A wild cheering rose at his words and all hell broke loose, men rushing about, grabbing chairs, shovels, tent poles, whatever was at hand to use as a makeshift weapon.

The Major smacked his cane across the desk, the sound ricocheting around the tent like a pistol shot. 'You'll do no such thing,' he snapped, and they halted as one at the authority in his voice. 'Fight with what? Sticks and stones? Those soldiers were armed to the teeth this afternoon. The cavalry. The infantry. Goddamn tanks!

There are women and children here, or have you forgotten?'

The call to action was abandoned. Fury turned to resignation, then grinding defeat as it began to sink in to the men that they were licked, that they'd reached the end of the road.

The Bonus March was over.

A delegation of veterans went to where the troops had halted near the camp. They were given permission to approach a gleaming black staff car, where they asked General MacArthur for enough time so that the veterans and their families were at least able to leave with some dignity.

The General granted their request. However, the evacuees would be allowed only an hour. One hour, no more; after that, the troops would move forward.

One hour.

The camp surged to life, veterans rushing frantically about in the dark, gathering families and possessions as the troops outside continued to fall into position. Tanks were stationed at either end of the bridge to deter traffic. A massive searchlight was assembled and aimed at the camp. A cone of light began to illuminate the shacks, so bright that it blotted out the moon, bleaching wood and cardboard alike to bare bone. Slowly, it moved from left to right, capturing in its white, blinding eye a veteran trying frantically to start his ancient jalopy here, a woman there, throwing clothes and a few chipped dishes into a battered suitcase, a child clasping a toy, his eyes still heavy with sleep.

The designated hour drew to a close with the camp still far from being empty. Slowly the searchlight swung, picking out husbands panting under the weight of mattresses and box springs, shouting at their wives to go on, hurry, quick, with the children. Families too poor to own a car, and with children too young to run very far or fast were rushing towards the garbage dump behind the camp for somewhere to wait out the night.

The Major turned to Connor, Angelo and the other veterans, offering to house for the night as many as would fit in the rooms where Jim and he were staying.

Connor shook his head. 'I want to watch,' he said slowly. 'We'll leave like they want, but I'm watching every last thing that these yellow bastards do to our camp. Jim,' he asked, 'will you drive us?'

*

Jim drove through the Anacostia neighbourhood, where residents had started to gather on the sidewalks, watching with morbid fascination as the troops readied themselves. He parked on a small bluff directly overlooking the camp as the first of the infantry marched in.

The soldiers paused at the first row of shanties, flinging open doors and shattering the flimsy windows with the butts of their rifles as they made sure that they were empty. Wadding newspaper into corners, they then set the shacks alight. The flames licked tentatively at the walls, sparked along the doors, grew bolder. With a great whooshing sound, the shelters collapsed, going up like tinder.

From row to row they went, systematically razing the camp to the ground. The replica of the White House, the lean-to with the carefully painted white picket fence, countless barrels, many with mattresses still inside – all of it, up in flames. They broke the jaunty, hand-painted wooden signs and threw them on the fires. The paint blistered in the heat, the words melting, erased into nothing. Scores of American flags burned too, Old Glory, writhing in the flames.

Veterans streamed panic-stricken from the camp. Still, they weren't moving quickly enough, it seemed. The small group on the bluff watched, sick to their stomachs, as the soldiers began once more to use tear gas, flinging canisters into the fleeing crowd.

'The same officers we fought for,' Connor said, 'those very same men. It was General MacArthur, wasn't it, who directed the operations in France? How did he forget the bullets we took for him?'

'They're not all bad,' Angelo said haltingly. 'You know how it works in the army, orders come from higher up, and . . .' his voice trailed away.

Clouds of smoke began to drift up from the burning camp.

'Never did find Rooster Curtis,' Connor said abruptly. His brow furrowed slightly as he stared at the camp. 'Must have landed in someone's cooking pot.' He laughed, a short, sharp bark. 'Tough old bird, right to the very end.' He picked up his suitcase. 'I've seen enough. Jim,' he held out a hand.

Jim shook it, unwillingly. 'Where are you going to go?' he asked.

Connor shrugged, trying to force a grin. 'Something will come up. It always does.'

'If you ever find yourself headed our way—' the Major began.

'Thank you, Major, that's awful kind and I'll surely keep it in mind.' He snapped his heels together and, standing to attention, Connor saluted the Major, who returned it, leaning on his cane.

'You coming?' Connor asked Angelo.

Angelo hesitated. 'Think I'll wait a while, till morning.'

Connor was walking away, when he stopped, struck by a thought. 'Hey, Jim,' he called. 'Remember when I told you that the camp lay on Good Hope Road? I didn't tell you the whole story, y'know. It lay at the intersection of *two* roads. One is Good Hope. Want to know the name of the other? The other road . . .' The camp was burning fiercely now. The glow from the flames fell across Connor's face, revealing the rotted stumps of his teeth as he began to laugh humourlessly. 'The other road is Asylum. *Asylum*!'

Jim and the Major left for Raydon as soon as it was daybreak, after dropping Madeleine with her mother. The road was thick with veterans. When they offered rides, just as they had only two weeks earlier, few of the men seemed to know where they were headed. Some asked to be dropped off a couple of towns ahead, some for a ride as far as they themselves were going. They barely spoke, neither the men in the back, nor the two in the cab, all lost in their thoughts as they stared at the road.

The Hoover administration had severely miscalculated the reaction of the public to the rout at Anacostia. Newspapers across the nation were filled the next morning with pictures of the ravaged camp and the aftermath of the evacuation. A soldier bearing a lit torch setting a shack aflame. Families sitting shocked and destitute along the roads leading from the nation's capital, wet rags over the eyes of the children to soothe the burning from the gas. Troops, posing for a picture around a large piano, cracked nearly in half. The same camp piano around which the veterans had gathered, so filled with hope and song.

The nation erupted in outrage. *US veterans herded out of Washington, like so many unwanted strays.* Newsreels of the evacuation began to play over and over in cinemas theatres, and audiences gasped in shock.

Amidst all the furore, one story gained particular attention. The morning after the camp at Anacostia was razed, the *New York Times* reported, a group of cavalry officers was gathered on the Flats, discussing the events of the previous night. Perched on the bales of hay that had been brought in for the horses, they were drinking the coffee issued by the makeshift field mess when a sergeant from the 12th Infantry approached Major Patton, a small, concave-chested man in tow.

The veteran with him had been part of the camp, the sergeant explained. Saying he was an old friend of Major Patton's, he'd asked to see him.

'Sergeant, I do not know this man. Take him away and under no circumstances permit him to return.'

The sergeant led the veteran away. Major Patton turned to the watching officers. 'That man was my orderly during the war. When I was wounded, he dragged me into a shell hole while under fire. I got him a DSC for it. Since the war, the family has more than supported him. We've given him money. We've set him up in business. Several times. Can you imagine the headlines if the papers got wind of our meeting here this morning?' He shook his head. 'Of course, we'll take care of him anyway.'

The veteran made his way haltingly through the remains of the camp. Joe Angelo stopped for a moment, at what had been the entrance. He looked back, at the soldiers and the horses, at the blackened, still-smouldering stumps of the shacks. A few veterans were shuffling among the ruins. Hats in hand, they pleaded for permission from the soldiers to sift through the ashes and salvage what belongings they could find.

Joe Angelo looked at all of this, but with unseeing eyes. He saw instead the camp as it once had been. A chimera built from broken glass and tipped metal, aflutter with a thousand flags. Housing within its rundown heart the fragile resurgence of a dream. Granting the men who had thronged here a brief respite from the hell they found themselves in, allowing them to relive old, half-forgotten lives, when they'd still been young, when they'd still stood whole. The mess calls, the army discipline, the *brotherhood.* The magical carving out of identity, from little more than mud and the pickings from a rubbish heap.

He saw all that the camp had stood for during the few months of its existence. A haven of purpose, of self-worth reclaimed. An asylum, filled with hope.

Turning around, Angelo trudged haltingly away.

massacred the twenty or so survivors who'd landed on the [illegible] ing they had been captured by the Japanese, they were [illegible] [illegible] paddle the [illegible] where a [illegible] [illegible] opposed [illegible] small [illegible] [illegible]

[illegible] with [illegible] from part of the camp [illegible] [illegible] [illegible]

[illegible] 'I don't know the [illegible] [illegible] [illegible] [illegible]

The [illegible] the [illegible] Major Ba[illegible] to the [illegible] The [illegible] during the war. When I was [illegible] he [illegible] [illegible] [illegible] family [illegible] [illegible] [illegible] [illegible] the paper [illegible] of [illegible] [illegible] [illegible] Hong Kong [illegible] [illegible]

The [illegible] the [illegible] the [illegible] [illegible] who [illegible] [illegible] [illegible] [illegible] the [illegible] still [illegible] were [illegible] and [illegible] [illegible] [illegible] and [illegible] time they [illegible]

[illegible] looked [illegible] at him with [illegible] [illegible] the camp [illegible] had been [illegible] [illegible] [illegible] [illegible] [illegible] [illegible] [illegible] the man [illegible] [illegible] [illegible] the [illegible] [illegible] [illegible] [illegible] when the [illegible] [illegible] [illegible] [illegible] [illegible] [illegible] [illegible] [illegible] [illegible] [illegible]

He saw [illegible] stood [illegible] months of his [illegible] of [illegible] [illegible] [illegible] [illegible]

Turning [illegible] [illegible]

ARTOIS AND CHAMPAGNE

France • 1915

FROM THE JOURNAL OF

James Arthur Stonebridge

16 June 1915

I lie on my back in the mud, taking in the night sky filled with Verey lights. Pick one, make a wish upon a shooting star. I follow its trajectory: the burning fuse, the tapering light, the halo that lingers in its wake.

It fills my mind again, the feel of the knife. Yet another lesson learned, from the May offensive. The Boche have tunnelled deep into this sector. Their trenches extend hundreds of feet below ground, far below those of the Allies. It was in these tunnels that they took cover in May, waiting for the first wave of the assault to pass before emerging in a lethal ambush from behind. This time, however, the Legion is prepared. Two men from each unit were assigned an extra cache of grenades this morning, and special, long-handled knives.

Grenades lobbed down slat holes, a dexterity with the blades. The roar of the beast in my ears.

I can feel it even now, as I lie here staring at the stars, the fit of the handle. The heft and thrust of the knife, the sickening, involuntary jerk at the other end, sometimes a panicked thrashing.

My mind drifts in circles, lapping at old memories. Hurrying along the edge of the Connecticut, the sound of its full summer flow rippling through the woods. In my hand, a long stake of maple. I have just read a book, the most wonderful yarn, about a shipwreck, and a single survivor marooned upon an island. It has gripped my imagination for days as I have lain on the carpet of the library, reading. When I tell Bill about it, he comes up with the idea of harpooning our catch, just like Crusoe might have done.

I haven't thought of that boyhood afternoon in years. It comes clearly to me now, the swift, downward thrust, the frenzied thrashing at the other end of the stake as the impaled fish tried desperately to break free.

So tired. All around me are the cries of the wounded, the fizz of blood-drunk flies. All the water's gone, and most of the ammunition. There's no food. Only now do I appreciate why Gaillard urged us to fill our canteens before each of the offensives, to hoard whatever bread we could before the charge.

Water, everywhere the cry for water from the wounded.

I hear Gaillard's voice again in my head, from when we first marched here to Artois. The pride in it as he recounts the old legends.

The defence unto death at Sidi Mohamed, twenty-seven legionnaires and their lieutenant facing down a thousand.

The enemies routed at Sebastopol and Inkermann.

At Magenta.

At Solferino.

Of that fight to the finish at Camerone, of the sixty-two legionnaires who stood shoulder to shoulder against nearly two thousand Mexican troops. Brothers unto such a valiant death, that when the paltry five who remained at the end attacked with bayonets drawn, in a final, gallant charge, the Mexican commander ordered their lives spared. A battle so gloriously fought the words 'Camerone 1863' are permanently inscribed upon all the flags and banners of the Legion.

We listened enthralled. This hallowed legacy of which we are now part, a ballast, lifting us from narrow definitions of self, to greater ideals. We are warriors, we are the Legion. We stand as one against tyranny, defending justice to our last.

Will they talk of us too one day, of the legionnaires who advanced at Artois, of all those who fought in these red fields of France? They will, they must; we sang as we marched in May, deep, full-throated, all the way here.

Different, this time around. Again that heightened sense of perception, of smell, on this, our second march to the Front. The warm musk of passing cavalry stirring up older, concentering memories, of hay and hillside barns. Whereas in May we saw ourselves at the epicentre, now it all seems oddly removed. The images push up against each other, now looming close, now blurred and receding. As if the moorings are already coming undone, the fastenings loosening to earth and body so that our shadows seem to fall off kilter, a half-step to the side.

The songs come to mind again this morning though, in the forward trenches as we await the signal to advance. For an instant, they don't matter any more, the insanities of this war. We stand there, together. There is rare beauty in this moment, such rough perfection in this fellowship of tempered steel. Touched as it is by the voices of ghosts, a harsh purity, such as that of a peregrine's scream, of wintered woods, of a bobcat, muzzle bloodied, feeding in the snow.

The whistle sounds for the charge; we swarm up the ladder as one.

Here I lie now in the mud, too spent to move. I shut my eyes, tired, so tainted, wanting only to sleep, to sink far into the deep.

The Verey lights keep going up, their flares stamped upon my eyelids. Make a wish upon a shooting star. From within that centre of light, the faint silhouette of a child. Jim, in the orchard, swinging from the old oak. The sounds of a summer afternoon. The swoosh of the tyre, the giving creak of the bough. A child's innocent laughter. I reach forward, to touch the sunlight in my son's hair.

Someone is calling my name, shaking my arm, slapping my face. I open my eyes with a start.

Obadaiah.

We are the Legion, brothers to the end.

I get on my knees. We crawl forward once more.

TWENTY-FIVE

Artois • 1915

The war don't end that winter. It spill over into January, and a cold, wet spring. The rain, she set our new uniforms to leakin'. Them generals back at headquarters, they figured the old red trousers be too easy a target for snipers. Only, these new blue ones been ordered in such a hurry that the dyes still raw, leakin' every chance they get. Reckon them generals ain't spent too much time in a trench either – red or blue, it don't matter down here – take hardly a day for everyone of us to be wearin' the same brown, mud colours.

The generals be right spooked too by all the Christmas canoodlin' between us and the Boche; they given orders for us troops to move from sector to sector so we don't get none too friendly no more with the other side. Hard to believe now that Christmas even happened; ain't no tellin' which part of the Front Hans Fitschen at now. On the Kaiser's birthday, the Boche send a powerful heap of shells our way.

'Just you wait till it's *my* birthday,' Gaillard yell afterwards, shakin' his fists at their lines. 'Just you wait and see the fireworks I send over then!'

We been long enough at the Front that our rawness, it start to smooth over. There's things we done learned. When we pass through villages now, instead of chocolate or tobacco, it be tins of Vaseline we first look to buy. A slick of grease on the barrel of our rifles keep the mud from stickin'.

We know to be real careful lightin' up a cigarette, and never to be third on a match. It bring bad luck. Three soldiers light up from the same match, the man that goes third, he sniper fodder. James though, he say it ain't got nothin' to do with luck.

'When the first man lights his cigarette, it gives the sniper the range to his target. The second soldier lights up, that gives the sniper windage. The third – well, that's the shot.'

Put that way, it sure make sense. I known from the day I met him that this here Yankee, he powerful smart alright.

We know now to wear our cartridge belts to the side, so they don't press into our backs when we sleep. We wrap our canteens under our blankets so they don't freeze solid overnight, and warm the biscuit rations by the small fires we allowed to build in the dug-outs when we find dry enough wood. Them biscuits, they be hard as iron – ain't no amount of soakin' in coffee or rum that do any good, but the fire soften them somewhat, makin' them nearabout decent.

Our appetites, they fallen off from when we first signed up. We eat only half our rations now, savin' the rest, like the *anciens* been doin', for later. Still, when the Boche patrols take to hangin' baskets on our wire at night, filled with wine, and cheese and meat, we be quick to take advantage. There's notes the Boche leave with the food – these here are their daily rations, they write, why don't we desert over to their side and see for ourselves? Them baskets, they left only 'bout a quarter full by the time they reach headquarters. And when headquarters send back baskets in reply, filled with fine French charcuterie and polite notes offerin' this small bit of 'charity' to the Boche, well, what's a legionnaire to do but follow System D and help hisself?

'Charity start at home,' I point out to James.

'And fortune favours the bold,' Karan agree from where he bendin' over what left of his robe, pickin' cooties from the folds and crackin' them, one by one, between his thumbnails. There's dirt all over those hands that once been so fancy, a thick black line under each nail, same as all of us. He laugh as a thought strike him. 'You know what they should issue along with the uniforms? Mess kit – check, rifle and bayonet – check, ammunition – of course, and three live monkeys, standard issue. To help pick the cooties, *jeune legionnaire.*'

'Well, I haven't seen a single cootie around here,' James say, strokin' his beard. When we stare at him like he boo coo crazy – 'Not a single one. Nope, all the ones I've met are married, with large families.'

Them devil-spawn cooties. In our clothes, in every bit of hair they find on our bodies – heads, armpits, the beards we been growin' all winter for warmth. Gaillard show us to run a hot wire through the seams of our uniforms to kill off the nits. He tell 'bout anthills too. Soon as we find one, near the reserve trenches, we tear off our uniforms and spread shirts, jackets, all our gear over the hill. The ants, they pick off the cooties in swarms. After they done, for the next few hours at least there ain't nothin' movin' in the seams.

Come April, and we still ain't seen no real action. Just this crazy-makin' trench life, livin' with the rats, just sittin' 'bout waitin' to get picked off by sniper fire and such. We figure out ways to entertain ourselves, durin' those long, soul-kill hours between the night patrols and the shellin'. We stick a hat on top of a bayonet and pass it this way and that along the parapet, till a sniper's bullet come tearin' into it. We let the hat drop, wait awhile, and just when that sniper been congratulatin' hisself on a hit, we start bobbin' it 'bout again. Card games, always a card game goin' on somewhere. We play for tobacco, or chocolate, or drinks when we get paid. Chevalier and others collect shrapnel and pieces of exploded shells. They worry at them with pocket knives and such, makin' rings and souvenirs to send back home.

James now, he start playin' the odds. He got a natural feel for numbers, makin' out patterns where I find only mumble-jumble. Sort of like me and music, just findin' rhythm where most others don't. Them losses we suffer, all the men lost, every time we hear tell of another casualty, all of it go right into that brain of his, and what come out is numberin' odds. Say we headed back towards the reserve trenches. It being a dark night, we figurin' to take a detour – climbin' up from them zigzag trenches, to cut out over open ground. The odds of makin' it without attractin' sniper fire 'bout twenty-four to one, James tell. Same exact detour with the moon up and shinin', the odds just 'bout nine to one.

'Given that there's more chance of artillery fire gettin' us right here in the trenches—' He shrug. 'We should just make the detour whenever there's no moon, and save ourselves some bother.'

We get him to set all sorts of gamblin' odds, of being shelled on a clear day with enemy planes crisscrossin' overhead, of makin' it through a night patrol dependin' on the wind and which way the Verey lights gonna sail, and if we turn right from the wire, or left.

It been a thing for play at first, but when a raid party gotten caught in Boche crossfire, and the only one to make it back was James, the officers sit up and take notice.

How is it, Gaillard want to know, that James make it back when even the two *anciens* on the raid, with all their nerve and experience, didn't?

'The odds of survival,' James answer slowly, 'had I stayed where I was in the grass, or run straight back for the trenches, were both poor. The best bet, and most logical course of action given the direction of the Boche firing, was to run *parallel*, along their trenches till I was out of range. Once I was, I doubled back around to our lines.'

The higher-ups, they got their eye on James after that. It don't surprise none of us, and put a great big grin on my mug when Yankee James Stonebridge promoted to Legionnaire 1st Class and then once more, to corporal, right before our marchin' orders arrive for Artois.

Rumours been steady flyin' around the trenches: a grand French offensive in the works. Goin' to be a humdinger we hear, pushin' the Boche right back to Berlin. We can't hardly wait to get ourselves some real action at last, to be done with trench life for good.

It like new life been injected in us all. 'Fraid? Sure we 'fraid a little of what out there, but anythin' got to be better than these months in the trenches. Gaillard and the other *anciens* tell of past wars won by the Legion, of Sidi Mohamed, Magenta and Camerone, till we all dreamin' of open charges across No Man's Land, fightin' like real soldiers, no more of this devil-spawn diggin' and shovellin', of hidin' 'bout below the ground. We sing as we march, the whole way to Artois.

Soon as we reach, damn if we ain't handed shovels and picks once more.

James stroke his beard. 'I believe it was Gaius Julius Caesar,' he says real dry, 'who said that he won just as many battles with the shovel as with the sword.'

We *feel* the war here in Artois, more than we ever done before. It press down like the air before a thunderstorm. All across our side of the sector, soldiers busy expandin' the trenches, layin' mines and makin' parallels for the attack. We work at night, layin' duckboards and such, sometimes so close to the bobwire that if a man stretch out his arm, he could touch it with his fingers. The Boche, they know somethin' up. Their machine guns are trained on our lines, spittin' yellow fire through the nights.

Taras, one of Gaillard's *ancien* buddies, hit through the chest and jaw at a listenin' post. He taken, resistin' fierce all the way, to the medics. We hear later that he wait just long enough for his wounds to be dressed. 'You have to rest,' the doctors say to him, 'give your injuries time to mend,' but Taras, he ain't havin' none of that. He set right back out, tryin' to get back to the Legion. He don't make it far. They find him later that evenin', fallen by the roadside, dead.

'*Une bonne mort*,' is all Gaillard say when he hear.

I don't see what so good 'bout this death, what so honour filled 'bout dyin' alone in a ditch. Poor devil, to get this close to the action we been waitin' on so long, only to catch one too soon.

His dyin', it make us shovel all the harder. The sweat pour freely as we lift sandbag after sandbag over the parapets, itchin' bad to be done and for the attack to finally begin.

We ain't got long to wait. Two days later, all patrols, every trench detail, is cancelled. There's no other orders, not yet, but we know what this mean all the same.

All hell break loose in our camp, as we prepare to attack.

We shave off our winter beards, polishin' our boots and washin' the red sticky mud from skin and kit the best we can. Everythin' that ain't mission critical is removed from our packs. Men busy writin' letters home. Chevalier bent for hours now over his pile of metal scraps, finishin' a vase for his wife. A thing of wild, bayou beauty it is: birds, so many birds, carved all around, wings spread wide as they fly.

There's big lines at the depot, legionnaires pushin' and hollerin', tryin' to lay their hands on whatever extra cartridges they can. Gaillard and me, we go on a special System D mission – it take some doin', and I ain't tellin' how or where, but when we get back to the camp, there so many grenades hangin' 'bout our belts, it a wonder we even walkin' straight.

I hand James three of the extra grenades. 'Wherever did these—?' he start to ask, then thinkin' the better of it, he don't.

*

'In cold blood!' Karan be bringin' up the Lusitania again. The torpedoin' of the ship been on all our minds, ever since news came last Wednesday. He fold his robe, tuckin' the ties real careful inside as he set it by for storage. 'Civilians on board, women and children, and still they sank her. American citizens, *neutral* citizens, and the Boche just went ahead and—'

'What were passengers even doing aboard that ship in the first place?' James snap sudden like, cuttin' him short. He been real quiet all day, so this burstin' out take us by surprise. 'The German embassy took out multiple advertisements, right beside the sailing notices: "Should the Lusitania be found in disputed waters, she will be considered an enemy target." It doesn't get any clearer than that. Still they went, disregarding the warning, and booking passage for their women and children too.'

He spit out a mouthful of chaw juice. 'Folks back home have no idea, just no idea of how bad things are over here. There's a war going on, for God's sake. A *war*. And yet there they go, booking passage on a ship that's plainly doomed. They might as well,' he say tightly, 'have come picnicking in front of our wire.'

It an uncharitable thing to say, I know he just worked up over tomorrow, but I want bad to laugh out loud at that.

'You're missing the point, Stonebridge' Karan protest. 'The Boche bombed American citizens. President Wilson *has* to throw his hat into the ring after this, how can he possibly remain neutral any longer?'

The conversation go on as James rise abrupt like to his feet and stride away. I go over my stash of grenades in my mind once more, listenin' with half an ear. 'Surely now, after the Lusitania, America will come to grips at last that there's a war on.' 'Yes, one we've been fighting for months now . . .' 'This could be good for everyone in the end. American troops alongside the Allies at last – unless we wrap it all up tomorrow, that is . . .'

I'm awful restless all of a sudden. All this waitin' 'bout, with so many hours to go before tomorrow. Thinkin' to stretch my legs, I wander over to the small knoll at the edge of the camp. Who do I find there but James, silent as a statue as he stare through the trees. The belt of bobwire just 'bout visible in the distance.

He turn at my approach, frownin'. 'The trees must all be in bloom now. The orchard,' he say. 'Back home.'

Verey lights start to shoot into the dusk. They hang in the sky for a moment before sailin' lazy like on the backdraught, trailin' white light over the ground. Somethin' beautiful and at the same time, cold and horror-filled 'bout that cotton-white light.

'The Romans were right around here somewhere. Over a thousand years ago. Digging trenches, watching the dusk over these very hills.' Another small frown. 'And now . . .'

He don't finish the sentence but I know what he mean. And now here we fixin' to make the charge ourselves An odd notion, to think of those long-gone Roman soldiers. Did they stand where we are, lookin' down into the dark? Did they wonder 'bout all that gonna happen when the sun rise from behind them hills, did they have these prancin' dancin' butterflies in their bellies too?

'Those flowerin' trees you talked 'bout,' I ask, to get my mind on somethin' else. 'Apple?'

'Baldwins,' he nods. 'Pippins. Kings. Pink and white flowers, sweet-scented.'

He shift the chaw 'bout in his cheek. 'We planted a tree for Jim when he was born. Should fruit for the first time this year.'

We fall silent, lost in our own thoughts and trackin' the paths of them Verey lights.

'He's been wanting a dog. Told him when I left for Paris that we'd get him one soon as I got back. I wrote his mother today though, told her to get him one even if—' he nod towards No Man's Land. 'Regardless of what happens tomorrow.'

It's the most the Yankee ever said 'bout his boy.

'You goin' to get him that puppy yourself,' I say. 'What kind?'

'English setter. Maybe a pointer, or a coon hound. A good hunting dog.'

We stand there, side by side, watchin' them Verey lights climb. The bobwire real clear, black and grey, passin' again into shadow as them lights drift away.

'Doesn't feel right. To talk about him here.' The Yankee, he talkin' fast, urgent like, the words fallin' one over the other. He look at me in the dark. 'You asked me why I never talk about my boy. He, my wife – they're part of a different world. Untainted. The mirror still upright, whereas we—' he flip his palm over, a quick, small movement.

He don't complete his sentence, but there ain't no need. I ain't fully reckoned what a mirror got to do with anythin', but the rest of what he tryin' to say, I get. See, there two different worlds – the one we left behind, and this one, turned upside-down and insides-out by the war. Make sense, to keep the two apart. So that no matter how hard this one get, he still got the memory of the other, untouched by the killin', by the filth and devil-spawn stink, that other world, just as he left it, waitin' to welcome him back.

That why he don't talk 'bout his wife or son. *That* why he ain't said nothin' 'bout me to his wife, I figure, thinkin' back to the socks and cap he given me at Christmas. Obadaiah, you sure a ninny, thinkin' 'bout such foolish things with tomorrow's advance comin' up, but all the same, a warm feelin' spread like butter inside me. The thorn that been prickin' these few months, the notion that our friendship, it just don't matter that much to Yankee James, that thorn, it just 'bout fold up and melt away.

'He's a good kid,' James say, his voice gone all quiet once more.

Them Verey lights keep goin' up, their glow on the trees.

'My father fought in the Civil War. Do you know what those veterans would ask each other when they met?' He continue without waitin' for an answer. '"Where'd you lose your grin?" That's what he told me they'd ask, the first thing they wanted to know – "Which battle did you lose your grin in?"'

A thought strike me, and soon as it come, it feel so right, I wonder why it ain't occurred to me before. I pull the gris-gris from my pocket. 'Here.'

He look surprised.

'Go on,' I say, 'take it.'

He open his mouth to protest but I cut him off. 'Ain't given you nothin' for Christmas,' I point out.

'Don't be a damn fool,' he say, frownin'. 'It's your precious magic voodoo mumbo-jumbo charm. I can't take it.'

'Sure you can – it a gift. And it called a gris-gris.'

'Don't be a fool.' He shake his head. 'I don't even believe in these things.'

'Well, I do. This here a powerful good luck gris-gris. For your boy's sake,' I say. 'Take it.'

He do then, reluctant like.

'Keep it on you when we head out.' He nod, head bent over the gris-gris, turnin' it over gently in his fingers.

'It got powerful juju,' I say again. 'Ain't nothin' too bad goin' to happen to you tomorrow, not so long as that gris-gris on you.'

James look up, with a sudden, shy sort of smile. It make him look young. 'I suppose we'd best stay close during the charge, then,' he say.

Talk start to wind down, until there silence through the camp. Gaillard tell us *jeune* chickens to rest up, get as much sleep as we can, that rooster goin' to call for us real early tomorrow. I try, but keep wakin' through the short night. For once, we ain't none of us complainin' when it come time to rise.

We all of us wired and jumpy, even the officers. They carry their watches in their hands, lookin' at them, then over at No Man's Land. They in full dress uniform. Medals won in wars over the past twenty years or more sit all polished and cocky on their chests. Most don't even carry no bayonets, just a swagger stick in their hands. They check their watches over and over, gloves shiny white as they tap them against their palms.

Dawn break with a crash of guns. Our artillery been lined up to give the enemy lines a poundin', softenin' them up for our charge. Shell after shell; sound buildin', then foldin' over itself like the music-filled pleatin' on a squeezebox. The tree line come into view with the first light of the mornin'. Then it gone, vanished into smoke. Sparks shoot from the branches as they fall. Three hours, our artillery keep it up. We can't see nothin' of the Boche lines no more, nothin' but fire and explodin' earth. At 10 a.m. sharp, we get our signal.

'Avancez!' the officers roar.

Four thousand men answer. *'Vive La Legion!'* We push forward, first the fourth line, now the third and now, the second line of the advance trenches. Wait, wait for the whistle. My breathin' sharp and shallow, the ground, it as if she buckin' and movin' from the force of them guns. Now the first line of legionnaires go out on to the battlefield. *'La Legion! La Legion!'* A shinin' line of bayonets through the dust and smoke. Then they and the men holdin' them are gone.

En avancez! Another shinin' line take the place of the fallen, pourin' out over the top.

Forward once more, this time to the front trenches. Our artillery still at it, the sound hammer at my bones. The ladders be covered in slicks of mud – red, wet. Hurry Obadaiah, don't you fall now and make no fool of yourself. James just ahead of me. He turn, search somewhere to the back and above our heads with a strange sort of look, then we racin' forward, up over the ladder, chargin' across No Man's Land.

No time to think, no time to be 'fraid, our legs goin' like pistons. *En avancez, mes enfants!* Goin' so fast, my boots ain't hardly even touchin' the ground. We shoutin' and yellin', what, I ain't got no idea, the shells so loud I can't hardly hear myself.

There's singin', swinging sounds I start to make out, shinin', whinin' sounds, and I realise they bullets. I'm flyin' through them, right past, and there, ahead, the roll of bobwire, when a shell burst right by me. A wave of heat, and I'm lifted clean off the earth.

I'm flyin'.

Everythin' go real quiet. I wonder if I'm dead. I can see smoke, so thick it like the mornin' sky gone dark. There, and *there*, a bunch of coats, the blue coats of the Legion, floatin' through the air like wings . . .

I land hard on my side and lie winded. The thin echo of metal in my ears.

I stumble forward once more. A legionnaire, what left of him, is gaspin' for air. I'm afeared as I look at his face, but even under the dirt and blood, I can make out enough to tell that this man a stranger. A sharp slide of relief in my belly. I stick his bayonet blade down into the mud, the signal for the medics that a wounded man lyin' here. Ain't much more I can do for him.

Where James? Gaillard, Karan, the others?

I go faster, and now I'm runnin' again, pushin' forward. Men fallin' all around me. So many, droppin' to the ground together, all at once, that I think the officers given an order for us to get down and take cover. I start to slow but then I look closer and see them men, they dead.

Still the whine of bullets, tearin' through bodies like paper. Bullets, and shells, still them shells, and it only now, when I turn a ear to their song, that I realise. Those shells tearin' into us, those shells are ours. They *ours*.

I 'member the look on James' face just as we gotten up the ladder, that disbelievin', anger-filled look. He done realised back there, just like I'm doin now – *our damn artillery got their range all wrong*. Along with poundin' the Boche trenches, they tearin' up No Man's Land, and us, their own soldiers, advancin' through it.

It set my blood to boilin' and make me want to laugh my guts out at the same time, but I ain't doin' either 'cause I'm still runnin', keepin' on chargin' and I'm past the wire. Sandbags through the smoke, the same sort of parapets on which them Christmas trees stood shinin' only a few months ago. Christmas trees, lit up with gold, and I'm rollin' over the sandbags, slidin' down the rubble. I'm inside the first of the Boche trenches.

The Legion's charge been so fierce, we taken ten kilometres of ground that day. Ten kilometres! Only, the generals back in the command offices never expected no such advance. One kilometre, maybe two, but ten? The reserve troops needed to hold the line we just broken through are delayed. We got no choice but to fall back, a killin' rage in our hearts as we ordered to give up all but four kilometres of this hard-won, blood-fought ground.

Dead and wounded everywhere. Of the four thousand who gone in this mornin', not even half have made it back. Two to one odds, and James and I, we been among the lucky ones: ain't one bullet that touched us.

Chevalier, we learn, has been killed.

Blue coats risin' through shell smoke, like wings.

My hands shakin' as I take a cigarette from the pack that James pass around.

I think I understand now, what Gaillard say 'bout Taras dyin'. '*Une bonne mort.*'

It *was* a good death. I figure it ain't where Taras died that been important, whether in a ditch by the road or here on the wire, what count is *how* he died. The same way that our dead gone today: facin' the enemy full on, set on not lettin' their buddies, their brother legionnaires down.

My hands – why they shake so bad? I got to try quite a few times before I can light up that cigarette. My skin feel like it don't sit quite right on me, the world ain't spinnin' the same.

James nod towards No Man's Land. 'They may as well,' he say dazed like, 'have come picnicking by our wire.'

He talkin' of them Lusitania passengers, of the comment he make last night, of folks back home havin' no idea of what it like over here.

A picture jump sudden like into my head, of little old ladies in their Sunday best, shakin' out red and white picnic cloths. 'Could y'all be a dear and pass the salt,' I say unsteadily, tryin' to make a jest.

His mouth twitch. 'Picnicking by our wire,' he repeat. It ain't funny, but we start to laugh all the same, laughin' so hard, there tears in our eyes.

We in reserve for a month, waitin' for new troops to take the place of those we lost. Us *jeunes*, we drink long and hard alongside Gaillard and the *anciens*. Turns out they don't treat us like *jeunes* no more. As if we seen enough, done enough, proven ourselves in this May offensive. We adjust to this new status, makin' believe that in those two-to-one odds we just gone and beaten, there be some hidden purpose, some higher meanin' around our makin' it through. We speak little of what we seen out there, of all that we done, of the dead who be patrollin' our dreams.

Come June, we headed once more for the Front. The banner of the Legion fly high above fields covered in wildflowers. Summer time in the trees, thick and green. Long lines of infantry and cavalry passin' in their shade, all headin' the same way. Allied troops everywhere. James point out a Belgian battery with English harness and Canadian mounts. I ain't no horseman, but even I can see how beautiful they are, them horses, their coats chestnut-coloured in the sun. James stop to rub their noses. They prick their ears, as if listenin' to our songs.

The mornin' of the attack heavy with summer heat and waitin'. The horses flick their tails at the flies worryin' their hides. Although I just went, I want bad to take a piss again. I stare at James' back, try and get my mind someplace else. There's sweat stains on the square of white cloth on the back of his shirt. Hopefully we cut those squares large enough. We each got one, stitched on to our shirts, so our artillery can tell us apart from the Boche. There's observers too this time, stationed on rooftops, so they can signal our advance and positions to the batteries.

Lord, but I want bad to piss. When's the damn whistle goin' to sound anyway? I bunch up a fist, practise my upper jab just for somethin' to do. I catch Gaillard's eye and he wink, givin' me a thumbs-up. He—

The whistle sound, on the dot. Again the mad rush up the ladders. Sprint-*drop*-sprint, run like madmen across No Man's Land. The noon sun on high; there ain't a single shadow of our charge.

Once again, the attack don't go to plan. Always room for fuck-ups at the Front. The observers, they been among the first to be killed. Those white squares of cloth ain't done much – once again, our 75s torn up their own.

Again, the generals gone and misjudged our advance. Come dusk, we holdin' on to Hill 119, waitin' desperately for back-up that ain't nowhere in sight.

Relief troops finally come the followin' night. Somehow we crawl back to our lines. When they take the roll call that night, only one in five men answer. Name after name called with nobody to claim them, only '*mort*', 'dead', left to be written beside. James, he got thrown into a trench. Banged up his shoulder, but the medic set it right. His left eye troublin' him ever since the fall. He don't say nothin', but I see the way he keep blinkin' to clear it, pressin' a palm against it to stop its waterin'. We each been wounded this time around – him hit through the arm, me along the side where a German bayonet gone through. Both lucky again – they only flesh wounds.

'*Je meurs content puisque nous sommes victorieux. Vive La France.*' The medics find this note on a young officer. He dipped a piece of shrapnel in his own blood, for pen and ink. 'I can now die happy as we are victorious.'

We victorious, the generals declare. We won. If victory be this, these few metres of land, then we won.

I want bad to smash up somethin', to bust my fists to the bone. This time, I known better than back in May. I know that after the shakes stop, after we take count of ourselves, we goin' to find that we left parts of ourselves out there in the mud. Ain't nothin' you could see, ain't nothin' to gather up and toss into the graves, but there a dirge in my head all the same.

'Une bonne mort.'

I understand fully now what Gaillard been tryin' to say. Out here, on these killin' fields, death is good, it be the only good. What left of the livin', it ain't fit to be called livin' at all.

A boxin' ring keep goin' in and outta my thoughts, the twisted rope, the pink canopy with electric lights. I don't pay it no mind at first, but suddenly I think of the Champ. I 'member the way Jack Johnson looked at the Velodrome last year, standin' in that ring. The stillness in him after he won, the dead emptiness in his eyes as if there weren't no value in the winnin', as if there weren't nothin' of worth left in all the world.

I think of him, of those flat, tired eyes, filled with all the sadness a man can hold. I think of all we seen, all we done here today, and I want to bury my head in my hands.

A dirge keep playin' in my head, a long, empty, mournin'-dove call.

A week later, what left of the regiment sent into battle again, defendin' our line against a Boche counter-offensive. We shelter behind a parapet of corpses. This time, my hands ain't got the shakes at all.

Them holes we hide inside, they slowly bein' filled, with cold, dark glass.

Groups of Boche prisoners taken through our lines. Christmas long forgotten as we spit and cuss at them. The Boche officer walkin' at the head of one of the groups, it as if he can't hear us none at all. Straight he walk, real tall. Gaillard step up to him, get real close, up in his face. Pullin' out his knife, he hold it to the Boche's stomach. We all fallen silent, watchin'. A cut downwards, and he snip off the buttons on the man's trousers. The officer grab at his pants, strug-glin' to hold them up in front of his men. We start to laugh. That Boche, he look at Gaillard, look at us, straight in the eyes. Holdin' up his pants at the waist in one hand, he salute us all. He walk past, best he can, in the sudden silence that follow.

*

Come 4 July, they give the Americans in the Legion a special forty-eight-hour furlough. We leave at once for Paris. I don't 'member too much of it, 'cept I drank so much, had it not been for James, no way I would have made it back to the Legion in time. I suppose I also gone ruttin' in places I shouldn't have, but all of the itchin' and leakin' that followed, it weren't too much worse than the cooties, anyhow.

TWENTY-SIX

The observation balloon drift far below and to the right. From where we standin', on the peak of the Ballon de Servance, it look like a slow, yellow, second sun over the Front.

'That's Mont Blanc.' James point to the huge mountain to the south. 'And those, the ranges of the Jura.' He turn east, pointin' out the Jungfrau, Wetterhorn and other names I ain't never heard of before, the snow-topped mountains of the Alps.

Just 'bout 4 a.m. when we headed out this mornin'. 'Whose damn fool idea was this anyway,' I mutter, thinkin' to get a rise out of James, but he turned awful quiet since Artois and don't seem to notice. He ain't said much on the hike up here either, eighteen kilometres with sacks and full gear.

It only now that he startin' to talk, as he look around at them mountains. Sure pretty up here. Everythin' feel real far, the war, the Front. Men are takin' off what gear they can and fallin' into the sun-warmed grass. A sharp drop to our right, down into a dark green valley and then the itty-bitty villages and sun-filled plains of the Alsace. A ribbon of a river, catchin' the sun as it flow. I take a deep, long breath, takin' in the fresh mountain air. Ain't no death stink here, just the smell of pine and mountain flowers.

Church bells start to ring somewhere, the air so clear, we hear them all the way up here.

James turn his head, listenin'. 'The bells here have names,' he say.

Gaillard stir from where he lyin' flat in the grass. 'Must have been ringing in Rodern too. They were standing right by the church, I heard.'

Far as we are from the Front, ain't no gettin' away from the war. It was one of the locals in Rodern, we heard tell. A company of legionnaires billeted there, and in the middle of a roll call, he signal to the Boche across the hill. Five lost, includin' the lieutenant; Ed Bouligny, though, he make it just fine, with only a hole in his coat.

'I don't know how to compute the odds of that,' James say quietly. He spread his hands. 'Neither the odds of the shelling – the serendipity of their position, the perfect calibration of the shells – nor of Bouligny's survival.'

The observation balloon sail slowly over the lines far below. A fat, yellow-silk sun, mockin' the stillness of the day.

Over a month we been in this sector, resting up after Artois in these quiet mountain parts. Ain't nothin' much to do here but a bit of drillin' in the mornin', and a march now and again to dig second line trenches – always the devil-spawn diggin' – nearer to the Front. There's games of Bridge and Manille in the square; we gather at the Cheval Blanc in the afternoons, takin' in the cool, clean air. James' eye, it still botherin' him. He don't say nothin', but I seen how he press a pocket square to it to stay the waterin'. Hardly says two words to no one, but least he startin' to write in that notebook of his again.

I come across a church organ once, on one of my wanderings through the village. It sittin' there by itself in that old, quiet church. It look so lonesome that I walk over and press a key, another, pleasurin' in the clear sound of the chords. I ain't thinkin' to do it, but I find myself sittin' down and startin' to play. I ain't played no hymn for many years, but this the music that come now to my fingers. A short piece, one I 'member from way back, when Pappy been takin' me, my hand in his, to church. The notes of that hymn, they fall from my fingers, floatin' through the empty pews, hangin' in the light from the stained-glass windows, red and green.

I sit quiet after I'm done, just starin' at the keys. When I look up, I see an old man, patiently waitin'. 'Can you play for us?' he ask. He turn his beat-up hat in his hands. The organ player, he at the Front, he explain, and it been a long time since the townsfolk have had a church service.

I play that Sunday, for him and his wife, and their three poilu boys fightin' in the war. For their neighbour, a sweet-faced young widow, shadows under her eyes. For the old man we seen pacin' 'bout his tiny garden. He pace all day, every day, from when reveille sounds till after the stars are out, anxious for news of his son, missin' since Champagne. For Madame Thibault from the Cheval Blanc. Her face gone bright red, same as when as she dry cloth labels on the counter of her bar. The address on the labels written real careful in capital letters; they meant for the packages she send her nineteen-year-old grandson. He lyin' in a hospital across the border, both eyes gone, but he alive. As she prepare each parcel, Madame Thibault go bright red from holdin' in her tears – how can she cry, when she luckier than so many others in the village?

I play for her, for all of them. Legionnaires start to wander in, drawn by the music. James, Gaillard, Karan. They sit off to the sides and at the back, starin' at the ceilin' or at the floor.

I play like I never played before, not even needin' to look at the sheet music. The notes flow like water from my fingers, washin' away, for a short while, the taint. Faces start to appear in the shadows. James and the others, I know they see them too. Ghost shapes in the walls, fillin' the pews. All those we lost, them that walk among us still, callin' out in our dreams. The music, bringing them back. I play on, the notes risin' and fallin', risin' then fallin', settlin' around our shoulders like an absolution.

The locals, they leave after the service, but we stay on.

'They were in a street beside the church.' Karan's face hard to see, part in shadow, part in light. 'Standing right beside the *church*, when they got it.' He talkin' 'bout the shellin' in Rodern.

His voice real flat, like he don't care one way or another. '*Got Mitt Uns.* God's With Us, isn't that what the Boche say?'

James stirs. 'The church bells here have names,' he say again. 'Marie Rosalie. Julienne Marguerite Marie. Marie Therese Josephine.'

'There's a story told in India.' The same flat tone to Karan's voice. 'An ancient story, dating back two thousand years, maybe more. There was a great war that was fought. A feud within the ruling family, cousins arrayed on either side. When Arjun the warrior prince saw his maternal uncles, a grandfather, his old teachers, the boys he had grown up with as brothers, lined up on the other side of the battlefield, he was overcome by grief. "How can I lift a finger against my own blood?" he asked. "Would this not be the greatest sin?"

'"It is your destiny as a warrior to fight, Arjun," Lord Krishna, the blue god, counselled. "To retreat from the battlefield would be cowardice, a mark of impotence that will tarnish your name for all time."

'"Better that than to spill the blood of a kinsman," Arjun replied.

He laid down his bow. "Better to live the rest of my life a coward than to stain these hands with the blood of my teachers."

'"Why do you fear?" Krishna said then. "The soul is indestructible. The body is born, it dies. It manifests, it is destroyed. What you kill is only the husk – the seed lives for ever. The wise mourn neither the living nor the dead. It is your religious duty to fight. Fight for the *principle* behind the war, without thought of personal victory or defeat. Fight in my name. By doing so, you could never incur sin."'

Karan smile tightly. 'In other words, if you fight in the name of God, in the name of good, then go right ahead. Fire at will because it isn't a sin. But what if *both* sides believe that God is with them?' His voice rise, echoing through the church. 'What then is the *point* to all of this, and on whose bloody side is God anyway?'

I'm still tryin' to work my way through all what he said when Gaillard, who sittin' by hisself, start to speak.

'I heard about this attack once,' he tell, 'from the colonial troops. They had been stationed in a village when the unit came under a heavy bombardment. *Salaud* Boche, they destroy the place, all the buildings torn down, the whole village turned into stone and dust. When the troops finally crawl out of the cellars, they see this one house that has taken a direct hit. Nothing of it left standing, not the roofs, not the door, nothing at all, except for a single wall. They go closer, and now they see that the wall, that one wall that has been left standing, it's got a crucifix hanging on it.

'One of the men says all excited to the group, "Do you see? Do you *see*? Why was this wall saved? Of everything else, why this particular wall? It's a sign, I tell you, a sign from God himself."

'He hurries over, to take a closer look at the crucifix; just as he gets there, the wall collapses right on top of him.

'God,' Gaillard say slowly, 'has nothing to do with this madness.'

He shake hisself, like a dog caught in the rain. 'Ça suffit!' Enough of all this, he exclaim. He crack his knuckles. 'Do you,' he ask me, 'know how to play "Alouette"?'

I surely do.

'Say James,' I call, after I'm done. 'You got any requests?'

He look startled. 'No.'

'Course he was goin' to say that. 'Okay,' I reply, 'how 'bout this?' and launch into Yankee Doodle.

It a right rousin' tune I knock out, thumpin' the keys, singin' aloud, and in spite of hisself, the Yankee, he start to crack a smile. I keep right on playin', faster and faster, teasin' and pullin' at the chords till those keys, they damn near start to smoke. James, he start to smile wider.

'Chorus!!' I call, and he start to sing along.

Now everybody start to request songs. I play them all, and some more, mixin' in some right hot jazz. More and more of our boys stop by the church, and before you know it, *laissez le bon temps rouler*, we havin' a powerful swingin' time. Let the good times roll, in the name of those lost at Rodern, for all those who are gone. *Laissez le bon temps rouler*, for we been to hell and back and surely headed there again soon, but tonight we together. Tonight we brothers, tonight there's song. We sing the 'Marseillaise', we roar along to repeatings of 'Alouette', the prayer candles all lit up, holdin' the darkness away.

When we finally get to our billets, I fall asleep nearabout at once. I dream of a lark, caught in bobwire. *Alouette, gentile alouette*, lark, gentle lark, just like in the song, but her body broken, wings all tore up. How she struggle to be free, singin' all the while.

We still in Alsace through the end of August, right into September. On 13 September 1915, we line up with the other regiments to be reviewed by the President de la Republique hisself. 'This a right big deal, I hear,' I tell James out of the corner of my mouth as we stand to attention. 'This battle flag they handin' out to the Legion, it real prized.'

'There's too many of us in one spot,' he mutter, eyes goin' first to the hillsides, then the open ground, and back again, as if he tryin' to map out every bit of cover. The left eye, it startin' to fill with water again.

'Yes, but we got good odds, don't we? We well behind the Front, beyond the range of them Boche batteries . . .'

The talk of odds, it work. He hesitate, then nod slightly.

It sure a fine evenin'. Mont Blanc in the distance, and the trees just startin' to colour. The blare of bugles pierce the air. Our commandant, he step forward to receive the battle flag. Somethin' 'bout Gaillard's expression catch my attention – such pride and seriousness in his eyes. I glance 'bout, and now I see the same look on

Karan's face, on James' . . . on mine too, I realise. The bugles blare again, raisin' the gooseflesh on my arms.

We watch in silence as our new flag run up the flagpole. The Croix de Guerre been added to our colours – the whole battalion being decorated today, on account of the way we fought in the Artois offensives. Our old motto, *'Valeur et Discipline'* been replaced. *'Honneur et Fidélité'*, our flag now say as it wave proud above our heads.

'It is written now on our flag itself – we are the Legion of the Honourable,' Gaillard mutter. He got tears in his eyes.

I damn near start to choke up myself. We are the Legion. For the first time in my life, I feel like I'm part of somethin', somethin' bigger than any of us alone. We are the Legion. We brothers, tighter than kin. Through thick and thin, brothers through blood spill.

The clap of our hands on our weapons like a thunderclap through the pines. Twenty thousand rifles fly up together as we present arms as one.

Soon after, we ordered back to the Front. The locals see us off, placin' gifts – a couple of boiled eggs, a pouch of tobacco, a ripe orange – into our musettes. Madame Thibault, her face go bright red as she pat our cheeks and say goodbye, tryin' her best not to cry. She and her girls, they gone and picked bunches of flowers that they place in the muzzles of our rifles. It hang over our column, a smell of roses, as we march slowly away.

We discuss the new flag as we go. Which be more important – valour or discipline? Which be more prized – honour or fidelity?

'Valour,' I say. 'Take the Champ. He ain't always that disciplined, what with his hard drinkin', hard partyin' ways, but he got real heart and that what been gettin' him wins all these years.'

'Fidelity,' Gaillard insist. 'Loyalty to the flag, fidelity to the Legion always, *Legio Patria Nostra,* the Legion is our Fatherland.'

'Honour,' James say. He adjust the strap of his rifle and the white rose in the muzzle fall on to the road. 'Honour,' he repeat as he bend to pick it up. Carefully dustin' off the rose, he place it in between the pages of his notebook.

'When a man lives by a code of honour, everything else follows as a matter of course. Fidelity, valour *and* discipline.'

We march on as the first stars come out. 'There's another story,'

Karan say slowly. 'About honour. From that same war. Arjun the warrior prince? My namesake, Karan, was his bastard half-brother. Born to their mother when she was yet an unmarried princess, he was secreted away at once. A lowly charioteer and his wife found the baby, and raised him as their son. Karan grew up outside the golden walls of the palace, without any of the trappings of wealth or privilege that were his birthright. All the same, even with the odds stacked against him, Karan became a warrior of great prowess, some say the greatest of all the stalwarts arrayed on the battlefield that day.

'Constantly ridiculed for his humble birth, Karan was never permitted to participate in the royal contests, where prince was pitted against prince in displays of strength and mastery. Arjun, it was always Arjun who won, while Karan watched from the sidelines.

'The one prince to show him any kindness was Duryodhan, Arjun's cousin. Duryodhan extended a hand of friendship to Karan, and in return he had the latter's unstinting loyalty. The men grew close. When Duryodhan appointed Karan the ruler of a minor principality, Karan ruled with a firm but just hand. A charioteer's son! It was as if, people remarked in astonishment, he had been born to the throne.

'When the threat of war first arose, Duryodhan and his kin were allied on one side, Arjun and his brothers on the other. Lord Krishna, the blue god, went to see Karan and revealed to him at last the circumstances of his birth.

'Were he, Karan, to align himself with Duryodhan, he would be fighting his own blood. Also, surely he could see that "Dharma", his moral calling, lay on the side of good, of Arjun and his brothers?

'"I know full well that just cause lies with the other side," a shaken Karan told Krishna. He knew too, that it was they who would emerge victorious. How could they not, when God Himself was with them?

'Karan smiled, and it was a smile filled with sadness. "All the same," he said, "my Dharma, my loyalty, lies first and foremost with my friend." He had given him his word and no matter how hopeless their cause, now that the chips had fallen, he would stand beside Duryodhan and fight to the very last.

'"Come with me," Krishna urged, "and meet with your brothers. They will be ecstatic to learn the truth. What's more, as the oldest brother, it is *you* who will have first claim to the entire kingdom, once the war is won. The entire land, the richest kingdom on earth will be yours."

'Karan shook his head. What good riches or fame, or the largest kingdom on earth, he asked Krishna, if a man had no honour? What good were any of these if he turned his back on his friend? No. He would do the honourable thing. He would stand with Duryodhan.'

'*Pour l'honneur*!' Gaillard roar at the end of the story, punchin' the air with his fist. '*Vive La Legion d'Honneur*!'

We take up the cry. '*La Legion*! *La Legion*!', it echo through the hills.

TWENTY-SEVEN

Bois Sabot • September 1915

We step off the 40x8 into a cloud of soot. The sun still some time from risin', but already in every direction, the chug and toot of trains. Freight 40x8s like ours, the carriages marked '*40 Hommes, 8 Cheval*', forty men or eight horses, into which naturally we been stuffed fifty or more to a carriage.

'I suppose we ought to be thankful,' James say, 'that some jackass clerk back there didn't think the "or" actually meant "plus" and have horses loaded into the carriages too.'

So many trains – the exhaust from their engines done turned the platform black. Little *Décauvilles*, requisitioned passenger trains, big ones and smaller locals, all carryin' men, cannon and materials on them newly extended railway lines.

'*Allez, allez*! *Grouillez-vous*!' the guides shout, movin' us along. 'The trucks will be here at 6 a.m.!'

James look at me. We both thinkin' the same thing: they sent the slaughtermobiles.

The Allies been gearin' up for one of the biggest offensives yet. We know we headed for some real hot water alright, 'specially from the long line of Fiats, Whites, Saurers and big grey Renaults rollin' into the yard as we wait. We been long enough at the Front to know that anytime they send *les autos* for transport, we bound for some special kind of hell. Not so much automobiles as slaughtermobiles is what James say they are.

There's all sorts of mutterings 'bout *les maudit autos* as we get in the cars, company by company.

The Fiat speed over the newly tarred military road – forty feet wide, smooth and straight as an arrow – aimin' to get to camp before daylight. More aeroplanes be flyin' over the lines these days. Both friendly and enemy planes, goin' this way and that all day long even with the anti-aircraft guns firin' away and the dogfights that end with one or the other plane fallin' smokin' from the sky. Movement of men and materials be done before sunrise and after sundown now, with troops told to lay real low and outta sight durin' the day.

From every station along the line, regiments be advancin' eastward, headed for this part of the Front. Actives, reserves and territorials, line infantry, hussars, dragoons and Zouaves. Mounted light infantry, other cavalry divisions, Senegalese and Algerian troops, Alpine and foot *chasseurs*, heavy and light artillery – every single branch of the Allied army, followed by their supply wagons.

Each courtyard, every farm and town square that we pass in this grey light, packed with artillery *caissons*, ammunition carts and Red Cross trucks. Pack mules tied to railings and poles; they don't so much as open an eye as the lights of the Fiat fall on them. The horses that gonna pull the huge batteries up the slopes of Champagne whicker nervous-like from the make-do stables, tossin' their manes. Herds of cattle – fresh beef for us troops – moo from behind the temporary warehouses. It still awful early, but men already at work in there, lit by the naked bulbs rigged along the elephant iron roofs as they unload crate after crate of tinned provisions and loaves of hard, army bread.

The driver take a sharp turn, sendin' our steel *casques* bangin' against the sides of the Fiat. The helmets, they new issue, along with gas masks and a special salve for the face, hands and neck to treat burns from the Boche flame-throwers. I spin the helmet in my hands, testin' the cold, hard weight of it.

'Just what we need,' I gripe, 'to go into battle with these big soup kettles on our heads.'

'*Merde*!' Gaillard agree. 'So pretty we will look too – with kettles on our heads, masks so we can't see shit, and hands all slippery from this damned salve!'

James tap the dome of the *casque*, runnin' a thumb around the deflector rim that meant to direct shrapnel away from our faces. 'I suspect we'll be glad soon enough to have these on us,' he comment.

Talk turn to the Boche arsenal. Machine guns, flame-throwers, hand grenades, the devil-spawn dumdum bullets that bust through a man like he made of tissue paper – all these discussed, with special detail around every terrible wound they can leave.

'Hardly matters though, in the end,' Gaillard say. He tell of this soldier he heard 'bout, from someone whose buddy's cousin, twice removed, been at the very same hospital when it happen.

This soldier he hear 'bout catch a dumdum bullet in the leg. By the time the doctors get to him, the wound bad enough that they got to amputate, 'bout halfway up the thigh. The operation go well, and this soldier, he recoverin' proper, when the hospital come under heavy shellin'. A shell drop clean through the skylight, straight on to the bed where he lie, right through it, and land with its nose buried in the floor.

Turns out, it was a dud.

A harmless dud. Thing is though, the shell, it fallen *exactly* where that man's amputated leg would have been. Did no other damage as it fell, but if that leg were still there – Gaillard waves his hand *'Au revoir!'*

We silent as we take it in.

'So what's the point of the story?' Karan ask.

'Point being,' Gaillard say, 'that a man can only be hit by the bullet – or shell – that got his name written on it. And if it's got his name on it, if his time is up, nothin' that anyone can do about it. As for the rest,' he grin. *'Ce n'est pas important.'*

The Fiat race on. A cher walks sleepy like by the side of the road, a pail in her hand; the war, it been goin' on long enough now that she don't even look up as we pass. It's us who watch, takin' in every little thing 'bout her as she grow smaller and smaller in the distance: the way she raise a hand to the scarf 'bout her head, the hip-sway of her walkin'. Small things, everyday things, but already they feel like they from a different world.

We near the lines now – I can tell by the newly set-up evacuation sheds comin' into sight. Enough light to the dawn now that I can read the signs nailed to their entrances – *'Blessés Assis'* on some, *'Blessés Couchés'* on others. The wounded who can sit up, and the wounded who layin' flat on their backs.

The dead, we know, will lie where they fall.

The explosions from the shells so many, so bright, it clear as day in the reserve trenches although it hardly 2:30 a.m. All summer long, the generals been readyin' for this attack. Three thousand French guns we got firin' on this strip of Front that ain't even fifteen feet long. Thanks to them aviators, every last enemy trench, earthwork and buttress has been mapped out. Each of our batteries got a target to grind into dust. Two thousand shells piled behind every battery, so they don't run outta ammunition. Cannon everywhere, and fat *saucisses* observation balloons fancied up with telephonic connections to guide the firin'. Ain't nothin' left to chance this time – at the briefin' last evenin', they even tell us the regimental numbers of the Boche facin' our line.

Four shells, per minute, per metre the order is. Four shells a minute per metre, for three full days and nights now, with no lettin' up. I ain't up to figurin' how many shells that is, but they make a noise so devil-filled, it seem to move and breathe. Thing of smoke and fire-tongue. We ain't none of us slept too much these past couple of days, and when our orders finally come at 1 a.m. this mornin', 25 September, we all been relieved.

So much shellin'. We can't hardly hear ourselves speak no more. James shout somethin'. I look over at him to read his lips and see the thin line of red comin' from his ears. Only now do I realise wetness is in my ears too; I touch my fingers to one and they come away bright with blood. I tear open my medical kit, orders be damned. Handin' some cotton to James, I stuff the rest into my ringin' ears.

The cold drizzle of the night don't let up none, fallin' from a sky the colour of gunmetal when mornin' come. 9:15 a.m., our artillery go dead quiet. The silence, it hurt my ears, so sudden that it feel like a hammer blow. My shoulders sore from the tension, nerves wire-tight as we wait. One second. Two. There – the sound of the regimental bands. My ears still ringin' somethin' awful; I *feel* the vibration of the drums instead of hearin' them. A sea of blue pour from the advance trenches, forward, into the smoke that hang over No Man's Land, thick as a stage curtain over the Boche lines. Slowly my hearin' come back. Trumpets and drums, and the rhythm of the 'Marseillaise'.

It the turn of the Boche guns to roar into action. Their gunners got the range, cuttin' down full sections of the advance. Just as quick, other troops take their place.

A cloud of smoke and dust in the reserve trenches; a shell, someplace ahead. We turn our faces, coughin'. Word come down the line: nine lost, includin' an officer, before we even gotten the chance to advance. Another shell. We duck, haulin' our musettes on to our necks to protect against shrapnel.

Ain't even stepped out into the battlefield yet, and already I'm thinkin' them soup-kettle helmets a powerful good idea.

The bugles now, callin' our cavalry forward. A wave of men and horses, tryin' to advance through the firin'. Three times they try, three times they forced to fall back. A unit of French 75s open up from somewhere in the back, tryin' to give them cover. Their firin' fall short, right into the reserve trenches. The horses, they rear and plunge, some goin' boo coo crazy, throwin' their riders from their backs as they leap into the trenches. One goes gallopin' terrified down the trench, men yellin' warnings, pressin' to the sides of the trench as it race past. A copper-coloured beauty, frothin' at the mouth. Gaillard grab its reins, sweatin' and cussin' from the strain, but he hold on. The horse swerve to the left, eyes rollin' in fright. Liftin' its tail, it let go a hot stream of dung as it come to a stop.

Our Captain scramble on to the parapet. '*Courage mes enfants*!' His voice high, clear as a bell as he walk along the length of our trench, tryin' to calm everybody down, his thin figure in full view of the enemy guns. 'Courage!'

We round up them runaway horses and put down the wounded; James, he use his helmet to cover their eyes, sparin' them the flash as he fire.

Wild cheerin' in the French trenches around noon. The line that the Boche said was so strong that it need only two washerwomen and a gun to hold it, that line just fallen.

'*Vive La France*!' '*Vive La Liberté*!'

Our orders come late afternoon. We supposed to advance in reserve and strengthen the French position in the enemy trenches. Forward, through the smoke-filled communication trenches. I make out shapes, faces as we pass. Them tortuosa trees from near Verzy . . .

Now the medic stations, marked with boards painted with a red cross. Already the stations crowded with the wounded and dyin'. A sweatin' priest bendin' double as he perform the last rites. He gone and pulled up his cassock to make it easier to get around; we see the hobnailed boots and army-issue trousers that he wear underneath.

A group of Boche prisoners being herded along. Many just boys, some look no more than sixteen. They torn through with shell, bullet and bayonet wounds, uniforms flappin' in its and bits, fire-scorched and still smokin' in places. The look in their eyes – I seen it in the horses of earlier this mornin'. That same crazed fright, a settlin' madness from being pushed to the edge of what they can take. Many openly cryin', like the children they are, skinny white arms tight 'bout a buddy's neck. The stink of vomit and explosive 'bout them, and fresh, barbecue char.

Out of the trenches at last, forward, through the break in our wire, across No Man's Land. The white limestone has been shot away by the shells – furrows of brown undersoil look like scars across the plain. A mess of litter – blooded bayonets, tangles of bobwire, cartridge casings, shrapnel, dented helmets, sheets of elephant iron, all twisted and shot through with holes, ridin' spurs, broken stakes of the Boche's *chevaux de frise*, detonated shells. All sorts of metal bent and beaten outta shape, some still red hot and glowin', like battle wreaths for the dead.

Closer now, to the Boche trenches. Their line so fully shelled, levelled so flat that there ain't no need for the sections of bridgin' our French 'genie engineers been stockpilin' to the rear. Bodies everywhere, lyin' so thick in places, ain't no way to advance but to run right on top of them with our hobnailed boots. In one huge pit, dozens lyin' twisted together, all killed by the same shells.

Into the Boche trenches, down into the earth along flights of stairs. Stairs, real stairs, made of concrete. The Boche done built an underground city, fully six to eight metres below ground. These ain't no itty bitty dugouts like ours, with chicken wire for beddin', but bedrooms proper, with bedsteads, washstands, tables and chairs. There's kitchens, bathrooms. Even a mess room, kitted out with a piano and phonograph, both gutted from the shellin'.

Broken glass crunch under our feet as we start to look around. A signboard hang crooked along one wall. James, he set the board upright – '*Schützengraben Spandau,*' he read aloud. The Boche, they gone and given their trenches names. This here been Trench Spandau. Two bottles have rolled against the wall, untouched. They filled with wine. Dustin' them off, I stuff them in my musette.

Most everybody doin' the same now, pickin' out treasures from the smokin' rubble and messes of bloodied bandage. System D in full swing – anythin' of use is ours. Luger pistols, still in their holsters, packs of cigarettes, lighters, tins of cherry jam, a tobacco pipe, its bowl painted with soldiers in what look like regimental colours.

Gaillard come whistlin' past, two boxes of cigars under an arm. He point at the string of dried sausages around his neck – '*Landjäger*!' he say happily.

James bend over somethin'. I mosey on over, curious to see what he picked out. He lookin' at half an arm. It lyin' there in the dirt, a postcard in its fingers. The fingers, they long and well formed I notice, long enough for the piano. I can read some of the words on the postcard – '*Mein schatz Ernst* . . .' Ain't no sign of the rest of the body, ain't no way of knowin' if Ernst among the wounded or just one more of the dead. Just his arm remain, with its piano-playin' fingers, holdin' tight to that postcard.

James dust his hands on his trousers. He look at me as if to say somethin', when someone casually kick the stump aside.

Word come late that afternoon. Only the first line of the Boche trenches has fallen; even with all that shellin', the wire belts of the second line, they stand untouched.

'Still,' Gaillard say stoutly, 'these trenches are ours.'

The look on James' face say it all. These trenches ours now, this day sure gonna count as a victory, but for all the men and ammunition lost, we ain't advanced no more than this thin bit of chalky ground.

The Front powerful restless all that night. Verey lights goin' up at all hours, and the crackle of rifle fire – short, sharp bursts through which we can hear the cries of the wounded and dyin'.

It keep drizzlin' through the night, leadin' into a mornin' all grey and fuzzy 'bout the edges. We get new orders, to double back part of the way we come, then head off at an angle towards a wooded ridge north of Souain.

The drizzle keep drip-drippin' on to our helmets, workin' past upturned collars as we make our way back through the captured trenches. The French 'genies, they sure been busy since we came through here last afternoon. Their crews gone and shifted the sandbags around overnight. Parapet turned into parados, facin' the other way, towards the Boche second line. Passage been cleared through the rubble. Too many been through here already but my eyes peeled to the floor all the same, for more wine, cigarettes or other stuff that might be worth a legionnaire's while, when:

'Fuck.'

He stop so sudden that I nearabout bump into James' back. Everybody ahead stopped too, starin' at a section of loopholes. Now that I look, there somethin' right odd-lookin' 'bout the shape of those loopholes. I squint through the drizzle, tryin' to make out what it is, and then it hit me – those loopholes, they framed in boots. Short of time, and needin' to turn these trenches around in a hurry, our 'genies, they gone and used the dead to fortify the walls. Two Boche, laid 'bout six inches apart, their boots flush with the wall of the trench. Another body placed across them. Dirt shovelled over, *et voilà*, both grave and loophole ready.

'Fucking System D,' James says, and begin to laugh softly.

It right hilarious, that 'genie version of System D. It crack us up proper. James laugh, we all do, eyes starin' wide, mouths white at the corners as we look at those dead-filled loopholes and laugh.

A few hours later, it's us lyin' in graves. When we get to the ridge, our orders are to draw the fire of the enemy batteries, so that our troops can make a flankin' move. Ain't no trenches in this part of the sector and so we dig shallow graves for ourselves, lined up side by side. Just deep 'nuff for a man to lay flat, with the walls thick 'nuff that if a shell falls in one, the men on either side still got a chance. The rain, she keep fallin' all the while.

Two days later, it still rainin' and we still lyin' here in our graves, gun bait for the Boche. Lucky for us, they don't have our exact location, but they got the range to do plenty damage all the same.

I run my fingers over the eyeholes of the canvas we each got for coverin', checkin' that the cartridges holdin' it down against this diabolic rain still in place. When all of this craziness done, I swear I'm headin' straight to the desert somewhere. Some place with white sun and hot sand, and I don't care none 'bout no *cafard* brain, I don't.

Verey lights start to go up, plenty bright through the canvas. I shift 'bout in that cold, wet grave, tryin' to get comfortable as the rattlin' of machine guns go on, all night, even louder than the rain.

When I wake up, it taken a second or two to figure out where I am. I think at first that maybe I gone and died sometime in the night. Lyin' there in the grave with the canvas over me, and everythin' so quiet, ain't no gunfire, nothin'. I throw open that canvas in a hurry.

A cold grey mist pour in. James, I hear James, whistlin' soft under his breath. I damn near jump up and do a jig right then 'cause the rain, that no 'count, devil-spawn rain, it finally stopped.

Visibility so poor in the mist that guns on both sides gone quiet. We get outta the graves, stretch our legs in the open. George the cook, he taken advantage of the cover and brought the mess kitchen right up to the ridge. We crack jokes and warm our hands around steamin' mugs of coffee into which a bit of rum find its way. George, he let go his royal manners to join right in the banterin'. He keep slappin' Karan on the back, like a long lost friend.

'*Alors*!' Gaillard cry, and like a magician with a hat, pull loops of that *Landjäger* sausage from his musette as we cheer and clap, along with a fat log of *Erbswurst*.

The mist start to thin. We're hunkered 'bout the stoves, enjoyin' the soup that George gone and whipped up from Gaillard's pickings and raisin' toasts to the Boche mammy who done sent her boy such delicious vittles, when the enemy albatross come into view. We scramble to put out the fires, lyin' still as we can. For a long, slow minute, ain't nothin' happen. Maybe he ain't seen us, I think hopefully, just as it come – the long tail of a smoke bomb, plain as an arrow in the clearin' sky. Two more come sailin' down, markin' our exact position. We race for cover as the Boche guns swing slowly towards us.

Their singin' start up once more, shells slammin' into the make-do kitchen, callin' to us by name.

Our losses from the bombardment are the worst since the offensive begun. Karan, he stand lookin' down at what left of George's body. Somethin' pass through his eyes, then it gone.

'Long live the King,' he say flat like, and turn away.

Our colonel riled up real bad by all the gun bait orders the Legion gotten so far, all the lyin' 'bout in graves and this mornin's shellin'. So badly he want a chance, just one chance, to get back at the Boche, to show them what the Legion all 'bout, that he practically beg headquarters for permission to advance.

He get his wish. We to engage with the Boche tomorrow afternoon: a blind attack, on the Bois Sabot.

The Bois Sabot, or Horseshoe Wood, is an earthwork fortification the Boche done built, shaped like a horseshoe around the Butte Souain. It one of the strongest positions the Boche got on all the Front, thick with machine-gun nests, and with plenty artillery support. These our orders: advance into the face of the horseshoe, divertin' enemy fire so that other French divisions might take the Sabot from the flank.

The Legion headed for a suicide mission.

TWENTY-EIGHT

Seem a waste, to leave them bottles of wine behind. I open them with the tip of my bayonet, settin' one to my lips and passin' the other around.

'*Prêts?*' Gaillard grin like a wolf as he call out to James and me. 'A fine pair of wind chimes you two are going to make, dancing from their wire!'

'Dance we surely will,' I return the compliment, 'but on *your* grave, that where.'

'Long as I go facing the enemy.' He shudder. 'No leaving arms and legs out there for me. A clean shot, that's all I ask for.'

We know not many of us goin' to make it back from the Bois Sabot but after all the gun-bait waitin' 'bout of the past days, it a relief to know we advancin' into attack at last. Maybe it the wine, but I feel sort of light-headed, like I can't hold on to no thought for too long. Time seem to rush past awful quick and slow down so terrible that a minute feel like it stretch for ever. I try and hold on to it, the notion that these here might be our last few hours on this earth, but it brush through my fingers, like a stone skippin' over a river, and go jitterin' off again. We laughin' a little too loudly, talkin' quicker, our jestin' touched with death-talk tonight.

'A clean shot,' Karan agree with Gaillard. 'And if I do have to donate a leg or an arm, I hope I get the *Medaille Militaire* or at least a citation in exchange.'

'I don't know about a citation,' James say, 'but we'll certainly get you a buskin' permit for the streets.'

I laugh. 'What do you reckon . . .' I ain't sure I want to know the answer. 'What do you reckon our odds are?'

James move the chaw 'bout in his jaw. 'Poor.'

I wait for actual numbers, but he ain't givin' none. 'The bobwire ain't been touched, I hear tell. Underbrush and long grass everywhere, hard to see much of anythin'. One patrol walked right into the Boche – got shot up all to pieces.'

James steady cleanin' his rifle, as if he listenin' to the weather forecast is all. 'They beat the rest of us to it by a day then,' is all he say.

He keep polishin' the rifle when suddenly – 'How come you don't get any mail?' he ask. 'Never seen you get anythin', not a letter, not a parcel.' He frown, as if this here question been botherin' him a while.

'Ain't nobody there no more. I got some distant family down South, but Pappy—' Ain't a story I told too much, but I tell it now to Yankee James. I tell him 'bout the brick they sent flyin' through the schoolhouse window. The same broken window with the rags stuffed into it at night, but this time, they been bold enough, hate-filled enough to throw the brick in the middle of the day. It come sailin' clean through that open window. Catch Pappy on the side of his head. He never the same after that. Couldn't teach no more, was in bed for months till he died, and after that, well, wasn't much point in me stickin' around there no more.

Yankee James don't say nothin' more. We go on readyin' our gear. They given us orders before in the reserve lines, to make real sure we got on clean underwear – 'It lessens infection if you are wounded.' Guess the generals ain't figured we be wearin' the same uniforms for days.

Gaillard, he takin' all what still left of his pickings from the Boche trenches into the attack. 'No way to send these for storage at the back,' he point out, 'and they will be worth some real francs in Paris.'

His sack bulge out at the back, filled to the top, but he hoist all that extra weight on his back easy as a feather.

We go real quick through the communication trenches. The French troops we pass look real surprised – who these men advancin' before they can? Hard to tell if they jealous or feel powerful sorry for us.

'Ah, *La Legion, La Legion,*' they mutter when they learn who we be.

Legion of Honour, Legion of the Brave.

There's somethin' I been meanin' to ask Karan. 'That war in India that you talked 'bout,' I ask urgently as we press forward. 'What happened in the end? Who won?'

'Arjun and his brothers did.'

Ain't realised that my shoulders been all tensed up till I feel them relax. They won. In the end, they won. That the answer I been hopin' for.

Karan still speakin'. 'It was a war unto death, though. Nearly four million men went out on to the battlefield. When it was over, only twelve were left standing. Twelve. They won, but their sons, relatives, friends – all were dead.'

Given me gooseflesh when he say that. Then the humour of it strike me. They won alright, but what exactly?

Feel 'bout right, it do.

Here now, our jumpin'-off point from the trenches. We got to go through a small scrub of pine and then out into a clearin' with no cover in sight. James hold out his hand as we wait for the whistle. 'Gaillard was right,' he say, by way of wishin' me good luck. 'A handsome wind chime you're going to make on the wire. Run fast,' he add then, urgent like. 'When the firing gets severe, and the columns break, run fast as you can, you hear? Either straight ahead, or off to the side, it doesn't matter, as long as you aren't in the centre of the advance. There's a reason why we've been lucky so far. Most soldiers, they aren't exactly sharpshooters, and so they aim for the general heart of the advance.'

Now what he say make sense, the Yankee awful smart, but I know the reason we be comin' back safe each time is the gris-gris. Ain't no time to reply though – the whistle sound, and we leave the trenches for a storm of bullets and shrapnel.

It like walkin' into a silver rainstorm. A high-pitched whine, as the Boche guns light into us. Its and bits of tree-hide and leaves still wet from that rain of the past days, fallin' all 'bout us. A hot sting through my thigh. Men droppin' in waves, so many bullets still slammin' into them that their bodies roll over and over on the ground, like leaves in a fall breeze.

I run fast as I can, slippin', slidin' down the slope. Faster, Obadaiah, pick up your ninny feet and run. Bullets swipin' around me, faster, across the valley at the bottom, part way up the next, its rise out of sight of the Boche guns. I throw myself to the ground, flippin' on to my back and pantin' hard. James just up ahead, a wildness in his eyes as he grin.

'Having fun yet?' he mouth at me through the racket.

A wetness down my leg, and I 'member the wound. Tear open the medical kit, tie a rough tourniquet to stop the bleedin'. Don't feel no pain, not yet, not with the rush of battle still strong in my blood. Wop, wop, wop, the steady sweep of the machine guns.

'*Avancez*!'

On our feet again, charge up the rest of the slope, past a knot of pines. Mud flyin' knee-high and more, bullets tillin' the earth. I'm jumpin' over bodies, so many, all ours, rollin' like they made from thistle weed and cotton down. I'm runnin' a little to the side, I find, just off the centre of our advance. James, where James? His voice in my head, 'Run as fast as you can.'

'*Avancez, mes enfants*!' I actually hear the Captain, through all of this noise. He just ahead of me, I see him sink to the ground. Roll, roll, roll. I nearabout trip over my feet: Karan, he liftin' into the air. I know it's him – what left of his robe, it spill from his torn musette, like a fire-coloured cape. *His robe, he carried his damn robe into battle*. I laugh out loud in the madness.

Maybe it the smoke, must be on account of the smoke, 'cause I only see the upper half of his body and arms. Just half of Karan's body, thrown clean into the air, the robe flyin' out behind him, all torn up at the bottom from those Russian socks he been steady cuttin' from it. His arms spread wide, as if blessin' us all.

Forward, Obadaiah, run. Men dyin' all around me, my brothers, goin' down like rag dolls. *James*, ahead, on his stomach, clippin' at the bobwire. He fine, I known all along he goin' to be fine with the gris-gris in his pocket. At the wire now, onward, followin' James through the break in the belt.

Forward, advancin', *to where?* We throw our grenades wildly before us – can't see too far with the smoke. Loose dirt ahead, the sandbags of a Boche outpost. James, half crawlin', half runnin' towards it. I'm followin' right behind, when my leg give way from under me. I grip my rifle tight, hold it above my head as I fall. *Une bonne mort*, a legionnaire's death. Pappy's voice in my head, callin' my name.

It dark when I open my eyes. I'm laid out near a water-filled hole, shell flash and Verey lights off to the side. The leg hurt now, throbbin' somethin' bad. My tongue stuck to the roof of my mouth. I work it loose, tryin' to swallow as I feel 'bout for my canteen, but it long gone, lost somewhere in the advance. I inch towards the edge of the hole, dip my head in and drink. Another flash of Verey lights and now I see that what I taken to be a floatin' log is a body. I rest my achin' head against the mud, just glad I drank the water before I seen he in there.

Where everybody? What happened to James? I raise up on my arms to get my bearin's. I see the observation trench we been runnin' towards when I fell. Its parapet directly ahead, sandbags torn, blasted by what must've been a direct hit of a grenade. I crawl towards it, my leg draggin' behind me.

Somethin' move in the half-light, near the lip of the trench. This, of all the devil-spawn horror of the battlefield, raise the hairs on my neck like nothin' else do before. The squat shape of it not human, not animal. I freeze. Verey lights go off again, and now I spot the bayonet, one of ours, stuck blade down in the earth.

The shape, it slowly sort itself. It human alright, men, two of them, one bendin' over what left of another. My heart start to pound as I crawl nearer, and I'm awful close to burstin' into tears. James, the man bent over the other is James. He taken a nasty hit to his head, an arm hangin' bent and useless as he try to get morphine into the shape on the ground, but he seem okay. The wounded legionnaire though, he ain't got much legs no more. The left arm shot away, from below the elbow. His face got hit too – most of the jaw is gone. He moan through the mess of bone and blood, turn towards me as I come closer.

Gaillard.

He look at me with the one eye that still open. I know at once what he want. I *know* what he askin' for, without sayin' one word.

Une bonne mort. I grip my rifle closer.

'Don't be a fool,' James say shakily. He point at the trench, its mouth open wide in the dark. 'We carry him there. I've had a quick look inside. Two dead Boche, and one wounded. We leave Gaillard there for their medics.'

Gaillard, he make a bubblin' sound like a man tryin' to talk underwater. I can't take my eyes off his face, what left of it.

'He ain't goin' to make it.'

'You don't know that. You don't *know* that. We have to give him a chance. The trench,' James say again. His voice, it tremblin'.

We shoot him full of morphine, tie tourniquets from what left of our medical kits. We half carry, half drag him down into the trench. Somehow, his musette made it through okay. It drag behind, spillin' open as we pull him into the trench. A Luger holster, cigarette lighters, spectacle cases, smokin' tobacco, a knife with a carved handle – all his pickings from Trench Spandau now spillin' into this one.

There two dead down there, just as James said. The third Boche, he sit with his back to the wall, an arm held against the leakin' in his stomach.

Gaillard make that bubblin' sound again. I know what he want.

James squeeze the last of the water from his canteen into what left of Gaillard's mouth. 'Courage,' he say, and his voice shake again. 'Courage.'

We settle him the best we can before we leave. When I turn at the lip of the trench to look back, he movin', somehow he *movin'*, tryin' desperately to crawl after us.

We try to find our way from the torn-up ridge and blasted tree line. Everythin' look different in retreat. The small hills that rose from the plains this mornin' been shelled so bad the landscape itself is changed. Everywhere, the dead. I keep hearin' Gaillard's voice in my head as we crawl through the long grass.

'Une bonne mort.'

I come to a dead stop. My leg botherin' me some, but it ain't the reason I can't go no further. I rest my cheek against the mud. *Une bonne mort.*

We left him to die in a Boche trench.

'Obadaiah,' James begin, but I shake my head. Turnin' around, I start crawlin' fast as I can, back towards the observation trench.

He made it partly up the slope of the trench. Pullin' hisself after us, inch by inch, with just the one huge arm.

Brother Strong Heart Mighty Oak.

He lie face down in the mud. The stars, they out now, and I see the wet stain newly spreadin' over his back.

He was shot. Gaillard, he shot in the back as he try to crawl after us, make it back to the Legion.

The wounded Boche still sittin' against the wall. There's a Luger lyin' by his side. I look at it, puzzled. I know it weren't on him when we were down here before. Then it strike me: Gaillard's torn musette, spilled open on the floor of the trench. That Luger, it Gaillard's, the spoils from Trench Spandau.

Feel like a strange, wakin' dream as I get down into that trench, real careful around Gaillard's body. 'Obadaiah!' James say urgently from the top. 'Obadaiah,' he call again, but there ain't no stoppin' now.

I stand before that wounded Boche, and all I can see is that Luger. The Boche, he push it weakly away. His lips move as I bend to pick it up. They cracked and dry and he got to work his tongue around the word.

'*Erbarmen*,' the Boche say. His eyes, real tired, wanderin' from my face to the pistol and back. '*Erbarmen*,' he say again.

I don't feel a thing as I pull the trigger. A single shot to the head. I lean against the wall, lookin' down at the body as James climb heavily into the trench.

'It weren't a good death. Shot in the back, facin' away from the enemy.'

James say nothin'. Ain't never seen him take a thing from the trenches before, but slowly he bend and take the helmet from the Boche.

We make our way out, past Gaillard's body, and head back for the French lines once more.

Only later, when we at the dressin' station, all shot up with morphine, that the pieces, they start to come together.

'What was he sayin'?' I ask James, without turnin' around. The Yankee, he awful smart, know all sorts of things. 'The Boche, what was he sayin', at the end?'

'*Erbarmen*.' His voice real quiet. 'Mercy. That's what he was sayin' – "Mercy".'

'Mercy,' the Boche said. I see his face again in my head, the way he push that Luger aside as if he done, as if he ain't never goin' to fire at nothin' no more.

'*Erbarmen*.'

Was he askin' for mercy, or tryin' to explain that he gone and killed Gaillard out of mercy? I see his eyes, so tired as they look into mine.

'*Erbarmen*,' he say again, tryin' to get me to understand.

*

We ordered to wait in the sector a few more weeks after the offensives. They start to bury the dead, so many dead, that for now, all they got for grave markers are empty bottles, stuck neck down in the mud.

An old man sit under a knot of trees, one of the locals, whittlin' branches into the battlefield crosses that gonna follow. I watch for a long time before I ask.

They all the same, he nod, each cross cut to exactly the same length and width. Whether for our dead or the Boche, the crosses, they made the same.

That Christmas of 1915, a couple of football matches break out here and there between the Allies and the Boche. Orders pass down at once, the generals makin' sure it brought to a quick end.

'No fraternising with the enemy this year,' newspapers on both sides report. The war, they seem to suggest, is on for real.

The war, this endless, bottomless war, the war to end all wars.

TWENTY-NINE

Raydon • 1932

'I asked her to marry me.'

Ellie looked up startled, a half-folded sheet in her hands. 'What?'

He fidgeted with the edge of the table, suddenly shy. 'Madeleine. She said yes.'

He'd proposed soon after they'd returned from Washington. The events of the 28th had played over and over in his mind. Their jaunt in the plane, the thrill he'd felt at winging through the sky. Her face, lit with laughter, eyes aglow as she watched him take it all in. The evacuations downtown, and his fear, the bone-chilling fear he'd experienced at the prospect of her coming to harm.

Later that same night, their small group had stood on the bluff in Anacostia, watching the burning camp. All that had been built with so much pride was lost in an instant, lives flipped inside out on the turn of a moment. He remembered looking up, at the three-quarter moon floating overhead. Fire below, ice above, and men, eking out what lives they could in between. Although barely twenty-four, with the prime of his life yet ahead, Jim was suddenly aware of a sobering sense of finiteness. He saw his life unfolding before him not as a wide open sea, but a river, bound by the banks through which it flowed, his years ahead dotted with a precious few interludes of true grace. Fuelled by the defeated faces of the Major, Connor, the other men on the bluff, Jim was seized by a sense of urgency, of the importance of recognising each benediction as it appeared, of taking firm hold before it swept permanently out of reach.

This woman, this particular woman, standing beside him. Of russet hair and ready laughter, a tic in her forehead when she was mad. The small, red mole between her breasts. This sense of belonging he felt, whenever she was near.

Madeleine had slipped her hand into his. Jim gripped it tightly, knowing he never wanted to let go.

A broad grin broke out on Ellie's face now. 'Well of course she said yes!' she exclaimed. 'She knows what's good for her, doesn't she?' She hesitated. 'Still, do you think it's all a bit too soon? You've barely known each other three months and—'

'Feels right, Ellie.'

Her eyes grew moist. Casting aside the laundry, she reached up and kissed him soundly on the forehead. 'Who'd have thought it? My little Jim poopie-pants, all grown up and about to be married.'

'Ellie!' he began indignantly. He paused, studying her face. 'Are you crying?'

She cleared her throat noisily. 'Of course not.'

'You *are*, Ellie.'

'Am not!' She turned back to the sheets. 'When's the last time you saw me sniffle, Jim Stonebridge?' she demanded, surreptitiously wiping her eyes.

'About two seconds ago.' He came up behind her and awkwardly put his arms around her.

Ellie started to tear up again, her glasses getting so fogged that she had to take them off and wipe them clean on her apron. 'Now see what you made me do.' She laughed, and patted his cheek. 'Have you told the Major?'

The Major had withdrawn into some dark and lonely place. He'd collapsed into his bed upon their return from Anacostia, and not stirred until well after noon the next day. He rose only briefly, before retreating beneath the covers again. For days he drifted in and out of sleep. He dreamed no dreams, there were no night sweats, just a bleak emptiness. Jim came upstairs time and again to check on him; each time the Major heard him on the stairs, he turned away and closed his eyes once more.

'It wasn't your fault,' Jim wanted to say to his father as he stood worriedly at the entrance to his bedroom. 'You did everything you could.'

The words did not come, remaining unspoken as had so many between them over the years. Jim knew instinctively that the unexpected camaraderie they'd shared in Washington was gone, the relationship between father and son falling once more into the patterns of old, conforming to the silences that webbed the contours of this house and the striped shadows of the barn. All the same, there lay a new understanding between them, a fragile, delicate thing, but there nonetheless, taking the brittle edge off their bond. The wariness that Jim had always felt around his father, as if he were walking on eggshells, was gone, and in its place, was a new-found empathy.

When finally the Major found it within himself to shake off his torpor, he'd aged, seemingly overnight. It had been early, the house thankfully silent as he'd limped haltingly downstairs. The light still so paltry that he could see nothing reflected in the black mirror, its glass a dark sheen against the wall.

Was it Obadaiah he'd seen in the camp, he wondered again. Just that one time, by the boxing ring, then he was gone. Or had he imagined it?

The Major searched in the mirror for answers. He shuffled closer, and now his image emerged from its centre, pale and attenuated. He looked at his reflection, filled with revulsion for the indistinct figure in the glass, a man with no more substance than a ghost.

Hands trembling, he opened the door of the long-case clock that stood ticking against the wall. He drew out the bottle of whisky hidden there, and twisting open the cap, tilted the bottle to his mouth. The immediate singe of alcohol obliterated the need for thought.

He headed for the orchard. It had rained sometime in the night, the grass wet against his slippers and the hem of his robe. A robin called unseen, clear and fluting. It halted its song at his approach and then called again, after a moment, this time from somewhere to the east, where among the banks of white starred pennyroyals, the Cortlands were beginning to swell rosily.

The grass had grown in while they'd been away and was beginning to crowd the trunks of the trees. Bending, he started automatically to weed. There was a simple satisfaction in the task, in the sharpness of the blades of grass, the cool brush of earth against his hands. The Major paused, slowly rubbing a clod between his fingers.

When he was a child, the family had summered one year in Cape Cod. It had been an idyllic time, of sun-warmed waves, of building sandcastles with Bill while their nanny read aloud to them, of all the shrimp a boy could eat and combing the beach for sea glass. At the end of the holiday, he'd brought back a small scoop of sand in his trunk, a secret souvenir that he'd not even told Bill about. He mixed the sand into the soil of the orchard. For some reason, they never did make it out there again. The nanny eventually left too, but when he walked about the orchard afterwards, he'd sometimes thought of that handful of seashore and smiled.

It so satisfied him, the quiet sentimentality of the gesture, that he'd repeated it over the years. Loess from Mexico. The red earth of Hawaii. A handful of Shropshire sod. Trench mud packed into a Boche helmet, the bullet hole plugged with cork. All carted home and sifted into this New England soil, a private mapping of his life, like the silver tracings of a snail.

The Major wished he'd brought back some of the mud from Anacostia. Things had happened so quickly . . . He was overcome again by the sense of powerlessness that had assailed him ever since the night of the evacuation. A sense of failure so acute it cut through the fog of alcohol, stressing upon him yet again of how little consequence he was. Like the discarded husk from a seed pod, emptied of worth. He sat down heavily in the grass, uncaring of its wetness. He pressed his hands into the topsoil. The earth yielding, but firm, steady beneath his fingers. A physical anchor to a world he'd given up trying to understand.

Jim told his father about his proposal, and Madeleine's acceptance. The Major nodded, aware that he ought to say something in response, but unsure what that ought to be. 'Excellent. She – she's a wonderful girl.' Rising from the armchair with some effort, he held out a congratulatory hand.

A few hours later, Jim came upon a round box of midnight-blue velvet resting on the breakfast table. In it, the asscher cut diamond ring that his mother had worn for all her wedded life. He rubbed a finger over the ring and the stone shot to life against the warmth of his skin, casting a solitary spark that hung trembling and rainbow-faceted all along the opposite wall. Jim looked through the open windows, at the quiet figure working among the apple trees, watching as a breeze gusted through the Major's scant hair, exposing the vulnerable pinkness of scalp below.

Caught up in the swell of public support for the Anacostia victims, the *Gazette* called to ask if the Major could resubmit some of his previous editorials.

'Why don't you speak with them?' Jim urged.

The Major said nothing, wholly absorbed in a patch of dandelions, in the spores beginning one by one to detach themselves from their moorings with such enviable ease.

Jim brought down the tan leather folder where he'd secretly saved every single one of the articles that his father had written. He sat in the library, riffling through the pages. As he turned the sheets filled with precise, copperplate script, rereading a line here, a paragraph there, Jim had the odd sensation of holding something sacral in his hands. In the aftermath of Anacostia, there was a poignancy to his father's words that had eluded him before. To get them published now seemed whorish, as if catering to cheap sentiment. Jim put the folder away.

Despite the brevity of the courtship, Madeleine's parents met the news of her impending nuptials with remarkable equanimity. Her father had rather liked Jim from the start, and her long-suffering mother was secretly relieved to be getting her daughter off her hands. Madeleine wanted to be married in the fall, just as the leaves were turning, she explained, twisting Jim's mother's ring on her finger this way and that, admiring it as it caught the light.

Freddie went into a fit of sulks when he heard about the wedding. 'Surely you don't expect me to attend,' he said. Madeleine kissed him on the cheek and said he'd better be there.

'How about I just fly my plane into the belfry instead?' he suggested morosely and she laughed.

'It won't last, you know,' he predicted with gloomy satisfaction. She smacked him lightly on the head and told him not to be such a sore loser.

When the wedding date was set, her parents placed a call to the Major. Would he send them his list of invitees, her father asked jovially.

The Major was nonplussed. There was no need for a list since it'd probably be just the four of them attending, including the groom, he said. Misunderstanding the surprised silence at the other end: 'It's Ellie and her kid,' he elaborated, 'she's been a surrogate mother to Jim . . .' What was that? Yes, only four, but perhaps Jim had some folks he wanted to invite. No, there was no other family. There were his wife's relatives in England, but he hadn't been in contact with them for years.

Madeleine wanted to know which of Jim's friends would be attending. 'None,' he shrugged. There were some folks from the local school he was still friendly with, but nobody he especially wanted to be there, he said. His college roommate perhaps, but he hadn't been in touch since graduation; the same went for his football teammates. It was Madeleine's turn to be taken aback. Now that she thought about it, although he seemed to know practically everyone each time they went into Raydon, Jim had never spoken of any particular friends.

'Just another thing that's passed down through the Stonebridge men,' he said caustically when she pointed it out to him. 'We like being left alone.'

Seeing him begin to bristle at her questioning, she let it go.

'I wish Connor and some of those guys could've come,' he said suddenly.

'Connor, from Anacostia?' Madeleine looked at him surprised. Her expression softened. 'I wish so too,' she agreed.

The wedding invitations arrived, embossed with a scrolling font on an ivory background. The first thing that Ellie did upon receiving hers was to head on over to the country store and wave it under Carla Dalloway's nose. Well, *of course* she'd been invited. She'd practically raised the boy, hadn't she? Yes, all the way to Boston!

Old Asaph and Jeremiah listened interestedly to the exchange from their seats on the porch.

'The Stonebridge boy be getting hitched,' old Asaph observed.

'Ayuh,' Jeremiah concurred. 'Right bonny little thing she is, his flatlander girl.'

'Very pretty,' Asaph agreed. 'Reckon she'll get the flatlander bits ironed out of her soon enough too, here in Raydon.'

There was a spate of celebratory soirees in Boston in the weeks leading up to the wedding, thrown by a seemingly endless procession of Madeleine's friends. Jim excused himself from most of them – the apple harvest was upon them, he pointed out. The few he did attend, he gamely endured, nursing a beer and standing resolutely by her side. When the inane chatter became too much, he put an arm around her waist, steering her to the dance floor.

'You dance?' she asked astonished as he twirled her expertly around.

'My mother.'

'She did a fine job teaching you, Jim Stonebridge.' She reached up to kiss his neck. 'I could get used to this.'

He grinned, pleased both with the compliment and this respite from the crowd.

They were married in late September, in the midst of a gentle fall, when Black Pete emerged once more from the woods with sacks of puffballs and a huge cluster of oyster mushrooms to sell, the coats of the horses starting to thicken while they ambled peaceably about the paddock, or stood in thoughtful contemplation of the red and orange hills.

The day of the wedding was as beautiful a day as anyone could remember, the trees outside the church a blaze of colour that matched the vibrancy of the bride's hair. She wore it in a low knot, its marcelled waves fastened at the side with a diamante pin that had belonged to her grandmother. In the bouquet of freesias and orchids she carried was a single peacock feather. It was her 'something blue', she said, pointing out the cobalt among its many hues.

The groom had touchingly chosen his father to be his best man.

Ellie made no pretence of trying to hide her tears, noisily honking into her handkerchief all the way through the ceremony.

Madeleine bought him a gold watch as a wedding gift. Jim was embarrassed and admitted he had nothing for her; she was put out at first, but then she laughed.

He set a trap line later that season, following a gully along a river bottom into a thick belt of wooded land. He trapped three foxes and skinned them himself, curing the pelts in the woodshed before sending them to a furrier in New York. When the package arrived, he stuffed it under their bed, bringing it out late that night.

Delighted, she tried the cape on, still naked, a faint glisten of sweat on her midriff and between the slope of her breasts. She posed before him, a hand on one hip. With her hair tumbling about her shoulders, she looked to Jim like a magnificent, wilding queen.

Amused to hear how miffed Carla Dalloway had been about not receiving an invite to the wedding,'Why don't we host a reception?' Madeleine suggested.

Ellie was thrilled at the prospect of a party in the house after so many years. Jim hesitated, glancing at his father. Madeleine slipped her arm through the Major's. 'It will be such a pleasant affair,' she urged, smiling, 'If you'd only agree, please would you?' The Major haltingly did.

They settled upon an elaborate tea. Ellie was busy in the kitchen for days. She showed Madeleine the rows of trunks in the cellar where the carved girandoles, the crystal and the good china had been kept in storage. They dragged it all upstairs where Ellie set about cleaning and polishing the pieces, soaking the crystal in soap suds to fully restore its sparkle.

Tables were set out in the orchard, under the green of the apple trees, the boughs of the Astrakhans and Porters heavy with ripening fruit. Madeleine foraged among the harvested apples, heaping mounds of the best in bowls of carved malachite and on massive, silver-footed trays.

'Nobody's going to eat that many apples,' Jim pointed out, bemused, to Madeleine.

'Those are the centrepieces, silly,' she replied, laughing.

The afternoon was an undisputed success. The Major slipped away almost as soon as the tea began, disappearing into the high reaches of the orchard where mercifully, the sounds of the revelry carried only faintly. Carla Dalloway pressed a bolt of cloth into Madeleine's hands. It was a wedding gift, she said, adding that the house and the grounds had never looked prettier, not even from when she remembered it as a girl.

It warmed Ellie's heart to witness Jim's small, throwaway gestures of tenderness towards his bride.

'Provence roses!' she heard Madeleine exclaim, over the row of bushes by the kitchen one morning. They had been particularly late blooming this year, and while the roses had all fallen now, there were still small piles of petals here and there on the ground.

'Cabbage roses,' he countered, just to be difficult. 'No need to get all fancy, cabbage roses is what we call them around here.'

He took the beauty out of everything, she said indignantly. Besides, whatever was this obsession with cabbage in these parts? Boiled cabbage, skunk cabbage, even this lovely flower . . .

Worried that Madeleine might not understand his particular

brand of jesting, not just yet, Ellie almost called out to him from the kitchen window to stop being so ornery. She held her tongue though, watching as he plucked a sprig of leaves, carefully stripping its stalk of thorns before tucking it behind Madeleine's ear.

'"A rose by any other name . . .'

'. . . would smell as sweet,"' Madeleine finished, smiling as she raised a hand to lightly touch the sprig in her hair.

The Major, Ellie continued to worry about in private, pulling out the bottles from all of his hiding places when he was outdoors, and monitoring just how much of the liquor he'd consumed.

In the presidential Elections that November, Roosevelt and the Democrats won a resounding victory over President Hoover. This was the first election since 1876 in which the Democratic candidate won the popular vote, and the first since 1852 in which he was declared the winner in the Electoral College as well. It was the Depression of course, but the tipping point, the pundits unanimously agreed, had been the appalling handling of the veterans and the Bonus March by the previous administration.

Ellie was certain the Major would be as pleased as punch at the news, but he only nodded vaguely when he heard. Seeing Ellie's worried eyes on him, he pulled on his gloves and avoided her gaze. Muttering something about needing to see to the Red Astrakhans, the Major retreated outdoors and spent the day among his trees once more.

THIRTY

1933

A brisk wind rattled the walls of the lean-to, whistling through the cracks. Connor muttered in his sleep, drawing the sheets of newspaper close. The wind blew harder still, gathering speed along the frosted banks of the Hudson then slamming into the shack. He woke with a start, cursing under his breath.

It was another mild winter, following on the heels of the one before. When you were hungry, however, so starved that your stomach seemed to be stuck to your spine, and the only covers you had were sheets of hoarded newspaper, even the mildest of winters cut to the bone. Connor sat up, blinking in the half-light. He stretched his arms, groaning as the muscles in his shoulders protested, stiff with cold. He needed to take a piss, but stayed a while longer in the swaddle of newsprint, loath to leave the relative warmth. The wind battered the walls again. 'Goddamned . . .!' Pushing the door of the shack open, Connor ventured outside.

Fog hung over the icy river, ballooning in the wind. Fog over the escarpment too. Thinner inland, parting here and there to reveal the lopsided shapes of the shanty town. His stomach growled. An image rose in his mind, of sausages cooking fatly over a fire, and he remembered that he'd been dreaming about them before waking so abruptly. A pan of sputtering links, the delicious smells as they browned . . . He sucked in his breath, so hungry he felt almost faint. There was the mineral taste of blood in his mouth. Connor hawked and spat. His teeth had become worse, he knew, his gums frequently bleeding, his breath so rank at times it turned his own stomach. He spat again in disgust, trying to clear the taste from his mouth, then shuffled towards the bank. A stand of weeds, stripped of leaves and coated in transparent, glass-like ice. Unbuttoning his pants, he aimed a stream of urine right at its heart, the steaming yellow flow washing away all the delicate beauty of the ice.

'Happy New Year,' he muttered to himself.

The sound of the morning reveille rose into the dawn, as behind him, the camp began to stir.

It was yet another junk-pile veteran camp, one that nobody had bothered to name this time, cobbled together on a patch of waste-land below Riverside Drive in New York. About eighty veterans had struggled here through the months following the evacuation at Anacostia, scratching out a living from selling pro-Bonus literature, and panhandling. There were only so many soft touches in the city, however, and now, at the very start of 1933, Connor, and so many like him, found themselves at the end of their ropes once more.

When word came later that day of a second organised march to Washington, Connor met the news with disinterest. Gradually, however, as talk of the march continued, his optimism began to stir. It was a new government after all. Maybe it would work this time around? One more march, to press their demands.

He rinsed his mouth with the last sip of coffee as he mulled it over, swirling the liquid about to make the most of its scant flavour. His stomach growled again, so loud that it startled him.

Connor joined the march in Philadelphia where nearly two hundred veterans had assembled. They set off hopefully on foot, on the one-hundred-and-forty-mile hike to Washington. Hardly anyone paid heed to this second Bonus March, however, all eyes trained instead on President-elect Roosevelt. Only six marchers were left by the time a lone reporter from Washington found them, gaunt and exhausted, thirty miles from the capital in Elkridge, Maryland. Five were huddled on the kerb, over a meal of bread and water. The sixth stood, clutching the American flag.

A New Deal, the President-elect promised the country, on the wings of economic reform and a balanced budget. On 30 January, he celebrated his fifty-first birthday with a grand party at the family home in Warm Springs, Georgia.

That very same day, Adolf Hitler was appointed the new Chancellor of Germany.

Spring came early that year, in a tumult of brightness and early-spawning trout. Everywhere, a sense of anticipation as the nation counted down with increasing fervour to the inauguration of the new president. The ice that had bound the hands of the town clock melted, the sound of the bell startling all of Raydon as it tolled once more. It was the earliest in the season that this had ever happened, as far as anyone could remember. As if time itself were buckling forward, hurtling towards the New Deal.

'Even the maples been in a rush this year,' old Asaph commented.

'Ayuh, and mud seasons's going to be something awful,' Jeremiah prophesied gloomily.

The date of the inauguration drew closer. Special committees worked day and night in preparation for the throngs of spectators expected to descend on the city. Connor had been sheltering in a flophouse since the aborted march. He was perilously close to running out of even the few cents required to pay for his squalid quarters, when he found work fastening the rows of loudspeakers that would broadcast the inaugural address.

An army of carpenters, handymen and construction workers hammered away, erecting stands and podiums on the grounds of the White House, the Capitol and all along Pennsylvania Avenue. Connor paused in the middle of lashing a loudspeaker to its pole, gazing down at the avenue as he stretched his arms. A memory, of soldiers in gas masks, horses stepping smartly through rubble. He froze for an instant, then resolutely turned away and resumed his task.

It occurred to him that the first words of the new president would flow through the very loudspeaker that he, Michael Liam Connor, was fastening. Buoyed by the prospect, Connor began to whistle, under his breath at first, then louder, cheerfully adding to the cacophony that filled the city.

'Did you see this, Ellie?' Madeleine pored over the magazine, fascinated. 'The gowns sound beautiful.'

Ellie shook her head in disapproval. 'I don't see how all these inaugural galas are supposed to help the country,' she said archly.

Madeleine smiled, still preoccupied with the article. 'My father would say that this is *exactly* what the economy needs. More people spending . . .' She continued to read, picturing the drape and fall of the blue velvet dress that Mrs Roosevelt was going to wear at the inauguration. 'Listen to this – "the dress is of crystelle velvet in a shade of hyacinth that has been named Eleanor Blue in Mrs Roosevelt's honour. The three-quarter-length, wraparound coat is of a dark-blue but not quite navy tint, that has, at Mrs Roosevelt's suggestion, been named for her daughter, Anna." I wonder,' she mused aloud, 'if Carla Dalloway might stock some material in these colours soon?'

Jim walked in and Madeleine jumped up, setting the magazine aside. Winding her arms about his waist, she reached up to kiss him on the neck. 'Let's attend the inauguration.'

'What?' He laughed. 'No.'

'Jim, the papers are all calling it an absolutely historic moment. There's going to be bands and firework displays and more parties and receptions than you could possibly imagine.'

They left the room, Madeleine still trying to convince him. Ellie paused in her dusting to rake a disapproving eye over the article. She shut the magazine, shaking her head again over the extravagance of it all.

'Still, I like her,' she said stoutly to nobody in particular as she beat the drapes. 'That Mrs Roosevelt and I, we share the same name after all.'

Madeleine continued to badger Jim about a visit to Washington. The papers were estimating that there would be more people attending this time than at any previous inauguration. Didn't he want to be there, right in the middle of it all? Besides, it could be *years* before Eleanor Blue and Anna Blue made it to Clara Dalloway's store in Raydon.

'Anna what?' Jim asked bewildered.

Finally, he took her to the cellar, and showed her the trunk, hidden behind a huge mahogany bed. He ran his hands over the jumble of antique silver inside, the creamers and tureens that he'd quietly been selling, a piece here, a piece there, to tide them over these past few years. A tray had gone last summer towards funding his and the Major's visit to Washington. Madeleine leaned against the wall, shocked.

'Are we short of money?'

His lips tightened. 'No. No we're not, but all the same, this is a working orchard. The yield each year is what it is, and we sell what we can sell, only prices haven't exactly been high of late, have they?' He shut the trunk, feeling strangely ashamed, and already regretting the impulse to share it with her. 'We're not going,' he said curtly.

She nodded unhappily. 'What's this?' In a bid to change the subject, she picked up a helmet lying on the floor. 'There's a hole . . .' she began, then realising what the neat, round aperture in the helmet was, flung it from her with a sharp cry of distaste. Turning, she stormed back up the stairs, not entirely understanding the sudden prick of tears behind her eyes.

Jim picked up the old Boche helmet from where it lay rocking on the floor. A stiff, closed-off expression on his face, he dusted the helmet against his corduroys and replaced it atop the trunk.

Feeling bad about the way she'd handled things, Madeleine set aside all notions of a visit to Washington DC, masking the twinge of disappointment she still felt. 'It was only an idea,' she said, smiling to Jim. All he did was nod non-committally in response, continuing to be cool and distant with her in the days that followed, still smarting over the way he'd opened himself up and how small she'd made him feel.

Upset by his reticence and suddenly restless, the silences of the house and the stark, winter-bound orchard filling her with claustrophobia, Madeleine decided to go home to Boston for a week. Jim dropped her off at the train station. 'Have a good trip,' he said, pecking her swiftly on the cheek. She nodded. He waited on the platform until the train pulled out from the station. She watched from the window as he strode away, craning her neck until he was lost from sight.

The whirl of inauguration-themed parties in Boston cheered her up, although she missed him constantly. To her surprise, more than dancing and carousing with her set, what she found most stimulating was the sparkle of conversation, the prolonged and animated political discussions she found herself increasingly drawn towards as her father and his cronies debated the new president and the changes to come.

All the same, if she were to be entirely honest, Madeleine admitted to herself, the highlight of her visit had to be the discovery of fat bolts of Eleanor and Anna Blue, freshly ordered in from New York along with rolls of velvet in the most delicious colours – Lanvin Red, Chianti Violet and Georgia Peach.

The 32nd President of the United States was sworn in on Saturday 4 March. He began the day with a short prayer at the Church of the Presidents, the historic St John Episcopal Church. Light filtered through the richly coloured windows over the family and entourage, as Reverend Endicott Peabody, who had married the Roosevelts almost three decades earlier, led the service.

'O Lord, our Heavenly Father, most heartily we beseech thee with thy favour to behold and bless thy servant, Franklin, chosen to be President of the United States.'

Later, a fanfare of trumpets, the Marine Band breaking out into 'Hail to the Chief' as President Franklin Delano Roosevelt stepped on to the platform. A massive roar erupted from the gathered crowd, the largest on record for a presidential inauguration, a hundred thousand voices echoing from the buildings, ricocheting off loudspeakers, amplified through the airwaves to be heard halfway across the world. The radio announcers briefed their listeners on the proceedings, and President Roosevelt went on air. All of America listened, gathered about their radios. With them, a sizable chunk of the civilised world, hanging on to every word.

The voice of the new president was calm but firm as he addressed the nation. 'There is nothing to fear,' he began, 'but fear itself.'

Madeleine returned, her face lighting up when she saw Jim. He'd missed her deeply too, her absence an invisible weight he seemed to carry about no matter where he went. Both were equally eager now to lay their discord, unarticulated as it had been, to rest.

She kissed him tenderly that night, cupping his face in her hands. Pressing her lips softly against his forehead, over each summer-bleached brow, his eyes closing as he submitted to her administrations. Over the contour of jawline and thrust of Adam's apple, delighting in the quickened sound of his breathing as she ran her tongue delicately along the side of his neck. Laying proprietary claim to the hollows above each clavicle, to the firm line of shoulder and the thin, silvered lines where the skin had stretched – football training, he'd said when she'd asked. She trailed her fingernails down his chest, gently circling the taut nipples. Lower still, over firmly muscled waist and abdomen, lower, caressing the turgid swell of him, fingers moving from root to stem.

Gripped with a wild, fierce ardor, he flipped her on to her knees, raising her haunches in one fluid movement as he straddled her from behind. She was startled at first by this abrupt switching around of power, muscles tensing at the animal urgency of his entry, but as he began to thrust inside her, Madeleine arched her back and shuddered, a primal spasm that passed seamlessly from her body to his, deepening the intense physicality of their connection as she gave in, gave herself wholly to him, burying her face in the pillows as she cried his name out loud.

THIRTY-ONE

Raydon • 1933

Just as old Asaph had predicted, the maples were early that year, the sap running freely all that spring. It slowed eventually, the candied air giving way to the fresh scent of new grass pushing its way through the mud. Wood and pasture alike were stippled in bright, jaunty green. Barn walls were fortified and fences creosoted, relieved of winter sag. The horses were let out early to pasture. They turned frisky, even the oldest and most staid among them, whickering in delight over this first forage after months of hay and grain. They tossed their manes, kicking up the yellow heads of dandelions as they cantered through the paddocks, shedding the shag of their winter coats in handfuls of fluff.

Madeleine was laughing over the antics of the newest foal as it gambolled through the grass when she had her first spell of lightheadedness. It was fleeting, lasting mere seconds, and she thought nothing of it. Two more episodes followed the next week, both of such cursory duration that she paid no attention to these either. It was only when she threw up without warning, out by the side of the barn, that it occurred to her.

Ellie summoned the doctor who cheerfully confirmed their suspicions – Madeleine was pregnant.

When they told Jim, he nodded, rubbed his forehead, nodded again, eyes widening first with surprise then flooding with joy. He grinned, a great, big, foolish grin that spread right across his face. In two long strides, he was at Madeleine's side and uncaring of his wet, mud-splattered clothes, he lofted her into his arms.

At first, Madeleine was caught up in the general whirl of excitement. There were congratulatory calls to take and a pile of mail to reply to, good wishes to the happy couple streaming in from Boston and New York. The Major had broken out his best cigars over the news, patting Jim on the back and offering Madeleine his compliments in an endearingly formal manner. He would graft a new apple tree in honour of the baby he said, just as one had been grafted for every Stonebridge boy before him.

'You've very sure it will be a boy,' Madeleine remarked, laughing.

'The odds are he will be,' the Major said quietly. 'There's a long line of boys in this family.' He hesitated as a thought struck him. 'Have you thought of a name?'

Jim shrugged. 'Not yet. James something Stonebridge, I suppose. If it's a boy.'

The Major tapped the end of his cigar on the ashtray. 'Would you . . .' he cleared his throat. 'Would you perhaps consider naming him James Henry?'

Jim looked up sharply at his father. *Henry*. He remembered how the Major had called this name aloud while delirious with fever at Anacostia. The way he'd denied it afterwards, and refused to discuss it any further. He took in the way his father was sitting in his armchair now, fiddling with his cigar, not looking at either of them as he awaited their response.

'It depends on what Madeleine thinks too,' Jim said carefully, 'but sure, I like the sound of it. James Henry Stonebridge, if it's a boy.'

'James Henry,' Madeleine repeated, rolling the name on her tongue. 'I like it too. So which one's Henry?' she asked, gesturing at the portraits and silhouette pictures on the wall.

Jim glanced at his father again, seeing beyond the impassive expression to the slow, vulnerable gladness dawning in his eyes. He shrugged. 'Just an old family name,' he lied.

The prospect of the baby seemed to energise the Major, seeding him with quiet purpose in a way that nothing else had, not since the rout at Anacostia. Rejecting out of hand the seedling catalogues that arrived with such regularity in the mail, the Major had Jim leave word in town for Black Pete instead. When that venerable emerged once more from the woods, the Major tasked him with finding a truly unique apple tree, one worthy of this as yet unborn grandson, from which a graft might be developed.

Pete came through magnificently, with two scions wrapped in moss. They came from a tree so special that they were the first folks he'd ever told about it. 'Edges a pond, far into the woods,' he divulged, glancing about him as if wary of who else might be listening. 'With that fresh, sweet water to drink, and these here apples to eat, a man wants for nothing.' The fruit so perfect of hue and taste, he added in a rare fit of drollery, that he wouldn't be surprised if it weren't the very tree that had got Adam and Eve into all that mischief.

The scions weren't all he'd brought with him. Fishing about in his sack, he handed a touched Madeleine a beautifully detailed stallion that he'd carved from butternut wood. 'For the wee 'un,' he said, nodding bashfully in the general direction of her midriff. He'd have gifted it when the baby was actually here, he explained, but it could be a while before he came into town again.

All in all, in those first few months of her pregnancy, Madeleine felt for the first time in her life as though she'd pulled off something truly worthwhile. It was only after the initial euphoria died away that the doubts began. She passed her hand over her still-flat belly time and again, examining the curves of bosom and hip for the slightest hints of tumescence. She'd lie awake at night, staring at the carved stallion just visible on the bedside table in the moonlight, following the detailing around the hooves and mane as she belatedly tried to come to grips with all the changes that had taken place in just over a year.

It was as if she'd been carried away on the crest of a wave, blithely riding its currents all this while, and only now, with the weight of responsibility, this new life steadily burgeoning inside her, was she finally taking stock of just how much her life had altered. Her mind touched repeatedly upon the vague, half-formed ideas she'd always harboured, their specifics indeterminate, but centred around a common theme – of going places, doing things. With her dancing perhaps, or maybe the theatre, just what exactly she'd never been quite certain of, but always a sense of something larger out there, something she could be a part of. It was just a question of finding it, she'd always assumed.

She wondered now if she ever would. She felt helplessly hemmed in, removed from the world by the stone walls that rambled endlessly around these hills, by the bucolic stretches of apple orchard and sugarbush, and quiet, dozing woodland.

Jim awoke one night to the muffled sound of her crying; when he put his hand to her face, her cheeks were wet.

'What's wrong?' he asked, bewildered, and she shook her head.

'You're not happy about the baby,' he guessed, flatly.

'I am. Of course I am, it's just . . . I don't know, it's all too much, so soon – a *baby*, Jim,' she tried to explain.

'Why marry me if you didn't want my children?' he said curtly, unsettled by the sight of her crying and more hurt than he cared to admit by what he perceived as her rejection.

'Is that the only reason you wanted to be married – so I could push out your children?' Her eyes fell on the butternut wood stallion. 'I'm not one of your brood mares,' she said, angered.

They lay in silence for a while after that. 'Madeleine,' he began, trying to make amends, and she turned blindly towards him, burying her face in his chest. They kissed, with a tenderness that he misread; he reached between her legs and she pushed him away, upset by the notion that perhaps this was all he wanted from her.

'Not one of your brood mares,' she repeated sharply. She dreamed of skunk cabbage that night, of the hungry spathes, bursting through the ice.

President Roosevelt set in motion a series of initiatives under the 'New Deal' that were designed to rejuvenate the economy. One of the very first was the formation of the Civil Conservation Corps – the CCC – a public works programme eligible to single men all across the country. They had to be willing to work in forest conservation, among other projects, and would each be paid thirty dollars a month, of which a minimum of twenty-two dollars was to be remitted to their families.

Connor cheered the initiative. It was almost a sign, he'd thought, them wanting single men, what with him and the missus having split up. The money wasn't much, but it was something. When he tried to enrol, however, he was informed that the upper age limit for eligibility was twenty-five. *Twenty-five*, an age that even the youngest of the Great War veterans had last seen over ten years before.

Veterans began to talk of marching yet again to Washington. About three thousand gathered there in May, under the aegis of a veteran's convention. This time, however, the Government was prepared. Determined to avoid another Anacostia debacle, they set up a huge camp to house the veterans at Fort Hunt, just outside the city.

Connor had run through the wages he'd earned during inaugural week, and was sheltering at the Salvation Army on Pennsylvania Avenue when he'd heard about the camp. He hurried there at once, letting out a low whistle of appreciation as he looked about him. Hooverville, this was not. Rows of eight-man tents were laid out in company streets of forty tents each. The tents came equipped with electricity; at the end of each street were sinks and running water. There were latrines, and even a bathhouse with a hundred showers. And the food! Connor stared disbelievingly at his plate. Baked ham. Potatoes. Peas. A hunk of bread, a generous pat of butter.

'There's rice pudding after, and coffee,' the veteran sitting next to him said. 'And more like this, at every meal. Bologna, potato salad, apple butter for supper. Oranges, eggs and potatoes for breakfast, with more bread, and as much coffee as you want.' He shook his head in disbelief. '*Oranges*!' he repeated happily, loosening his belt.

Connor wolfed down every morsel and went back for seconds. He noticed the battery of armed soldiers patrolling the perimeter of the camp, keeping a close watch on the veterans, but he was too hungry to care.

He was still there when Mrs Roosevelt surprised the veterans with a visit. She listened to their grievances, speaking in turn of the many battlefronts of the Great War that she'd visited, and leading them all in a rendition of 'Long Trail A-Winding'. That small gesture, of empathy, of a woman's touch, of just *listening*, went a long way. 'Hoover sent an army. Roosevelt, his wife,' a veteran commented wryly.

Soon after the First Lady's visit, the Government, in a conciliatory gesture, made twenty-five thousand slots in the CCC available to veterans, married or single. There were those who said the Government could go screw itself. 'Fuck the CCC and fuck this dollar-a-day pay' they said angrily, what about the bonus that they'd already earned?

There were many like Connor, however, who figured that one dollar was better than none. 'Sign me up!' he said eagerly, and was one of the first of over two thousand men at Fort Hunt who enrolled.

*

'Let's drive over,' Jim suggested to the Major, 'make a day of it. Maybe some of the folks from Anacostia are there.'

He'd gone looking for his father as soon as he'd heard about the CCC veteran camp that was being set up right there in Vermont, in nearby East Barre. He'd found the Major in the cellar, checking in yet again on the two precious scions that had been left to rest there until the grafting could begin next spring.

The Major's eyes momentarily brightened at the prospect. Then images resurfaced in his mind: the burning shanties, the defeated faces of the men. It reared up again, the sense of shame, the feeling that he'd let them all down by not lobbying hard enough, or with sufficient heart. The guilt, unreasonable as it was, that he was partly to blame for the catastrophe. 'No,' he said baldly to Jim, turning away.

Unwilling to give up so easily, Jim drove up there alone. Maybe he'd come across Connor or one of the others – it would cheer the Major up, he knew it would, to meet them again. The site was teeming with newly arrived veterans, almost two thousand so far, a camp official informed him. When he asked after Connor, Angelo and a few of the others from Anacostia, however, the man shook his head. 'There's too many come in all at once, so the paperwork's still getting sorted. You could leave word at the registration office,' he suggested.

Jim drove away, disappointed. He started to brood once more about Madeleine on the way home. He was yet to forgive her for that barb about being a brood mare. Yet again, by tacit agreement, they'd left the argument of that night unaddressed, pretending it had never happened, but her words still festered. He couldn't understand her ambivalence over their baby; it cut to the heart of him to think she might not want this child. He reacted in the only way he knew how, from all his childhood years of growing up without his mother and subject to the vagaries of the Major's moods. Jim withdrew into himself, masking his hurt under a cover that alternated between reserve and a cool flippancy.

When she'd pushed her supper around the plate, saying the very sight of it made her feel ill, 'There's bread if you can manage that,' he offered.

'Bread will make me even fatter.'

He'd gone back to his food without comment.

'No, Madeleine, you aren't fat,' she said for him.

'You aren't,' he pointed out, 'just heavier now that you're pregnant,' and was genuinely baffled when she called him a boor.

Madeleine had continued to swing between cherishing and chafing at her pregnancy as the summer wore on. It made her feel guilty, the internal back and forth, as if she were already failing this child. She called a girlfriend, hoping for reassurance, a woman a few years ahead of her at school who'd recently birthed her second. 'Oh, it's all worth it, but say goodbye to your waistline,' she said briskly. 'The hips too, they never quite sit the same again.' There was a mind-scrambling list of leaking bladders, flabby stomachs and other post-partum mementoes. Madeleine asked, horrified, why she'd never talked about any of this before. 'Didn't want to scare you girls off,' was the cheerful response.

In a fit of desperation, she called her mother, who told her not to be silly. 'It's what one does – get married and have children.' When Madeleine asked why her parents had stopped at just the one child, 'One was *quite* enough,' her mother replied definitively.

'I might never be able to dance again,' she'd said tearfully to Jim that night. 'The hipbones, sometimes they never quite come back together the same again.'

It would turn out just fine, he said, choosing his words carefully. Women had been giving birth for centuries, hadn't they?

Maybe they'd had an easier time of it because their husbands had petted and fussed over them, she said petulantly. 'My girlfriend's husband,' she informed him, 'is taking her to Italy as a birthing gift.'

Jim eyed her laconically. 'Well,' he said, 'there's the cattle fair next spring . . .'

Despite herself, Madeleine had started to laugh.

When she heard, Ellie had gone up to Jim as he was brushing down the horses and whacked him lightly on the head. 'She's not a country girl, she's still getting used to our ways,' she told him. '*Show* her you care, and James William Stonebridge, I've seen the way you look at her when she doesn't know you are, so don't you go shrugging your shoulders at me now.'

Jim mulled over what Ellie had said as he drove back to the farm. He thought again of that brief time in Washington DC with Madeleine, before the rout at the camp. That flight they'd taken, soaring through the skies. The look of sheer joyousness on her face as she'd turned to him. 'Do you like it?'

He remembered too, how disappointed she'd been that they couldn't go to the inauguration. Maybe it wasn't a bad idea, to enjoy a weekend somewhere before the baby came, he mused, calculating how much it might cost. Unknown to Madeleine, he'd taken up an opportunity to be a guide for some rich flatlander tourist who'd wanted to go fly fishing in the Connecticut. When the man had asked around in town for someone who could take him to the best spots, it was Jim's name that kept coming up. It was an easy gig, just a few hours for a couple of days.The 'hoppers had been hatching and the fish readily taking the bait; the flatlander had amassed a haul of brook, brown and rainbow trout, one among them so oversized that he'd tipped Jim handsomely.

Jim had set the money aside thinking it would come in handy for when the baby was here, but now he wondered otherwise. The orchard had done well this year, and folks everywhere were saying that the Depression was drawing to a close, that it was only a matter of months . . .

He turned on an impulse down a side road that led to the river, just a few yards from the sinkhole. He walked down to the shoreline, shading his eyes as he looked up at the overhanging ridge. It was just over a year ago that they had both swum here with such abandon. Like a bird swooping midflight she'd been, arcing gracefully into the water. *My Venus Anadyomene.*

Jim made up his mind. He walked back to the truck, spirits lifting as he began to contemplate their holiday. Maybe it could be an early anniversary gift from him to her, he thought as he drove. He wound the window down further, letting in the summer sun, starting to whistle as he drove through the hills.

Thinking he'd surprise her with it, Jim started to plan their getaway in secret, calling up hotels for the best rates and scanning the newspapers for bargains. He'd very nearly finalised everything, when Freddie called for Madeleine.

'We're having a theatre workshop, Cookie, and we miss our star. How about you come down too?'

Madeleine listened with growing interest as he outlined just what the multi-week programme would cover. 'Come on down,' Freddie urged again. 'That is, if you aren't already too much of a fat cow, darling, we can hardly have you waddling about the stage.'

She told him not to be so catty, and said maybe, but it was a long time to be away. She'd have to think about it.

'How long?' Jim asked.

'Five weeks,' she told him.

Angered that she would even consider staying away for so long – 'You should go,' he said distantly, saying nothing to her at all about that surprise trip to New York City that he'd been planning, about all that he'd lined up for them to do. Things he'd thought she might enjoy – a horse carriage ride through Central Park, the picnic at sunset there that he'd arranged through the hotel, the Broadway shows he'd shortlisted, based on the reviews, dinner at the Waldorf Hotel since her friends kept going on and on about how *wonderful* it was, a trip to the top of the Empire State Building, just like King Kong had done in the motion picture they'd both enjoyed so much that they'd watched it twice.

'I'll drive you down,' is all he coolly said to her.

Upset that he didn't seem to care whether she was gone or not, Madeleine said breezily that the train was perfectly fine; if he could drop her off at the station, she'd have Freddie pick her up in Boston.

Hemmed in and isolated as she'd begun to feel on the farm, to her chagrin, Madeleine was equally restless in Boston. She was enjoying the workshop, but all the same, she couldn't help thinking it was all a little trite, a piece of frippery in a world where there was so much more to explore. Slowly, as she lay in bed night after night, absently massaging her belly and unable to sleep, Madeleine started to gain insight into her angst, gradually tracing its roots all the way back to the events of last summer. The pregnancy had brought it into focus, but the restiveness had begun well before that, she realised.

Anacostia.

Being there, actually being right there when the camp was routed, had awakened something within her. All those half-articulated thoughts melding together into a desire to do something of substance in this world, to participate in it as wholly as she could.

And Jim . . . He'd been central to that burgeoning impetus, their marriage the supposed anchor from which to explore the world with all its possibilities together . . . What she hadn't bargained for was how shuttered he could turn, as if there was a hidden core of him that she never could seem to access, and how lonely it could make her feel.

Freddie shadowed her, constantly by her side at the rehearsals. When she compared him with Jim, he seemed unbearably boyish and immature. Remembering then that Jim had barely even called since she'd left for Boston, she took Freddie's hand playfully in hers. He tried to kiss her, and she hesitated a moment before pushing him away.

The episode so unsettled her that she called Jim to say she was coming home, two weeks earlier than scheduled. He'd still been angry with her for leaving in the first place, blue eyes cold as he watched the train chug in. But then she stepped on to the platform. The baby had grown, a rotund belly beginning to emerge from her slender frame. Madeleine was aglow, russet hair lustrous; it took Jim's breath away to see how beautiful she looked. Fecund, fertile, bursting with life.

He kissed her forehead that night, tenderly, her eyelids. Kneeling before her, he placed his arms around her and rested his head against her stomach. Gently he began to kiss her again, across the protuberance of skin and belly button. He parted her legs, slowly lifting the silk of her nightgown and she trembled. He dipped his tongue lower, lapping at her; tears came to her eyes at the tenderness, the near reverence in his touch.

The first killing frost of the season swept in unannounced, freezing shoots and leaves overnight. When the Major watched the sunrise the next morning through its reflection in the mirror, it reminded him with a jolt of the woods in France after a shelling. The same wan, bleak light, and the stubs of trees, jagged and charred.

Snow set in soon after, drifting over the wooden rafters of the old covered bridge, settling on shingle and stone alike. Madeleine went unexpectedly into labour, so early that she was unable to get to Boston for the delivery as planned.

'Jim!' she called in a panic, as her waters broke, and he rushed from the shed, tossing the pile of firewood aside.

So it was that on a brilliant November morning, James Henry Stonebridge came into the world, in the very same room where a long line of Stonebridges had been born before him. He arrived perfectly healthy, squalling and crying, tiny red fists balled in protest against the cold. Ellie brought the baby out to meet his grandfather. 'Go on, hold him,' she urged, smiling.

The Major took the baby hesitantly in his arms. He looked down at the tiny, blanketed form. 'James Henry,' he said softly. The baby blinked sleepily as if in response, gazing up at the Major as he opened his mouth in a big, lopsided yawn. The Major chuckled. 'James Henry,' he said again, and his voice shook.

Late that evening, the snow started to fall again, carpeting the hills in pure, untarnished white, and staying on the ground all that winter.

THIRTY-TWO

Spring 1935

'You see?' Major Stonebridge murmured in satisfaction, pointing out the tiny green leaves sprouting atop the apple sapling. He looked over his glasses at his grandson. 'New growth.'

Jimmy bent precariously forward from his perch in the Major's arms and tried to pluck at the leaves.

'Don't do that!' Major Stonebridge laughed and swung him around. 'How do you expect your apple tree to grow if you destroy all its leaves?'

Jimmy chortled, revealing two nascent teeth. Throwing his podgy arms around his grandfather's neck, he gave him a wet, sloppy kiss. Major Stonebridge hugged the little body closer. 'Do we remember our grafting lesson? The rootstock from the oldest tree in the orchard, and a scion from within the woods. Together, a new tree, for James Henry Stonebridge.'

Jimmy squirmed in his grandfather's hold and tried to tug on his glasses. 'Now, now,' the Major admonished solemnly, as he continued to lecture the child on fruit buds and cambium.

Ellie shook her head fondly by the kitchen window. Barely a year and a half old, and Jimmy had accomplished what none of them had been able to, rousing the Major from the depths of his despondency. The child had gravitated towards his grandfather almost from the time he was born, his fretting quieting as if by magic when seated in the Major's lap.

The Major still drank like a fish, far more than was good for him, but it had been a while, Ellie recalled thankfully, since one of his binges. Instead of his solitary rambles about the orchard, he now went with young Jimmy tucked into his arms. And that sapling he'd grafted! The way he fussed and mussed over it, you'd think its roots were dipped in solid gold. He'd not let Jim do the cutting, shaping the tips of the two scions and the rootstock himself, binding the exposed layers together with special care. Right upset he'd been all that week when one of the scions had not taken, withering away on the graft. Thankfully, the remaining one was doing well. Not a morning passed without the Major going out to pet and admire it.

She watched as Jim appeared from around the side of the barn. He tousled his son's hair and was rewarded with a two-toothed grin.

'Ootstaw,' Jimmy said importantly, pointing at the sapling.

'That's right, rootstock.'

Their voices floated down to the house and Ellie thought of the Major's wife with a sudden lump in her throat. How she'd have loved to see the three of them, standing there together, silhouetted against the red of the barn, the apple trees, and the clear, blue sky.

The baby's arrival had brought Jim and Madeleine closer too. It still frustrated her, the way he could withdraw so fully, the impenetrable nature of his silences, but their mutual love for their son further cemented the elemental bond that had always existed between them.

Motherhood had instilled Madeleine with new confidence, settling her in a way she hadn't foreseen. All the doubts that had assailed her during her pregnancy had stilled as she gazed at the newborn in her arms, Jim steadfastly by her side.

On a whim last year, she'd taken up a short stint assisting one of her father's university colleagues, a professor in the political studies department, in editing his essays for publication. She'd thoroughly enjoyed the work, and the literary debates that had followed equally so. At a reading hosted for the professor, an acquaintance had suggested to Madeleine that she might do a spot of fundraising for the local library. The gala she organised was such a success that she found herself much in demand, travelling regularly to Boston now to fundraise for a select group of charities and organisations whose ideologies she believed in.

'You let her go now,' Ellie had counselled Jim. 'Madeleine needs to get out of these hills every now and again. She's a city girl after all.'

'Flatlander, you mean.'

'How would you feel if you had to stay all cooped up in one of those townhouses there in Boston?' she demanded, hands on her hips. She nodded with satisfaction at the look of horror that crossed

Jim's face at the prospect. 'I thought so. Well, it might be the same with her, just the other way around.'

He still hated it. when she left, but slowly adopted a grudging acceptance.

As for the Major, little Jimmy Henry was a miracle, wholly unexpected and entirely undeserved, but one that he marvelled over every single day. 'He's the spitting image of Jim at that age,' Ellie kept saying. Try as he might though, the Major could not remember Jim as an infant. Those memories were all tangled up in the war years that had come so soon after. Only hints remained of the time that had elapsed before.

When the Major would limp into the nursery in the morning only to find little Jimmy already up, standing impatiently in his crib, it sometimes brought back a faint imprint of memory. It was the same crib of burled walnut, worn smooth over the decades and passed down from generation to generation, that Jim had slept in. As he stood over the crib, chuckling at Jimmy tugging at the bars, the Major would be gripped by a sense of déjà vu. A shadowy imprint in his mind of his younger self, standing exactly here, with Jim, not Jimmy, gurgling in pleasure as his father reached for him.

The specifics, however, this sweet-scented mix of milk and talc, the innocent trust of a child curled asleep on his lap – these the Major did not recall at all. The early years of Jim's childhood tacked instead on to the edges of other memories: that winter of 1917–18, for instance, when the temperatures in Raydon dropped to thirty below and did not rise above zero for forty consecutive days.

He remembered with crystal clarity the bite of those mornings that he was home on furlough, frost piling in the corners of the window panes like sawdust. Stepping outside on those sleepless nights, with icicles glittering all along the eaves, the cold a balm against the rawness of his leg. A whoosh of wings against the moon – a migrant great horned owl, one of so many that winter, fleeing the great white north. The gleaming gimlet eyes, the tiger stripes, the hoot of its six-tone songs.

Surely he was imagining the child by his side?

1918. The sharp memory of coming home for good and the sight of the thinned-out orchard. Apple orchards up and down New England had been decimated by the cold that year but these old, hardy breeds, the McIntoshes and Malindas had held stubbornly on. Even the graft that had been planted when Jim was born, even that tenderling doggedly stood. In these battered survivors, the faint mirroring of his story.

The Major had poured himself into the orchard in the months that followed. He could rattle off, even now, the names of the grafts he'd initiated then, could recall the precise shape and texture of each of their leaves. And like a hint of colour just beyond the edges of a daguerreotype, a blurred sense of his young son, toiling faithfully alongside.

It filled the Major with sadness, these shell holes in his memory. The stretches of darkness, the unaccounted days mired in loss. The faces from the past that he sometimes saw, phantom images in the black mirror, in the crowd beside a boxing ring.

It was only when he was with his grandson that he felt somewhat restored, those guileless, blame-free eyes easing his inner turmoil. Bit by bit as little Jimmy grew, the Major began to take an interest in the world about him once more. The Bonus Bill was submitted to Congress for the sixth time in January 1935, and he began to pore over the newspapers as before, tracking reports of its passage. That spring, when Major General Smedley Butler published a book on veterans and their plight, the Major promptly put in an order.

He was sitting lost in the book when little Jimmy toddled over. The Major hoisted him on to his lap. The child pointed at the cover. 'War is a Racket' the Major read aloud. Jimmy jiggled his bottom up and down, bouncing on his grandfather's lap in encouragement. The Major obligingly began to read aloud:

'. . . Thus, having stuffed patriotism down their throats, it was decided to make them help pay for the war, too. So, we gave them the large salary of thirty dollars a month.'

The Major sighed and tried to put the book aside, but Jimmy bounced up and down again until he continued.

'Half of that wage (just a little more than a riveter in a shipyard or a labourer in a munitions factory safe at home made in a day) was promptly taken from him to support his dependants, so that they would not become a charge upon his community. Then we made him pay what amounted to accident insurance – something the employer pays for in an enlightened state – and that cost him six dollars a month. He had less than nine dollars a month left.

'Then, the most crowning insolence of all – he was virtually black-jacked into paying for his own ammunition, clothing, and food by being made to buy Liberty Bonds. Most soldiers got no money at all on pay days.

'Enough,' the Major said abruptly. 'No, Jimmy,' he said firmly, when the child pouted, 'that is quite enough reading for now. Look!' He pointed at a barn swallow dipping and wheeling outside. Jimmy stared in wide-eyed fascination, mouth agape, clutching on to his grandfather's thumb. The Major hugged his little body closer and, shutting the book, began pointing out yet again all the varieties of apple trees in the orchard, teaching his grandson each of their names.

There was something so endearing about the two of them sitting companionably there that when Jim came in from the barn, he paused in the doorway to watch. Madeleine came sleepily down-stairs, pushing the hair back from her face. He glanced coolly at her, still angered by their recent argument.

She'd returned from yet another trip to Boston last evening and he'd been at the station a good half an hour early to get her, just from missing her so. When she'd stepped from the train car, it had given him a start, the new shortness of her hair. She'd laughed, linking her arms about his neck. 'Do you like it?'

He did, actually, once he got over the surprise of it. What got him irritated was the faint tang on her breath. 'Have you been drinking?'

She'd risen up on her toes and kissed his cheek. 'You might say that. An impromptu get-together last evening, and,' she gestured at her purse, 'a small going-away gift inside, to while away the hours on the train.'

He knew without asking that the odious Freddie had been in-volved. 'Let's go,' he said curtly.

'Don't be such a stick-in-the-mud, Jim Stonebridge, it was only a glass or two.' She kissed him again. 'I missed you, you know.'

He'd picked up her bag without comment, striding towards the truck.

'I missed you too,' she muttered for him, under her breath.

They'd slept on the far sides of the bed. He'd been the first to wake this morning. He looked at her, watching the light fall on her skin, the shorter hair highlighting her cheekbones, the etched jut of her jaw. He put a finger to one creamy arm, tracing the pattern of light and shadow; when she stirred, however, he'd taken his hand away and walked into the bathroom without a word.

Madeleine smiled now as she watched the Major and Jimmy, taken again by how much they were alike. She leaned gently against Jim. 'I did miss you.' He glanced at her, looked away.

'Well, that makes one of us,' he said. She paid no mind, resting her head against his arm and after a moment's hesitation he raised it stiffly about her waist. She leaned closer, and he drew her in, holding her close. She smiled, again, contentedly.

As they stood there watching little Jimmy chortle in his grandfather's lap, it gradually dawned on Madeleine that for the first time that she could remember, the Major had moved his armchair from its customary position before the fireplace. It was angled in such a way now that sitting in it, one still had a clear view of the black mirror, but one could also, as the Major was now, look directly out on to a large section of the apple orchard. The verdant, buzzing vista of flower and fruit, the brilliant yellows and reds of finches calling from the trees, the colours vivid, vibrantly alive.

THIRTY-THREE

That summer, they had a surprise visitor. On a sun-soaked July afternoon filled with the chirp of song-sparrows, Connor walked up the drive.

'I'm headed to Washington,' he explained, grinning as the Major slapped him on the back and shook his hand. 'Thought I'd take a bit of a detour and look you folks up.'

'You staying a while, I hope?' Jim asked.

'Just the night, if you'll have me.' He jerked a thumb at the barn. 'In this heat, a pile of hay to sleep on will do me just fine. Well, that and maybe a beer.'

'I think we can do better than that,' the Major said wryly. 'Come on inside and let's get you that beer for starters.'

Madeleine came to see what the hullabaloo was about. 'I'll be . . .!' Connor exclaimed, as he removed his knapsack from his shoulders. 'Look who we have here. Mrs Stonebridge then, I take it?'

'That's right,' she said, laughing. She kissed his cheek. 'And there's someone in the nursery who you ought to meet as well.'

He'd been in the CCC veteran camp up in Vermont for a while, he told them, building dams over the Winooski.

'I went up there,' Jim interjected, and the Major looked at him, surprised. 'I drove up to see if you or any of the others had signed up.'

'Got your message,' Connor admitted. 'Took me a while, I know, to get here, but I've been moving around some.' He hesitated. 'After Anacostia . . .' A hummingbird flapped in the honeysuckle vine along the porch. He followed the blue flurry of its wings. 'Not been in touch with anyone in a while,' he said by way of explanation. He squared his shoulders, mustering up the cheerful, stump-toothed grin that Jim remembered so well. 'Well, I'm here now, aren't I?'

'Yes, and let's drink to that,' the Major said.

*

The three men sat late into the night, long after Madeleine retired upstairs. Connor did most of the talking, spinning yarns and repeating old, half-forgotten jokes as he worked his way through hard cider and whisky, his laughter ringing through the pall of cigarette smoke.

He'd gone back to see his wife, he said, to see if they couldn't pick up where they'd left off. It had worked for a few months, but all the old stuff started up again and one day, he'd just upped and left. 'Ain't been back since, and she ain't been looking for me either, I don't think,' he said matter-of-factly.

'The dynamite,' he confided at one point, talking about the CCC camp in Vermont. 'The explosions did me in.' He lit a fresh cigarette. 'We cut granite up and down the Winooski, in all sorts of weather. Blisters on our hands every day, the size of marbles. Still, I was fine with it, even in the . . . bitch of a winter you folks have around these parts. All winter long we worked, the ground like iron and the freeze rising from the water until our balls just about fallen off. They'd drive us to the river in open trucks with the wind coming in from everywhere. Kids would throw snowballs at us as we passed through the towns, through Waterbury and East Barre.'

He grimaced. 'Just kids being kids, but those snowballs stung, made some of the men real mad.' He drew on his cigarette again. 'It was when the blasting started that I had to leave. The sound of it . . .' He looked at the Major. 'Couldn't take it,' he said simply. 'Too much like France.'

He'd dropped out of the camp in Vermont last year, wandered some, and when his dollars ran out, footed it back to Washington. Figuring that he'd had about all that he could take of the cold, he'd signed up for a veteran rehabilitation camp way down South, near Charleston.

The rehab camps had been set up the previous fall. Loath to enlist additional veterans into the previously initiated CCC projects, not when there were so many younger, able-bodied men across the country eager to enrol, the Roosevelt Government had instead formulated a plan targeted specifically at veterans. The men who signed up at these rehab camps would be assigned public work projects. All meals and board would be taken care of, with pay ranging from between thirty and forty-five dollars a month.

There was a fundamental difference between the CCC and the rehab camps though. The latter were filled not only with down-on-their-luck doughboys, but a sizable number of veterans who'd previously been claiming disability benefits. In the wake of the budget cuts implemented by the Roosevelt administration, veteran benefits had been affected across the board. Those with physical disabilities and service-related illnesses had their benefits reduced. Those with 'neuroses' that could not irrefutably be connected to their time served in France lost their benefits entirely.

'A lot of head cases,' Connor said now. 'Wasn't anywhere else for them to go, after their benefits were taken away. Good men, some better than others, but real messed up from the Front. There was this engineer, not two whiskers on his face, although we must have been about the same age. Babyface here was real polite, real pleasant, but a couple of drinks in him and he'd just about turn inside out. He'd go looking for trouble, pick fights with just about anyone – the bigger the better – get himself beat to a pulp on purpose.'

He chuckled as he poured himself another shot of whisky. 'Not that the rest of us were much better. All sorts of trouble they have down there in the South, and we found it all. Come payday, this guy who owned a bar in Camden would send down a bus for us; in between, there were sellers of moonshine. And the women! This one time, a buddy was up to his eyeballs in booze, so pickled that he goes wandering off into some stranger's house. He goes right on upstairs and when the homeowner returns, who does he find but this weary-ass doughboy, all tucked up and snoring in his bed!

'That one, the police laughed off. But when a bunch of us got into a fight with some of the locals last month, that didn't go down as well.' His face twisted. 'You know what happened in Washington around then, Major.'

'The veto.'

It had been a crushing disappointment. When the Bonus Bill had passed with such ease through Congress in January, veterans across the country had come to believe that their bonuses might at long last, be in sight. For months, it was all Connor and so many more like him had talked about, the BONUS, the *Bonus!*, spinning dreams around all that they'd do when they finally had it in their hands.

On 22 May 1935, however, President Roosevelt stood before

Congress. In an unprecedented move, he explained in a fifty-five-paragraph speech just why he was compelled to veto the Bill. It was one thing, the President maintained, for the Government to provide financial support to those veterans left physically disabled by the war. It was quite another entirely to be expected to accord special compensation via the Bonus Bill to the able-bodied. Those veterans, he said, ought to be treated exactly the same as other American citizens, on a par with all those who did not wear a uniform during the war.

Yet again, victory had been snatched from the veterans. In this cruel, see-saw ride, the Bonus Bill was now dead until 1936, when the next session of Congress would convene.

Connor had fallen into a black mood after the broadcast. The veto had been bad enough, but what made it worse were the President's words.

'The veteran who is disabled owes his condition to the war. The healthy veteran who is unemployed owes his troubles to the Depression.'

The statement had picked at a deep-rooted sense of shame. What of the years *before* the Depression, then? Everyone around him was making money hand over fist, while nothing had seemed to stick with him. The drifting, the falling in and out of jobs, the troubles at home – he'd been one of the lucky ones, practically unscathed in France, and yet, he'd racked up failure after failure all the years of his return.

Men like him had returned from the Front entirely capable, the President had stated with such firm conviction. The parts inside of him that felt shot through to pieces, those then, Connor thought, must be entirely of his own making. A fault of character, an abject failing of strength.

'I rounded up a bunch of us for some hard drinking that evening,' he recounted now to the Major and Jim. 'We piled into a couple of beat-up old cars and headed into town. Every last penny we had, we put it on the counter and told the bartender to keep 'em coming. The mood we were in, didn't take much to get into an all-out brawl with some locals. The police came, blowing their whistles and laying about with batons. Next thing you know, they put us doughboys behind bars. We were still so cut up over what we'd heard on the radio, we broke that jail.'

Connor waved his cigarette about with boozy pride. 'That's right, we *broke* the damn jail. The entire top floor – smashed the panes and broke the screens, pissed all over the walls. The captain in charge of the camp was a real decent sort. He sprung us out of there, but told us there wasn't much more that he could do for us, not after the trouble we'd stirred up. He paid us for the rest of the month and said we'd have to move on to someplace else.'

He gave a bitter laugh. 'So here I am again, moving on, back on the road again. You know the best part of it, though? They had us all working on a new golf course while we were there. A golf course, when I bet you anything that there weren't one set of golf clubs in all of that rundown little tank town. *A fucking golf course*! Busting our backs and knees for one dollar a day.' Connor barked with laughter again. 'We doughboys should be treated no different, the President said, than those who did not wear a uniform. When we shipped out to France, we went ready to fight for this country. Went ready to die. You tell me, Major, just how are we the same then, as the ones that stayed behind?'

The Major rose from the table, and reaching for his walking stick, limped from the room. When he returned, Jim recognised the book in his hands.

'You seen this?' the Major asked quietly. Connor shook his head.

He thumbed through the passages of Major General Butler's book, until he found the one he wanted. He began to read aloud. 'I have visited eighteen government hospitals for veterans. In them are a total of about fifty thousand destroyed men – men who were the pick of the nation eighteen years ago. The very able chief surgeon at the government hospital at Milwaukee, where there are three thousand eight hundred of the living dead, told me that mortality among veterans is three times as great as among those who stayed at home.'

The Major paused, his voice raw. He coughed, cleared his throat. 'Boys with a normal viewpoint . . .' he rasped, breaking off into another bout of coughing.

Jim stood up, and looking over his father's shoulders, took up the narrative. 'Boys with a normal viewpoint were taken out of the fields and offices and factories and classrooms and put into the ranks. There they were remoulded; they were made over; they were made to regard murder as the order of the day. They were put shoulder to shoulder and, through mass psychology, they were entirely changed. We used them for a couple of years and trained them to think nothing at all of killing or of being killed.'

Jim paused, disturbed. Connor sat in rapt concentration, staring at the table; even his father, despite having read the book from cover to cover, was listening intently to the words.

'Then, suddenly, we discharged them and told them to make another "about face"! This time they had to do their own readjustment, sans mass psychology, sans officers' aid and advice and sans nationwide propaganda. We didn't need them any more. So we scattered them about without any "three-minute" or "Liberty Loan" speeches or parades. Many, too many, of these fine young boys are eventually destroyed, mentally, because they could not make that final "about face" alone.'

'You've got a place here, you know,' the Major said gruffly the next day, as Connor prepared to leave. He'd head down to New York, look up a couple of buddies there, he said. Maybe Angelo in New Jersey, and then onwards to Washington. There was a rehab camp in Florida, he'd heard about; maybe it was time he checked out that part of the country.

'It means a lot to me, Major, but no.' He grinned. 'Don't think I can take another one of your winters.'

The Major nodded without comment, understanding, however, the real reason behind Connor's reticence.

'Maybe you could come for apple picking season then, in the fall,' Jim suggested, helping Connor with his knapsack.

'Nah. I'll be in Florida then, sitting by the water, a knockout by my side.'

'There are storms in Florida,' Madeleine pointed out, and he laughed.

'Hemingway lives down there,' the Major remembered. 'Ernest Hemingway,' he said, as Connor looked at him blankly. 'Famous writer. He served as an ambulance driver in France.'

'Well I'll surely say Hello if I run into him. Maybe he can write a story about me and my buddies, huh, Major?'

The Major smiled. 'Should you change your mind,' he said again, 'you always have a place here.' He hesitated, wanting to address what he knew was Connor's true concern, but trying to find the right words.

Giving up, he looked the younger man in the eye,'We're *all* fuck-ups, Connor,' he said then.

Connor looked away, fiddling with his hat. 'I guess I just don't want to fuck up around folks I know,' he said, barely audibly. Although he was not yet forty, Connor suddenly looked like a very old man. 'Been fucking up a long time, and I'll not do it no more around those I know.'

On 28 July, the third anniversary of the Anacostia evacuation, Connor was in Washington yet again. He was part of a contingent of two hundred veterans who marched across the Potomac river to Arlington National Cemetery. The two veterans who had been killed during the riots that day in 1932 lay buried here; the veterans laid wreaths at their graves.

Almost immediately after, Connor enlisted with the camp in Florida. He soon found himself headed down the coast, all the way to Matecumbe Island in the Florida Keys.

THIRTY-FOUR

Matecumbe Island • 2 September 1935

It had already begun to rain when Connor awoke. He groaned and rolled on to his back, his eyes adjusting to the leaden light as water dripped down the window panes. The barracks were rank with booze and sweat. He sat up gingerly, wincing as he reached for the bottle that lay beside him. There was hardly anything left, but he tilted it to his mouth all the same, draining the last few drops. He swayed upright to his feet. Men lay slumbering around him, in various stages of repose and undress. One of the women from the previous evening was still there, he noticed, snoring gently on somebody's bunk. Connor let his eyes move over her, dwelling on the naked flop of her breasts, the undulation of waist and thigh. He passed a hand over the semi-hardness of his crotch, and sensing the urgent pressure of his bladder, lurched unsteadily towards the door.

The wind was brisk enough that he had to lean against the door to keep it propped open as he unzipped his pants. He urinated into the wind, letting the rain wash against his face. It felt good.

'Shut the damn door,' someone yelled from inside the barracks. 'Your piss – it'll all wash inside.'

Connor let rip a loud fart in response, continuing to watch the streaming palms, the wind whipping caps of frothy white from the waves. The storm that they'd been talking about at the bar, it was here.

The first warnings about bad weather had appeared in the evening papers on Saturday. A 'tropical disturbance' had been detected east of the Bahamas and was headed in the direction of the Keys. At Sloppy Joe's that evening, folks had talked of the approaching storm with resigned annoyance. What perfect timing, to hit the Keys squarely over the long Labour Day weekend.

Ernest 'Papa' Hemingway sat at the bar in a black mood, hunched over his Teacher's. 'He was in the middle of a story,' Skinner, the huge, three-hundred-pound bartender explained to an amused Connor, 'and now he can't work until the storm's past.'

'Hey, Papa,' Connor called, 'how about I buy you a drink and cheer you up?'

'You keep on buying drinks for folks, doughboy, and you're going to be broke faster than I can empty this glass.'

Connor laughed. 'It's the end of the month, remember? Payday, Papa, I got plenty.'

He bought a round of drinks and sat beside the writer, admiring once again the mural of General Custer that dominated the wall. The veterans had become a fixture at the bar ever since the camps had opened, adopting the dark, cavernous interior, the floors slick with spilled drink and melted ice, the pool tables as their own. Papa Hemingway was here almost every evening, drinking alongside them, swapping yarns and entering friendly pissing contests in the trough that served as a urinal out the back.

He eyed Connor gloomily. 'You staying local for the weekend?'

Connor shrugged, drumming his fingers on his glass. 'Ain't decided yet. Might go up to Miami for the game with a bunch of the boys tomorrow.' He tilted the glass to his mouth, draining it empty.

Those dime-priced shots of gin and fifteen-cent glasses of whisky had a way of adding up, and as things went, Connor had found himself sufficiently depleted of funds on Sunday morning that he could ill afford the trip to Miami. A bunch of them elected to stay on in the Keys for the weekend. Some of the women from the carousing of last night had come back to the camp with them. What was a trifling storm when you had plenty of cheap booze and women to while away the hours?

At 10 a.m. that Sunday, the Coast Guard received a weather forecast that warned of increasing winds, possibly of hurricane force in the Florida Straits. They had a seaplane fly around the Keys, dropping wooden blocks that warned of the potential change in the weather to hurricane status. The pilot made several trips, even using paraffin-coated ice-cream cartons when he ran out of blocks. Assuming that the camp authorities had things under control, he did not, however, bother to drop warning messages around the veteran camps.

Oblivious that the storm they were expecting was now an impending hurricane, the veterans in Matecumbe spent all of Sunday in yet another booze-soaked blur.

It began to rain in earnest late Monday morning, the wind roaring eerily through the mangrove swamps. Still the camp authorities waited to act. The camp trucks that could have been commandeered to get the veterans off Matecumbe had been locked up for the holiday weekend. The only evacuation measure that remained was to order a special train all the way from Miami; this they were loath to do until they were certain that it was indeed a hurricane they were dealing with.

The rain poured incessantly, whipped by the wind into sheets of water that slammed with startling solidity, first vertically, then at a slant and sometimes almost horizontally, into the work camps. Finally, at 2 p.m., an order was put in for that train. A crew had to be mustered, however, a task complicated by the holiday.

By the time the train left, it was already 4:25 p.m.

Word was at last sent to the veteran camps: the status of the storm had been changed to a hurricane, and it was making straight for the Keys. The men were to wait at the railway embankment for the train that had been sent for.

The wind rose by the hour, battering the hurricane flags – red, with a black square in the centre – that had been raised all along Key West.

Connor huddled against the embankment, lying low to the ground. The barometer had steadily continued to fall, heralding the approaching centre of the hurricane, as he and the other men had thrown their few belongings together, latched the barrack doors shut and headed out. The wind was so strong they'd practically crawled to the embankment, the waves pounding so forcefully now upon the island that the very ground seemed to tremble.

The rain beat down mercilessly, shorting flashlights, making a mockery of the few raincoats they had among them as it soaked the men through and through. Connor pulled the lapels of his coat tighter about his neck. The wind gained even more speed, flinging handfuls of sand, stinging faces and hands and drawing tiny spots of blood. Connor drew his sleeve over his fingers and shielding his face with his arm, peered cautiously through the aperture, startled and not a little awed by the ferocity of the storm. An arc of lightning crackled overhead. Three trash cans were dancing in mid-air.

Every little while, someone would raise his head. 'I hear it, I hear the train,' he'd shout, his words all but swallowed by the storm. Each time, it was only the roar of the wind, blowing faster and faster through the mangroves, sounding cruelly like the shriek of a locomotive engine. Still they waited, as the barometer continued to drop.

29.55

28

27.5

Men began to scatter, crawling into the darkness to seek refuge where they could; in the mangroves, belting themselves to the palms. Connor stayed where he was. He began to laugh, taken by the irony of it all. The train wasn't coming, not any time soon it wasn't. Once again, they were on their own, just a bunch of beat-up doughboys crouched in this parody of the trenches, cowering for their lives in the sand.

He'd wanted to see a storm, he thought to himself, he'd actually *wanted* to see this! The thought made him laugh all the more.

The eight-mile eye of the hurricane drew closer still to Matecumbe, sending the wind into a howling frenzy. A sapodilla was uprooted and flung against the rocks as if it were no more than a toothpick, the roof of one of the barracks lifted clear off and was thrown, splintering, into the sea. Pieces of lumber were carried from the construction sites, and sent slamming against the embankment, as a two-hundred-and-fifty-mile-per-hour gust began to churn the beaches, turning sand into tiny missiles that flayed clothes from bodies and the skin clear off faces, the fingerprints from hands. All around Connor, men began to scream.

He tried to rise to his feet, and was knocked down by something that hit his legs. Stubbornly, he got to his knees when the wind shifted direction for a brief instant, permitting him to stand. 'I'll not go lightly,' he shouted, although there was nobody to hear. 'I'll not—' The wind picked him up effortlessly, shrieking in his ear as it flung him through a curtain of sand, tearing the voice from his throat.

Connor saw a wave rear up over the island, a huge body of water, dark and oily, all-encompassing, large enough to swallow the world.

*

Connor was right. The train never did arrive, its progress so impeded by fallen debris that by the time it reached Islamorada, the eye of the hurricane had just made landfall on the Keys. The train was blown clear off the tracks, with only the locomotive left standing.

The weather stayed so rough that it was not until Wednesday that the first rescue boats reached Matecumbe. None of the buildings of the camp remained. Veterans lay everywhere, their bodies rolling back and forth in the surf of the now calm and glassy sea, slung impossibly high from those trees that still stood, dozens found in the mangroves where they had sought shelter, the mangroves themselves brown, stripped entirely bare of their leaves.

THIRTY-FIVE

Raydon • 1936

The Labour Day Hurricane, the press called it. It was the strongest recorded to have ever hit the United States, setting a new barometric low for all of the Western Hemisphere, of 26.35 inches.

Jim searched the lists of the dead for Connor's name. 'Maybe he never did go to the Keys after all,' Madeleine said hopefully.

Maybe, Jim thought to himself. Or perhaps he had, but was lucky enough to have been away when the hurricane hit. It had been a long weekend after all – maybe he'd gone to Miami and ridden out the storm in safety there, drinking and carousing in a bar someplace.

Maybe he'd been blown out to sea, yet another veteran whose body was never recovered, their deaths never included in the final toll of fatalities.

'Who Murdered the Vets?' Hemingway asked in an emotional piece, calling to justice all those who'd so callously abandoned the men on Matecumbe until it was far too late. Jim recalled that brief conversation on the porch between Connor and his father, and wondered if Connor had indeed run into the writer on Key West.

'Maybe he'll write about my buddies and me,' he'd wisecracked then; how he'd roar with laughter now, laugh until he was doubled over, at the cruel irony.

The rich, Hemingway pointed out bitterly in his essay, knew better than to visit the Keys during hurricane season. Why then, had veterans been sent there in droves? There was a stench that hung over the islands, he wrote, the stench of the dead and the rotting, that he last remembered from the war.

The Major studied the photographs of the carnage published in the papers. Bodies lashed together on a cart and towed behind a car. Rows of wooden boxes into which the decomposing remains had been dumped before being taken away to be burned. He pored over them in silence, raising a hand now and again to wipe away the water dribbling from his damaged eye as he took in every minute, horrific detail. The missing shoes and tattered remnants of clothing, an arm flung over a face, as if to shield it from the wind, dead veterans arranged in long, efficient rows, head to toe.

The Major's face was expressionless as he studied the images, only the fluttering left eyelid betraying the raw despair welling up inside. Like a crack opening along an ocean floor, everything he'd kept so long unspoken, all that he'd tried so hard to keep in check, was coming loose, revealing the fault lines that lay beneath. The twitching of the left eye worsened, a trickle of water coursing steadily down his cheek. He lifted a hand to brush it away, but the fingers locked, and now the wrist, a paralysis swimming up one side of his body so that he could no more move his left arm than deny the pressure building within his chest. A centrifuge of sorrow and helplessness pulling so inexorably that the Major imagined he might collapse into himself. He called out, but the words slurred in his throat.

'Jim,' he managed with great effort, but it was only a rasping whisper.

He tried to rise from the armchair and fell headlong, the pages of the newspaper with their stark, black-and-white images scattering about him. 'Jim,' he slurred again through the one side of his mouth that he was still able to move, 'Jim . . .' the sound no louder than a sigh.

The Major let go, a great surge of grief crashing through him like breakers in a storm. The waters sucking him under, beyond the layers of loss and riddling guilt, down, deep under, to where there was nothing but a vast stillness. No more ghosts, no more voices from the past, just a floating, pelagic silence.

'A stroke,' the doctor diagnosed, and they were lucky it had been a mild one. With rest and enough time, he fully expected the rictus in the Major's face and side to right itself. Jim nodded, trying to hide his relief; after the doctor left, he stood over his father's bed for a long time, silently watching the rise and fall of his chest as he slept.

In the face of the outcry that erupted over the hurricane disaster, the Government launched an official inquiry. It was a hasty affair with a quick verdict: there had been no negligence. The Government had acted out of good faith; the deaths were classified as an 'Act of God'.

Public sentiment stayed firm, however, in support of veterans and their cause. Not four months later, in the dawn of 1936, of what was an election year, the Bonus Bill was finally approved.

Blood money, Jim thought with disgust, as he listened to the news on the radio, unable to contemplate the bonus without thinking of Connor. So many like him, fallen by the wayside during this fourteen-year-long petition. He looked at his father, trying to gauge his reaction. The Major had recovered sufficiently from the stroke last September that the downward pull on the left side of his face was barely noticeable any more. Jim noticed the differences all the same, saw with bitter sadness the slow decline in the man he'd known. He watched now as the Major cut a plug of tobacco, his face completely blank as the newsreader on the radio went on. Shavings slopped from the tin on to the Major's clothes. He seemed neither to notice, nor care.

There began to be more instances, as the months went on. Shirts left untucked, one side of the Major's braces hanging loose from the waist of his trousers. It was because of this damn heat wave that they'd been experiencing, Jim told himself. When the Major forgot to shave a couple of mornings in a row, he brought it casually to his father's attention, pretending not to notice the start of embarrassed surprise, quickly masked, as the Major reached a hand to his stubbled cheeks.

Minor things, each of them, but brought into sharp focus by the eerie passivity that seemed to have taken hold of the Major, a silent, glassy calm, like the sea after a storm. The Major drifted through his days, only brightening while muddling through the orchard with little Jimmy. When Ellie came in especially early one morning, to avoid the summer heat and get a head start on the day, it gave her quite a turn to find the Major sitting in front of the black mirror.

'You haven't slept all night, have you?' she asked, worried.

The Major turned distant, unfocused eyes on her. He looked bewildered as he tried to recall her name. 'Good morning,' he said hesitantly then, and turned away.

*

The bonuses were paid out in the middle of June, with an immediate rash of engagements, weddings and divorces that followed among the veterans and their women. A few men put their bonuses into savings accounts. Many others bet it on the race track or on gold brick, get-rich-quick schemes, promptly losing it all. Much of the money would go towards settling accounts and old debts; there was many a doctor, a reporter wryly commented, who slept a little easier these days. The papers were full of stories of veterans and their plans: some talked proudly of clothes and shoes for their families, a new overcoat perhaps for themselves, others put the bonus into a new truck, or repairs.

'Boy, that's all going on a first payment on a decent shack made of brick instead of lemon meringue,' a veteran named Frank told the *Los Angeles Times*, beaming from ear to ear.

Pete, a partner in a service station, had a 'Santa Claus' list of wishes: a new set of teeth for his wife, an encyclopedia for his son, and for himself, a set of rare cactus plants.

'Never owned more than three pairs of underwear in all my life,' yet another veteran happily told a reporter outside a haberdashery store in Chicago. 'Now, I'm gonna get twenty.'

The Major stood confused in the hallway, unable to remember whether he'd been entering or leaving. 'Do you need something, Major?' Madeleine asked. He mumbled unintelligibly in response. She stepped closer and took his hand, flinching slightly at the ripe, unwashed smell of him. He followed without protest as she gently led him to his armchair.

'Wasn't Jimmy with you?' she asked, puzzled.

They found the child still happily playing where his grandfather had left him in the grass. 'No harm done,' Jim said quickly, before Madeleine could get upset. He played down her doubts when she told him about the expression on the Major's face when she'd come upon him – the blank confusion, and the stench on his clothes.

'It happens,' Jim shrugged. 'What do you expect a man to smell like anyway, after a morning spent working in the sun?'

He kept an even closer eye on his father after that, alerting him to an undone fly, keeping tabs on him in the orchard as much as he could. Nothing particularly untoward happened for the next couple of weeks, and Jim was just beginning to hope that his father was taking a turn for the better, when he happened upon the Major sitting in his armchair, fiddling agitatedly with one of Jimmy's wind-up toys.

It was an old, battered tin bear, one that the boy was especially fond of. Jim remembered the child clutching it closely as he'd stepped out to the orchard that morning with the Major. 'Where's Jimmy?' he asked tightly, not waiting for a response as he ran out the door.

Behind him, the Major looked distressed, turning the toy over in his hands, as if trying to remember something important, something that tugged faintly at his memory. He cranked the key in the back, winding it until it would not turn any further. He set the toy on the floor, intently following its progress as he drummed his fingers on the arm of the chair.

Jim found his son inside the paddock. Pulling him out from under the fence, he headed back towards the house, his face dark with worry. Jimmy squirmed from his grasp as soon he spotted the Major. 'Gran'pa!' he shouted eagerly.

The Major turned, his face transformed with delight as the child clambered on to his lap.

'Ellie,' Jim gestured towards the Major. 'Have you noticed . . .' He swallowed, unable to complete the sentence. The toy bear was still marching forward.

'Yes,' she said simply. The bear bumped against the fireplace and ground to a halt with a clicking, whirring sound. Ellie looked at Jim, her eyes beginning to well. 'He's worn out, Jim. He's just plain worn down and worn out.'

Madeleine walked out to the orchard where Jim was watering the trees. He pretended to splash her and she laughed and ducked. 'How much longer?' She ran a hand down his bare back, which was damp with sweat.

'A few minutes more.' He gestured at the apple sapling that the Major had grafted for Jimmy. 'The young ones, too much sun and they can dry out, never quite grow right after that.'

She nodded, trying to find the right opening for what was on her mind. 'Ellie says it's so hot this year that berries have been baking right on their bushes – wrap them in a little sugared dough and we might well get pie.'

He grinned. Madeleine hesitated, watching as the spray caught the sunlight. '... she also said that the Major hasn't been doing so well.'

Jim stiffened. 'He's fine.'

'Maybe we should get him a nurse,' Madeleine suggested gently.

'He's fine.'

Upset by the notion of his father being perceived as an invalid, Jim would brook no more discussion on the matter. Madeleine tried, a few times more, before giving up in frustration. Jim began to shield the Major all the more, filling in his pauses, shepherding him through his day, as if by his constant, unwavering vigilance, he could somehow make his father better.

The Major continued his decline well past the summer. There were good days, when he was withdrawn but lucid and present. Then there were others, when he mistook Jim for his uncle Bill and reminisced with him about pretty Samantha Lockhart who'd summered in Maplebridge back in 1901, with eyes like greenest sea glass.

Things came to a head when he stumbled one night into Jim and Madeleine's bedroom. He stood disoriented in the dark, dimly aware that he wasn't in the right place. Before he could turn around, however, his bladder gave way. With a pungent splatter, the Major urinated over himself and across the parquet floor.

Madeleine sat up with a scream of fright, holding the bedclothes to her chest. Jim rushed his father into the bathroom, angry and embarrassed. In his hurry to get there, he nearly slipped in the puddle of urine, which only made him angrier. He stripped off the Major's nightshirt, and the Major acquiesced without a murmur, sitting in the bathtub with the touching trust of a child as Jim poured water over his head. He held out his arms and Jim soaped them down. He scrubbed the pink, wrinkled flesh, filled with a raging sadness at the soft sag of skin, the helplessness that his father had been reduced to.

As the Major watched the back-and-forth motion of the bath brush, its tiger-striped handle triggered a memory. 'So many owls,' he said suddenly. 'The winter of 1917. Great flocks of them, migrating from the north. Went out into the woods once after them. There was a full moon, and icicles—'

'I was there,' Jim said, cutting him off. 'Don't you remember? You took me with you.'

The Major looked confused.

'You took me with you,' Jim repeated, his tone softer. 'Woke me up, and bundled me into my coat and boots. You're right, it was a full moon. You pointed out the icicles along the barn.' He paused in his washing and looked at his father, his eyes tender. The Major was listening intently, as if to a story he was hearing for the very first time. 'You held my hand all the way. We went deep into the woods, and when there were no more owls, we saw a brace of hares, dancing, upright on their hind legs.'

'Hares,' the Major repeated, wonderstruck, 'dancing under the moon.'

The end when it came, was peaceful. Jimmy had just woken from his afternoon nap. Despite having spent the entire morning toddling about in the orchard behind the Major, he'd immediately asked for his grandfather again, sleepily rubbing his eyes. Jim gathered his son into his arms, smiling as the child snuggled his face into his shoulder and yawned.

'Gran'pa!' Jimmy called as they headed downstairs.

'I think your grandpa's asleep,' Jim said, shushing him. He could see the back of his father's head, as he sat in the armchair.

'Gran'pa!' Jimmy called in response, even louder.

The Major didn't so much as stir. A prickle of misgiving went through Jim. He strode forward, Jimmy still in his arms.

His father's eyes were shut, a look of such peace, such infinite calm on that worn face, that Jim knew, even without touching him, he knew.

'Gran'pa?' Jimmy asked uncertainly.

'Your grandpa . . .' Jim's voice shook. He tried to smile at the child. 'He's been very tired, Jimmy. He's been tired for a long time and he's going to sleep for quite a while now.'

The child nodded solemnly. 'Sleep awhile,' he echoed.

Jim looked down at his father, tears brimming in his eyes. A breeze gusted through the open window, touched with the first scents of fall. Jim reached forward to smooth down his father's hair. His fingers stayed, caressing the Major's cheek, gently shaking his shoulder, stroking a motionless arm. 'Dad,' he called softly. His voice broke. 'Dad,' he said again, choking back his tears.

*

They buried the Major in the family plot. The *Gazette* composed a long, glowing obituary about their local veteran. Half the town came out to pay their respects at the wake. Black Pete too, extricating himself from the woods, clutching a handful of wild ferns and moss. Saluting the coffin, he stood quietly to the side during the service, placing the bouquet, such as it was, by the headstone after it was done.

Soon after President Roosevelt was re-elected for a second term that November, Jimmy turned three. Madeleine threw an elaborate party for him in Boston, but despite the best efforts of the clowns and the magician, he cried inconsolably all the way through, asking over and over for his gran'pa.

THIRTY-SIX

Paris • May 1940

Drôle de guerre, they been callin' it, the phony war, one full of drollery and jest. Germany gone and picked a fight with France once more and with England too this time, but for months after that first declaration last September, ain't much more that happened. After that first shock, folks been goin' 'bout their days, livin' and lovin' just the same. The shops still open, the market at Les Halles as busy, the stalls filled with eggs and butter and fruit. Even when the Government done put wartime rationin' in place, allowin' meat to be sold no more than four days a week, there still plenty to be had. Montmartre look strange in the practice blackouts, without the lights of the clubs and the shiny signs over their awnings, but behind them darkened windows, folks be boozin' up a storm still, dancin' and carousin' same as before. A fat Thanksgivin', a right merry Christmas, with turkey and chicken, oysters too, if you knew where to go, and the city crowded this Easter with tourists and soldiers on furlough. Soldiers with polished buttons and new-pressed uniforms, and smilin', happy dolls on their arms.

Drôle de guerre all through winter, and the spring.

Truth be told, I never seen the jest in it. Sure I tried to shrug it off like most others done, but I known all along. I been feelin' the war from the start, a hot, dry wind stirrin' the leaves. I be hearin' its tread, in the thin light between wakin' and sleep, be seein' its skeleton shadow among the audience as they clap and holler and call '*Encore*!' How many years in Paris now? I been back a couple of times to America, when the old hankerings taken over. Followin' the music trail in Harlem, goin' down South, wanderin' 'bout as my fancy taken me, but things there, they ain't changed all that much, not for folks like me, and each time, I just turned around and moseyed on back to Paris once more. How many years now? I stare at the stage, tryin' to work it out in my head. Nineteen? Twenty?

Ain't never been too good with numbers. Many years, enough for the stubble to come out white each mornin', for a stiffness to set into my fingers and knees, a creakin' and crackin' in them that weren't ever there before. A long time, a lifetime, in these up-and-down streets of Montmartre, claimin' this itty bit of Paris for my own.

A sudden hush fall over the room, breakin' into my thoughts. The band finish settin' up on stage and Django walk to his chair in that grace-filled, don't-care-none style he got. He pluck casual like at his guitar. The A string, a low E. The audience clap. He look up briefly, at nobody particular, a quiet, knowin' sort of smile on his face as he start to play.

Django Reinhardt one of the few musicianers still left in Montmartre. Most others gone, headed for America, leavin' for Spain, Lisbon, London, even, anyplace away from the war that now be beatin' on the doors of Paris. *'Drôle de guerre'* they said, but I known better. It been whisperin' in my ear from the start. Like a thing woken from winter rest, with the first flowers of May, from among them quiet, grass-covered graves, the war risen again in blooded hunger. Not three weeks and Belgium fallen, the Allies beaten back to Dunkirk, the Boche surroundin' Amiens and Arras like they did once before.

Paris a changed city since. Shutters on shops, restaurants closed, thousands fleein' to safety. Saint Germain gone quiet, Pigalle deserted, Montmartre an empty shell. *Drôle de guerre,* they call it, all through the winter and the spring, but there been nothin' phony 'bout this war. I seen it waitin' in the shadows, felt its fire eyes in my sleep. I known from the start, in the hurts that started up again, in these old, old wounds, opened and leakin' once more.

Django play on, smilin' that small smile. The strings he pluck be the same as on any other guitar – simple A and D and G – but in his fingers they turn magic. The notes be liquid, fallin' like rain. The melody a river, a broad, rushin' river with hidden depths and secret ripples, and in its waters lie the stories of all our lives. The Government, they done retreated from Paris this mornin', they gone and left the city to the Boche. Better occupation than bombin', better a fallen city than one lost for ever to rubble and dust. This city be forsaken, our Paris surrendered to the Boche, and Django, he pick at the hard knot of pain in our hearts, layin' it open with his playin'.

Music, such music flowin' over the room, gatherin' up all manner of thoughts and things unspoken, things a man ain't even realised been lyin' inside of him until he hears it mid-chord. It wash over the silent audience, deep into me. Tellin' the things I ain't got no words for, sweepin' up all that be lyin' broke and splintered, things I tried so hard to forget, bringin' them together once more. I hear it again, the roar of war, but it from all those years ago. Here – the tread of marchin' boots. We young, we strong. *Vive La Legion! La Legion, la Legion,* we brothers marchin' along a road touched with gold.

I turn blindly, stumblin' in the dark as I make my way from the club. The music follow me outside as the door swing shut; even after it fade from hearin', I feel it swellin' inside. Brown silk water, of riff and arpeggio. Storm river, haint river, filled with all the glory and sadness of the world.

The streets lie quiet, so empty. Paris under blackout once more. The streetlamps painted a dark blue so it harder for attackin' aircraft to see them, their wartime light throwin' strange shadows into the night. A dog sniff at a stoop. The buildin' all dark; ain't no doorman to shoo away the dog tonight. It look up cautious like at my approach, give a small wag of its tail. Doorway after doorway, all lyin' silent, windows painted over or draped in heavy black. Some gone and taped strips of paper over theirs, crisscrossin' this way and that, all over, so the glass don't shatter too badly in a bombin'.

Most Americans gone too – Gene Bullard, Bricktop, the Baker girl, all the bands, the singers and dancers, bouncers and bartenders, all upped and left before the Boche get here. 'You ain't leavin'?' they asked me, surprised, and I grinned and made jokes 'bout being a comer, not a goer.

'The Nazis ain't colourblind,' Gene warned. 'Things ain't going to be the same in Paris no more, going to get real ugly for us folks once they get here.'

Think I ain't known that? The Boche this time, they ain't just soldiers. They got Nazis among them, hatin' on Jews and black folk and pretty much anythin' that don't look and sound like them. There been this exhibition in Dusseldorf couple years back. Real big affair I heard tell, on what the Nazis be callin' 'degenerate music'. All the dangerous, devil-spawn music that goin' to take their culture right back to the dark ages if they ain't careful. *Jungle music,* they call it, all the beautiful, soul-touchin' jazz that be playin' in Harlem hotspots all the way to Montmartre. Heathen jungle music, thought up by backward, degenerate folk.

The poster for that exhibition, it was a paintin' of a man of blackest skin, with the face of an ape. A black monkey-man with native hoop-rings in his ears, ape lips curled 'bout the mouth of his saxophone and a Star of David on his chest.

Jungle music, they call it. I wonder what they goin' to make of Django's gypsy tunes.

One by one, most everybody gone, but this degenerate still here, waitin' for what, I can't clearly explain. As if . . . as if by stayin', by tryin' mule-headed like to hold on to this life I done built for myself here, a life around melody and beat, this world of music and song in the up-and-down streets of Montmartre, maybe this war, somehow it go away. It just go away, this phony war, this war of tomfoolery and jest. So I stay, but each day the sound of war grown louder, and it feel like the years done rolled back with its roar.

The call of the beast, just like I heard from behind prison bars at La Santé, all those years ago. Only this time, ain't no thrill in the hearin'. This time I know better. I done fought the war to end all wars and there a deep, deep hurt in my bones.

There this piece I read in the *Matin* yesterday. Paris under siege again, it say, same as way back in 52 BC. Turns out that two thousand years ago, this Roman general named Labinius, he try to take Paris. His legions come along the Seine in nearabout the exact approach the Boche usin' now. Two thousand years! I read that article, and damn if I don't almost turn around to ask James, him what was always talkin' of Romans and Vikings and such, just what he think of that. The past jumbled with the present, all mixed up in my head. I think of James, I 'member the way we marched once, like so many are marchin' now. I know what lie ahead for them, and it bring a chokin' to my throat.

Damned, devil-spawn war, bringin' up all the old things, all the set-aside, buried things. Like river silt, they come pushin' up once more.

I walk down these blue-lit streets, lookin' at empty corners and barricaded walls. A man stand alone on the quay ahead, fishin' in the half-light. He turn as I come closer and our eyes meet before he turn back to his line. He too be holdin' on, I figure, hangin' hard as he can to the life he known before. Who can tell what this day goin' to bring, who knows what tomorrow hold. So here he stand, on this empty quay, before everythin' change, a last time, fishin' in the Seine.

Somewhere across them bridges, the Boche steady advancin'; there's the smell of rain in the air.

I walk along the flowin' river, and from the heart of this watchin', waitin' city, I start to hear her song. The song of Paris, a song of love, of war, the music spillin' from Django's guitar.

A thin light breakin' in the east, and faces in the mist along the Seine. Karan, Gaillard – Brother Strong Heart Mighty Oak, the Captain. I see them in the chords, feel them in the music; James, he look up from his book and smile. I hear it now, the bass note, I hear the distant call. All that I been turnin' away from all these years, come alive now with the war.

I keep movin', one foot after the other. There's a feather-tail of black smoke risin' into the sky across the river, like smut against the grey. I ain't got no more to say, got no more fight left in me. I'm just followin' the music, lettin' the chords lead me home.

Music, it be a road. Ain't no tellin' where it begun, ain't nobody can say how it goin' to end, but once it get hold of a man, ain't nothin' he can do but follow it along. And sometimes, maybe sometimes, for it to move ahead at all, the music, it got to go way back, windin' back on itself.

The music, it be a road.

THIRTY-SEVEN

August 1916

Which one of us seen the mirror first? When I think back on that mornin' now, I ain't none too sure. Maybe it were me? Or was it James? Maybe we seen it together – I don't 'member clearly, 'cept I looked up and he was starin' at it too.

It was real late by the time we reached the village the night previous. We been a long time on the road, so tired that the *jeunes* fallen dead asleep on every ten-minute break we taken on the march. Hell of a thin' to wake them too, with some near sleepwalkin' even after. Me, I ain't slept. Ain't been sleepin' too much at all, not since Champagne. My eyes feel like they stuffed with sand, all gritty and burnin'.

We march through the empty streets, the sound of them hobnailed boots loud against the stones. A dog bark somewhere in the dark, stop. The village is empty. Shellin' turned real bad in this sector, and all civilians have been moved out in a hurry.

We passed them on the march here. Old men. Children. Women. The rich ones ridin' in hay carts, but most on foot, pushin' handcarts, the sort used in gardens and such, stained orange with rust. Hoistin' on shoulders and backs the few things they got. A loaf of bread, a wheel of cheese, one a ham, tied in string.

Some of the chers quietly weepin', others got faces blank and hard as stone. Sets me on edge to see the ones who cryin'. I'm suddenly angry – 'Ain't no room for tears,' I want to tell them, '*C'est la guerre*,' it the war, just the war and what cryin' or feelin's got to do with any of it? It only when pain shoots through my fingers that I realise how tight I'm holdin' my rifle. I loosen my grip, easin' the skinned knuckles still sore from the most recent brawlin'.

A few of the folks, they nod weary like at us but most just shuffle by in silence. Ain't nobody cheerin' us on, and for this at least, I'm thankful. The war, it gone on too long for no cheerin' or clappin', taken too much already from both soldier and civilian.

There's a shift in their column, and my shoulders go tight. Only a woman, steppin' off to the side of the road. Her stomach hang round with child; she set a hand down in the dust to steady herself as she try to squat. She stare straight ahead, no expression in her eyes, as if she ain't here at all, like it got nothin' to do with her, the pool slowly spreadin' from under her skirts and darkenin' the dust.

We keep goin', James a little ahead and to my left. We ain't talkin' much, him and I. Things ain't sat quite right between us for a while now. Gaillard, that wounded Boche officer I gone and shot . . . I was sure that James goin' to report me back then, seein' how particular he be 'bout everythin'. He don't, and it shame me even more, make me bitter angry. We ain't spoken of that night since, and our silence, it stretch between us.

All that rain durin' the Champagne offensive, it given James pneumonia. The officers done forced him see the medics who packed him off to the hospital for a couple of months. We ain't said much before he left, ain't been in touch all the time he was gone, and when he come back to the Legion earlier this week, I was powerful glad to see him, but again, the words, somehow they just ain't come out right. Too much to say, and so we ain't said nothin' at all, just noddin' stiff like at one another and keepin' outta each other's way.

I watch as he dig some chocolate from his pocket on one of our breaks, snappin' it into itty bits that he hand to the children we pass. They take it from him, lookin' away, down, at the road. A little girl, led by her mammy who look so bone-tired, she don't even notice when James hand out the chocolate. That little girl take it, quickly, as if James might change his mind. She tug on her mammy's hand and offer that chocolate to her instead. Her mammy, she look like she wakin' from her dream. She carry a framed photograph in the other hand, holdin' it real close. She try to smile at her daughter as she shake her head – no, you eat it. '*Merci*' she say, real quiet, as she turn and look at James.

An old man comin' up behind them, bent low over his pushcart. He got things piled every which way inside – pots, pans, a jug of wine, rope, two pails, and on the handle of that cart, a parrot. That bird now, he hoppin' mad. All red and green and puffed up mad, twistin' his head this way and that and cussin' up a storm.

'Cochons! Quels salauds!'

So ridiculous that bird sound, so outta place in that silent, done-in column, that my mouth start to twitch. James glance at me, and I know he amused too. I make like I ain't noticed, watchin' that mother instead as she go past with her daughter, huggin' that photograph close.

That parrot, it go right on squawkin' and yellin', and it 'bout the only thing sayin' anythin' at all. *'Cochons!'* We hear it long after it gone from sight. *'Salauds!'* Screamin' into the night.

Hungry and footsore by the time we get to the village, we billet in the dark, in and around the empty houses. I wake in a sweat in the middle of the night, same as I been doin' these past months, not sure at first if it a dream. The whisper *'Erbarmen. Erbarmen,'* in my ears, Gaillard's laughter fadin' into the night. I lie still, waitin' for the rattlin' in my chest to ease. Breathe in, breathe out.

'Erbarmen.'

The moon, she sail slowly past the open windows, leakin' silver everywhere.

I'm up before dawn, even though my bones full of achin', my tongue as if wrapped in cotton. At least it shapin' up to be an easy day – reveille, a spot of drill in the square, and then we let off with orders to build a first line of defence around the borders of the village, usin' whatever we can find. There still a shell or two that the Boche send over our way, but few and far enough for us to ignore.

We break off into groups. I set off clean the opposite way from James, again, why, I can't fully explain. The sun warm on my shoulders, easin' the stiffness from them as we poke 'bout the village. In every home, signs of a quick leavin'. I light a pipe I find by a fireplace, filled nearabout to the top with decent tobacco. An open bottle of jam, the spoon still standin' in it, knittin' left on chairs, the needles still pokin' from them. Socks, a hat, a scarf maybe, meant for some loved one at the Front. I finger each piece, but ain't nothin' finished enough to be of use; annoyed, I toss them aside.

From house to house, gatherin' up mattresses, chairs, tables, just 'bout anythin' that might stand in for bobwire and slow down a Boche attack, even for a bit. The shell holes in roofs and walls look like mouths, open wide in surprise. Beside one front door that hang all crooked, a heap of postcards, the sort kids like to send each other, thrown all over the floor.

I pick one up, readin' the large, scrawly writin' on the back.

'Chère Mathilde . . .'

Easy to imagine the scene. The little girl told to hurry, to help get the important things together: deeds and such, food, what money they got in the house, 'Hurry, be quick, we have to leave.' And Mathilde, bitin' her lip, being real brave and tryin' not to cry. She pick up this most important of all her things, this here collection of postcards. Her poor mammy smackin' them from her hand at the door – ain't no room for trifles, not at a time like this.

I stare at Mathilde's postcard. The darkness that been risin' up inside, more and more of late, that feelin' like there ain't no hope, ain't not much point to anythin', the feelin' I be tryin' to keep locked away, it come bubblin' up again like river sludge. More legionnaires come troopin' through the door just then, and I rise to my feet. James with them; I turn away, lettin' the postcard drop real casual from my fingers, as if it don't matter none. He say nothin' either and we start to work on the door in silence. We take it off its hinges and a couple of the *jeunes* haul it away for the barricade.

Right restless all of a sudden, I cast 'bout for a joke. Somethin' to make us all laugh, bring some cheer into these empty homes, but the words, they don't come. We searchin' through the bedrooms upstairs when I find the clothes hangin' in the armoire. It take 'bout two shakes of a duck tail for me to tie on a bonnet, pull on a petticoat and put on a show for the men.

James, he start to grin, wider and wider, the other legionnaires, they roarin' with laughter as I mince and prance 'bout. The Boche, they still sendin' over a shell or two as I sashay out the door and up the street, poppin' open a pretty pink parasol at each fresh burst of shrapnel.

Pretty soon, everybody gone and caught a case of jester fever. We swan in and outta them houses, outdoin' each other in our pretty frippery. Skirts and hats and old tweed coats; we got straw baskets on our heads and bonnet ribbons trailin' past our chins. James begin to laugh proper; findin' a spare bonnet, he jam it on his head.

Even the officers get a laugh outta it all. For a while, that ghost village, it filled with merrymakin', some of the men even startin' a mock weddin' party in the square. We all joinin' in when the shellin' get worse all of a sudden; James and I, we still laughin' as we pick up our skirts and race for cover.

That how we first got to the chateau, James and I. We ducked inside its grounds to wait out the shells.

They slow down soon enough, with no real damage done other than a couple more roofs torn and the steeple of the church destroyed. We sit up and look around where we are. The wall around the chateau got shell holes through it. The two gateposts still standin' though, with a lion on the left, an eagle on the right, starin' down at us. We make our way through the garden. A shell gone through the roof at the back of the chateau sometime. When we push open the door, James start to cough from the dust lyin' thick on the floor.

We look around us in surprise. Everythin' covered in black net. Yards and yards of the stuff, draped over the chairs and tables, coverin' the paintings and the chandelier still hangin' fine from the ceilin'. It unsettle me to walk through the rooms. Black everywhere, over the mantel, along the curtains, across them carved armoires and canopied beds. It dull the sounds of the day, the buzzin' of bees and such, the birds callin' in the trees outside. I kick at a small pile of broken tiles. They fall apart, even their clatter soundin' far away, the dust risin' just a bit before sinkin' back to the floor.

So much black. I seen this sort of thing often enough in the great houses down South to know what it mean: the chateau, it a home in mournin'. The mourners, like the dead, gone now, leavin' only memories and shadows in all this net. They even got it coverin' the mirror on the wall.

'I'm gettin' the hell out—' I start to say, when I stop.

That mirror, it ain't covered in no net at all. It 'bout the only thing in here that ain't been covered up; *that mirror, its glass itself is black.*

It given me the shivers, right from the start.

'A Claude mirror.' It was used by painters and such James say. He touch a finger to it and the glass, it look like a well of dark water.

Voodoo water.

I ain't said nothin' to him then, but I known right away. That mirror, it ghosted. I want nothin' to do with it, but my feet, they move on their own. I get near, real near to it; when I'm right up to the glass, it's Pappy's face I see lookin' back at me.

Pappy, as he looked in the end years, with his cheeks all lined and drawn, and the eyes sunk deep in his head. The colour gone from his face, leavin' only the grey mask of the dyin'. I stare into those night-shine eyes, so dark and heavy with meanin', and I ain't got no words to speak. My mouth dry as I stumble backwards, crashin' into a table just behind.

'There's the dead inside that thing,' I manage, real hoarse.

James look at me amused like as he start to take it down. It right heavy, that thing, settin' his arms to strainin' as he lift it from the wall and set it on the floor. The mirror lie at our feet, like an ink-black stain.

A sudden movement off to the side catch my eye. I'm spooked enough by this silent, mournin' house, and I swing around sharply. 'What the—' I begin, rifle already liftin' when I stop, completely thrown.

A kid stand there.

A boy, 'bout nine, maybe ten years old. Out of nowhere he come, and it a right good thing that mirror lyin' on the floor. Had I seen him in that black glass, I'd have gone and given myself a heart attack, I would, figurin' him for a haint.

The kid, he stand real easy in the doorway, stretchin' his neck to see over the large white dog that just 'bout fit in his arms. James and I, we just stare at him. No kid got any business being here in this empty place.

He don't look one bit shook up. 'Bread?' he asks, from over the cayoodle that growlin' and waggin' its tail at us, as if it can't quite make up its mind.

It James who gathers his wits first. 'You speak English?' He frown. 'What in God's name are you doing here, son? Where's your family?'

Shakin' off the hand the kid got on its muzzle, that dog, it start to bark.

'*Non*, Gaston, shhh.' The kid rocks back and forth, nearabout fallin' clean over from the weight of the animal. Now I see it, the dirty, stained bandage around the mutt's leg.

'Bread?' the kid ask hopefully again.

*

We fish in our pockets for what chocolate we got. The kid take it hungrily.

'What's your name?' James ask. 'Where's your family?'

'Jean Henri,' he say, in between his chewin'. 'English . . .' he pull a face. 'Little bit. *Comme ci, comme ça. Parlez-vous français?*'

Seems his pappy been the caretaker of the chateau. He done enroled in the war soon as it started, he and the two sons of the chateau. The kid's pappy been the first to be killed; word of the sons' deaths come a few weeks after. The old lady of the house, she taken it real hard, her children's passin'. Jean Henri touch a finger to his temple. '*La vieille dame est allée un peu coucou folle,*' he say.

He bend to let the dog outta his arms. Gaston stand there a moment, testin' his bum leg on the floorboards. He bark a couple times more just to prove his point, then limp over to us, sniffin' at the hand James offer him, and waggin' his tail.

The kid look at us real curious. 'London?'

'Vermont,' James correct, the same time as I say 'Louisiana.'

A small pause. 'America,' we say, together.

'*Des Americains*!' The kid's eyes go wide. 'New York!' he exclaim, and damn if he don't start buildin' skyscraper shapes with his hands. It tickle me proper, and James, I know he got a twinkle in his eyes too.

'*Pourquoi tu n'es pas parti avec les autres?*'

The kid shrug. Leave with the others and go where, he ask. Besides – he nod at Gaston who sniffin' at the black mirror still lyin' on the floor. The dog was awful spooked when the shells first hit the town. Barkin' his head off all the while they were fallin', and jumpin' outta the kid's arms just as that bit of roof done fallen in. Part of it catch his leg. The doctor said it'd heal, but that the cayoodle needed to rest it.

Right on cue, Gaston cock a leg against the mirror. '*Non*!' James and the kid yell together, and the cayoodle change his mind, settin' down on the floor to scratch his ear instead.

Well, if the leg needed some rest, better then that they stay put, *non,* the kid continue. He hid in the cellar while the others left. The old lady was still too cut up over the death of her sons to pay much attention, to wonder where he was as the carts pulled away. He'd kept aside a bit of food when loadin' her cart; there was water in the well behind.

'It is a good thing you came,' he say to us all cheerful. 'We have finished all our food.'

'And what if we *hadn't* come when we did?' James look awful stern. 'No food, all alone—'

But you did, Henri point out, grinnin'. He wasn't sure when he heard us tramp through the streets last night, whether we were friendlies or the Boche. He figured to have a proper look at us this mornin', but he couldn't make out the uniforms under all the dresses. 'Why are you dressed as women?' He point to the skirts we still got on.

James clear his throat, tearin' that bonnet from his head and even without lookin' at him, I know that the Yankee, he goin' all shades of red. Old soldier tradition, I tell the kid. When we 'bout to pick up no 'count little runaway kids like him, that when we play dress-up in women's clothes.

'*Mais*—'

'Enough with the questions. Where did you learn to speak English?' James want to know, headin' off the conversation before it go any further.

Well, that how he known we were friendlies, he explain, when he heard us in the chateau, talkin'. The old lady, she had friends from London who visited the chateau each summer. Before the war, that is.

'Big Ben! London Bridge!' he say, grinnin' cheeky as a monkey.

'That's all very well,' James say, tryin' to look all serious, but there a twinkle in his eyes, 'but we've got to figure out what to do with you.' He hoist the mirror back on the wall. 'Come along now, let's get you – yes, yes, and Gaston – out of here.'

The legionnaires gather around, exclaimin' over the kid. Gaston get plenty attention too. That cayoodle, he been born for a circus, so happy he is to play to an audience. Henri call out a command in between stuffin' hisself with his sandwich, and Gaston offer a paw.

'Sit!' and he crouch, the torn-up leg stickin' stiff out to one side.

'Play dead!' 'Roll over!'

Everyone so impressed with the show that all sorts of treats come out. Gaston take them all happily, his tail waggin' so fast, it just a white blur. It make us laugh and that only make him wag it all the more.

'Alright, alright,' James say, 'we need to change his dressing. Here boy,' he click his fingers. '*Viens, Gaston, ici.*' Gaston hop over on three paws.

'*Assieds-toi.*' Gaston listen, droppin' first on to his behind then stretchin' out his front legs. His tongue hang from jaws open so wide it look like he grinnin'. '*Bon chien,* good boy . . .' James press a gentle hand on the animal's ribs and he obey again, topplin' over on to his side. He start cuttin' away the dirty bandage and Gaston let out a small yelp. 'Good boy, good boy.'

'Don't worry,' I tell the kid who startin' to look a bit anxious, 'we do this all the time.' It ain't just the kid who anxious. All sort of butchery I've seen in this here war, all kind of terrible wounds, and yet here I am, feelin' all faint over a rough-haired cayoodle. Goin' by the sudden silence, I ain't the only one either. Gaston whine again, thump his tail weakly against the ground. A mutterin' of sympathy rise from the crowd.

James glance at us, amused. A quick mop of the wound, a dustin' with antiseptic powder, a clean new dressin', and *voilà*! Gaston stand up slow and tender, to cries of '*Bon chien*! *Bon Gaston*!' from us all.

Henri whoop out loud, and throw his arms around James as he thank him. The Yankee look taken aback. He smile then, pattin' the kid awkward like on his head.

We stuff Henri and Gaston full of food till both can't eat no more. Best to send the kid to local headquarters with the evenin' motorcycle dispatch, James decide. They'll know what to do with him.

'No! I'm not leaving,' the kid protest. He not a child, he say, just a few years older and he could've been at the Front, fightin' right by his father's side. He want to stay here, he insist, with us.

'Well, judging by the way the war's dragging on, I'll be sure to put in a good word in a few years, when you're old enough to enlist,' James say amused. 'However, until then—'

'I'll run away,' Henri threaten angrily.

'You'll do no such thing.'

'It's Gaston, he needs to rest,' the kid plead, changin' tactics.

'You can show his leg to the doctors at the dressing post,' James point out calmly.

Henri look at me for support, but James, he right. This ain't no place for no kid.

'I'm not a child!' the kid say again, so mad now that he all but stampin' his feet. Jim lift him in one arm, the dog in the other, and set them both down in the motorcycle carrier.

'It's for your own good,' he say. He ruffle Henri's hair. '*Au revoir*, kid.'

Henri still hollerin' as the motorcycle roar away.

Ain't even noon the next day but who do we see teeter-totterin' up the road that lead to the village, but the kid, Gaston in his arms.

'It was Gaston,' he say quickly, before either James or I can get in a word. 'He ran away, and well, what choice did I have but to follow him?'

I'm tryin' real hard not to grin, but James, he ain't amused. 'He ran away,' he repeat disbelievingly. 'Gaston.' The cayoodle prick his ears at the sound of his name, tail goin' wag, wag, wag.

Henri set him down. 'Yes, so fast that I could hardly keep up,' he say, without a hint of shame.

That cayoodle done ran so fast, so far, he claim, that by the time he caught him, it made more sense to head for the village than turn back for the dressin' post. They hitchhiked over, plenty dispatch couriers on the road . . .

'Here boy!' James snap his fingers and the cayoodle do his three-leg hop. He put his bum leg down a moment, rest it on the ground then lift it up real quick again.

'Oh, he's just tired now, from all the running he done since this morning,' the kid explain. He grin. 'Is there any food?'

Two more time we send him away. Both time he find a way to come back. His pappy waitin' for him at the village, he lie to the first dispatch courier. He come to the dressin' post to get his pet's leg looked at, he explain, and now he need a ride to get home.

He signed up with the Legion, he tell the second, who chuckle at that but drop him off all the same.

'Jackasses,' say James, annoyed. 'They should know better, what business does a child have here?'

'You're going back,' he tell the kid firmly.

Henri cross his arms and stick out his lower lip. 'You send me away, and I'll just make my way here once more,' he vow.

They stand there, glarin' at each other. It make me want bad to laugh to see them: full-grown Yankee and little French tyke, each mule-headed as can be.

The matter of the kid, it go up to the officers. Messages go between them and local headquarters. Ain't nobody sure what to do with him. The Captain order Henri to be brought to him, along with James and myself, seein' as we the ones who found the kid in the first place.

'You know you're not supposed to be here,' he say to the kid in French.

'But I want to join the Legion,' he reply.

The Captain grin. 'Join the Legion, eh? You know what we do with soldiers who disobey orders? We throw them in the *boîte*.'

'I will never,' the kid promise, 'disobey a single order from you, *mon generale*.'

The Captain burst out laughin'. '*Capitaine*,' he say, amused, '*capitaine*.'

'Maybe he stay?' I suggest as we foot it back to our billets. 'Only for a bit,' I quickly add, at the look on James' face.

'The village was evacuated for a reason.'

'Shellin' gotten less over the past week,' I point out. 'The Boche, they've let up some.'

'Sure they have,' he agree, 'and that's probably because there's a full-blown offensive in the works.'

'Maybe they figure to leave this part of the sector alone.' I pull out my ace card. 'Besides, odds of the kid gettin' hurt here with us to look out for him sure lower than if he go trampin' 'bout out there alone.'

The talk 'bout the odds gotten him, just as I known it would. James glare at the kid, and at the cayoodle, who promptly hold out a paw.

'Fine.' James shake his head, knowin' when he licked. 'Fine. The kid stays. Yes, and Gaston,' he confirm, even as the question formin' on my lips. 'They both stay until we're sent back to reserve, and then we take them to wherever it is that they can be kept out of trouble.'

The kid tryin' hard to follow what we sayin', screwin' his eyebrows together as he try to make out all the English. 'You're stayin',' I translate for him, shakin' Gaston's paw. 'For a bit, till we can take you someplace safe ourselves.'

He jump to attention, and throwin' a right smart salute, '*Vive la France*! *Vive* New York!' he whoop.

'Vermont,' James mutter, the same time as I correct – 'Louisiana.'

We glance at one another, look away.

'*Vive La Amerique*,' we say then, together, as Gaston bark excitedly, waggin' his behind. '*Vive La France, Vive Liberté, Vive La Legion*!'

It feel like the most we said to each other, James and I, in months.

THIRTY-EIGHT

The next couple of weeks pass slow and easy. Shelling's still light, sometimes a whole day goin' by without a single one sent our way. Summer lie fatly on tree and meadow, the sky clear and worry-free. When we drill in the park, there's birds singin', and flowers in the uncut grass.

It do us good to have the kid around, even if it only goin' to be for a bit. Henri act real tough, but he just a little boy, still unspoiled. That innocence, it make us all 'member another world. A better world, the one we left behind, the world that still be turnin' out there beyond this war.

And Gaston – even the most ornery among us plenty taken with the cayoodle. His leg mendin' real nice too. He set it down more and more when he walk, and even taken off right across the park a couple of times, chasin' squirrels. Someone gotten the idea to twist ribbons found in one of them houses into a thick collar for him. Red and green, the same colours as the *fourragère* braid that was presented to the regiment after the offensive at Belloy Santerre this July. A star tied to the middle of the collar, the sort that go on Christmas trees, all sparkly and made from tinsel, big as both my fists together.

James frown. 'Talk about giving the snipers a target. You may as well paint a bullseye on his back.'

'Ain't been no sniper hearabouts, not since we came,' I point out.

He mutter somethin' 'bout there surely being an attack in the works, the Boche been just too damned quiet, but he let it go.

The kid, he taken to followin' James and me just 'bout everywhere, even wakin' with the reveille. He copy us when we drill, helpin' much as he can with the diggin' of trenches and strengthenin' the barricade. He become a bridge of sorts between James and me. We still ain't talkin' that much, but havin' Henri with us give us an excuse to fall into the old patterns of patrollin' together, even billetin' next to each other at night.

Through it all, Henri, he got questions, questions, and more questions.

What America like? Which one bigger, London or America? We seen Big Ben yet? What Paris like? No, he ain't been there, not yet anyhow. Do you get *chocolat* in America? How do you get from here to there – could you swim? He learned to, in the village pond. Oh. Well, how old you got to be to get work on a ship? Do they allow dogs?

Damn but the kid sure can talk. I want bad to laugh each time I catch sight of James' face. Like a cat in a room full of rockin' chairs with no way out he look, as the kid go on and on, but all the same, Yankee James answer. Pretty much one or two words is all he answer with, or a grunt when gruntin' will do, but every single one of the kid's questions to him, he answer.

He still replyin', weary like, as we foot it up the narrow slope of road that lead to the chateau. The battalion scoutin' for bomb shelters, and when the kid hear, he tell 'bout the cellar attached to the chateau. Room enough for a hundred, even two hundred men, he claim. That where Gaston and he hid when the rest of the village left.

We goin' over to check it out. It give me a turn to walk through them gateposts. We ain't been back here since that first day, and it give me the willies, just thinkin' of all that mournin' net and that black voodoo mirror inside.

Nicer out here in the grounds. The sun in the trees, bouncin' from the iron gate. James, he perk up at the sight of the fruit trees in the garden. Now he the one firin' questions at the kid.

Those trees, why they planted alongside the wall? Is that all the support they given? How old that one? And that? How much water they need? What the soil like in these parts? Do they need manure? How much the trees be yieldin' each year, does the kid know?

They still talkin' as they head around to the back of the garden.

The stone rim 'bout the old fountain a sun-warmed yellow. I set myself down for a bit, below the winged angel baby carryin' a flame torch in his fat little hand. Water still tricklin' from the tip of the torch, a gentle, peace-filled sound.

Gaston come trottin' past, nose pressed to the ground. '*Viens,*

Gaston.' He leave off the scent and come on over, tail waggin'. He offer a paw and I shake it. I run my fingers through the thick, white coat, scratchin' his back. He flop down by my feet with a sigh.

A slow peace come stealin' over me. I sit there by the fountain, lettin' the warmth of the day into my bones, and slow, real slow, I start to hear it once more. The music of the stones. A sound I ain't heard for way too long, a song gone quiet in the war, turned silent by too many deaths, by a wounded man who stare straight in my eyes as he whisper for mercy, by the callin', mockin' shadows of the night. Now, at last, on this sunny afternoon, the music, it come tricklin' into my heart again.

Here, the melody, the faint plink-plink of strings, growin' stronger as I listen, the music part mine, part from these drowsin', 'memberin' stones. I see the chords, teasin' from behind my eyes. They start to dance, they spin. I tap my feet, hesitatin' like, drum my fingers against that sun-warm rim of the fountain, Gaston beatin' his tail against my legs as I start to hum the tune out loud.

The sound of voices; my eyes open, the tune flowin' away, but it leave behind the markings of its passin'. They round the corner, James and the kid. Henri gone back to doin' most of the talkin', I see, amused, and James, to gruntin' in reply.

I see also how the kid, he gone and tucked a hand into James', and the Yankee, he ain't makin' no move to shake it free.

'You going to keep sunning yourself like a jackass, or would you care to join us?' James say it light and don't-care as can be, but I know the Yankee long enough to hear the small pause in between the words, as if he not sure how this olive branch he holdin' out gonna be taken.

I nod in reply and follow them inside.

It cool and dim inside, the sudden drop in temperature sendin' a shiver through my bones. I got to blink a few times for my eyes to adjust, after the brightness of the garden. That mournin' net, it just as I 'member it, yards of it, like the web of some powerful-big spider. Gaston, he come hoppin' in just then, and seein' him, that tail held so high and jaunty without a care in the world, settle me some.

You a ninny, Obadaiah Nelson, I silently scold myself. *Ain't nothin' to be 'fraid of here but spider webs and bird shit.*

James and Henri, they already halfway down to the cellar, the kid's voice floatin' up the stairs. Do they have cellars in America? Do they keep coal there? Apples?! What sort of apples?

Gaston stop at the head of the stairs, unsure of his leg. He take a half-step, stop again. '*Viens*, Gaston!' Henri call, and he whine.

'Come on, boy,' I say. 'Come on, together.'

I slip a hand through that *fourragère* collar, guidin' him down. He climb down one step, real slow, one more, then findin' his leg holdin' up just fine, let out an excited bark. He give me a quick lick on the wrist as he pull free from my grip and go racin' down the stairs.

James tap the walls of the cellar. 'At least a couple of feet thick,' he guess. 'We'd have to clear out all the junk, but this one's the best so far, I think.'

'Plenty room for at least fifty men,' I nod. 'Don't see much damage being done to this place even with a couple of Jack Johnsons hittin' directly above.'

'Jacque Johnson?' Henri ask at once. 'Who's that?'

I look at him, not knowin' what to say. After that win at the Vel d'Hiver in Paris, there was another fight for the championship in April this year, in Cuba. This time, though, Jack lost. He was beaten bad by Jess Willard, beaten fair and square. His picture in all the papers afterwards: Jack, my champ, *Jack Johnson* lyin' flat on his back in the ring, a hand coverin' his eyes.

I kept that picture a long time. Taken it out again and again from my sack, tryin' to figure out what he was thinkin' as he lay there, tryin' to read them hidden eyes. A hurt in my gut as I looked at it, if I gone and lost somethin' real important too.

'He a boxer,' I begin. 'He . . . Jack, he . . .'

'Jack Johnson is the best, the strongest, a champion among champions,' James say quietly. He start to tell Henri 'bout that glory-filled, long ago fight in Reno. I listen, drinkin' in every word as if hearin' the story for the very first time, as we head on back upstairs.

That mirror, it sit on the wall where we left it, black and still. This time though, ain't nothin' I see but my own mug, starin' back at me. I realise I been holdin' my breath; I let it out and it form a small patch of film on the glass.

'Say, kid,' James ask, 'did you know a girl called Mathilde, here in the village? Seemed to have a collection of postcards, over in that brown-and-white house?'

I guess he ain't the only one to 'member that postcard collection we seen, scattered by the door.

'*Oui, bien sûr,*' the kid nod, of course he know her, she in his school.

I'm just 'bout turnin' away from the mirror when James look my way and I catch his eye in the glass. A thing of only a moment, but somethin' 'bout his reflection make me pause. It as if that black mirror, it gone and stripped away the top coverin' of ourselves, this outer coatin' that we present to the world. What reflected in the glass is all them hidden, secret things, the truth that lie beneath. Shoots growin' under the earth, a cotton field in the moonlight, raven wings, beatin' against the wind. I see empty spaces and things unspoken, a lonesomeness that lie thinly between evenin' and night. All the broke and shifted parts rattlin' 'bout inside me, I see in James' reflection too; I stare at my friend, at this livin' ghost so brimful with guilt and sadness, and I guess he seen the same in me too.

I hear as if from a distance, Gaston's tail goin' thump, thump as it knock against a table. Henri still talkin' 'bout Mathilde. 'Such an annoying girl,' he gripe. 'Always at the top of our class, going on and on about books and stuff. Why,' he exclaim in disgust, 'she's even scared of Gaston! *Gaston*!'

So riled up the kid look at the notion that anyone could be scared of the cayoodle, that it lift the melancholy from us.

A joke, I need a joke. 'Who dat?' I ask, noddin' at James' reflection. It's 'bout all I can think to say.

James don't miss a beat as he add the question to mine. 'Who dat who say who dat?'

I chuckle. James, he starts to grin too.

The kid slip his hand into James' as we walk out into the sun. 'The old lady of the chateau,' the kid say real matter-of-fact, 'she thought she could see her sons in the mirror. After word came of their deaths, she'd sit starin' into it for hours. She was a kind woman, but *un peu folle*' he say, shakin' his head.

'Enough of all that.' James firmly change the subject. 'Obadaiah here has a poem to teach you, all the way from Louisiana.'

We teach him the words, and he find them awful funny. He yell them out aloud, all three of us do, all the way back to the billets:

'Oo dat?'

'Oo dat oo say oo dat?'

'Who dat who say who dat when ah say who dat?'

The fire burn beside the wall, hidden from enemy eyes by a bunch of trees. The evenin' so calm, so peace-filled and drowsy-makin' that we billetin' out in the open tonight. There a small chill to the air, an itty bit of mist that trail under the stars, like to remind us that soon the season gonna change. The outer corner of the sky light up dim now and then, from some faraway shell. I lie on my back, watchin' the slow-movin' moon, the fire warm against my side.

'So how would we get him across anyway?'

Startled, I raise up on an elbow to look at James, ain't sure I heard quite right.

He nod at the kid who fallen asleep curled up against him. 'Henri,' he say gruff like. 'How would we do it?'

'Across where? To America?'

'Yes. Home.' He glance at me, like he ain't sure of my reaction. I suppose I'm still lookin' thrown, and his next words, they come out in a rush. 'I've been thinking. The kid's got no more family around, at least that's what he says. Maybe he could come back with me. After all of this is done. Come live on the farm.'

After the war. A strange notion, to think of this war as ever havin' an end. What was it we used to say, back when we were *jeunes* at the trainin' camp in Toulouse? Six months we given it, six months at the most, for the war to be done.

The fire flare in a sudden draught, sparks shootin' orange and red against the wall.

James, he waitin' for a reply. 'Sure,' I shrug. ''He'd be happy there, I reckon.'

The small loosenin' of his shoulders. 'He would. My own boy's only a few years younger, they could grow up together.'

'Well, you better take Gaston too, or the kid, he goin' to go jumpin' off the ship soon as he can and swimmin' right back to shore.'

He grin.

We fall quiet, lookin' into the fire as it burn down.

'In the hospital – when I was there – the pneumonia—' he gesture with a hand. It the first we've talked of the previous months. 'There was this Tommy they brought in. Lost a foot, and with a bad case of shell shock too. He'd convinced himself that this was just a motion picture we were in. A really terrible one that did not make much sense at all, but a movie, that's all it was, the war. When the nurses came in each morning, he'd bark at them, demanding to see the director, demanding changes to the script *at once.*'

It make me laugh, the story.

'I made it to the *boîte* six times while you been gone,' I share.

We fall silent for a while again.

'How long since we signed up? Toulouse . . . it been what – two years now?'

He nod again. 'August 1914.' He reach forward to stoke the fire, careful not to wake the kid. 'You going back down South once we're done?'

There he go again. How you so sure, I want to ask, even as I shrug my shoulders in response, that we ever goin' to be done with this? That there ever goin' to be an end? Ain't no reason for it, but I'm angry, sudden like, as I search the sky for more shell burst.

The kid stir in his sleep. James lift his head gently from his arm, shiftin' him on to the blanket.

He smilin' as he look at me. 'Maybe we could do that trip we talked about. Cross country, in a covered wagon, like they did in olden times, you, me and both the boys.'

After the war.

I search, but the night sky is undisturbed, the moon sailin' real calm through the mist. My eyes move lower, past the tree line, past the shadows on the wall and the low-burnin' fire, comin' to rest on the face of the kid. Asleep, with sass and spunk at rest, he look even more of a child. Young, so open, full of trustin' and innocence. As I watch him sleep, that sudden anger, it start to uncoil, pullin' away. I let it go, feelin' the weight of it leave my chest.

After the war.

I take a deep breath. The night air feel cool in my lungs. I nod. 'From Montana,' I agree, 'all the way down to New Mexico.'

THIRTY-NINE

When we spot the plane, it still only a twinkle of silver. Away to the west, so far that at first we ain't even sure if it a plane or just a trick of the light. I shade my eyes and look harder. That twinkle, it movin' across the horizon towards us.

Someone grab a pair of field glasses. 'Boche!!' The *alarme* sound through the streets. Men race for cover, runnin' into cellars, huggin' the long grass in the park and jumpin' into the trenches we been diggin' around the village. The small clink-clink of metal as bayonets sheathed in a hurry, so their shine won't give us away. The telephone operator start tryin' to get headquarters on the line.

That twinkle grow closer, larger. 'Where the hell are our guns?' James mutter. We hunkered down in a section of the trench that lie a short distance away from the chateau, the kid and Gaston too. 'Come on, come on . . .'

We search the sky for signs of our guns openin' fire, waitin' for the Boche plane to be downed. Now, anytime now, our guns goin' to get into position, shoot the *salaud* down.

It only static we hear, cracklin' down the telephone line.

The Boche plane make a slow circle past the church, cruise over the length of the town, away, behind a hill.

'He ran away!' the kid whoop.

We don't say nothin' to correct him. That pilot, he ain't gone nowhere, not so soon, he ain't. James grab the telephone from the operator, pressin' it to his ear. Still just static. He scan the sky, mouth tight. There, them twinklin', shinin' wings as the plane turn from around the hill, headin' back towards us.

'Restez en bas,' James say tightly to the kid. Stay down.

The whine, the high-pitched whistlin'; Gaston start to bark as the first of the shells slam into the church.

*

It clear pretty soon that this ain't the one or two, itty-bitty, How Dee Do things the Boche been sendin' our way these past couple of weeks. This here the real thing, a right powerful shellin' of the village. That plane, it keep on circlin' above us, the pilot radioin' in the targets. The shells come singin' over, smashin' the houses into nothin', stone, brick and tile crumblin' into dust. Gaston, he got the shakes real bad, he barkin' his head off at the noise. The kid's eyes are wide with fright; he tryin' his best not to show it as he hug the cayoodle close.

'Courage!' I yell into his ear, and he nod, tryin' to smile.

James bent in the dirt, a finger in one ear, the telephone pressed to the other as he yell down the line to headquarters. He slam down the receiver, eyes fixed on that plane we can still see flyin' above the smoke. 'Bastard!'

We hunker down, Gaston barkin', whinin', shakin', goin' boo coo crazy as the shells fall, and all the while, that plane, it fly calmly above. Impossible to tell from here how much damage being done, or where the rest of the battalion is. Previous instructions from headquarters been real clear: 'Stay down, stay out of sight during a bombardment, do not give away your positions.'

We there a long while before them shells finally slow, their devil songs fadin'.

Gaston finally go quiet, but he shiverin' from nose to tail. Now there just one or two shells at a time, and even that slow until there silence. The sort of silence that follow a shellin', a thin, metallic quiet, coloured the same silver as that Boche plane still circlin' above the smoke.

We gettin' to our feet, takin' count of ourselves, dustin' off our weapons and readyin' for a ground attack, when Gaston, he pull free from Henri's grasp. Leapin' up the slope of the trench, he go racin' through the smoke-filled village, makin' for the only safety he know, runnin' fast as he can back to the chateau.

Before anyone can react, the kid take off after him.

'Henri, *non*!' I jump up to go after them. James yank hard on my rifle strap, spinnin' me around.

'No.'

'We gotta get them back.'

We shoutin' at each other, tryin' to hear above our still vibratin' ears.

He shake his head, eyes fixed on the kid as he run up the street. 'No. The shelling's stopped. They'll be better off inside than out here when the ground attack begins.'

Our eyes still followin' the kid, with Gaston just ahead of him. The cayoodle beginnin' to slow on account of his leg, but he chargin' forward all the same, that gold and silver star in his *fourragère* collar shinin' through the smoke. The same thought occur to both James and me as we look up at the sky. We watch as the plane turn as it track a winkin', shinin' star racin' through the ruins.

For a long moment, ain't nothin' happen. It as if time itself gone slow. Maybe he ain't seen them, I tell myself. Or maybe he has, but he flyin' low enough now to see it only a kid, chasin' his frightened dog. The dust slowly start to settle. The sound of someone coughin', that plane circlin' above. Then it come, the slow whistle of a shell. I hear its music, I hear it, and I know where it goin' to land.

We take off from the trench together, James and I, runnin' fast as we can towards the chateau. There, straight ahead, the left wing fallen in now, but the rest of the façade still standin'. Closer still, the whine of the shell in our ears. 'Henri!' I see Gaston, just disappearin' inside the doorway and now Henri hear us callin' his name. He turn to us in the doorway, we so close now, I can see the tear stains on his smoke-blackened cheeks. He a kid, just a little child. He try his best to grin. 'Gaston,' he say, just as the shell land.

It a direct hit, perfectly called in. A sick-makin' *thump*, the chateau stand upright for a moment and then it crumble, in a huge outward burst of shrapnel and stone, blowin' us off our feet.

FORTY

New York City • December 1940

The Christmas tree towering at the head of the ballroom was ablaze with colour, the red, white and blue theme of the ball replicated in the twinkling lights and glowing balls of plastic that hung from every inch of its branches. Madeleine twirled the stem of her glass between her fingers. Was that a chip in her manicure? She frowned, drawing her hand closer, but it was only the light, skimming her red nail varnish, shimmering from Jim's mother's ring. She lifted her finger, a graceful, barely perceptible movement. The diamond sprang alive, turned incandescent and radiated fire. She stared at it, the melancholy she'd been trying to stave off all evening washing over her again.

'A dance, milady?' Freddie bowed before her, grinning as he held out a cut-out star.

She shook her head, amused despite herself. 'Another? Freddie, how many of those *did* you buy?'

'Well, if you must know,' he pulled a fistful of stars from his pocket. 'Let's see, what have we here – 5, 6 . . . 9 dances lined up with the loveliest woman in the room.'

'Freddie, Freddie.' She shook her head again, smiling, and not a little touched. 'Why ever wouldn't you go dance with one of the girls over there instead?' She gestured towards the debutantes and models surrounding by wooing, admiring men. Each girl was a taxi dancer for the evening, wearing, as Madeleine did, a sash over their gowns emblazoned with the words *Dance With Me!* in an elaborate red, blue and white font. The sashes had grown increasingly pinned with stars as the night had progressed. A star for a dollar, a dance for a star, with all the proceeds of the ball going towards the Aid Our Allies Fund.

A choice handful of married women had been tapped for dance duty as well. Madeleine tilted her chin, a hand holding her sash in place as Freddie pinned the star on to her shoulder.

'Could we sit this one out?'

'You sat out the last two,' he pointed out. 'Besides,' he waggled his fingers towards the band as they struck up the opening notes of the next song. 'Hear that? They might be playing especially for you. Come on Cookie, cheer up.' He held out his hand, and resignedly she took it, following his lead on to the crowded dance floor as the band launched into a rollicking version of 'Lookie, Lookie, Lookie, here comes Cookie'.

Not yet midnight, and already the ball was shaping up to be an unqualified triumph. Patrons spilled from every corner of the Waldorf, the five-dollar tickets having sold out weeks in advance. All the same, Madeleine felt oddly removed from the gaiety, her gaze drifting about the room as she danced, as if searching for someone who wasn't there. She registered only marginally the glitter of jewels, the well-known faces from celluloid and stage manning the crowded bar, the giant grab bags that dotted the room, filled with donations from the most exclusive stores in New York City.

The massive board that occupied half of one wall was surrounded by guests clamouring for a chance to pin the 'tache on Herr Hitler's face while women shrieked with laughter from the debunking beds at the other end of the room. A young lovely sat balancing on each wobbly bed, men gladly paying for the privilege of lobbing a ball at it and trying to unseat its occupant from atop her precarious perch.

The entire evening had been months in the planning. Madeleine knew she ought to be pleased with its obvious success. Her eyes rested on the Christmas tree again. It towered over them all, a Norman spruce nearly thirty feet tall, thoroughly bejewelled and adorned into a vast triangle of sparkling, tricolour light.

An image rose unbidden in her mind. Of another tree, decidedly more modest in height, hung with well-worn ornaments, some of which had the glitter rubbed from them and were chipped here and there from the years. She could almost hear the orange crackle of the fire in the grate, its sound particularly loud in the winter stillness of the orchard. The scent of pine, slivers of green in the uneven floorboards where so many needles had slipped into the cracks. Christmas carols playing in the background, Jim humming along under his breath as he sat polishing his rifle, glancing now and again out the windows at the snow-bound hills.

She turned her head, fighting the despondency welling inside of her.

'I can't believe he wouldn't come,' Freddie shouted above the band, leaning in to make himself heard.

She shrugged, forcing a lightness into her voice. 'It's only a ball.'

'Only a ball? This is *the* event of the year, darling! And you helped organise it.'

She shrugged again, nonchalantly. Her feet moved of their own accord to the music. She couldn't help but picture Jim, however, in full evening dress, cool and commanding by her side, more arresting by far than anyone in the room.

'No,' he'd said flatly when she'd broached the subject. 'You know where I stand.'

'Couldn't you make an exception, just for one evening? We wouldn't have to spend a penny—'

His face tightened. 'No.'

'I didn't mean . . . you know that isn't what I meant. You don't have to make a donation of any kind, participate in any of the fund-raising. Just come. Be there. With me. It's one of the biggest events of the season. You don't have to make it into a political issue, for God's sake.'

'It *is* a political issue, it's nothing *but* a political issue. The "Aid The Allies Fund"? It's warmongering, plain and simple. No,' he repeated flatly.

Her voice rose ever so slightly. 'War, in case you hadn't noticed, is already upon us.'

'Upon Europe,' he corrected.

'Yes, upon Europe. And soon upon America as well, unless we do something about it.'

'Warmongering. Meddling in something that's none of our business. Last I checked, Hitler's made no move to declare war on America, or have I missed something?'

'As yet. He hasn't declared war on us as yet, but it's only a matter of time.' She turned away, suddenly exhausted. 'The ball – I'm going to go – I have to, I'm one of the organisers.'

'Enjoy yourself,' he said coolly.

It felt as if they had been at loggerheads for months, ever since war had broken out in earnest in Europe once more. The dissent between them was the same that had rent the entire country in two. On the one hand, there were those who championed active and immediate involvement. Stand alongside Britain and her allies, the interventionists urged. Throw the weight of the United States into the ring, stamp out the scourge of Nazism before it spreads to America's shores.

Why expend an ounce of energy on an issue that wasn't theirs, the non-interventionists countered? Why spend American resources, why risk American lives in a conflict that was still largely European in scope?

The argument had drawn a line right through their marriage. Madeleine stared at the full-page advertisement in the papers – 'STOP HITLER NOW!' – and reached unconsciously for the flag pin she wore in the lapel of her blouse. If Hitler won in Europe, the advertisement warned, America would find itself alone in a barbaric world. She tried to imagine the prospect and shuddered. She didn't understand how Jim could stand by and do nothing, especially when the Major, his own father, had been one of the earliest from this country to volunteer for the Great War.

It filled Jim with a bitter anger that she and her friends could be so blind. How quick they were to forget the previous war, an entire generation of men decimated, their lives forever twisted out of shape. Especially Madeleine, after she'd witnessed first-hand the damage it had wrought upon his father, on Connor, on all those at Anacostia, so many soldiers used up in the war and then callously cast aside.

It felt to him like a betrayal, an ultimate forswearing of the Major's despair over how shabbily those doughboy veterans had been treated, now to endorse this war that wasn't theirs, to offer up an entire new generation to experience the same hell those doughboys had.

This wanton rabble-rousing, the paranoia that seemed to spread daily . . . Charles Lindbergh was one of the few who made any sense these days, Jim thought disgustedly to himself. The aviator had come out strongly against active intervention by the US.

'We must stop this hysterical chatter of calamity and invasion,' he said in a radio broadcast. He scoffed at the danger of an imminent German attack. 'If we desire peace, we have only to stop asking for war.'

His speech only served to further divide the country. Lindbergh was a Nazi spy, his detractors claimed. Look at all the time he'd spent in Berlin before war broke out. Wasn't that proof enough of his true intentions?

Back and forth, between co-workers and neighbours and former friends. Everywhere, talk of the war, this rampant, heated argument over America's involvement in it. Jim and Madeleine went to the movies, where she was nearly reduced to tears by the newsreel and its coverage of the London Blitz. They'd been tuning in to Edward Murrow's radio broadcasts from London each evening, listening intently as he described the eerie, pitch-black darkness broken by a single searchlight as it swept the sky, the stoic calm of the people while air-raid sirens sounded in the background. His words had been distressing enough to Madeleine, but to see the devastation in London, real, actual images up there on screen – the fires leaping from curtained windows, the billowing smoke, the rescue ladders leaning against blackened buildings, brought it all terribly to life.

The RAF were fighting valiantly, the voice-over said, standing their ground against the ferocity of the German onslaught. Madeleine was overcome by sadness, their dogged bravery and staunch determination to fight this David and Goliath battle. 'We have to do something,' she thought helplessly to herself. 'We've got to pitch in.'

Shaken as Jim was by the images, it only strengthened his conviction. It was madness, what was happening in Europe. It would be insanity to invite this wanton destruction upon American heads too.

Madeleine turned to him, shaking her head. Even in the darkened hall, he could make out the distress on her face. His expression softened as he gave her his handkerchief. She leaned against him, resting her head against his shoulder.

She was quiet on the ride home. Jim glanced at her as he drove, but said nothing to break the silence, glad for the absence of an argument and savouring the warmth of her leaning against him.

He was watching her comb out her hair later that night when

she turned to him with troubled eyes. 'Would you ever consider enlisting?' she asked tentatively, almost afraid of the answer.

And there it was again, the collective differences between them raising a head once more. He looked at her, suddenly tired. 'To fight someone else's war? No. And who'd look after the orchard if I left?'

She said nothing, turning back to the mirror as she tried to sort out her conflicting emotions. Part of her deeply thankful for his response, part ashamed, both of his stance and her relief.

He saw only the shame in her face and was stung. 'It isn't our war,' he repeated coldly as he strode from the room. 'And I'd like to see just how many of your flatlander lot rush to enlist.'

War clouds continued to gather, the looming threat weighing heavier and heavier on the nation's collective heart. That October, in the heat of election season, and just a month before he would be elected for an unprecedented third term, President Roosevelt announced the first peacetime conscription in the nation's history. All able-bodied men between the ages of eighteen and thirty-six were called upon to register.

Jim reported at the draft office, doubly irritated by the long lines and the waste of a perfectly good morning right in the middle of hunting season. He easily passed the medical examination, and handed the title deed of the orchard without comment to the registration clerk. He was classified accordingly, in category II-C.

Registrant deferred in support of agriculture. (Agricultural occupation). Fit for unrestricted military service.

The first number of the draft lottery – 158 – was drawn with great ceremony a few weeks later by the blindfolded Secretary of War, Henry Stimson. The blindfold was the same one that had been used in 1917 by the then Secretary of War Newton Baker, and was a strip of upholstery, the newspapers reported, taken from a chair that had stood in Independence Hall at the signing of the Constitution of the United States in 1789.

There was nobody, Madeleine couldn't help but notice, not a single person in all her Boston crowd who'd been drafted. Clara Dalloway's grandson was thrilled to find he was.

'It's the first time I've ever won a lottery,' he explained to the reporter of the *Gazette*, beaming with pride.

'Poor bastard,' Jim said as he read the interview.

*

'I declare this ball a resounding success.' Douggie Garland sat down beside her, interrupting her reverie. 'Congratulations, my dear.'

'It took a village.'

'I imagine it did. That's what it takes. A village, many villages, and hopefully soon all of this country will come together in doing what needs to be done.' He rolled his cigar against an ashtray. 'Surely you aren't alone?'

'No, Freddie's at the bar.'

'Stonebridge isn't a supporter of the movement then, I take it?'

She smiled wanly. 'The Great Debate has spilled into our home it seems. The husband anti-war, the wife rooting for the Allied cause.'

'If there were a way to avert the war, we would be for it, of course,' Garland said. 'But after the horrors of the London Blitz, and with the dire straits that our allies find themselves in—' He sucked on his cigar. 'We can't be ostriches, sticking our heads in the sand.'

'Jim's hardly an ostrich,' she said at once, rising loyally to his defence. 'Sometimes, when I think about it – I don't know, it makes a certain amount of sense, doesn't it? Why brook a war that has nothing to do with us?'

'Because England is our ally. Because we must fight against tyranny.'

She smiled ruefully. 'Except it isn't you and I who are going to be doing the actual fighting, are we now?'

She decided to call it an early night.

Freddie escorted her out. They stood in the lobby of the hotel as she fastened her cape.

'Are you sure you won't stay longer? Lily Pons is about to go on.'

'I know . . . it's just – I'm just tired, I suppose.'

He nodded. 'Cookie.' He cleared his throat. 'Been meaning to tell you all evening – I'm headed over to England.' He tugged boyishly on his ear. 'I've enlisted, as a pilot.'

Madeleine stared at him in shock. 'Oh Freddie,' she said, at a loss for words as she raised her hand to his cheek.

'I figure there's only so many times I can ask you to run away with me,' he said. 'And since you're never going to say yes—'

She laughed tremulously. 'You may as well run away by yourself, to England?' She hugged him fondly, trying not to cry.

The clock struck midnight. The first strains of the 'Star Spangled Banner' came over the loudspeakers, Lily Pons' operatic tenor swelling through the lobby and spilling out into the streets in so beautiful a rendition that even the cabbies paused their honking and momentarily slowed down to listen.

FORTY-ONE

Raydon • August 1941

After a singularly wet past few weeks that had spoiled the patch of wild strawberries – the fruit rotting on their stems – the thistledown had finally begun to fly in earnest. Ellie stood at a window upstairs, watching the wisps float through the garden, the sun warm on her arms as she sorted the linen. 'Summer snow,' she mused wistfully, at once embarrassed by her unaccustomed sentimentality. She sighed. August already. Soon fall would be around the corner, and 1941 would be gone, just like that. What was it about the years that made them go faster and faster the older one got?

All the talk about the war too. It was never-ending. The radio, the newspapers, at the general store and at church suppers – everywhere, the war. Why, even old Asaph and Jeremiah had had a falling-out over it, one calling for action, the other equally dead set against getting involved. At the small memorial service that Carla Dalloway had hosted in the general store after Black Pete passed away, both had nearly come to blows, cursing at one another at the tops of their reedy voices, each trying to whack the other with his cane until folks had intervened.

Another of Madeleine's magazines had come in with the mail a couple of days ago. The cover story featured the draftees of last October. Carla Dalloway's grandboy had been sending her letters telling her how sick and tired they all were of boot camp, and the article in the magazine said much the same. Nearly a year on, here they were, these young men who'd so eagerly enlisted, holed up in army camps around the country. Instead of fighting for their country, they'd found themselves digging latrines, endlessly drilling and peeling mountain after mountain of potatoes. All for thirty dollars a month, they complained, when they could have been making six or seven times that amount working in the defence factories.

They were thoroughly disillusioned, the magazine reported, and anxiously waiting for their contracts to be completed come October. They'd even coined a term for it – OHIO – Over The Hill in October, scrawling it in white chalk across walls and over camp beds, a reminder as they counted down the days.

It was this that had caught Jim's eye, 'OHIO', splashed across the cover page. He'd flipped through the article, and of course couldn't resist rubbing Madeleine's nose in it.

Ellie sighed again, staring out the window. Things had been fairly good between those two all these past few months. A family Christmas, and Madeleine here for most of the spring. It was just all this talk of the war . . . They had begun to avoid overt discussion of it now, both wearied by their bickering. Their dissent, however, had taken on other, more insidious forms; an iciness between them as each held firm to their ground. The thing about ice, Ellie brooded, was that it had a way of splitting things apart. Working its way into the smallest nooks and crannies so that even after it melted away, like a crack down a rock face, things stood permanently altered. It was almost better, she thought unhappily, when they used to row outright.

That time a month or so ago, over the prophecy. She'd been poring over Eleanor Roosevelt's newspaper column one afternoon. It was her daily ritual, to read 'My Day' – Ellie liked to follow the doings of her famous namesake, secretly picturing herself in her stead. Travelling one day to New York, setting off for Tucson the next, shaking hands here, cutting a ribbon there, giving speeches and saying all these important things . . . She'd been particularly enjoying the column that afternoon – Mrs Roosevelt was describing her recent visit to Vermont, and Ellie was nodding in approval over an account of waffles with maple syrup and sausages, when she exclaimed aloud.

She looked over her glasses at Madeleine. 'Have you seen this?'

The First Lady had referenced a translation that someone had sent her. It was an ancient French prophecy, made in medieval times:

'I have seen the terrors of forests and mountains. The unbelievable has frozen the people. The time has come when Germany will be considered the most belligerent nation of the world.'

Madeleine had pounced on the article. She'd rung her professor father who'd obligingly searched out the entire translation for her, and she highlighted sections of it for Jim to read.

'It is the time when Germania will be called the most belligerent nation on earth. It is the time when there will spring from its womb the terrible warrior who will undertake war on the world, and whom men under arms will call 'Anti-Christ', he who will be damned by mothers in thousands.

'His arms will be flamboyant, and the helmets of his soldiers be topped by points throwing off lightning, as their hands will carry flaming torches. It will be impossible to list the victims of his cruelties. His winged warriors will be seen, in unbelievable attacks, to rise up to the firmament, there to seize the stars to throw them on towns from one end of the universe to the other and light gigantic fires.'

'A prophecy?' Jim said incredulously when Madeleine showed it to him. 'Is this what the great warmongering front is hanging its hat on, these days?' He read only a couple of paragraphs before handing it back to her. 'And where exactly does it say that it is about this war anyway? It talks of spiked helmets – the Germans wore those in the Great War. The war,' he added mockingly, 'to end all wars.'

A few heads of thistledown caught a stray draught and wafted higher, through the pink sprawl of the cabbage roses, past the old apple tree, silhouetted against the faded red of the barn. Ellie followed their progress, past the eaves, a brief sighting at the lip of shingle and blue sky, and then they were gone. She continued to shake out the linen, her gaze drifting along the imagined arc of their flight, over the smudge of upland and out to the far, mauve-tinted hills. Her gaze wandered, closer now, over the stubble of pasture and the rolls of newly mown hay. It had been a busy couple of days here on the orchard. What was it the Major used to say?

'When the thistledown starts to blow, 'tis time for the grass to go.'

Her eyes softened as she remembered, the corners of her mouth lifting. She glanced at the sky again, her hands automatically folding and sorting. Clear and cloudless, with no threat of rain. 'Still,' she mused, 'better Jim brings in the hay. All it takes is a bit of damp and—'

A movement at the end of the drive caught her eye. From this vantage point upstairs, she could clearly make out the man who stood among the foliage. An older man, from the stiffness of his movements. He shifted position again, raising his fists in an improbable boxer feint. Ellie watched in surprise. Whatever was he doing?

Left. Right. Left.

Obadaiah lowered his fists, shaking them out by his side, trying to ease his nervousness. He looked yet again towards the drive that snaked up and away from where he stood. Removing his hat, he fanned himself with it, then jammed it back on his head.

'Quit being a ninny, Obadaiah Nelson,' he muttered to himself. 'You ain't come all this way only to turn back now.'

He fished the small square of paper from his pocket. This was definitely the place they'd given him directions to in town. He took off his hat once more, set it back on his head. Upper hook, lower jab. He bounced creakily from foot to foot, then, taking a deep breath and squaring his shoulders, he picked up his suitcase, and to Ellie's consternation, started to walk up the drive.

'Ellie! Hey, Ellie!' Young Jimmy shaded his eyes and squinted up at her from the dooryard. 'Can I have some more pie?'

'You most certainly may not, young man!' She hurriedly set aside the linen. 'That's quite enough for one morning. Go on now, get your father, quick, we have a visitor.'

She hurried downstairs, eyeing the poker in the fireplace. All this talk of the war, it was doing strange things to folks. Interventionists watching pacifists with suspicion, as rumours of German spies embedded deep within American society spread like poison all through last year. There had been incidents of vandalism, of folks losing their jobs overnight for saying the wrong thing, sometimes not even for that. There were even those who'd barged into their neighbours' homes, questioning their loyalty and demanding they salute the American flag. Flatlander craziness, with almost none of that going on here in Raydon, still . . .

She was being unduly alarmist, Ellie decided. The stranger was likely just another of those oddballs found occasionally wandering these parts. It was probably a meal he was after, or perhaps he was lost.

She opened the door just as Obadaiah was lifting his hand to the knocker. 'Yes?' She looked at him, even more puzzled than before. A man of colour, and certainly not dressed like too many around here.

She took in the silk hat on his head, the fit of his clothes – well worn and travel-soiled, but there was no mistaking their expensiveness. A real fancy-pants, this one.

'Yes?' she asked again, tartly.

Obadaiah removed his hat. 'James . . .' He cleared his throat. 'I'm lookin' for James Stonebridge.'

'Ellie?' Jim came striding from the orchard, Jimmy scampering alongside.

'Someone's here for you,' she said, as Obadaiah turned around. Jim saw something familiar about him.

The stranger smiled. 'You be little Jim, I'm guessing? Only, not so little now, are you? No, it your pappy I'm after. Captain James Stonebridge, of the Foreign Legion.'

'*Major* Stonebridge,' Ellie corrected at once. 'He's passed on.'

Obadaiah's face went grey, crumpling in shock.

'I'm sorry,' she was saying. 'Three years now since he left us . . .'

Obadaiah looked away, dazed, at the roses sprawling across the dooryard, seeing as in a slow-moving dream, the red-painted barn topped by a wedge of summer sky, the apple trees covered with bloom. With the war on in earnest, it had taken him a while to make it here from Paris. He'd finally managed to get on a boat from France, with multiple changes through Europe until the ship to New York. Picturing in his mind all the while the very vista that lay before him now – this old, graceful house, the rolling orchards, brought alive from the rare reminiscences that James would suddenly share with him, all those years ago. He'd stood at the foot of the driveway for an eternity, imagining just what he and the Yankee would say to one another.

'Damn fool!' the Yankee would explode when he laid eyes on him.

'Who dat?' he'd counter innocently at once.

'Who dat who say who dat . . .' and they'd start to laugh in unison . . .

'Always was talkin' 'bout them trees, he was.' Obadaiah gestured with his hat, trying to smile. 'Goin' on and on 'bout graftin' and hybrids and such.' He swallowed painfully. 'I hadn't heard. The other legionnaires . . . we keep in touch, some of us. Nobody said nothin'.'

'He didn't have contact with anyone from the war. Wouldn't speak about it at all.' Jim hesitated, puzzled by the stranger and still trying to place where he'd seen him. 'Won't you come in?'

'No . . . no, I should get goin'.' Obadaiah shook his head, tryin' to find his bearings. 'But here. This be . . . *was* his. Yours now by rights, I reckon.' Reaching inside his jacket, he drew out an old, leather-bound notebook. Dirt and time had ground their way into the brown cover, obliterating some of the gold lettering, but the name inscribed on the spine was still clearly legible.

James Arthur Stonebridge.

Young Jimmy, who had been observing the proceedings with great interest, poked his head forward.

'Hello!'

'Why, hello there, mister. And you are?'

Jimmy stuck his chest out with pride. 'James Henry Stonebridge,' he said.

A flare of shocked recognition in Obadaiah's eyes at the name, and suddenly Jim remembered. The camp at Anacostia. Beside the boxing ring – it had been him, this tall, stooped stranger, standing by the ropes, staring with such intensity at the Major.

'Anacostia,' he exclaimed. 'I saw you at Anacostia. Sir,' he asked urgently, 'how did you know my father?'

Obadaiah stood in a trance before the black mirror. It had given him a turn alright to see it there, squatting on the wall. He'd stumbled, his limbs filled with trembling.

Jim noticed. 'He brought it back with him.'

Obadaiah's eyes were fixed on the mirror as he nodded. '1916.' His voice shook. 'Trois Fontaines. A small village, just beside the Front.'

'Were you—' Jim began, brimming with questions, when Ellie caught his eye, waving frantically from the kitchen. He frowned impatiently. 'Excuse me.'

Obadaiah barely noticed him leave. He stepped forward, closer to the mirror. Again that feeling, of floating through slow-running water, of moving through a dream. James gone, so many years lost, but this, the mirror, surviving still, conjured directly from their past. He took another shaky step forward. The room around him seemed to blur about its edges, dissolving into another, older room that took its stead.

The chateau, muffled and silent, swathed in black netting. 'This here mirror is spooked,' he declares and James glances at him with that swift, sideways look of amusement. 'Haints?' his expression seems to say. 'There's no haints in here – it's a mirror, jackass, that's all.'

Obadaiah raised a hand to the glass, remembering. A wash of light across the surface of the mirror, the glass seeming to buckle and swell at his touch. A ripple, as on silken black water, shadows stirring towards him.

He only vaguely registered the hushed exchange in the kitchen. 'What do folks like him eat?'

'Ellie! The same as folks like us, or any other folks, for that matter.'

A burst of indignant whispering from Ellie. 'Well, how should I know? There haven't been many like him around these parts, have there? Although, there was that lot who looked just like him, in the veteran camps up in East Barre . . . Still, I had to ask, didn't I, or would you rather I served something he wasn't going to eat?'

Their voices seemed to come from a long way away. Obadaiah stood transfixed before the mirror. It was James he could clearly hear, *James*, and the others, behind him. Karan, Gaillard, the Captain . . . all of them, together, marching in perfect sync. The flag aflutter, the slow roll of drums, and voices, rising in song.

'J'avais un camarade, De meilleur il n'en est pas;
Dans la paix et dans la guerre
I once had a comrade
A better friend, there was none.'

Obadaiah's eyes filled with tears. James was right, he thought to himself. Yankee James, he was right all along. There never were any ghosts in the black mirror.

'In war and in peace
Were we brothers,
Marching with even pace.'

There was no voodoo magic, neither haints, nor any hexes placed upon it – all it housed were the sorrows of the man looking into it. All that was forsaken, every hollowing regret, all those who had once touched his days and infused them with meaning, all who were gone – these were what a man saw staring back at him, encased in smooth, black glass.

'After the war.' What was that James used to say? *'We'll drive, from Montana, down, all the way to the ocean. The wind in our faces and salt spray stinging our skin.'*

After the war, he'd say, after the war, holding it out like a promise. After the war, when the world would right itself, after the war, this war to end all wars.

Grief tore into him afresh, a small, inarticulate sound escaping his throat. His hand shook as he raised it, the fingers trembling as he wiped his eyes. When he looked again at the mirror, a face came slowly into view.

A face he remembered well, the same blue eyes, reserved, questioning, the stubborn set of jaw. The gently receding hairline of a man neither young nor yet old, the first lines about his mouth hinting at loss, at the battles, both large and small, that life had thrown his way.

Obadaiah turned around to face Jim.

FORTY-TWO

Jim sat in the old leather armchair, the journal in his hands. It was late, closer to morning than to the night before, but he was wide awake, mind still racing from the events of the day. He touched the gold lettering on the cover, fingertips lingering over the loops and curlicues of his father's name.

He'd accepted the journal without comment when Obadaiah had handed it to him that morning, stuffing it into a pocket of his overalls with a casualness that had belied his shock. A journal. His silent, reclusive father who had not once spoken of any of the war years had actually kept a *journal* all the while he'd been in France. Jim had carried it about with him all day, reaching now and again to touch its cover as if to reassure himself of its presence.

He'd been burning with questions, but the pain in Obadaiah's face as he'd turned around from the mirror stayed him. They'd stood in silence for a moment.

'You got the look of your pappy 'bout you.' Obadaiah gestured vaguely. 'The eyes . . .' He tried to smile, but once again, it was a poor attempt and he looked away, through the open window where the gnarled old apple tree stood framed against the barn.

'Maybe I could show you around the orchard?' Jim offered.

A brief hesitation, and Obadaiah nodded. 'Always was goin' on 'bout Reds and McIntoshes, he was . . .'

They paused in the dooryard while he lit up a cigarette and Jim saw the slight tremor in his hands. 'How did you—' he began again, but before he could say anything further, young Jimmy came tearing down the slope towards them.

He'd been dispatched to the barn under protest – 'But we have a visitor! Someone who knew Grandpa!' – and now, chores finally done, he came galloping towards this intriguing stranger.

'You knew my grandpa!'

'I sure did.' Obadaiah pulled on his cigarette, grateful for its comfort. 'From a long time ago.'

'How long ago?'

'Years ago. With him being 'bout the age your pappy is now.'

Jimmy frowned in puzzlement, trying to reconcile the memories he had of the Major, limping and bent, with the image of a much younger man. 'Did Grandpa have any hair back then?'

A tired gleam of amusement stole into Obadaiah's eyes. 'Plenty hair, the same colour as yours, and blue eyes the same as well. Although,' he added solemnly, 'he didn't talk nearly as much as you.'

'Yes, well, he has his mother's genes,' Jim said dryly, reaching out to ruffle young Jimmy's hair.

Jimmy kept up his guileless barrage of questions all through their walk around the orchard. Jim watched the older man, the way Obadaiah seemed to lower his guard around the boy reminding him with a pang of the Major, the way the air of fragility about him seemed to dissipate as he talked with the child. Once or twice, he even threw back his head and laughed out loud. Ellie called out that dinner was ready, and they turned back towards the house.

She had brought out the good china and even arranged a bunch of roses in a glass jar.

'This look mighty fine,' Obadaiah said quietly.

Suddenly self-conscious, Ellie fiddled with the gingham tablecloth, smoothing a non-existent crease. She moved the platter on which the roast rested, a tiny quarter-inch to the side, the better for the light to fall on its beautifully burnished front. 'It's just simple fare.'

'Simple fare, it suit simple folks just fine.' A sudden twinkle in his eye. 'Folks such as me, same as folks like you.'

Ellie went beet red with embarrassment, all the way to her roots. 'So you overheard me then, earlier. Well, what would you have me do—' she began, bristling, and Obadaiah grinned, holding up a placatory palm.

'I'm just having some fun, Miss.' He sat down at the table. 'All this look powerful fine. James, he was always goin' on 'bout your apple pie, he was.'

'Was he now?' Ellie smiled with pleasure. 'The Major was fond of my cooking.' She hesitated. 'And call me Ellie, do.'

'Did Grandpa go on about me too?' Jimmy wanted to know, still confused by the timelines of the past.

'Well, it was still early days for that.' Obadaiah pointed a fork at Jim. 'He talked 'bout your pappy though.'

Jim looked up sharply, blue eyes round with surprise. 'He did?'

'Carried a picture 'bout with him all the time. No more than knee-high to a duck you were, and your hair falling in your eyes.'

Jim nodded impassively, but there was a strange lump in his throat. He continued to eat, keenly aware all the while of the journal in his pocket, of its rectangular bulk, resting solid and comforting against his frame.

'Maybe it weren't nobody's fault,' Obadaiah said slowly. His eyes followed the last swoop of a barn swallow as it headed to roost, a dark, arcing arrow in the dusk. 'Not James', not mine, not anybody's. *C'est la guerre.*'

Jim and he sat on the porch, watching as the first stars began to light the sky. Behind them, the house lay quiet and peaceful. Young Jimmy had gone to bed, cheered by the prospect of Obadaiah staying with them a few days. Ellie had railroaded all of Obadaiah's earlier protests.

'I'm setting up one of the spare rooms,' she'd announced and Jim nodded in agreement.

'Damn fool thing to do, to come all this way only to leave so soon,' he pointed out, and Obadaiah had finally capitulated, amused and still a little taken aback by the similarities between Yankee James and his son.

He drew a deep breath, taking in the balmy scents of summer bloom and freshly mown hay. '*Country scents*,' James used to call them, and somehow Obadaiah had known, even in the filth of the trenches, he'd known just what his friend had meant, picturing in his own mind the pleasant scents of ripening apples, of mulched earth and warm animal hide. Grief filled him again, disorienting in its force, and Obadaiah looked down at his hands.

'*C'est la guerre*,' he repeated haltingly. 'We known, of course we did, James and I. It was just the war, the 'no count, devil-spawn war, swallowin' both men and boys the same.'

A breeze sifted through the sugarbush, stirring the tops of the trees.

'But maybe I should start at the beginnin'. Way back, at the very start. The summer of 1914, before the war, even. A golden light upon Paris and her streets filled with song.'

The moon rose, gliding over hill and copse. Obadaiah did most of the talking, Jim interjecting only occasionally with a question. The older man paused now and again to light a fresh cigarette, the ash-tray balanced on the railing filling steadily with stubs as the hours went on. At first his speech was rusty, the syllables disjointed, guttural, but soon they began to meld together, in a cadence both story and song, flowing in unfamiliar, deeply affecting rhythms into the night.

Jim felt the gooseflesh rise along his arms, events from twenty-five years ago unfolding frame by frame before his eyes.

Here, his father, a young man so filled with purpose and idealism at the onset of the war. The rough camaraderie of the Legion, the unlikely friendship forged between these two men from such vastly differing backgrounds. The blue uniforms, the *kepis rouge*, marking a field of wooden crosses, the painfully swollen feet after yet another marathon march. The welcome heat of a bonfire at the night's halt, its flames leaping against the ancient stone façade of the abbey where they'd camped. A crate handed out in welcome by the monks of the order; bottles popped open with alacrity, and his father's voice, commenting dryly on the virtues of fine champagne consumed under the stars.

The tip of Obadaiah's cigarette was an orange phosphorescence in the dark. The presence of the two men sitting there in the porch was cautiously assessed and deemed safe, and the scrabble and scratch of small night creatures resumed in the grass and the woodpile. Obadaiah continued his soliloquy all the while, speaking-singing this paean to his friend, an ode to his truest brother. Jim heard the roar of motorcycles, felt the dust of the roads in his lungs. A row of ancient poplars along the banks of a canal, set afire after a shelling; water the colour of molten metal, and the look upon his father's face as the trees shrivelled and burned, toppling one after the other into the quietly flowing stream.

Obadaiah talked on, painting pictures with his words. The rich, musical timbre of his narrative filling in the gaps of all these years, bridging the man the Major had once been to the shell he was reduced to in the end.

Jim saw himself, tied irrevocably to his father. As the Major had in turn been to his, backwards through the years, a long, unbroken line of Stonebridges, with an identical love for these purpled hills, for apple trees in bloom, for the tinge of snowmelt in the Connecticut, and walls of rambling stone.

He saw the invisible spiderweb of threads that joined them all, the myriad ways, subtle and overt, that the experiences and choices of the past shaped the present. Like the spathes of a plant, the older encasing the younger, a multitude of generations tucked one inside the other, beneath the quiet earth.

He thought of his uncle Bill, whose name Jim still carried in his own, his untimely passing permanently altering the course of the Major's life when it was he who signed up for the war instead of his older brother. He began to realise too, for the first time, just how much he was his father's son. Not merely bearing his name or born with the same blue Stonebridge eyes, but a deeper mirroring that had been shaped by the Major's silences, by the cold withdrawals that had been the only way his father had known to cope with his pain.

Jim felt the jagged edges of the Major's guilt, all the festering rot from the war. He saw a young French boy, the shelled and smoking village. His father calculating the odds, the naked fear in his face, Obadaiah racing alongside, calling frantically for Henri to stop, turn around, stop, goddammit, *it ain't safe*.

His father again, that winter of 1933. The wonder in his face as he held his grandson for the very first time, hugging the baby close. 'James Henry.'

Obadaiah's voice lapsed into silence. They sat there, lost in their thoughts as they looked out on to the moonlit orchard.

'C'est la guerre,' Obadaiah repeated slowly, leaning forward to stub out his cigarette. 'It was the war, the madness of it. Just the knowin' though, it wasn't 'nuff. It wasn't goin' to bring the kid back, it wasn't going to right all the wrongs. Maybe it was our wrong too. The kid, he had no business being there in the first place after all.'

He drew a shaky breath. 'Afterwards, maybe there been other ways, but I done the only thing I knew. I ain't never spoken of that day to nobody, not until now, and I ain't never spoken another word to James. Wasn't his fault and it wasn't mine, but it broken us in two all the same, what happened to the kid. The silence, that been our punishment.

'That shellin' of the chateau, I gotten caught bad in the blast. Landed me in the hospital for months. James, he sent me letters. I ain't never opened a single one and I ain't never replied, and them letters, they stopped. April 1917, America finally entered the war, while I still been recoverin'. When I gotten discharged, I learn that James, he transferred over to one of the Yank regiments newly arrived in France. Me, myself, I stayed on with the Legion.'

He paused, lost in the past. 'He gone and left a package for me before he left. The first and last time I ever gotten a package, in all the years of the war, and it was from Yankee James. 'My name written real neat on top, and the whole thing tied with string. In it, I find two things: the rabbit foot gris-gris I once given him for luck, and his journal, the one he always scribblin' in.'

Obadaiah went to bed at last, but sleep was the furthest thing from Jim's mind. He sat in the Major's armchair, the old leather journal in his hands. He held it tenderly, as if the unexpected gift were valuable beyond measure. He ran his thumb over his father's name again, picturing him bent over it in the cold, waterlogged trenches.

'Always was scribblin' in it,' Obadaiah had said. 'Said it was for the novel what he was goin' to write, after the war.'

He never did, thought Jim, not a novel, recalling with a pang all the articles the Major had repeatedly sent to the *Gazette*. The novel had never come.

He looked at the journal, imagining his father's face, the set blankness of it as he prepares to leave the Legion. He's readying a package; in it, the good luck charm that he'd once been gifted. He doesn't deserve it, is unworthy of any sort of good fortune, not after what happened to Henri. He feels wholly responsible: the boy was under their care. He knew the odds, knew exactly what he should have done, and yet, when it mattered the most, he froze.

Much as it has hurt him, he understands the silence. There is too much that has happened between him and Obadaiah, too much that they have endured. The silence is their penance, lying heavy between them, a gravestone marked with the dead.

He picks up his journal, his constant companion ever since he enroled at the start of the war. Page after page is filled with his writing, a meticulous account, an attempt to remember, through the mindless slaughter, just why he and so many like him signed up, an effort to make sense of the insanity of this war. He holds the journal in his hands, his heart heavy now with knowing.

There is no making sense of any of it. For him, for so many like him, there never will be an 'after the war'. There is only this: the bottomless hunger of the beast and their obeisance to its roar.

Filled with sudden revulsion, he tosses the journal aside. His eye has been troubling him; it starts to twitch again and he cups a palm over it, willing it to subside. He places the gris-gris in an empty tin of tobacco, then he turns to the journal again. Somewhere deep down, perhaps he isn't willing to accept that all of this has been in vain. It seems inconceivable to him, the notion, but a minuscule part of him still wants desperately to believe.

Picking up the journal, he slowly places it in the package. He fastens the package with string. *Obadaiah Nelson,* he writes on the top, addressing it to his friend.

He sits there a long while, holding the package in his hands. A thin rain starts to fall. He sits in silence, listening to the sound of the rain against the corrugated elephant-iron roof. He tries to discern a pattern, make out some sense of order in its staccato beat, a hint of some larger, greater meaning, but there is none. It is only rain. He rises painfully to his feet. There is nothing more to say, nothing more to do but leave.

He places the package on the table. Hefting his backpack on to his shoulders, he turns up the collar of his overcoat and steps out into the rain.

FORTY-THREE

Beacon Hill, Boston

It was entirely too early for the doorbell to be ringing in so diabolical a fashion. Madeleine hurried down the wide curve of stairs, fumbling with the silk tie of her dressing gown. The fundraiser last night had gone on forever before she'd been able to make her excuses and slip away. A few hours of sleep, she thought murderously, that was all she asked.

She could make out the blurred image of a man outside, through the bevelled glass of the door. She yanked it open, her annoyance evaporating when she saw Ellie's son standing on the stairs.

'Chris?' She looked automatically over his shoulders, as if expecting Jim to appear around the corner. 'What's wrong? Is Jimmy alright?' she began, worried, and he nodded.

'It's early, I know,' he said, grinning apologetically. 'I was headed to Boston for some tools, and Jim had me run this over to you.'

Madeleine looked at the parcel in surprise. 'What is it, do you know? I'm headed back in a few days anyway – I wasn't expecting anything.'

He shrugged. 'He didn't say. Just that I was to get it to you first thing today. And to take special good care of it on the ride over too, or he'd know the reason why.'

Turning down her offer to come inside – he had a lot to get done before heading back, he explained – he touched his hat to her and bounded whistling down the stoop.

She was barefoot, Madeleine realised. She flexed her red-painted toes absently against the stone, still bemused by the package. Chris started up the engine and the old truck belched and spluttered to life, the neighbour's dog starting to bark at the unaccustomed racket.

'You've got a guest at the orchard,' he called, as he backed up. 'Some Frenchman. A real fancy-pants, Ma said he was.'

'What? Who?' Madeleine asked, now thoroughly bewildered, but he was gone, careening down the cobble-stoned streets of the Hill.

She looked baffled at the parcel in her hands, tearing it open as she turned back inside.

It was an old journal; the Major's, judging from the name on the spine. A spurt of irritation went through her. What was this all about? An encore, after that OHIO article?

'Who is it, Cookie?' Professor Scott came down the stairs.

'Chris. Ellie's son, from Raydon. It's nothing,' she said, reaching up to kiss her father on the cheek.

'I thought it might be Jim.'

'When is it *ever* Jim?' she retorted, and at once regretted the sharpness of her tone. 'Ellie's boy,' she repeated, smiling to soften her words.

She ignored the journal all morning, leaving it lying unopened on her dressing table while she made calls, finalised arrangements for the next evening's 'Bundles for Britain' charity auction and attended to her correspondence. It remained on her mind, though, her gaze repeatedly turning to the telephone in the hallway. Maybe she should call Jim?

Or maybe he could have called her, she thought indignantly, countering herself. Typical, to just send this without so much as notice or explanation. And whoever was this mystery guest? They barely ever had anyone over at the orchard, and here she was gone not three days and there was someone actually staying over?! Couldn't he have at least called to let her know?

Eventually though, her curiosity got the better of her and she picked up the journal. 'He could've called,' she thought again to herself.

She flipped through the pages filled with the Major's small, precise hand, still annoyed, and not really taking in the words at first. Gradually, however, the sentences started to catch her attention. Madeleine ran a hand over the cover of the journal, recalling her father-in-law, a fern stuck in the brim of his hat, breaking into the most ridiculous dance to the tune of 'Yankee Doodle'. She shook her head, filled with a sudden sadness at the memory. It all seemed so long ago.

She turned a page, another. Settling down on the bed, Madeleine began absorbedly to read:

There come times in a man's life that change everything. He looks about him afterwards and sees that the leaves have turned, as if in an instant. The river has altered its course, no longer flowing southward or anywhere familiar at all. It is changed, the ripples from hidden trout seeming to flow up-current, the stones in its bed flipped over, exposing pocked bellies so long buried in the mud.

At first, a man is afraid. He keeps count of losses both small and large, tallying the hours spent without sleep, the weeks since he last bathed, the number of friends he has lost. He recalls the life he has left behind, and is fearful of its loss. He waits in his trench, goes over the top when he hears the whistle, and prays, to whatever God will listen, for succour.

The days mount, however, and he cannot seem to pray any more or believe that there is indeed a God. The dead lie in the open. He sees their filmed-over eyes, the milkiness of their gaze as they stare unblinking into the sun. It seems ridiculous to believe that something alive and human once beat within those mangled bones, and that it was something human, with will and conscience, that did this to them.

He waits, he goes over the top, he fights. He smells the rot of decomposing bodies on his skin and gradually it dawns on him that the sun will rise and it will set but never will there be an end to this madness. The fear inside him sinks deeper; slowly, it metastasises to ice. In the pit of his stomach and the back of his skull, a barricade against the shells bursting about him in nightmare splendour.

Ice, cutting him off from everything he once was, from any notion of the future, each moment of the present expanded into an eternity in its stranglehold.

Eventually, that is all that comes to make sense. A moment, that is all a man has claim to, the space between this breath and the next. A moment, that is all, and it matters no more whether he lives, or dies, or who he once has loved.

She read all afternoon and into the evening, skipping supper so she could continue uninterrupted. The Major's words seared into her, his eloquence all the more haunting for his refusal ever to speak of the war after it was over.

The Major had laid bare the horror of all he'd been through in his writing. Madeleine saw the blackened fields, the shattered trenches and the broken-doll sprawl of the dead. War, as it truly was, stripped of the romantic ideals of honour, of glory, of epaulettes and ribboned medals, brought to life, page after page in his journal. She saw the countless rows of men, and boys yet barely men, the innocence knocked so devastatingly from them, she felt the bottomless grief of their mothers.

Madeleine broke down and wept. For the Major, for every fighting soldier, for Freddie, poor dear Freddie, coasting somewhere over the Atlantic, for London and Belgium and the dead at Dunkirk, for all that was pressing down now upon American shores.

Her heart ached as she remembered the Major, sitting day after day before the black mirror. 'Who did he see in there?' she'd idly wondered.

How little they'd guessed at the burden he'd carried. Him, and so many like him, chained for ever to the past, the war tainting everything that had followed, all that was yet to come. A dark and poisonous pool, it held up a reflection to them, like looking in smooth, black glass. They had desperately sought redemption, but were haunted by the dead; they finally deemed themselves undeserving, believing that they were damned. Madeleine wept for their families, for all those who loved them, but never could understand.

She didn't sleep at all that night, grieving for the Major, for Jim, and the father he had been denied. For a young French boy, so needlessly lost, his memory living on in the name of her own son.

As soon as it was light, she headed back to Raydon.

It was early enough that he was still in the barn. Jim paused in his mucking-out of the stables, blue eyes guarded as she entered. She held out the journal.

'Why?' she asked unsteadily.

'Thought you were coming back on Friday,' he said, sidestepping the question.

She came closer, placed the journal on a ledge. 'Why did you send it to me?' she repeated.

A sudden vulnerability in his eyes. 'I read it all night long,' he said, haltingly. 'It was the first time I've ever felt like I really knew him. The Major.' He set down the shovel, trying to articulate the words.

'Judy. My dog,' he said abruptly. 'I told you about her – we gave her away.' Madeleine nodded, remembering the setter from the photograph of him as a boy, surprised by the change in subject but knowing instinctively that it was important.

'We were out in the woods, the Major and I. Judy too, she went everywhere I did. About three years old, pretty as a picture, but with some of the puppyhood still in her.' He paused, remembering. 'It was a warm day, the sun bright on the river. Judy, she spotted a bird, or maybe it was a squirrel – and took off after it. Flat out, down the ridge and across level ground. Disappearing at times in the underbrush, but the sun was so bright that day, it kept reflecting off of her collar. Leather, with brass and silver studs.'

He paused again, still unaccustomed to opening up the past and finding his way through the words. Madeleine knew better than to prompt him, waiting instead for him to pick up the narrative, which slowly, he did.

'It made me laugh to see her go. Something so free and unfettered about the way she took off racing . . . I was still laughing as I looked up, at the Major. He wasn't laughing at all. He was lifting his gun to his shoulder.'

Jim raised his arm, absently mimicking that long-ago motion. 'He was aiming it straight at her. At Judy. I don't know whether I shouted out loud or not. I think I did, as I launched myself straight at him. We fell, the both of us, the shot going wide.

'The Major never spoke of what happened, but he never did go into the woods again after that. All the same, my mother had me give Judy away. It was for her own good, she said. It was what I should do if I loved her.'

'Jim—' Madeleine's eyes began to fill with tears once more, thinking of him, of the boy he'd been, just a young child, so hurt and bewildered. 'How much you must have hated him for it.'

He smiled, a twisted smile, filled with pain. 'I tried,' he said simply. 'He was my father. I couldn't. I thought it was because maybe I hadn't trained her well enough, because she barked so much at times. That somehow it was my fault that he'd raised a gun on my dog.'

Again that smile. 'You see what he was doing though, don't you? He was playing out the odds. The odds from that day, in France.' It wasn't Judy he was aiming for at all. Like stars it looked, a collar of gold and silver stars, as she took off through the brush. That morning in France, when Henri ran after his dog – all the Major needed to do was to shoot down Gaston, to take aim at that shiny star on the dog's collar and odds are the Germans would no longer have had a target.

'I read the journal all night long,' he said again. He looked at her, blue eyes vulnerable, so exposed. 'I read it, and all I could think about was how much I wished you were here, by my side.'

She stepped wordlessly into his arms. She had no answers, no longer knew right from wrong. Should America join the war, should they stand aside? She no longer knew. All she did know, with perfect clarity, was that she was grateful.

Grateful for this sun-kissed morning, for each additional day of peace. For these ordinary scents, of hay and earth and wood, and for the feel of her husband's arms.

'Are you staying?' he asked against her hair.

She pulled his shirt free from the waistband of his trousers, running her hands beneath his undershirt, across the smooth, warm skin of his back.

FORTY-FOUR

Raydon • December 1941

The fire in the grate cast an ochre light over the floorboards, its warmth coaxing a deeper perfume from the Christmas tree that had already been set up in the corner. The fire wasn't really needed, the afternoon being unseasonably warm. Not that anyone was complaining, Jim thought wryly, not about near seventy-degree highs a week into December. Half of Raydon was lingering about on Main Street today, Ellie had said, after attending Sunday Mass. Even old Asaph and Jeremiah, taking advantage of the balmy temperatures to sun themselves – on opposite ends – of the bench beside the church.

He nudged a stray pine needle with his foot, paying only partial attention to the game. The Dodgers had just scored in the second quarter, but with eight wins this season, the Giants already had the championship under their belt. He stretched out his legs, listening with half an ear as Ellie and Obadaiah bantered in the kitchen over the elaborate meal he'd fixed for them this afternoon.

He'd offered to cook Thanksgiving dinner, but Ellie was having none of that. 'Sunday supper, then?' Obadaiah had suggested, undaunted.

'A feast,' he'd promised, as Ellie looked dubiously at him from over the top of her glasses. 'A grand banquet, with the best French cooking you folks ever had.'

It was a feast alright. Deeply flavored chicken, cooked in onions, mustard and hard cider. A generous heaping of the mushrooms that Ellie had canned in the fall, sautéed golden-brown in butter; a burnished potato gratin rich with fresh cream and studded with roasted garlic and tiny cubes of ham.

'Delicious!' Madeleine exclaimed, spearing another bite.

'Sure is,' Jim agreed, glancing indulgently at her. Unlike her previous time, when she was carrying Jimmy, Madeleine's appetite was particularly robust with this pregnancy. She took another spoonful of the stew, chewing with obvious pleasure.

'*Le Cordon Bleu* good,' she praised.

Obadaiah grinned. 'You gotta try it with them French chickens,' he said. '*Poulet de Bresse* – they just melt in your mouth.' He turned to Jimmy. 'Them birds, they got blue feet, you know.'

'Blue?' Jimmy echoed in surprise.

'Don't talk with your mouth full, dear,' Madeleine mildly admonished.

'That's right, blue. Red combs, and feathers white as snow.'

Jimmy digested this information, eyes wide as he pictured these wonderful, tricoloured birds. 'Fourth of July chickens!' he exclaimed.

'Victory chickens,' Obadaiah agreed, chuckling. 'James—' he paused, a shadow crossing his face. He looked down at his plate. 'Your grandpa tell me 'bout them,' he said simply.

'Well, it's very good,' Ellie said. 'And you better be teaching me how to make it too,' she threatened, waving her fork at him.

'So these chickens,' Jim asked interested. 'Do they sell well? We've got space here on the orchard. Maybe one day—'

In many ways, Jim thought, it felt as if Obadaiah had been here for ever. Jim would remember for the rest of his life, in sharp, angular detail, the morning when he'd first walked into their lives. After the initial shock of his arrival, his presence had quickly come to feel entirely natural, his staying on an organic progression of events that felt just right.

Ellie and he were like a pair of old wives, bickering back and forth, but there was no denying the deep and genuine fondness that had developed between the two. Like the Major had before him, Obadaiah took special joy in Jimmy, spending hours with the boy as he told him stories about his grandpa from a seemingly inexhaustible supply, talking to him about boxing and Jack Johnson, teaching him to play the harmonica and sing the old marching songs of the Legion.

Jim in turn took comfort in the presence of the older man. They worked companionably in the orchard, a natural rhythm to their labour all through the picking season, pausing to watch a glowing sunset as they brought in the rowen hay. There was still a bleakness he sensed at times in Obadaiah, a deep and unfathomable sadness in his eyes. Sometimes he wouldn't sleep, sitting out all night on the porch and playing his harmonica; it would wake Jim sometimes and he'd lie in bed listening to the soft, haunting notes. In the morning, Obadaiah would be quieter than usual, but they never alluded to it, and gradually the mood would begin to lift from him, and he'd start to hum again as they worked.

Laughter drifted in from the kitchen. No doubt Obadaiah was staying close to the woodstove, Jim thought, amused. He always seemed to be cold, him and Madeleine both. The fire this sunny afternoon had been lit at her behest, with Obadaiah enthusiastically championing the notion.

As if on cue, a log shifted in the fireplace in a shower of sparks. Still plenty of wood on there . . . He glanced at the clock on top of the mantelpiece. There were still a few minutes to go before half-time. Continuing, idly, to follow the game, he swivelled the armchair slightly, the better to take in his wife. Madeleine had pulled her chair as close as possible to the fireplace, absorbed in cutting out paper angels for Jimmy's Christmas play at school.

He was struck again by how luminous she was, as if lit from within.

'It's going to be another boy,' Ellie had pronounced, taking in her expectant glow.

A deep contentment stole over Jim. Registering every detail, the burnished sweep of hair, the delicacy of her wrists. She looked up, sensing his gaze on her, and smiled.

'We interrupt this broadcast to bring you this important bulletin from the United Press.'

The reporter's voice crackled over the radio, halting the commentary of the game mid-sentence.

'The White House announces Japanese attack on Pearl Harbour.'

FORTY-FIVE

Jim rowed in the middle of the river, a ripple at the prow as it sliced through the steel-grey waters of the dawn. He went at an even pace, neither fast nor slow, an assured rhythm to the oars so that they made barely a sound. The unseasonable warmth that had heralded December had rapidly given way as winter staked her claim, the river still free-flowing, but with ghost tracings of frost that gleamed along the banks. A mist hung over the water, damp and chill, but Jim rowed steadily all the same, from memory, familiar with every bend and riffle and deep, bottomless pool. Nothing else seemed to move, the trout that still remained holding to the bottom of the seams as the boat slid smoothly overhead. The whole world seemed to be silent and waiting, an almost ethereal calm over the woods after the rollercoaster of the past weeks.

They'd sat in shock around the radio, as most of the country had, turning the knob from station to station as news continued to filter through the airwaves.

'It's a hoax,' Ellie said appalled. Her voice trembled. 'Surely it's just a hoax?'

Jim remembered looking up at the black mirror, as the newsreaders continued urgently to report. The pale cast of their reflections, as if in a tableau, the leached colours of the warm afternoon, of bare bough and pallid sky, as if it were all already slipping from him, turning into a dream. The grim surety: this was no hoax. Pearl Harbour had happened, and the world as they'd known it had just changed for ever.

The newspapers came that evening, an emergency print run confirming what he'd known in his bones. Details began to emerge of the carnage. Thousands dead and wounded, multiple ships destroyed in a deadly, premeditated blitz. Everywhere, across the length and breadth of the nation, the same sense of shock, and a mounting anger. America had been attacked.

The Great Debate ended, as if a switch had been pulled, isolationist and interventionist banding together in the face of their country's need.

'Where *is* Pearl Harbour?' old Asaph asked bewildered, as news first broke.

'Someplace off Boston,' Jeremiah hazarded a guess. He paused, unsure. 'America,' he qualified, with angry certainty.

Old Asaph looked sombrely at his friend. 'This means war.'

Jeremiah beat his cane on the ground. 'We'll knock them senseless,' he vowed.

'We have been stepping closer to war for many months,' Charles Lindbergh, the most visible face of the isolationist movement said in a statement. 'Now we must meet it as united Americans, regardless of our attitude in the past.'

Ellie's boy, Chris, had practically raced out the door, he and so many like him, called up immediately for active service. 'They need me, Ma,' he said, and she nodded, kissing him on the forehead and failing miserably in her attempt not to cry.

Madeleine saw the fixedness in Jim's expression. 'You have a deferral from the draft,' she reminded him tremulously. Her hands went instinctively to her stomach, cradling their unborn child. 'You're exempt,' she said again.

Jim looked at her, blue eyes clouded, but said nothing in reply.

As staunchly as he'd opposed meddling in a war they did not belong in, now that it had been brought home to them, Jim knew there was only one thing to do. To stand up and fight, for his family, for this country, for freedom, for all that he believed in. He'd known with perfect clarity, as soon as the news had broken, just what his father would have done, and what he now needed to do.

Obadaiah had tried to talk him out of it. 'Ain't no shame in stayin' outta it,' he said. 'Maybe the bravest thing a man can do is turn his back on the madness.'

'Would you?' Jim asked simply. 'After this?'

Obadaiah sighed, slowly fishing about in his pocket to draw out a small box. He handed it to Jim; in it, the rabbit foot gris-gris.

Jim had silently accepted the gift, trying not to show how touched he was. He'd kept it on him ever since; it was tucked into the pocket of his flannel shirt now as he rowed. A band of light appeared to the east. A faint flush, of rose and orange, an opalescence to the mist as it faltered and started to fray. He pulled further along the river as the sunrise grew stronger, crowning granite and sugarbush alike, painting colour into the water that dripped from the ends of the oars. Young Jimmy yawned, rubbing the sleep from his eyes.

'Remember this,' Jim wanted to say to his son. 'Hold on to this morning, you hear? You and me together, on this free-flowing water, this river that will run for ever. No matter what happens, no matter what the future holds, know how deeply I love you. No matter how things may change, no matter how different they might become, know that I will always love you, and we will always be bound by blood.' He caught Jimmy's eye, and smiled.

He stopped rowing at last and pulled in the oars, the current in this part of the river was too feeble to do much more than lap gently at the boat. 'I saw your mother for the first time here, you know,' he said. 'I was fishing, and she,' he pointed upwards, 'she was flying in an aeroplane. She had a bunch of balloons in her hand, dark-red balloons, streaming from both sides of the plane.'

The boy stared at the sky, imagining the sight. 'Like apples!'

Jim chuckled. 'Apples,' he agreed. He looked at his son, a great tenderness in his eyes. He wanted to hold on to every last detail – the way his hair flopped over his forehead, the rounded innocence of his face, the scabbed and banged-up knees – imprinting in his mind every last inch and ounce of his boy.

The sunrise grew stronger still, gilding the water and scattering what little mist remained. These were the last few hours, Jim thought to himself, of the life that he had known.

Madeleine had held on to him all night. He'd looked at her this morning, at that auburn pelt of hair. *My Venus Anadyomene*. Placing a gentle hand on her swollen belly, he had felt the baby kick.

Young Jimmy dipped a hand in the water, swirling patterns through the gold. He rested his chin on the wooden rim and watched with childish absorption, the sway and shift of his reflection in the current. Jim looked at his son again, tracing his features in his mind. Then pushing aside the tarp lying at the bottom, he hoisted the black mirror into his arms.

*

He'd asked Obadaiah if he'd stay on at the farm while he was gone. 'And if I don't make it back—'

'You keep that gris-gris on you,' Obadaiah interrupted. 'It be powerful magic. You keep it close, you hear?'

Both men shook hands. 'Damn fool Yankee,' Obadaiah muttered, voice choked with emotion as he clapped him on the back.

They said no more, but Obadaiah was awake especially late that night. When Jim finally fell asleep upstairs, it was to the soft tune of his harmonica.

He'd woken this morning and lain in bed for a while, watching Madeleine sleep. All the preparations were made, with only one thing remaining to do. He'd dressed quietly and, going to the mirror, had hoisted it off the wall. He didn't know what lay ahead, if and when he would return. But what he did know with utmost conviction was that the past that had held sway over this house for so long must at last be buried.

He had traced the scalloped outline that the mirror had left on the wallpaper, the distinctly brighter patch where it had rested all these years. A stab of pain shot through him as he thought again of his father, sitting captive in his armchair as he stared into the glass, so tightly bound to loss.

He had wrapped the mirror in a tarpaulin and placed it in the truck. He was about to leave, when Jimmy came stumbling out. 'Dad?'

'What are you doing up so early?' Jim had asked gently.

'Is it time?' The boy had looked at him anxiously, rubbing at his eyes. 'Are you leaving already?'

He ruffled his son's hair. 'Not yet.' He hesitated. 'Hey, you want to come down to the river with your old man?'

The mirror caught the morning sun, gleaming like polished jet. Jim thought of the Major again as he tipped it slowly over the side of the boat. It bobbed incongruously for a moment, the water lapping at its gilded edge. Then a quiet sigh, a murmur that seemed to spread through the river. Jim watched it sink below the surface, feeling his father close and hoping he'd at last found his peace.

*

He was lowering the oars into the water once more, when, 'Dad! Look!' Jimmy pointed wide-eyed towards the woods.

Jim turned, and saw the bobcat sitting between the trees. Still as a statue, just sitting there and watching them, its pelt like smoothest velvet and frost bearding its face.

ACKNOWLEDGEMENTS

First and foremost, my deepest love and gratitude to my mother, for her rock-steady support, for multiple readings, for her ideas and encouragement at every stage of the writing. My husband, for his unwavering championing, my father for advice on all matters battle-related, my in-laws for their support and especially their understanding. My sister, for her incisive, unstintingly honest assessments, and Arjun, with me in so many ways through the writing.

Merrily Weisbord, for her uncommon grace and boundless generosity. My aunt Dr Leela Chengappa, for drawing on her many years with the Veterans Administration Medical Department to share her knowledge of PTSD. Biswarup Chatterjee and Jeff Willner for early read-throughs and suggestions. My cousin Shirod, for multiple pickings of his brain and whose service with the French Foreign Legion I freely leaned upon. Barry 'Baz' Joseph for sharing his insights, and the friendship that came about as a direct result of writing this novel. Doug Patteson, for his detailed review and hospitality at his New England farmhouse. Andrea Wetzler, for her large-hearted help with all things French. Sampriti Ganguli, Dave Volman and Maya Vijayaraghavan for myriad kindnesses. Lakshan Appachu for taking me flying and being my on-call aviation expert. Jim Crimmins, whose experiences on a naval submarine were a springboard to imagining life in the crowded trenches. Gautham Appaya, Eric Gibbs and Trevor Jacobs, for answering even the oddest of research questions. Professors Bill Labov and Gillian Sankoff, for their tips on dialect. Sukanya Dasgupta – you know why you are here. Polly Kelekis and Vrinda Deval, for egging me on through the long haul. Deepali Bagati, Sangeeta Modi and Vimmi Singh for being in my corner.

Kirsty Dunseath, editor extraordinaire, for helping make *Good Hope Road* better, including coming up with this title, and for going to bat with so much conviction. I am truly fortunate to have her. The lovely Lisa Milton, for her staunch and enthusiastic support over the years. Jennifer Kerslake, Craig Lye, Rebecca Gray, Steve Marking and the team at Weidenfeld & Nicolson. David Davidar, for his frank and unsentimental guidance, Pujitha Krishnan and Aienla Ozukum at Aleph. The team at Juritzen Forlagen for their confidence in this book. David Godwin, my formidable agent, Heather Godwin, and the women of DGA, both past and present – Amy Mitchell, Caitlin Ingham, Lisette Verhagen – thank you all so very much.

Read on . . .

AUTHOR'S NOTE

I grew up an army daughter, surrounded by the officers and soldiers of the Gorkha battalion that my father went on to command. This is where I first formed a deep and abiding respect for the men and women in uniform everywhere who selflessly serve their countries, prepared to make the 'ultimate sacrifice' if need be. *Good Hope Road* was born of a desire to pay homage.

In initial concept, the story began in the Sixties, weaving back and forth between the Korean and Vietnam wars. As I began the research process, however, I stumbled upon an account of the Bonus March, a startling episode of history and one with echoes in the present. Including this in the narrative would mean a shifting of time periods, to World War I and the years leading up to World War II. As I started to dig around for American volunteers at the outset of the Great War, I discovered a number of highly educated young men from privileged backgrounds who'd signed up with the French Foreign Legion starting in 1914, filled with noble ideals and determined to fight the good fight in this, the war to end all wars. There were African American volunteers too – Bob Scanlon, the boxer, and Eugene Bullard, who went on to become the first African American military pilot. It is all of their experiences that form the collective backdrop of James and Obadaiah's stories.

In terms of canvas, while the larger brushstrokes are those of the war, the details lie in the special kinship of the battlefield, in the unlikely friendship that grows between the two men. And then, in the aftermath of the war, the backdrop shifts partly to the Bonus March, all the while maintaining the focus on James, now a decorated veteran still haunted by his experiences, and his son, Jim, who struggles to connect with his father. I hesitated a long while with post-war James, trying to get inside his head. It was the image of the Claude mirror that I went back to over and over. It is a metaphor for his altered self, his pale, leached reflection revealing the extent of the damage that the war has wrought.

While *Good Hope Road* is a work of fiction, it sits upon the foundation of much that actually occurred. David King, the brothers Paul and Kiffin Rockwell, John Bowe, the poet Alan Seeger, Henry Farnsworth, Edmond Genet and Victor Chapman are but some of the many American volunteers who left behind letters, diaries and memoirs detailing their time with the Legion. I am forever in their debt. In reading David King's memoir in particular, there was a strange feeling of things coming full circle. After the war, King actually moved to India for a while. Here I was, nearly a hundred years later, having made the reverse journey, from India to New York, and now reliving his days in the Legion.

It was while researching the Bonus March of 1932 that I first happened upon the story of Joe Angelo. While I've imagined his camaraderie with Mike Connor, a fictitious character, and indeed, all the details of his stay at the Anacostia camps, the accounts of his relationship with General Patton are based on reported facts. As for the March itself, I drew much from Paul Dickson and Thomas Allen's painstakingly detailed work, *The Bonus Army: An American Epic*. The New York Public Library proved, as always, to be another valuable resource. An especially treasured find was a collection of copies of the *BEF News*, the newspaper that was published by the Bonus Marchers. Their pages, fragile, tattered and falling to pieces, but bringing the

Anacostia camps to vivid life in accounts of a certain Rooster Curtis and the daily BEF cartoons.

Last, but not least, the fiery Major General Smedley Butler was cause for inspiration. His 'War is a Racket', extracts of which are quoted in *Good Hope Road,* dates back to 1933. Shamefully, over eighty years later, and in the aftermath of Iraq, Afghanistan, Kargil and more, his words still hold true. Our soldiers set off to war much fêted and praised, and frequently under the dazzle of media spotlights. When they return however, all too often it is to societies eager to forget, and ill-equipped to offer them adequate rehabilitation support.

We've made strides in the right direction, but we need to do so much more. Beginning, perhaps, with a better understanding, an improved accounting of the true costs of war. One that takes into consideration not merely the lost lives and damaged limbs, but the hidden internal scars borne by all too many of those who do make it home. One that assesses the impact not only on our soldiers but on the *families* of those who serve.

Good Hope Road is an attempt, however humble, to explore some of these themes.

IN CONVERSATION WITH SARITA MANDANNA

Q: *Good Hope Road* is a work of fiction that deals with real events in twentieth-century history. What came first for you, an interest in the Bonus March and an awareness that you would like to write about it, or a sense of the characters, of the Major and Obadaiah and their stories?

A: The first seeds to implant were those of the Major and Obadaiah – I began thinking of two men of very different backgrounds and motivations, and what the long years of war might do to them and their friendship. As for the setting, when I set out researching *Good Hope Road,* I wanted to place much of the story in the 1960s, specifically the years between the Korean and Vietnam wars in the US. I was giddy at the prospect of exploring the era – the music! the clothes! – when I happened upon a throwaway account of the Bonus March of 1932. I couldn't believe what I was reading. That was the turning point: I had to include the Bonus March in the narrative. This in turn meant shifting the canvas of the novel to an earlier period, to that of the Great War and the years afterward that led to World War Two.

Q: How did you create Obadaiah's voice?

A: Obadaiah Nelson popped into my head fully formed – I can close my eyes and see him. I knew how he would react to situations, I just knew what he would think, he arrived on the page brandishing his particular perspective of wisecracking street smarts. What I worked on though, was how he said what he did. It quite terrified me at the outset, to be honest. I was very aware of being both the wrong race and the wrong gender, and I spent a great deal of time trying to make his voice as authentic as I was able, to capture the particular lilt and syntax of it without reducing it to caricature, or according him any less than his due. I studied African American Vernacular English (AAVE) grammar, read novels, both from the turn of the century and later, that centred around African American characters, consulted with a widely respected professor of linguistics at the University of Pennsylvania and even watched reality television for current usage of AAVE, trying to capture the rhythm and flow of his dialogue.

Then, there were the other aspects of Obadaiah's character. His feel for music, for instance. Again, it was books that helped – Sidney Bechet's detailed, lyrical memoir for instance. I watched documentaries, read news clippings, sourced copies of songs that African American soldiers sang during the Great War and listened to grainy recordings on YouTube. I visited New Orleans and Paris (go ahead, twist my arm) and pored over old photographs. The more I understood his fictional background, the better equipped I'd be to act as his spokesperson. I don't know if I got him completely right, but hope I came close. This much I do know: Obadaiah Nelson is someone who will stay with me a very long while.

Q: How much research did you do before starting to write the novel? Did you find some of the scenes difficult to write, knowing that so many soldiers lost their lives during the war and that those who did return were traumatised by their experiences?

A: There was a significant amount of research that went into *Good Hope Road*, primarily because the story is woven against a backdrop of actual events. If you don't get the details correct, or at least the vast majority of them, the narrative will never sit quite right. Take the sections set in the French Foreign Legion, for instance. I tried to ensure that Obadaiah and the Major would be in the very sections of the Front that the French Foreign Legion would have been in during the time. The uniforms, the food, the bonhomie – all these came from multiple memoirs and personal accounts left from the war years. Gaillard is an amalgam of the Legionnaires I came across in these accounts. There was so much I wanted to include but couldn't for lack of space. For instance, Gaillard could balance an egg on its end. He knew to sing 'La Marseillaise' backwards and a hundred and forty ways to tie a knot . . .

All of the war scenes were difficult to write. Not just because of the suffering of so many, but also how do you really know what these men went through when you've not experienced the horror of combat first hand? How then do you do their stories justice? I'd play the sounds of shells on multiple devices, amplifying them in an attempt to mimic the sounds of incessant shelling. I stood out in the snow in summer clothes, and extrapolated the emotional disassociation caused by extreme sleep deprivation to the dissonance these men under constant duress must have experienced. None of what I did can ever begin to approach what these men suffered, but it was a starting point.

Finally, some of the lighter aspects of research involved the sections of *Good Hope Road* set in the 1930s and early 1940s, other than the Bonus March, of course. The fascination with aviation at the time, the magic of Broadway, the beautiful clothes and haberdashery – I spent a good many evenings merrily going down rabbit hole after rabbit hole on the web, all in the name of research.

Q: The narrative strands interweave between France in the First World War and America in the 1930s. How difficult was it to create a balance between the two threads?

A: It was difficult and took some fiddling with, because of the difference in tone, context as well as setting, moving as the story does between the trenches of Europe and bucolic, verdant Vermont. After some experimentation, I settled upon a linear process, writing chunks of the sections set in the Great War, and then following those up with a sizable amount of the other portion of the story. The process of interweaving them came at the end. All the individual chapters were laid out on the carpet in the bedroom and then I began arranging and rearranging them in an order that switched between the two periods while still maintaining narrative flow. This was tweaked once more when my editor, the lovely Kirsty Dunseath, had a go at the draft, and then we were done.

Q: Could you tell us a little about your daily writing life? Where and when do you write? Do you have any writing rituals?

A: I wrote most of *Good Hope Road* as a full-time writer. This was different than when I worked on my debut novel, *Tiger*

Hills – that was done in fits and bursts of time, mostly at night. With *Good Hope Road*, I took a couple of years off to write in earnest. For the first time in my adult life, I was home during the day. I'd begin writing around 7.30 a.m. at the dining table, with a view of the ivy-covered brick Victorian next door. There were breaks for (a lot of) food, working out (see note on food) and email. I tried to restrict email to once or twice a day, but failed miserably with that. Eventually, I found it easier to just keep email open so I knew what was coming in. I would answer when I was done with what I was working on. I'd keep writing until 7.30 p.m. or if the writing was going well, until it wasn't. If the writing wasn't going well – and I had a good many days of writer's block – then I'd spend the hours researching. After I went back to a full-time job during the day, I completed *Good Hope Road* late at night and on the weekends (with even more breaks for food).

I need to be absolutely alone when I write. It doesn't matter where, as long as I'm alone. I was sentimental about starting and finishing *Good Hope Road* on the same laptop. It was an old one to begin with, and during the course of the writing, the battery died, the power cord had to be replaced and the cover came unhinged. Still, that was the only laptop I would write on, my old, rickety faithful, all the way to the end.

Q: Who are your favourite writers and whose work inspires your own?

A: There are so many writers I admire, but there are a few that especially resonated as I wrote *Good Hope Road*. Pat Barker's Regeneration trilogy has been an epiphany of sorts for me. I read it in my twenties and that was my first exposure to the

Great War. It has stuck with me ever since. So too, Sebastian Faulks' *Birdsong*, especially for the heart-rending bonds he describes between the soldiers at the Front. Jim Harrison, for the strength and beauty of his words. I'd dip into his novels as I wrote, seeking a male perspective, a brawnier rendering of phrase and sentence. Finally, Michael Ondaatje, especially *In the Skin of a Lion*. Part poetry, part prose, I browsed through it often, taking in afresh the luminosity of his work.

Q: What's next? Are you working on a new novel?

A: I'm beginning to ponder one. There is this period between finishing a novel and starting the next that for me is like a big gulp of fresh air. You are living in the real world once more, without fictional people whispering in your head. This past year after finishing *Good Hope Road* has been exactly that, and more. Gradually though, I feel something stirring once again. Something is brewing inside, what exactly, I don't yet know.

DISCUSSION POINTS

– What drives James Stonebridge to sign up with the French Foreign Legion, and how do his beliefs change as the war progresses?

– In many ways, the friendship between James and Obadaiah is an unlikely one. Discuss the similarities and differences between the men and how they are able to support each other through the conflict.

– How important are memories in the novel?

– We experience the trenches through Obadaiah's account and the Major's journal entries. How far do their views of war differ, and do you feel that one voice affects you more than the other? If so, why?

– What does the Major see when he stares into the Claude mirror, and what significance does the mirror hold in the novel overall?

– There are a number of songs in *Good Hope Road*. What effect do they have on the characters?

– Were you aware of the Bonus Army and the protests in Anacostia in 1932 before reading *Good Hope Road*? What do you think about the way in which veterans of the First World War were treated in America? Compare this treatment with the reception soldiers returning from war receive today.

- How does Sarita Mandanna portray the emotional and psychological damage of war and its effects on ordinary men and their families?

- *'Men eating, walking, marching together with little thought of race or background, recognising a deeper fraternity in all they had gone through together, in the scars, both exposed and hidden, that they bore.'*

  Does anything surprise you about the way in which race is presented in 1930s America?

- Trace Jim and Madeleine's love story through the novel. How does Madeleine help Jim to understand his father? What effect does the Major's journal have on Madeleine at the end of the novel?

IF YOU ENJOYED *GOOD HOPE ROAD*, YOU MIGHT LIKE TO TRY . . .

A Place Called Winter by Patrick Gale

Regeneration by Pat Barker

Birdsong by Sebastian Faulks

The Kindness of Enemies by Leila Aboulela

A God in Ruins by Kate Atkinson

Summertime by Vanessa Lafaye

The Narrow Road to the Deep North by Richard Flanagan

Atonement by Ian McEwan

The Help by Kathryn Stockett

Testament of Youth by Vera Brittain

The English Patient by Michael Ondaatje

Goodbye to All That by Robert Graves

HAVE YOU READ *TIGER HILLS*?

'She knew her child was special, had known from the very day of her birth, the day of the herons . . .'

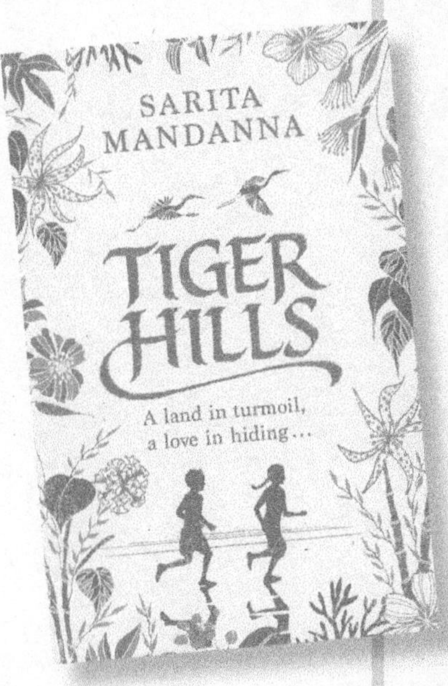

1878, Southern India. As the first girl born into the family for over sixty years, beautiful, spirited Devi is adored by everyone. And when she befriends Devanna, a gifted young boy whose mother died in tragic circumstances, the two swiftly become inseparable.

Their futures seem inevitably linked until one night Devi meets 'the tiger killer' – and makes a decision that has heartbreaking consequences for generations to come . . .

'Lavish . . . Mandanna's fusion of history and romance makes for an aromatic blend' *Independent*

'An epic and extraordinary debut from an astonishing new talent' *Daily Express*